About th

Stephen Mumford is a retired builder with a vivid imagination and a lifelong fascination with automatous machines. Ten years ago, he conceived a story set in an imagined Victorian London that quickly took on a life of its own. This inspiration led him to surprisingly tell all his close friends and family that he intended to write a book.

Without trying to sound too clichéd, *IRON JACK* was written and, as they say, 'the rest is history'.

Iron Jack

To Judith

S. [signature]

2nd December 2024

Stephen Mumford

Iron Jack

Olympia Publishers
London

www.olympiapublishers.com
OLYMPIA PAPERBACK EDITION

Copyright © Stephen Mumford 2024

The right of Stephen Mumford to be identified as author of
this work has been asserted in accordance with sections 77 and 78 of
the Copyright, Designs and Patents Act 1988.

All Rights Reserved

No reproduction, copy or transmission of this publication
may be made without written permission.
No paragraph of this publication may be reproduced,
copied or transmitted save with the written permission of the publisher,
or in accordance with the provisions
of the Copyright Act 1956 (as amended).

Any person who commits any unauthorised act in relation to
this publication may be liable to criminal
prosecution and civil claims for damage.

A CIP catalogue record for this title is
available from the British Library.

ISBN: 978-1-80439-986-6

This is a work of fiction.
Names, characters, places and incidents originate from the writer's
imagination. Any resemblance to actual persons, living or dead, is
purely coincidental.

First Published in 2024

Olympia Publishers
Tallis House
2 Tallis Street
London
EC4Y 0AB

Printed in Great Britain

Dedication

Apart from the few close friends and family that have taken the time in reading many raw, unedited versions of my story, there is one person who has never once said I should give up. So, with that said, this book is dedicated to my wife Lorraine, who has stood by me through the whole process, typing numerous versions and never once faltering in her faith in me or the story of *IRON JACK*.

Acknowledgements

First of all, thanks to Jaquie, my sister, who I unceremoniously gave five hundred unbound handwritten pages of my first draft and asked her what she thought of my story. Not to forget my daughter-in-law, Jessica, and her mum, Gina, for their tireless efforts in helping me edit and structure the book. My dad and Sam and Stevie, my two sons, who all constantly encouraged me to never give up on my dream of getting *IRON JACK* published and last but not least, the friends and family critics who took the time in reading my story and spurring me on. Victor Runacre, Janice May, Pat Laidlaw and Jaquie Mcginley.

Chapter One

Finding Hubert Wells

Professor Ernest Postlewaite closed the impressive gates of his grand Georgian mansion as he had done a thousand times before; however, this time, something was different. Feeling an inexplicable urge, he pressed his face against the ornate wrought iron barrier and peered around to survey the fruits of his labours in a way he imagined any inquisitive passer-by would do. There was no doubt his accomplishments had brought him much fame and wealth, but looking over his magnificent abode as a stranger would, he suddenly felt a waft of sadness come over him as he looked towards his lovely wife, Emily, her shoulders down and appearing lost and unhappy as they had tried many times to have a baby but after two harrowing miscarriages they both knew it just wasn't meant to be.

That poor girl, it must be hell to live with these days, thought Ernest admitting to himself, he was far from the ambitious, passionate man his beautiful wife Emily had taken to be her husband. *I mean, it's not her fault I feel such a wretch. Well, maybe this is the distraction I need and if nothing comes of it, I vow here and now I will cheer myself up and try and make a success of my marriage. I'll soon have that grand old house full of our friends and make it the positive and happy home it was intended to be.*

Suddenly, Ernest was distracted by a distant rattling sound coming from high above his head that caused him to instinctively looked upwards and squinting into the bright morning sky, he instantly recognised one of 'The Hand's' distant carriages swinging gently, as precise as clockwork it continued its regular journey across London.

Ernest, with his mood lifted, decided to give himself a bit more time to take in the sheer magnificence of the impressive structure he had actually invented. Trailing his eyes from the bottom to the very top of one of 'The Hand's' solid iron main supports, he could see the full scale and splendour of the five hundred foot high iron dome that encompassed the entire metropolis. It was at that precise moment he fully understood why all of London's citizens affectionately called his ingenious aerial rail system 'The Hand'.

Giving himself a virtual 'pat on the back' and taking in the grandeur and spectacle of his greatest achievement for a few more precious moments, he eventually pulled himself away full of enthusiasm focused on his main objective. *I can't stand here all morning gawping; if anyone sees me, they will think I am showing off. Oh well, let's get this done*, thought Ernest, as with a newfound verve and vigour and with a spring in his step, began the short ten-minute walk to 'The Hand's' Hampstead station.

Ernest Postlewaite, by thirty-five years of age, had done far more in society and achieved higher accolades than most people would in a lifetime. He had also become fully aware that the turmoil of unsuccessfully trying to start a family, along with the stresses and responsibility that came along with a man of his stature, had caused him to act in the manner of someone who was much older. In reality, he was in the prime of his life, but his fuddy-duddy ways, along with the constant stress of his lifestyle and extreme loss of weight, made this once kind, jolly, round-faced man appear gaunt and emaciated, giving him a stern look that to people who didn't really know him, believe he was an aggressive, unapproachable man. This 'well-held' view couldn't actually be further from the truth, and it was there and then that Ernest knew things would have to change. This was going to be the day when once and for all, he was going to find out if the heavy drinking, scruffy Hubert Wells he had been reliably informed was working as a lowly boilerman at the London Hospital could somehow, unbelievably, be the same the Hubert Wells that he had studied with at Oxford University.

It was 1887 and fifteen years since his last acquaintance with his old friend Hubert Wells. *What if his mental and physical state has deteriorated so much by his excesses that he wouldn't be up to any task I set him?* thought Ernest worryingly.

Oh well, if that were the case, I suppose I would have to put a brave face on everything and spend the rest of my days as a gentleman of leisure, in what is it the villagers call it? 'The Big House', thought Ernest, making a joke of what to most people would not really be a bad alternative.

Professor Ernest Postlewaite, to all outsiders, seemed to have everything, but today's meeting was not about wealth or prestige. It was about fulfilling a dream he'd had since his early days at Oxford University. In those days, Hubert Wells had listened to Ernest's fantastical theories and imaginings on many occasions. *Could this reunion spell the beginning of a partnership capable of making my dream a reality?* thought Ernest as he prepared to board one of 'The Hand's' ornate carriages that had just completed its five hundred foot descent and arrived at his platform.

Ernest climbed aboard the empty carriage and sat down. *I'm glad, really, they all mean so well, but on a day like today where I'm full of trepidation, I am not really up for small talk.* thought Ernest, glad that he hadn't set out earlier and got caught up with 'The Hand's' thousands of passengers going about their early morning work commute.

Ernest spent the short ten-minute journey on 'The Hand' taking in the sights of London. This magnificent aerial railway was the envy of the world's transport systems; in the centre of its sturdy iron dome structure was its heart, the massive steam boiler that was dominated by its towering chimney that billowed out a steady stream of thick smoke high into the atmosphere. It really was a sight to behold.

And just think, before I submitted my plans to parliament, they had proposed building an underground railway transport system, Ernest thought as he chuckled to himself, imagining commuters coughing and spluttering with their black soot-stained clothes as they emerged from the oppressive subterranean station. With a satisfying jolt, Ernest felt his carriage come to a halt as it reached the Whitechapel station destination. Stepping out of the 'Alight' side of his carriage, Ernest began the short walk towards the renowned London Hospital.

All those months of investigating have led me here; it just has to be him; how many Hubert Wells could there be residing in London, Ernest thought, trying to convince himself he wasn't on a wasted journey.

What did my informant say? When Hubert Wells is not working, he spends all his leisure time frequenting the local pubs and houses of ill repute. It actually could be my Hubert Wells because the way he was behaving before he was asked to leave was very similar. Who knows what the outcome would have been if he had stayed on? Such a waste of talent. Sighed Ernest as he took a few more steps and very soon found himself standing a few feet in front of the impressive brick-built London Hospital.

Ernest's stomach started tying itself into knots as he approached the entrance with trepidation. As he began to wonder what kind of state his old friend could possibly be in.

"Ah, Professor, and what do I owe this pleasure for your visit here?" asked the hospital's burly doorman, who had instantly recognised the world-famous Professor Ernest Postlewaite.

"Oh, all a bit hush, really, but between you and me, I've been asked to survey The East Wing to see if it has the potential for an annexe," answered Ernest, tapping his nose as he told a lie that he believed would allow him to walk around hospital grounds without arousing any suspicion.

"Oh, you just go ahead, Professor. It's so nice to know that with you involved, we will at least get a 'Proper job'," said the doorman, completely duped by Ernest's deception.

Ernest courteously tipped his hat and began to walk through the many winding corridors of the impressive hospital complex. Following his instincts, after a short while, he found himself in front of a door labelled.

MAINTENANCE ROOMS. NO UNAUTHORISED ACCESS.

Quickly looking around, making sure no one was watching, Ernest pushed open the door and took the short flight of stairs that would lead him into the bowels of the hospital. Immediately, Ernest felt the warmth of the boiler and exposed pipes and became aware of a distant hum of machinery and a strong smell of burning oil. Approaching what to him must surely be the boiler room, he knocked hard on the sturdy iron door.

Getting no reply, Ernest thought to himself, *I'm not coming all this way to be stumped at the last hurdle.* With that, he gave the heavy door a firm push. Unexpectedly, the door showed no resistance and swung wide open. Ernest could clearly see standing in front of him, illuminated by the glow of the boiler furnace, the striking figure of his old friend Hubert Wells. The unmistakable sharp bone line of his handsome friend's face was highlighted by black smudges of coal dust that disturbingly made his eyes appear sunken and dead. As Hubert Wells hauntingly stared out at Ernest, he still did not utter a word.

Ernest came over with a strong feeling of sadness at the sight of the pathetic-looking boilerman standing before him. This work-battered individual was undoubtedly the same Hubert Wells he had studied with at Oxford University but his overall demeanour was nothing like the confident, cocky, suave individual that Ernest had remembered.

In an effort to break the uncomfortable silence, Ernest blurted out, "Hubert, it's me, your old friend Ernest Postlewaite." Surprisingly, Ernest did not get the reaction he was expecting.

Hubert Wells just gave out a sarcastic laugh, followed by a sneering reply, "Oh, I know You; you are the Great Ernest Postlewaite, the 'Mr Big of London' I wondered how long it would be till our paths met again; as you can see, I haven't done quite as well as you." He sneered as he began throwing his arms around and pointing in all directions. He swayed drunkenly from side to side. "Still, it keeps me off the streets," he continued as he gave out another loud cackling laugh.

"Hubert, dear friend, please try and calm yourself; I haven't come here to gloat," Ernest uttered in a soothing manner. "At least give me a chance to explain why I am here. I have come here to offer you employment worthy of your full potential; I, of all people, know that you have a most brilliant mind, and excuse me if I sound rude, but you are definitely not showing your full potential in this place. I know that if you had knuckled down at Oxford, with your superior intellect, you could have gone on to design and build wonderful inventions equal to my own. To put it simply, I recognise your brilliance and need your help. You see, I have ideas and plans that I have had to accept I simply cannot achieve on my own. Hubert, with your help on my proposed project, we could build something that has the potential to be more beneficial to the citizens of London than even my Aerial railway transport system has proved to be."

On hearing this, Hubert calmed down and straightened himself up; using his fingers as a comb, he ran them through his greasy, matted hair. Ernest's rousing speech had seemingly lifted Hubert Wells out of a rut. Pulling the lapels of his oil-stained boiler suit and brushing down his trouser legs, the unkempt boilerman, trying his hardest to sober up, attempted to become the gentleman character he knew he should and could be.

Giving a loud cough to clear his throat, Hubert spoke to his old friend, "Before we leave here, I would like you to meet the two people who have shown me true companionship, far more than the tavern louts I usually associate myself with."

Ernest gave a nod of agreement, just happy in the fact Hubert had accepted his offer to work alongside him and with that, followed his old friend down a series of steps to a small corridor where they both walked a short distance until they reached the two doors in front of them.

"These rooms," said Hubert, "are rarely visited by outsiders." As he proceeded to open the door that was to the left of them. As the old wooden door creaked open, a dull gas light barely illuminating the room threw an eerie light into the small hallway. Ernest's senses heightened with fear as he could distinctly hear a deep grunting sound accompanied by heavy breathing, a disconcerting sound not unlike heavy snoring.

"It's all right, Joseph; It's only me. Don't worry. No one is going to hurt you; it's someone I trust that I want you to meet," said Hubert, hoping he had convinced Joseph it was not just a voyeuristic 'Peep Show', as others had subjected him to in the past. "You see, Joseph, things are looking up for me, and this could possibly be the last time I will be able to visit you."

Ernest's eyes had by now fully adjusted to the dull light and he focused his attention on what could only be described as the most horribly disfigured soul imaginable; this tragic figure's head looked barely human, at least three times the size of any regular person he had ever seen. One of his eyes was completely covered by mounds of lumpy skin, the other eye bright and piercing, focused on Hubert.

With a grunting, rasping voice in a sad tone, Joseph struggled to speak, "Hubert, please do not worry about me any more; each day and night is becoming harder to endure. I frequently dream that this cruel life I have been dealt with will soon be at an end, and in a short while, I will find myself in a better place, free from pain, judgement and torment."

Joseph struggled to roll his huge, deformed head slightly to one side until he could focus his one good eye on Ernest, continuing speaking as loud as he possibly could said, "Hubert, I can see a genuine kindness in your friend's face." As he cryptically added, "Just remember this is his strength, not a weakness." With that, Joseph shut his one good sparkling bright eye and quickly descended into a deep sleep.

Hubert and Ernest left the poor tortured soul alone for what would surely be one of his final sleeps and, once more, standing outside in the corridor, approached the door to the right. At that moment, Ernest decided to ask Hubert a question about something Joseph had said that perplexed him. "Why do you think of all the things to say? Joseph stated that my kindness is a strength and not a weakness?"

Hubert stayed silent for a split second; it wasn't the time to say anything that could alienate his possible benefactor and slyly thought to himself, *There are a lot of things about my life I don't think I would ever divulge to Postlewaite. Let's at least get settled in before he finds out anything about me.*

Eventually replying, Hubert said in a rather stern voice, "Look, Ernest, I am willing to make a new start, but during my time here as a boiler man, I have had to carry out many unsavoury duties for a senior member of staff who shall I say, has a degree of control over me. You see, Ernest, you appearing at this time could prove to be my saviour and not a minute too soon."

This response had left Ernest with many questions, but he decided he would leave them for another time.

Ernest and Hubert made their way to the second door and standing outside, Ernest's heart began pounding in trepidation on who or what, for that matter, he would find residing in this room.

"Ernest," said Hubert in an upbeat but cautionary tone. "I must warn you, this person you are about to meet is not like anyone else you would have encountered before. You must put any preconception of the human form to one side for now and accept the person you will meet purely as a truly remarkable human being that I know simply as Quinn."

Ernest thought to himself, *Hmm, human being, well that's a good start*, his mind by this time had been conjuring up all sorts of monsters.

"No, by all means, proceed, Hubert. If he's a trusted friend of yours, go ahead and enter, dear fellow," said Ernest, preparing himself for the worst sight he could imagine.

Hubert gave the ominous door a sharp rap with his knuckles. Ernest waited to hear a reply, but instead, moments later, he heard the distinctive sound of a lock being turned from inside the room. Giving it a few seconds, Hubert turned the doorknob and entered the room, beckoning Ernest to follow.

This room, as before, was very dimly lit, but Ernest, struggling to focus, peered around and eventually spotted, standing in the corner, a figure of what appeared to him to be a tall, slim, built, smartly dressed man. Hubert, in complete silence, walked over to the intriguing individual, proceeded to place his hands on his shoulders and begun to what looked like whispering. Ernest, all this time, had been scrutinising the mysterious person and could see something was not quite as it should be but could not put his finger on it. Unable to not quite make out what was different, Ernest walked over to join Hubert and his friend. As Ernest studied harder, the enormity of what he could see finally dawned on him and caused him momentarily to black out.

"Ernest, you've taken a bit of a turn," said Hubert, attempting to console his friend. Ernest, fully conscious, pulled himself together and began to look over in great detail the bizarre-looking man that Hubert had simply called Quinn.

Initially, Ernest had thought he had been looking at the back of a bald fellow's head, but when peering down at Quinn's feet, he could see they were pointing towards him; it became obvious that this pitiful creature, unlike all other human beings, was completely devoid of any facial features, no ears, eyes, mouth or nose. His head was just a blank expanse of skin, which gave it a bizarre look, not unlike a huge thumb.

Ernest, getting to grips with himself, began to study Quinn in more detail and noticed that in his neck was a small, sore-looking orifice, which Ernest could only assume was how this abomination of a human must breathe and eat.

Suddenly, from outside the room, a loud, stern, deep voice could be heard, "Wells, where are you? I told you to stay in the boiler room; what have I told you before about fraternising with those two freaks."

Hubert became animated in what appeared to be panic and quickly proceeded to pull back a small rug, exposing a metal cover. Quinn lowered himself calmly into his seat and, sitting bolt upright, turned his strange head towards the door in what appeared to Ernest a well, practised scenario.

"Follow me, Ernest," whispered Hubert as he lifted the heavy cover to one side and climbed down a short metal ladder. "Hurry along, old man. Quinn will cover our tracks," continued Hubert, as gradually the dim light from above diminished.

Standing in complete darkness, Ernest hung onto Hubert's coat tail when, after a few moments, Hubert produced a vesta box and a candle from his pocket. It became obvious to Ernest that everything that had just happened had happened before. Hubert, it seemed, was well prepared for this situation.

The dim candlelight partially illuminated the array of dark tunnels that stretched out before them. Sure-footed Hubert led the way along a section of London's complex sewage network.

Turning to face Ernest, Hubert spoke, "One day, when the time is right, I will explain everything, but until that day comes, I would like you to respect my wish that we do not speak of The London Hospital again until I am ready."

Ernest was just pleased he had coaxed his old friend to work with him, although leaving the hospital by ways of a sewage system, he had to admit, felt more like an escape.

The pair proceeded to walk along the tunnel, keeping their feet out of the steady stream of foul-smelling water.

Occasionally, a rat would scurry between their legs but Ernest completely trusted Hubert to find their way out. After walking for about fifteen minutes, Ernest was about to ask a few questions about Quinn when suddenly Hubert spoke excitedly, "There, just ahead, can you see it? That long ladder will lead us to a waste area just behind Bethnal Green Aerial Station."

Ernest was so pleased they would soon emerge from the putrid-smelling sewer into an area of London he knew very well.

Hubert proceeded to climb a steep vertical ladder and, letting out a grunt, he pushed the heavy metal cover, allowing beams of moonlight to illuminate their claustrophobic chasm. As they both climbed out and touched the damp grass, Hubert closed the heavy lid behind them. Standing up, they both instinctively gazed into the night sky where towering high above them was the magnificent sight of 'The Hand'. With a plume of thick smoke billowing from its towering chimney, its massive gas spotlights sent beams of light that cut through the smoke and fog to pinpoint 'The Hand's' five main stations. The hundred individual carriages sparkled and lit the night sky. In a constant and measured fashion, the cranks and pullies gracefully moved them to arrive and depart from their destination in perfect, precise timing. Ernest, full of pride, stared towards the centre of the massive iron dome and took in the grandeur of what he had invented. As he glanced over to Hubert, he could sense a feeling of admiration from his old friend.

Breaking the silence without warning, Hubert spoke in an authoritative way. "Come on, man, we can't spend all night gawping at the sky; use a bit of your influence and authority and get us to your warm, cosy house that a man of your standing must have acquired by now," he said in a tone of sneering sarcasm.

Ernest had felt this jealous streak previously and was

beginning to think that maybe this new partnership might not be 'the bed of roses' he was hoping for.

The pair entered the Bethnal Green East London Aerial Station Entrance, where Ernest proceeded to take out his punch card pass and push it firmly into the station's sturdy metal clock. With one full rotation, a gentle ping chimed and the tall ornate entrance gate slowly opened, where they both proceeded to make their way to the platform to where their driverless carriage was waiting. It would be just a short twenty-minute ride to Hampstead Heath and after entering the carriage, for the first few minutes, there was an awkward silence due to the many questions Ernest had promised he would not ask Hubert about his time at the London Hospital.

Suddenly, abruptly and against Hubert's wishes, Ernest could not contain himself any longer and blurted out, "Hubert, what is wrong with that Quinn? How did he become such a thing?"

Hubert, annoyed that Ernest had broken his promise of delving into his past so soon, reluctantly answered, "Honestly, I don't really know, but he has told me he has lived there his entire life. Now, can we just relax this whole ordeal is beginning to drain me," said Hubert in a stern voice.

Ernest couldn't relax as he began having worrying thoughts about the consequences of luring his friend away from what was actually a very responsible job. Unable to keep it to himself, he put his fears to Hubert, "You, sir, may only be a lowly boiler man, but as you know full well, upkeep of the boiler is an integral part of the hospital's infrastructure. With you unable to maintain and feed its furnace, then surely the hospital will very soon be plunged into cold and darkness."

Hubert, in an effort to alleviate his friend's concerns in a calm, authoritative voice, spoke, "Ernest, I may be, as you say, a lowly boilerman, but I am still the same Hubert Wells you knew at Oxford University, so I assume you do not think of me as stupid. I had been working on a complex theory that would fully automate the boiler system. After many months, I realised this was even beyond my intellect; in fact, there were many times I thought or wondered if old Postlewaite could do better."

Ernest laughed to himself but politely asked Hubert, "Pray continue, old friend."

"You see, there were times when I almost gave up until one day, God knows why I thought of laying out my problem to Quinn. Well, you must admit, Ernest, you probably felt the same when you first saw Quinn; he might be a big ugly thing, but you can sense he is very intelligent. Let me tell you, my assumptions were right. Within one week of setting out my task to Quinn, he had produced a brilliant blueprint plan that, once I had converted to a practical mechanical working section of my boiler system, it could now ignite itself and run on a fraction of fuel, allowing the system to be left unattended if needs be for at least one week. Plenty of time for anyone to notice that I have absconded and to find a replacement for me. You see, Ernest, the moral here is never judge by appearances; Quinn, far from being the pitiful freak I originally thought him as, is, in fact, actually a mathematical genius."

Chapter Two

Betrayal

This particular morning breakfast time at the 'Big House' was like no other. Ernest had got up and dressed before anyone else.

How will I explain our new guest? Hardly the type I usually associate myself with, he worried. *Still, Hubert is an educated man and with clean clothes, a nice wash and a shave. Let's hope when he appears, he will be a semblance of the old Hubert Wells. Maybe when I pluck up the courage to tell Emily he is to be our new long-term guest, hopefully, she won't be too shocked,* thought Ernest, not convincing himself it was going to be that easy.

Ernest removed the speaking tube from the wall and called down to his housekeeper, Mrs Beddoes. After a short while, the portly, faithful employee brought up three freshly prepared breakfasts. Emily, having briefly been updated, sat in her usual seat at the table and waited in trepidation, not really knowing what to expect.

"Ah, the beautiful Emily, honestly Ernest's description of you really doesn't do you justice," said Hubert, entering the dining room as if a celebrity of the Music Halls on a premier night.

Emily stunned at this exuberant performance, stared on and had to admit to herself this was undoubtedly an extremely handsome figure of a man. Looking immaculately groomed and smart in clothes she recognised as her husband's, Emily waited to see how events would unfold.

Ernest showed an expression of relief, as Hubert had not let him down, appearing all the English gentleman, just the sort of person expected would socialise with the distinguished Professor Ernest Postlewaite.

Settling down to eat their breakfast, Ernest began to lay out his ideas and plans he had for them. Emily, not wanting to get heavily involved and bogged down in 'man's work', made her excuses and left the table. Emily had always been proud of herself that she was good at judging people and what she had just witnessed during that last half hour, she could never divulge to her husband. She had noticed that every time Ernest had looked away, Hubert Wells focused his piercing blue eyes on her so intensely it was enough to make her blush. She was no mind reader but was experienced enough in the ways of the world to see that Hubert Wells was not an honourable man; in fact, she decided there and then it would be best for all that she kept out of his way as much as possible.

Ernest and Hubert stood in front of the dining room's huge circular window and as they both peered out, Ernest spoke. "You see Hubert, down there just to the left of the driveway, just before you get to the big gates. If you stare hard enough, you will see a roof that belongs to an outbuilding. Well, old friend, this particular building was built for one purpose only. This will be the workshop of a project I have dreamt of for many years and hopefully, with your help, Hubert, we can make my dream a reality."

Sitting back at the breakfast table, Ernest began to elaborate on his plan, "Put simply, my man, this will be what I have tagged as The Iron Guardian Project, a venture most would dismiss as an idea of fantasy, but in this worrying time of increasing crime in our capital, I feel that one day could be an essential part of our Police Force. What I propose to build is a mechanical machine, a contraption not like a steam tractor or a train that needs a driver, but a machine so advanced it will be able to think for itself and patrol London unassisted by any human and capable of making its own decisions. Of course, we will need practical help with its construction but these persons will have to be individually vetted as none of this confidential work can ever be divulged until such time it has been rigorously tested."

Hubert Wells, always a practical thinker, sat stunned in silence as Ernest continued laying out his plans and, at the same time, gradually filled the table with complicated blueprints and mathematical equations.

Two hours passed, Hubert and Ernest, looking ruffled, hair tousled and waistcoats undone, were frequently fed vast amounts of strong coffee from Mrs Beddoes.

"Tomorrow is another day, Hubert; let's rest now; you may treat my home as you would any good hotel and first thing in the morning, I will take you down to the workshop," said Ernest in an excited tone.

*

Over the ensuing months, work on the Iron Guardian Project progressed at a staggering rate. With the help of the Stroud family of mechanics and boiler makers, a local company that had glowing reports on their workmanship, they soon proved their worth. Eventually, between them all, they produced a machine of pure technical brilliance that, although looked magnificent, sadly had not reached the level of artificial intelligence Ernest had dreamt of. Ernest, believing the key to making his dream of creating a machine that basically could think for itself and be trusted to roam the streets of London unassisted, concentrated on developing a complex command system, something he was finding impossible to achieve alone. Sadly, for Ernest, Wells was proving to not be the helpful partner he had envisaged. Instead, he seemed to want to build a basic machine capable of only understanding a few simple commands.

*

London in 1887 was a frightening, foreboding city with levels of lawlessness and criminality at an all-time high. Ernest and Hubert's Iron Guardian would be a solution to this plight, but in its unresolved unsatisfactory state, it was a lingering failure and something that Ernest Postlewaite was not prepared to accept.

One morning, Ernest decided to enter the workshop alone. As he stared at his and Hubert's creation, looking magnificent, silent and still, a shudder sent tingles down his spine as the reality dawned on him that all they had built between them was merely a façade. This massive iron beast with its dead eyes giving it a haunted expression, this machine that he had given so much of his time and effort to look as impressive as he had ever hoped and yet, in other ways, so disappointing. The six-foot-tall metal juggernaut in the guise of a bulldog was no more in some ways than a steam roller used by road-building navvies. There was no way he could trust 'firing up' this gargantuan contraption without Wells around.

Oh, how has it come to this? he thought solemnly, *My idea, my project, and yet somehow, through my own weakness, I've let that dominating Wells take over.*

Time had shown Hubert could look all the gentleman you could imagine but this was a thin veneer; underneath there lay more of the scruffy alcohol and dependant person that Ernest had reacquainted himself with not that long ago at The London Hospital.

Back at the house, Ernest pondered on the predicament he had got himself into. All the early signs he should have picked up on, Wells's room unkempt and littered with empty bottles of all sorts, not arising from his bed sometimes till midday and most worrying of all, his evermore attentive behaviour towards his wife, Emily.

How have I allowed it to get to this, he thought, kicking the hall side cabinet loud enough to alert Mrs Beddoes.

"Are you all right, sir?" she asked in a kind, respectful way.

Ernest, not one for stuffy protocol and snobbery, trusted his long-standing housekeeper enough to open up about his true thoughts on Hubert Wells. "Oh, it's nothing really. I shouldn't allow Wells to dominate me, but I would like to know what you think of my guest."

Letting her kind employer finish speaking, Mrs Beddoes felt it was the right time to respond, "Sir, it's not only me; it's all the staff and even the Stroud boys who have noticed it; that Wells fellow will be the breaking of you. We've all noticed he doesn't work with you any more, but he's definitely up to something; he's in that workshop for hours at a time but never in the daytime. You must have heard the racket coming from the workshop in the early hours; God only knows what he and that machine…"

Ernest stopped her there; she wasn't supposed to know any details on his and Wells's work. "You have seen it then?" he asked meekly.

"Seen it!" she answered loudly. "It is like nothing that should be on God's earth. Honestly, sir, I thought of you as a Christian man, but to me, this is the Devil's work." As she shook her head and cupped it as if she was about to cry.

Ernest pulled himself together and, showing his authority, thanked Mrs Beddoes for listening to his woes and lovingly escorted her from the room.

Mrs Beddoes peered back in a gentle but clear voice and added, "Sir, that Wells is not right; be very careful with him; his ways towards Emily are not noble. I don't blame you if you haven't noticed, with all your working out and scribblings, but he has taken to escorting Emily on her daily trips to the city and who knows what goes on there, now I've said too much, you know I love you as a son and would not want to see you hurt."

Ernest, shocked but not wanting to show any emotion, bid Mrs Beddoes a good day, turned around and entered his study.

How could I let it get to this point, my weakness and let Wells basically take over my life? He has made me feel more like a guest in my own home. No wonder Emily is drawn towards his strong character and not the wet blanket I've become; let's hope not too much damage has been done and there is a chance of repairing my marriage. Perhaps taking Emily away on a much-deserved holiday would be the answer, maybe two weeks abroad and when we return, I will do the right thing and tell Hubert we have reached the end of our road together; after all, he's a grown man and the worst way, he can go back to similar employment as when I found him at The London Hospital, Ernest thought positively to himself.

*

The holiday in Venice away from 'The Big House', with all its issues, was the best thing that had happened to Ernest and Emily for years, or so he believed. On their return, at first, all seemed as it should, but it wasn't long before the Stroud brothers and all of his household staff noticed Emily was once again in Well's company more than she was with Ernest.

After one particularly hard day, wrapped up in his work setting about trying to fathom out the problem of what was preventing his iron guardian from obtaining a true artificial intelligence, Ernest accepted that disappointedly had not made any real gains and should make a fresh start in the morning. Trying in vain to get to sleep, thoughts of how he was being treated by Wells rattled around his brain and unable to rest, he decided there was no time like the present and headed towards Wells's room to confront him. As he knocked on the bedroom door, with no answer, he proceeded to enter and, as he looked around, was shocked to see the room in a worse state than he had ever seen it before. Empty bottles were strewn everywhere, strange powder marks on the bedside cabinet surfaces and most alarmingly, he spotted discarded needles on the floor and blood stains on the sheets. It became increasingly apparent to Ernest that this man, with whom he had shown friendship and given free board, was not deserving of his trust.

Hmm, where is he now? This is the straw that's broken the camel's back. I've got to sort this out, Ernest thought worryingly before he left the filthy room and set out to find Wells.

Mrs Beddoes was in the hall going about her daily duties and as their paths crossed, Ernest couldn't resist. Taking advantage of the opportunity, asked her what on earth had been going on.

"Sir, I warned you, he gave me and all the staff strict instructions to never enter his room; he is practically nocturnal.

We never see him in the day, but from around two a.m. until six a.m., there are all sorts of terrible noises coming from the workshop; I'm telling you, sir, while you were away on holiday, he's got a lot worse."

Ernest shocked at what his loyal housekeeper had just told him, made his excuses and asked Mrs Beddoes to run him a bath whilst he pondered on his next course of action.

After his bath, Ernest quietly got into bed next to Emily and lay there deep in thought, being careful not to fall asleep as he waited for Wells's inevitable return.

Just as Mrs Beddoes had stated, around two a.m., loud rumbling noises could be heard from the workshop area.

Luckily for me, Emily is a heavy sleeper, Ernest thought as he slipped on some clothes and crept out of the bedroom and, silently as he could, made his way to the front door and, once outside, headed in the direction of the commotion.

Once at the workshop's small window, Ernest peered in and could see the giant mechanical beast had been brought to life, its eyes and mouth glowing crimson red. Its massive iron body was rocking side to side as if ready to pounce. Ernest noticed that the beast wasn't chained or shackled in any way and he began to wonder what was actually holding it back. Scrutinising the room, Ernest could clearly see it was, in fact, Hubert Wells, who was keeping the beast at bay by using a form of sign language.

It was at this moment that Ernest saw something so horrific; it would be the final signal that would end his and Hubert Wells's friendship forever. As the iron beast's eyes glowed with increased intensity above the rushing, pulsing sound of its raging furnace, Ernest could just hear the familiar sound of a whimpering, yelping dog. Shockingly, in Wells's hands were what appeared to be a terrified small Yorkshire terrier.

"Hold back, or as you know, I will immobilise you!" shouted Wells sternly at the increasingly agitated enormous metal bulldog. "Do exactly as I have taught you and there will be plenty more of these for you to play with."

Ernest's instincts told him to intervene but he knew with their mechanical beast completely in Wells's control, it would be too dangerous for him to enter. Somehow, without Ernest's authority, Wells had made their proposed iron guardian into his slave, a killing machine with just one master. For a split second, thinking of putting his safety before him, Ernest prepared to run into the workshop to save the pitiful-looking small dog, but alas, it was too late for this helpless creature. All he could do was watch on as the monstrous iron beast at full power, obeying its master's theatrical arm gestures, dropped its huge metal jaw, exposing the raging furnace inside its enormous mouth.

With the heat intensifying, scalding the hair from the helpless howling terrier dog, moments from its merciless death, the metal monster's huge jaw snapped shut, ripping the defenceless creature to shreds, sending portions of blood-soaked flaming fur and flesh into the air, whilst Wells watched on laughing maniacally.

Ernest, helpless to do anything, left the horrendous scene and ran towards 'The Big House,' all the while covering his ears in an attempt to black out the terrible noises coming from the workshop. It was there and then he decided that at first light this morning, he would banish Hubert Wells from his house and, moreover, from his entire life. Sadness flooded over him as he couldn't help thinking it was such a shame as he remembered, in the early days of their 'Iron Guardian' project, they had already given a name to their creation, 'Barker', the mechanical protector and servant, a name not fitting of the unthinking killing machine that Wells had made it become.

Back at his bed, not wanting to worry or concern Emily, traumatised at what he had just witnessed, Ernest fell exhausted into a deep sleep. Waking later than his usual time, he noticed that Emily was not beside him and got up and walked towards the main bathroom, thinking to himself, *Directly after my bath, I will confront Wells, telling him I have seen everything he had been up, to and want him out of my life.*

After his bath and getting dressed in his bedroom, in the distance, Ernest could hear unfamiliar mumbling sounds coming from Wells's room; intrigued by these sounds, he approached the door. Deciding not to barge in silently, he waited outside, eavesdropped, and heard a male voice speaking.

"But you have to do it this way for full effect." Ernest could hear the slurred mumblings of an inebriated Wells. Choosing to continue listening, intrigued by what on earth was going on, he suddenly felt nauseated and sick, as though he had been punched in the stomach, as the next voice he heard was unmistakably that of his wife, Emily.

"I fear if I take any more, I will burst with excitement. I am so glad you have introduced me to this powder; perhaps one day you will let me take it as you do, you know, with that needle." She giggled.

With that, Ernest burst through the door and, full of rage, he went to attack the part-naked Wells, but more shockingly, glancing over, he could see that his wife Emily was completely nude. Both Wells and Emily's reactions were not what he had expected; they appeared not at all shocked at being discovered in this betrayal but instead just gawped at Ernest mockingly. Wells, breaking the silence, gave out a loud, sneering laugh accompanied by a sickly, slightly stupefied giggle from Emily, like a small child who had been caught doing something naughty. Suddenly, Emily gave out a mocking laugh at Ernest and at the same time Hubert began shouting out derogatory names.

"Boring, tedious, dull old Ernest," he chanted over and over.

At the same time, Emily, barely able to stand, made an attempt to dress herself and fell into Wells's lap. As a final humiliation, she leaned over and gave him a full kiss on his lips.

Ernest, incensed at this, went to swing a punch at Hubert but, being a tender man and so hurt by this treachery, just turned his back on the pair of them. As Ernest left the room in a voice that even he did not think he was capable of, he shouted angrily, "I want both of you despicable creatures out of my house immediately! You heard me! Now!"

Wells, never the one for not getting the last word, retaliated and shouted out, "Don't think this will be the final humiliation you get from me, Postlewaite, you see. It's not jealousy that led me to behave in this manner; let me explain: it's simply my love for life, something someone as stuffy as you could never understand. You may be successful and wealthy, but in fact, you are just one of life's great bores. Ask Emily who she prefers," sneered Wells.

Ernest was not prepared to listen any more and having said everything he needed to, he just walked away. A short while later, sitting in his study, Ernest heard the front door slam, a sound that signified to him that, sadly, his marriage was over and this would have to be a new beginning. Not usually a man who needs a cliched quote, but this one was so fitting his recent bad experience he began to repeat it in the form of a mantra: 'The darkest hour is just before dawn' letting the comforting words swirl inside his head, over and over until gradually soothing him he found a semblance of peace.

Chapter Three

Walter Sheridan, Detective Extraordinaire

Two months had passed since Ernest had banished Wells from his home. Sadly, that frightful period in his life had also spelt the end of his marriage. Ernest had still not mustered the motivation to continue with his 'Iron Guardian Project' and was beginning to feel morose. One glorious spring morning, an ominous letter arrived from his bank manager, requesting an urgent meeting.

As Ernest sat in the bank's small office, he stared at Smyth, a small balding man smartly dressed but wearing the same well-worn clothes he had been dressed in on every occasion Ernest had visited.

As Ernest tried to get comfortable, Smyth, in an authoritative voice spoke, "It seems, Professor, your current projects are costing you a small fortune."

"What do you mean," interrupted Ernest, shocked at what Smyth had just told him.

"Let me put it this way: if you carry on spending at your current rate and without a new source of income, I am afraid that very soon you'll be on the verge of bankruptcy," continued Smyth as he proceeded to produce the detailed statements of Ernest's recent withdrawals.

A sick, nauseous feeling overcame Ernest as he began

reading the documents and realised, they could only be accounted for by the treacherous Wells forging his signature. It seemed his unlawful withdrawals had started from the very first time Ernest had brought him to live at his house.

Not willing to divulge his theory to Smyth and wanting to leave the bank manager on a positive note, Ernest said, "I will shelve my latest projects and promise there will be no more extravagant spending for the foreseeable future."

Smyth gave Ernest a stern look and said, "That is fine but be assured I will keep you informed if this problem escalates." He stood up, preparing to shake Ernest's hand and bid him farewell.

Standing outside, away from the bank manager's stuffy office, Ernest took a deep breath of the fresh spring air. With his head clearing somewhat from the traumatic news he had just been given, he vowed to himself there and then that Wells would not get away with this embezzlement and near ruination of him. Knowing he needed to press on with his 'Iron Guardian Project,' he was very glad that the bank was not his sole means of saving. Never being a man to keep all his 'eggs in one basket', he had managed to keep a large amount of cash in a concealed safety box in his house. Ernest's thoughts focused on what he should do next.

I will need to track down that traitor Wells and my disloyal wife, but also, I cannot let this consume me and be my sole purpose in life; I have more satisfying things to get on with; hmm, maybe I should use a private detective, I know it's more expense but if I am to legally rid Emily from my life, it would be worth it in the long run.

Back at his house, in his study, Ernest began trawling through all his old newspapers, scrutinising the advertising sections until he found exactly the sort of agency he was looking for.

"There it is," he said to himself with a satisfied grin on his face. "Walter Sheridan, specialist in photography and private detection, fits the bill perfectly," speaking to himself, a bad habit he had gotten into since finding himself virtually alone rattling around the increasingly solemn 'Big House'. Making sure this time he didn't speak out loud, he thought to himself, *I shall travel to Sheridan's office first thing tomorrow morning.*

*

Ernest, with an optimistic spring in his step, emerged from the main exit of the Brixton Aerial Station. Walking briskly whilst using his local map, he soon found himself standing outside a modern, smart-looking shop; above in gold lettering on a black background was the impressive sign 'Walter Sheridan Photographic Specialist'.

On entering, Ernest is confronted by what was one of life's great eccentrics. Dressed in the garb of the previous century stood a striking redheaded fellow sporting impressive mutton chop side whiskers. His eyes were framed by a pair of blue-tinted, wire-rimmed spectacles.

"And what can we do for you today, sir, perhaps a family portrait," spoke the extravagantly dressed proprietor.

Ernest initially felt a pang of sadness as he began thinking, *Family portrait, not much chance of that happening in my current situation.*

"Perhaps at a later date," he answered, not wanting to elaborate any more on his life just yet.

Hmm, I will have to ascertain if this Sheridan fellow is the right man for the job before I go into more detail, the thought flashed through his mind.

"No, not photography today. I am actually here for your detective services," continued Ernest. "But first, sir, if you have an office of some sort, perhaps you could show me some references of your previous work."

Sitting in a small office above the shop, Walter Sheridan, looking all the more eccentric, having still not removed his emerald green bowler hat and burgundy frock coat, sat himself down at his desk. Before getting down to his proposal, Ernest spent a short time studying in more detail the eccentrically fellow dressed in full eighteenth century attire. Wearing a white ruffled shirt and black and green broad striped breaches, the look was completed with highly polished black leather riding boots, whilst perched by his side was a smart silver capped ebony walking stick. The epitome of one of Beau Brummell's London 'Dandy's.

After thirty minutes of intense discussion and perusing over some of Sheridan's fine naturalistic photographs, Ernest had to admit to himself this albeit highly eccentric fellow, Walter Sheridan, would be the perfect man for the job.

Ernest was highly impressed by what he had seen, spoke, "Walter, to be honest, in this pioneering field of photography, I have never seen such true-to-life naturalistic images in all my life."

"Let me stop you there, sir," interjected Walter. "I believe wholeheartedly there is not another person in the world as advanced in photography as me; you see, sir, I am the son of the late Albert Sheridan; you may have heard of him, the most respected photographer of the modern age. Since I was eight years old, I was my father's apprentice and prodigy. I am in possession of many photographic devices that are not yet available to the general public. In many ways, we are kindred spirits because although you haven't boasted about it, I recognise you as the great Professor Ernest Postlewaite, the inventor of our capital's world-leading Aerial Rail System. I, too, sir, am an inventor. If we reach a mutual agreement and you would like me to proceed to work on your proposed case, I will give you an exclusive demonstration and show you how I achieve photographs that are so realistic and informal. OK, Ernest, stand up," said Walter loudly.

Ernest did as he was asked and began thinking to himself, *Oh, here we go; am I in for a long, boring photographic session? The big box will appear, the black cloth over the head and that long wait keeping still, whilst the photographer prepares his solutions and arranges all sorts of paraphernalia.*

Walter proceeded to pull out a small device from his desk drawer and before Ernest could prepare himself, his eyes began to sting as a bright flash of light almost blinded him. After a few seconds, Ernest's eyes began to recover and he watched on as Walter pulled out what appeared to be a small card from the side of the strange, unfamiliar-looking box.

"Right, prepare to be amazed!" exclaimed the striking-looking eccentric fellow as, from the other side of the box, he removed a lilac-tipped pencil and proceeded to vigorously rub the pencil-like stick over the card.

"Fifty-seven, fifty-eight, fifty-nine, sixty, there, that has worked a treat!" exclaimed Walter as he waived the card excitedly in the air, occasionally stopping to gently blow over it. With a beaming smile on his face, Walter turned the card around and faced it towards Ernest.

Shocked at what he observed, the Professor lowered himself back into his seat and stared at the card in more detail, where he could see a perfect picture of himself squinting from the bright light that had flashed into his eyes.

"There you are, the first person apart from myself to actually see a demonstration of the world's first instantaneous camera," said Walter, quite sure he had managed to truly impress his client.

Over the next half hour, Ernest told Walter the entire story of how his former friend Hubert Wells had betrayed him and embezzled most of his money, making very sure to explain to Walter that he still had enough funds to cover his services.

"Ernest, it's been a pleasure to meet you today. May I add I feel privileged that you have chosen me to find the whereabouts of Hubert Wells and your wife, Emily? Perhaps, give me two weeks before I contact you with any information and hopefully photographic evidence of their infidelity."

Ernest agreed that this was an excellent plan and stood up about to leave.

"Ernest, you don't have to rush off. Would you like some tea or coffee, whichever you prefer?" asked Walter in a kind tone.

"Well, I admit that would be nice," replied Ernest, beginning to unwind from the day's stressful events.

After a short while of chatting about things in general, a slim, pretty-looking woman appeared, holding a tray of tea and biscuits.

"May I introduce my beautiful maid, Miss Rose Morely," said Walter, giving his employee an admiring glance.

After tea and more chit-chat, Ernest bid his quirky associate goodbye and asked him to bid farewell to the lovely Rose Morely for him. It was at this point in time he couldn't help sadly thinking to himself, 'I have to admit Rose is very pretty and so demure, not unlike my dear Emily was before that Wells had poisoned her.'

Ernest made his way to the Brixton branch of 'The Hand'

and reflected on a most satisfying day, having met two wonderful people, a genius photographer and his very attractive maid.

Stepping onto one of 'The Hand's' carriages, he made himself as comfortable as he could. Taking a deep breath, he gazed out the window as it began its ascent to the top of the dome, picking up fellow passengers as his journey to his destination in Hampstead continued.

Suddenly, Ernest felt many of his fellow commuters whispering and staring at him. It wasn't long before he realised, he had been recognised.

Oh no, I'm not really in the mood for chit-chat, he thought, as one of the passengers, a jolly middle-aged woman, couldn't help herself and spoke.

"It is you, isn't it? Professor Postlewaite? sir, you must be so proud, 'The Hand' is the envy of the world, you know and look at that view. Thank God they never approved that underground railway. All that smoke! You would have never have caught me travelling on that," she concluded.

"Thank you, Madam, I have to admit, you do get a stunning view from up here," said Ernest, full of pride, as the gentle clunk of 'The Hands' drive gears changed over to enable the carriage to make its steep, steady descent towards the Hampstead Village station.

Back home, Ernest suddenly began thinking about what was to become of the great hulking giant metal bulldog that lay currently immobilised in his workshop. 'Hmm, the basis is there, but if I am to give that artificial intelligence he deserves, I will have to drastically modify its command system. Something I fear even I couldn't achieve on my own. What I need is some sort of mathematical genius.'

With those words flickering into his mind, he pondered and

tried to remember where he had last heard that phrase.

Yes, I've got it, that first journey I shared with Wells on 'The Hand'. What was it he said about Quinn? That's it.

"Never judge by appearances, Quinn, far from being the pitiful freak of nature as most people would perceive, is, in fact, a mathematical genius."

Ernest's head cleared because he had now found what he believed was the key to his 'Iron Guardian Project'.

So, it seems it was Quinn, not Wells, that I needed as my associate. Let's hope he's still at the London Hospital and I can convince him to join me on my project. Now, where is that, Mrs Beddoes? I feel I have a lot of explaining to do, thought Ernest to himself, glad that he had one person in his life that he knew he could trust.

Chapter Four

Quinn, the Enigma That Is

Ernest, for the second time in his recent history, entered The London Hospital without the doorman batting an eyelid,
That was simple; I guess I am so well respected around these parts; no one would ever suspect me of any wrongdoing, he thought to himself, glad he hadn't stumbled at the first hurdle.

Ernest had come fully prepared with a detailed map of the London Sewers system along with a vesta box and candle as he knew there was no way he would be able to leave by the front door accompanied by the strange-looking Quinn.

Making his way to the basement, as Ernest walked past the boiler room, he felt a strong urge to push open the door, in the possibility that Wells would be inside working at his old job. Knowing this was his imagination getting the better of him and would never actually be the case, he fought off his urge and continued down the small flight of steps in front of him.

OK, I've only been here once, but I distinctively remember this leads me to Joseph and Quinn's rooms, he confidently thought.

Ernest's previous encounter with Joseph and Quinn had left an indelible impression on his mind and standing in front of the two basement room doors, Ernest, although knowing it would be a distraction from his mission, felt compelled to enter the room on the left, Joseph's room to see how he was doing.

Poor fellow, I must admit he didn't look as though he had much time left for this world, thought Ernest as he opened the door and entered the room.

Instantly, he could see that Joseph wasn't there and the bed was made up. Peering around, he spotted on a small desk a number of intriguing-looking books and he proceeded to open one of them.

'Hmm, very interesting, diagrams of all kinds of surgical procedures, well I suppose not really a surprise, I am in a hospital,' he laughed to himself as he reached over to the largest, most impressive book, a black leather-bound example he carefully opened it up.

What Ernest observed shocked him to his core. Each page showed detailed images of babies and small children, all displaying numerous deformities. As he took a seat and studied the book more intensely, suddenly stopping him in his tracks, he heard a voice outside the room. Quietly, he readjusted his position and laid on the floor at the side of the bed in an attempt to hide.

"Wells, my work here is done," a loud voice came from close outside the room.

Ernest recognised the tone as the same stern, authoritative voice he had heard the previous time he was here. Laying, frightened that they were about to enter, Ernest slid a little more under the bed and nervously continued to listen to the conversation.

"Never try and contact me again; although you are a man of means these days, you are still an addict."

The other person, whom Ernest instantly recognised as Hubert Wells, in a sneering tone, responded. "I may be an addict, but who else could you find to carry out your heinous work? It looks like we are stuck with each other."

As the voices, thankfully for Ernest's sake, became more distant, he listened on.

"Wells, don't you worry, I will keep you supplied. I said my work Here is done. I did not say I won't need your services again."

Ernest continued to lay still until he could hear nothing except his own heart pounding. When confident Wells and the mysterious, authoritative man had left the vicinity, he stood up and left the room and, quietly shutting the door behind him, walked the short distance to the second room.

All I know for sure is that he is called Quinn, but how can I introduce myself? Should I knock? Can he even hear me?

These many questions began to dart around Ernest's mind. Before he even had time to react, the door opened and he was confronted by the frightening vision of Quinn. The grotesque, featureless head facing Ernest caused him to shudder.

Oh, my Lord, he is more bizarre than I remember; well, at least I haven't passed out this time, Ernest thought, trying to keep calm.

With that, Quinn placed his hands on Ernest's face and, in doing so, proceeded to walk backwards, gently pulling Ernest into his room. All the while, Ernest is aware that somewhere in his head, he can hear a kind, comforting voice talking to him.

"Don't ever be afraid of me." Ernest noticed that as the words appeared, Quinn's fingers were gently tapping at the side of his face in a rhythm inexplicably connected with what he could hear.

"If I could have communicated with you on our last brief encounter. I would have warned you that Wells is not to be trusted." The uncanny sensation of speech continued to waft all inside Ernest's head. "I have over time realised that all humankind, as I perceive them, consider me disabled. The truth of the matter is, I have ascertained that the senses that most humans rely on I have no real need for."

Ernest began to pull his head back from Quinn's hands as the whole process was beginning to make him feel uncomfortable. Expecting the words in his head to disappear, he was amazed when the conversation continued.

"Ernest, you may count yourself as privileged as there are only a few people I have, shall I say, 'shown myself' in this way. By making this connection with you initially it is an exhausting procedure for me, but trust me, our conversations in the future will be a lot easier, as I can hear your thoughts and enter your mind without the need of any physical contact."

Ernest spoke to Quinn by projecting his thoughts, "Bringing Wells into my life turned out to be the worst decision I have ever made."

Suddenly, a tingling sensation was felt on Ernest's neck as once more Quinn's words appeared in his head. "The very first time I made the connection with Wells, I could feel a darkness, but I have such a small circle of acquaintances, I did not want to cut him out of my life, but believe me, loneliness is a bigger burden than an ill-judged friendship, you could say some contact is better than none at all."

As the tingling stopped and Ernest's head cleared, he once again trained his thoughts towards Quinn, "I get your sentiment entirely and with the way my life is heading, I myself need all the friends and help available. Quinn, would you agree to come with me now and help me with the project Wells and I had begun? The thing is, we had started to make good progress but Wells' evil nature had steered our project on the wrong path. Quinn, I believe with your help and your vast mathematical knowledge, together as a team, we could achieve results that are all I have ever dreamt of."

Before Ernest could say any more, the tingling started, signifying Quinn was about to speak, "I would love to experience the world beyond these four walls, so without hesitation, I accept your offer but we must go now as it is around this time the doctors are doing their rounds and sometimes check on me."

With that, Ernest watched on as Quinn pulled across the small rug, exposing the metal cover he and Wells had escaped down previously. Quinn prized open the metal cover from the floorboards and, using hand gestures, beckoned Ernest to descend into the dark tunnels below them. Standing at the bottom in the pitch black, Ernest watched on as Quinn closed the lid behind them. Remembering he had brought his vesta stick and candle, Ernest prepared to remove them from his pocket but suddenly felt sick as a loud splash was heard as the vesta stick slipped from his hand into the foul-smelling water. In a frantic attempt, in complete darkness, Ernest fumbled about, but to his dismay, the flowing water had seemingly washed the only means of lighting the candle away.

Feeling a mixture of being useless and helplessness, suddenly, the familiar tingling and comforting voice of Quinn entered his head. "Ernest, when you are with me, you will not need any map or any of the senses you usually rely on; all I need you to do is think hard about the address of your house,"

Ernest concentrated all his thoughts towards Quinn 'Hampstead'.

Instantly, the tingling sensation appeared along with Quinn's voice, "Do not say another word; from here on, you must stay silent; this is very important, as I need to concentrate."

Ernest, even in this virtual darkness, could see that Quinn was leaning his head back and was letting out a strong rush of air from the orifice on his neck, where soon after, he heard Quinn's voice enter his mind and say, "Hold on to my coat and stay close to me."

With that, Ernest followed close, watching Quinn as he moved his head in a slow, rhythmic swaying motion, stopping occasionally as he decided what path to take of the eerie labyrinth of tunnels that stretched out before them.

The long walk in complete silence gave Ernest a great opportunity to let his thoughts wander, *There has recently been a spate of violent murders in Whitechapel; this city has done a lot for me; what a brilliant way to repay it,* as he began to visualise Barker, his mechanical 'Iron Guardian' as the obedient and trustworthy machine that he had always dreamt of patrolling and policing the streets unassisted.

Suddenly, Quinn stopped walking. "Over there, that should bring us out in Hampstead Village," Quinn's words entered Ernest's head. Feeling extremely relieved on hearing this as the long walk in complete darkness had started to drain him. Quinn, using his knuckle, rapped on something metallic sounding. Speaking in his inimitable way, he continued, "This ladder should lead us to wasteland a short distance from the Hampstead Aerial station."

Ernest was beginning to think his companion with his unique senses was even more amazing than he could ever have imagined. In complete trust, he followed Quinn as they both climbed the steep ladder. Quinn, on reaching the top, pushed hard on the metal cover; a glow of moonlight filtered through as Ernest followed and clambered out of the manhole.

The comforting glow of 'The Hand's' carriages high up in the sky shone a soft glow onto Quinn's strange thumb-like head.

As Ernest stared at his deformed companion, he began to worry. 'This could be the hard part; how will Mrs Beddoes or any of my work companions react to Quinn? Oh well, it won't be long until I find out.'

All of a sudden, Quinn's voice entered his head, "We are in your territory now; you take the lead."

Ernest strode ahead, knowing this area very well, even in the dark of the night. "Keep up, Quinn!" shouted Ernest as he looked back and wondered, *How does he hear and see? Definitely not in the usual way; however, he seems to cope very well. I am still not comfortable with the way his words can just appear in my head; oh well, there is plenty of time to get to know him better. Hmm, that's as long as he doesn't know everything I'm thinking.* Ernest worried to himself.

As though Quinn had waited until Ernest's mind was clear, he spoke in his unique way, "Much further to go?"

"Nearly there, just beyond those trees," Ernest answered, quickly realising that what he had just said would only apply to a fully sighted person.

Before he had time to apologise, Ernest heard Quinn's voice in his head, "I may not see as I am told you people can, but I am always aware of my surrounding environment. I must admit this light rain helps a lot to give me a more detailed picture; I take it you are talking about the large oak tree to the left and not the sycamore tree directly ahead."

Ernest, stunned into silence, marched forward in the direction of his house.

*

Upon arriving at 'The Big House', Ernest, as quietly as he could, unlocked the front door. "Quinn, follow me; I will show you the guest room," he said, surprising himself by how good he was getting at telepathy, continuing, "Good, the beds made up; we have had quite an eventful evening. I am very tired and expect you to be too. Let us get some sleep now and we can go over the finer points tomorrow," said Ernest as he bid his strange companion a good night.

The following morning, Ernest knocked on his guest room door and waited for Quinn to respond. With no answer, Ernest entered the room. Thoughts flashed through Ernest's mind. *It feels as though Wells has contaminated this room; I can still feel his obnoxious presence.* Peering down at Quinn lying still on the bed, Ernest thought. 'Is he asleep? How can I tell?' Before he had time to bend down and give his guest a gentle nudge, he heard Quinn's voice enter his head.

"I've actually been awake quite a while," Answered Quinn in his own way.

Ernest was still concerned about how others might react to his strange guest's appearance. "Quinn, my man, I was thinking of introducing you to my housekeeper, who, after all, whilst you are staying here, will have to tend to all your culinary needs. I would like to add that in the past, whilst working on my Iron Guardian project, I have used the services of two wonderful Blacksmiths, the Stroud brothers, Samuel and Frederick. For our work together to proceed, you, sir, will have to work alongside them, so maybe it's best you meet them today."

"Ernest," replied Quinn, "my life, as you can well imagine, has been one of almost total solitude. Apart from the occasional visit from Wells, the only other person I have had any physical contact with at the London Hospital is the premier surgeon, who goes by the name of Bamforth."

Ernest could see that the very mention of this Bamforth character had physically drained Quinn, who was by now sitting up on the side of his bed cupping the wrinkled forehead section of his featureless head as a slightly disturbing rasping sound could be heard as though he was gasping for air.

"Sorry about that," said Quinn into Ernest's mind, continuing, "You are right; I will have to get used to meeting new people."

At this moment in time, Ernest felt it best he didn't pry or make too much fuss over Quinn's breathing difficulties. Changing the subject, he asked, "Is there anything I could get you to make you feel comfortable?"

Quinn, grateful for Ernest's concern, answered, "Yes, thank you, my friend. Some soap, hot water and fresh underwear would be perfect if I am not being too presumptuous."

Ernest was amazed that in such a short time, he had got used to Quinn's way of communicating and felt he should give his guest time on his own to adjust to his new environment. With that, I decided to leave him in peace. "Shall we say four p.m.? I will come for you then and as I promised, only my three closest companions will be at the meeting," said Ernest to Quinn in an upbeat tone.

The large sitting room of the big house emitted an excited burble of voices as Samuel and Frederick Stroud sipped their tea and chatted to Mrs Beddoes.

"I suppose it will be more adaptations of that great mechanical beast we built for the professor," exclaimed Samuel, quickly realising he might have divulged something Mrs Beddoes should not have heard.

Picking up on Samuel's discomfort, Mrs Beddoes interjected, "Oh, don't you worry, Samuel, there's not much getting past me around this house." As she laughed to herself and recalled all the strange loud noises she had heard coming from the long-abandoned workshop.

All became silent in the sitting room as the door slowly opened and Ernest walked in and addressed his guests. "Mrs Beddoes, Samuel, Frederick, it's nice to have you here all together," continuing, "in a short while, I will introduce you to the man who has kindly agreed to be my new work partner. I have to tell you here and now that this man, who, in many respects, is of superior intellect to mine, I must warn all of you, has an appearance like no other man. I fear you will all be shocked at how he looks, but I am appealing to your good natures that you let him communicate with you before you judge him."

Mrs Beddoes, Samuel and Frederick sat poised as Ernest called out for his new mysterious friend to enter. "Quinn, you can come in now, dear fellow."

Audible gasps are heard from the seated ensemble as they all stared at the tall, featureless freak of nature that stood before them. Samuel Stroud made the first reaction as a simple, straight-talking man; he stood up and pulled at the shoulder of his brother in a gesture as though about to storm out of the room.

Frederick, a strong-minded individual, in a forceful way, pulled Samuel back and said, "Sam, you are showing me up. You heard the professor explain we'd be shocked when we first saw him!" He coaxed Samuel to calm down.

With all sitting comfortably, they listened intently to Ernest as he requested that they free their minds of any distracting thoughts.

Instantaneously and inexplicably, Quinn spoke to all of them at once and as his words filled their minds, he explained, "I have never had the opportunity to try this before but it seems that, at times, I can even amaze myself."

The entire group sat trancelike as the strange-looking fellow talked soothingly into their heads. Continuing the conversation, laughing and joking, as if they had known each other all their life, they set out plans for how they should all work together.

Worryingly, Mrs Beddoes had a fleeting thought, *What food will I have to prepare and as I can see no visible mouth. How does that strange fellow manage to eat?*

Suddenly, there was a loud knock on the front door that abruptly brought them all out of their trance-like state.

Ernest, not expecting anyone, left his guests to enjoy each other's company and proceeded to answer the door. Standing before him with his shock of red hair and impressive mutton chops, dressed in his customary outlandish, dandy attire, stood the highly eccentric Walter Sheridan.

"Walter, I thought you would have sent me a telegraph to arrange a meeting and not just turn up at my house. This is a rather inconvenient time, you know," said Ernest, at the same time thinking that, fortuitously, this could be a perfect opportunity for him to introduce Quinn to him. "Walter, I presume the reason for this unexpected visit is that you have updates and hopefully photographic evidence of my wife's infidelity. You do realise this is a matter I would like to keep just between the two of us and as I have guests at the moment, it is inconvenient for us to go into detail right now," said Ernest firmly.

"Of course, I understand; look, if you don't want your guests privy to this matter, we'll leave that for another time, but whilst I am here, I am sure at the very least you would like to see the pictures I have obtained. I must warn you, though they might come as a bit of a shock once seen, I think you will agree they are certainly explicit enough for you to file for a divorce, as by this evidence, it seems that Wells fellow has taken your wife to the depths of depravity."

With that, Walter produced from the inside pocket of his frock coat a small pile of photographs. One by one, as he carefully laid them out on the hall table and as he described to Ernest exactly where and when he had taken them, he disclosed, "I know for a fact that the pair of adulterers are not living at any fixed address but are constantly moving from one hotel or boarding house to another."

Staring at the images at first, Ernest felt quite underwhelmed that what he could see was not as graphic as he had expected, only showing Emily and Hubert engaged in close embraces. "Walter, honestly, if I am to obtain a divorce, I will need more than this to convince the magistrate of gross misconduct on my wife's part. I am afraid these photographs are just not good enough." Whilst angrily shaking his head in disappointment.

"Wait!" exclaimed Walter sternly. "I told you at our initial meeting that I am no ordinary photographer; you see, my good man, using my 'Extended distance, focus adjusting camera', I have secured very upsetting photographic proof that highly unacceptable behaviour has occurred between them."

With that, Walter produced a second series of images showing Wells and Emily during various stages of extreme drug abuse.

Before Ernest had time to react, unexpectedly, in a loud voice, he heard Mrs Beddoes call out in a worried tone, "Professor, is everything all right out there?"

"Yes, I am fine. I will be in soon. Would you explain to the others I won't be long?" said Ernest, annoyed with himself at leaving his guests unattended for all this time but also extremely worried about what Walter had revealed to him.

The first photograph showed Emily laying back on a couch with one of her arms exposed and Wells apparently tying a tourniquet around it.

The second photograph, sadly for Ernest, was even more graphic, showing Wells heating up what appeared to be brown powder on a small spoon until it turned to liquid.

The third shocked Ernest to his core, as it showed Wells injecting the liquid substance, probably heroin, into Emily's arm as she laid down stupefied with a sickening glazed look in her eyes.

Wiping a tear from his cheek, Ernest looked pathetic and helpless as he admitted, "Yes, Walter, this will indeed be all the evidence I will need," as he proceeded to place the pile of damming photographs in the inside pocket of his jacket.

Ernest, never really knowing if he would need Walter's services again, decided this would be an excellent opportunity to introduce Walter to the enigma that is Quinn.

Escorting Walter to join his other guests, not really preparing him for what he was about to see, in a similar fashion to Ernest's first encounter with Quinn, Walter reaction was just as dramatic.

Mrs Beddoes frantically wafted smelling salts around the eccentric flame-haired man, who was currently lying unconscious on the living room floor.

Groggy but recovering, Walter pulled himself up and bent down to retrieve his blue-tinted spectacles. "Eh, Hum," – clearing his throat before speaking – "don't faff woman, I am perfectly well."

Mrs Beddoes, knowing her place, made her excuses and left

the room and thought, *I am a good judge of character and as long as Ernest does not invite that rude fellow to live here, I will keep my opinions to myself, but for me the less I see of him the better,* as she entered the kitchen to prepare the liquified mush of vegetables as Quinn had requested.

Back in the sitting room, the Stroud brothers had bid farewell to Ernest, Quinn and Walter, leaving them to discuss matters that they had accepted were none of their business.

Quinn had struggled to make a good 'connection' with Walter. He could feel a strong resistance but, for Ernest's sake, persevered. Very soon, it became apparent to Quinn that this particular individual would never want to be his friend and feeling ever more exhausted with the black wall of resistance blocking his thoughts, he eventually decided he could not endure no more.

Quinn, nodding his strange head politely, bid his farewell, but before leaving the room, focused his thoughts towards Ernest and said, "Definitely not my favourite of your acquaintances, but I can see you have much to discuss with him, so with that said, it has been a tiring day for me, goodnight Ernest we will continue our conversation tomorrow," as he closed the sitting room door behind him.

"My God, man, you warned me he was strange looking, but how could you invite that thing into your house," said Walter rudely.

Feeling obliged at putting Walter in his place and beginning to regret he had invited him to see Quinn, Ernest replied in a serious tone, "I think you forget that you are only my employee; it is not for you to tell me, in my house, who I can entertain. More importantly, whenever you are in my company, never refer to Quinn as 'That Thing'; in fact, I do not like your attitude at all."

Walter, not wanting to break his ties with Ernest, spoke meekly, "I do apologise, sir, this whole experience has left my manners somewhat waning. I hope you can forgive my ill-judged outburst." All the time sneakily thinking to himself, 'Quinn, you say, well, in my mind, that hellish abomination doesn't even deserve a name and, in my mind, he should never walk on God's earth,' as he slyly glanced at Ernest, hoping that his insincere response had been believed.

Changing the subject, Walter once again spoke, "I will say, Ernest, this case you have given me has incurred quite a few expenses. Stalking those two has had me travelling to every corner of London. More to the point, I don't know if you are aware, but in our city, especially at night, no gentleman or decent woman could feel safe. There has been a third brutal murder of one of the street harlots. Also, I am fearing our savings and financial investments are no longer safe. Have you seen in the local newspapers apparently a giant machine has smashed to pieces Coutts and Co bank in The Strand? Luckily, no one was hurt, but all the money and valuables were taken. According to witnesses, the safes were crushed and torn open as though they were made of tin. So, if you are on the verge of building something that can protect London, what did you call it? Your iron guardian project, then sooner rather than later, I say. Anyway, good luck with your new partner, although I can't imagine him accompanying you around town with those looks," said Walter, who couldn't resist another hurtful snipe at Quinn's appearance and bid Ernest farewell.

Ernest began to take a distinct dislike to Walter and started thinking it would probably be best that the less he had to do with him the better. With this in mind, he reluctantly shook the spiteful detective's hand and escorted him to his front door.

As Walter walked up the drive, he turned around and, in a jeering, somewhat disdainful voice, shouted out, "Oh, by the way, my bill will be in the post. Don't worry, I won't divulge anything I have seen here today." Giving a salute, in what Ernest felt was a mocking gesture. "We will meet again, as I'm sure there will be an instance you will require my services," he added cryptically as he slammed the huge iron gate behind him and disappeared into the distance.

Chapter Five

Building Bonds

"OK," said Samuel to his brother Frederick as he carefully descended down the stepladder that was securely propped against the giant iron bulldog. "I can't remember which one of us christened him 'Barker', but it has certainly given him more personality. Anyway, that's him completely cleaned and prepared. I must say, although it's Ernest's invention, it has to be our finest work to date," he continued, extremely proud of their achievement.

The past two weeks at the big house, particularly around the workshop, have been a hive of activity. The Stroud brothers had been tasked with giving Barker a complete overhaul, removing and reapplying all the riveted sections, undoing every nut and bolt before cleaning and oiling, and eventually reassembling the great machine.

"Funny," said Frederick. "We always refer to this machine as him, something I never remember doing with any of our other creations," he quizzed, waiting for Samuel's reply.

"Well, you see, Freddie, my boy, our skills are merely to bring machines to life. Ernest's unique skill is that somehow he can give his projects a personality; why do you think 'The Hand' is so iconic? It's not just the means of getting from A to B; it is something the whole of London has grown to love. You see,

Freddie, I think we are both really privileged to be part of this project and once Quinn and Ernest are satisfied with Barker's new command system, mark my words, seeing this machine come to life will be something to behold," said Samuel excitedly, as he gave the huge metal bulldog's cranium section a final dust and polish.

Quinn and Ernest's work on Barker's command system had also reached a crucial stage. Using the biggest guest room as their workshop, the pair gave the gleaming, complex command system, Barker's brain, its final dry run.

"Tell me again, Quinn, why isn't it in one piece?" asked Ernest, who by now took for granted the telepathic way he and Quinn communicated.

"It is in two sections because I have based our innovative artificial intelligence machine on the same principle as the human brain. I have split the right and left side of the cerebrum into two cerebral hemispheres," answered Quinn in a very superior tone.

Oh, I thought it was so we could easily get it through the door, thought Ernest, being flippant.

"Please try and be serious," Quinn's voice flashed into Ernest's head, causing it to sting.

I hate that. Did he actually read my subconscious mind, he thought, hoping Quinn was out of his range? *One thing is for sure, Quinn may be a true genius, but I do not believe any side of his brain possesses a sense of humour,* giggling to himself as he followed Quinn to the front door.

With Samuel and Frederick's assistance, eventually, they managed to manoeuvre Quinn's delicate, complicated mechanical brain into the workshop and lowered it into the great iron bulldog's cranium. Wiping the sweat from their brows after what felt like a particularly strenuous task, the Stroud brothers, having done all they could, sat down for a quick rest.

"Phew! I was beginning to think it wasn't going to fit with all those delicate and intricate components of the brain sections Quinn had built; I must admit there were times I thought all your hard work was going to be destroyed anyway. Whatever happens next is out of mine and Freddy's hands," said Samuel to Ernest cheerfully.

Frederick, seizing the opportunity, hoping Ernest was in his best mood, decided to speak. "Oh, did we mention to you that we need to go home early today?" he continued nervously. "Apparently, our Bassett hound Stanley needs our attention. I think he is pining for us and he is barking all day and night; well, that's according to Mrs Marems in the corner shop and she knows everything."

"No, that will not do," replied Ernest, exasperated that on what could possibly be the most important day for months, they were effectively asking for time off work. Suddenly, Ernest's mind was working at great speed, recalling Frederick had told him he had a Bassett hound dog, hatched a cunning plan that was completely out of his character but could push forward his project at an incredible pace. *Hmm, Wells had used a real dog in his experiment with his version of Barker. As I am convinced that our improved version will be the polar opposite of the killing machine he had created, then surely there is no risk,* he thought, trying to convince himself.

"Boys, you must realise I cannot allow you this day off, but I have an idea; why don't you invite your sister Lilly and your pet dog Stanley to come and visit you here." Ernest knew they would agree but felt slightly sick at his deception.

Frederick allowed a few hours off, left his brother working on Barker and set off in the traction engine to pick up his sister

Lilly and her pet dog. After a few hours, arriving safely back at The Big House workshop, Lilly, holding Stanley's lead, went over and introduced herself to Ernest and Quinn, whose unusual appearance she had been briefed on. Frederick joined his brother in checking that all of Barker's vital components were as they should be.

Suddenly, Ernest, in a loud, authoritative voice, spoke, "Samuel, I hope you have added that emergency stop lever as I requested."

"No, not quite finished yet," shouted back Samuel as, knowing he was behind schedule, frantically welded a heavy bar onto Barker's main oil reservoir pipe.

Ernest, looking admiringly at the striking-looking woman shaking Quinn's hand, was immediately impressed by Lilly's appearance and attitude and thought to himself, *Yes, most certainly a true Stroud. I must say that short boyish hairstyle suits her very well and topped off with that bowler hat, a very modern look, ha, she wouldn't have known, but that tweed trouser suit is perfect for today's activities.* Ernest couldn't help noticing how well Lilly had connected with Quinn as she stood by his side, holding tightly onto Stanley's leash; with her trance-like expression, he could clearly see that Lilly was in deep telepathic conversation with Quinn.

Continuing to take control of proceedings, Ernest announced in a loud voice, "So, I think a quick checklist is in order. Samuel, slide open the observation portal on his cranium and check the command system pipes are all connected while you are at it, torque wrench all the major support fixings and check that the fuel levels are as required, oh and Frederick, the last and most important function you will have to do is hold tightly onto that emergency cut off lever but before doing so you must make sure that the fuel ignites switch is on and the gauges show full pressure, only then turn the 'engage pistons' key but don't forget you must wait at least five seconds before you and Samuel simultaneously press the two big green 'all systems engage' buttons. Myself, Quinn and your sister will be waiting just outside the big double doors. I believe we should all be perfectly safe and I am very confident that all should go well because Quinn has incorporated a 'loyalty connection' device. If this works as we hope, then once activated, on my command, Barker should walk towards myself and Quinn in a steady fashion."

Going through the long, complex activation process, the magnificent ten-foot-long, four-ton giant iron bulldog burst into life. With its huge jaw barely open, all watched on as the glowing coal embers began to flicker inside Barker's huge mouth. As the temperature of his furnace reached maximum steam pressure, the metal dog's huge eyes began glowing crimson red.

With that, Ernest shouted out loudly the command, "Samuel, Frederick, when you are ready, press the all systems to engage buttons!"

With that, the floor of the workshop shuddered as the massive machine reared up on its haunches and, with a thunderous din, gave out a blast of scalding hot air.

Shouting loudly above the noise of Barker's engine, Ernest yelled, "Barker, follow my voice!" Whilst Quinn, Lilly and her dog Stanley stood waiting with apprehension outside the workshop.

Completely ignoring Ernest's command, Barker stood firmly on the spot. This clearly was not the response Ernest and Quinn wanted or expected and they had to admit to themselves that something was not working quite as it should. Suddenly, with a massive jolt, taking Frederick by surprise and throwing him off the 'emergency stop lever' Barker lunged forward. At the same time, Lilly, startled by what she had seen, dropped her pet dog's leash and with Stanley free from the tether, the agitated Bassett hound ran, not as expected, away from the fearsome iron bulldog, but instead towards him.

Ernest's thoughts turned to panic, *No, this cannot be; how could I have allowed this to happen,* fearing Stanley was about to be burnt to a crisp before being mercilessly ripped to shreds.

It was then a very strange thing happened, whether Quinn, in his unique way, had managed to intervene or something of a much baser level came into play. Barker abruptly stopped, his gigantic jaw fully closed shut and his eyes dropped to a soothing, warm orange glow; he then proceeded to lower his haunches and sit in a submissive position.

As Barker's giant bulldog face cooled, Stanley, feeling it safe, approached the fearsome iron bulldog and seemingly, instinctively knew that no matter how big this mechanical canine was, he was still merely a pup and that Stanley, as the elder in this situation was in fact 'The Top Dog'. With a gentle nuzzle and pushing his pore softly into Barker's huge front foot, Stanley waited patiently until the iron beast once again stood up. Turning his head slightly, Barker fixed his eyes on Stanley and waited for his command. Showing all the respect to his new Top Dog friend, with a loud shudder, Barker engaged his sturdy metal legs and marched forward, following Stanley until they both sat obediently at Lilly's side, all the while excitingly wagging his tail, expressing how clever he was.

Ernest, relieved and feeling his mechanical creation was no threat, stood by his side and gently patted the enormous metal bulldog's head. Quinn, Lilly and the two boys, all feeling ever more confident, proceeded to do the same.

Ernest, above all the jolly chatter, spoke in a loud voice, "I truly believe what all of us here have just experienced is something no person, dead or alive, has ever witnessed," he continued, full of pride and emotion and said, "we, my friends, have just seen the first true bond between a living creature and a machine with artificial intelligence, albeit a purely a dog's instincts."

Wiping tears of joy from his face, Ernest called for Stanley to heel and watched on as the clever Bassett hound led the fearsome metal bulldog and walked towards the workshop's large double doors.

Once inside, Ernest called out with his voice full of laughter, "Samuel, Frederick, come here, boys; I need your assistance for the shutdown sequence. Thankfully, that emergency cut-off lever was not required after all."

*

Over the following weeks, The Big House became a hive of activity. Ernest had asked Samuel and Frederick that, during the early trials of Barker, would they mind, along with their sister Lilly and her pet dog Stanley, staying for a few weeks at the Big House, explaining to them he had already informed Lilly that she and Stanley were to be an important part of acclimatising Barker to his surroundings.

"Sir," said Mrs Beddoes to Ernest in a concerned tone, "There is a lot of gossip in the village that normally I wouldn't bother you with. Although only 'tittle-tattle', I think it's important enough for you to hear. You see, sir, it's the noise, Stanley's loud woofing and Barkers engine roaring and hissing, I suppose is acceptable and explainable at midday, but at two a.m.

in the morning, it is causing quite a stir and the few excuses I have given, sound barely believable." Becoming quite emotional, she continued, "You see, sir, I am not a very good liar and not for one minute do I think they believe me when I told them our guest dog had escaped and we needed the traction engine to look for him."

Ernest almost laughed out loud but decided to suppress his inappropriate response and instead gave his loyal, much-loved housekeeper a hug. Addressing her using her Christian name as he had done before in similar circumstances, he said, "Margaret, there, there, please do not upset yourself, leave it to me and I will sort this out. As soon as they are available, I will send Samuel and Frederick into the village and have them put out, shall we say, more plausible explanations. I am sure they are much better liars than you," he concluded, trying to put a humorous atmosphere into the conversation.

Back in his study, Ernest pondered on how best to proceed with his Iron Guardian project. '*Hmm*, I wonder if Barker is ready for the next stage as I am sure he would be a great asset to the Metropolitan Police Force,' thinking to himself as he picked up the latest issue of The London Pictorial Times newspaper. After initially reading a long article documenting every aspect of the Whitechapel murders, on the opposite page, he noticed a report stating that there had been another bank robbery in the capital. Certain details of the report grabbed his attention, especially the part explaining how the robbers had broken into the bank.

The article read.

During the early hours of Tuesday morning, at Alexanders Cunliffe's and Co,30 Lombard Street, there had been a catastrophic robbery culminating in the entire front section of the bank being destroyed, torn apart, brick by brick. The iron volt was smashed open and every item of cash and jewellery was stolen.

Hmm, thought Ernest, *an incident like this is far more than any 'Peeler' on the beat could handle; perhaps a meeting with the chief of police should be my next course of action.* Continuing with his thoughts, taking on a sense of urgency, *I will ask him to bring along his most trusted and reliable police constable, as it will be imperative for Barker to form an instant bond with a prospective partner.*

The evening before the arranged meeting with the chief of Police and his PC, as things turned out, would be quite emotional.

It was in the early hours of the morning at two a.m. that, as planned, Ernest and Quinn had woken themselves and got dressed. They had both decided that before it was time for Barker to leave for his new post with the Metropolitan Police, they wanted to see and experience for themselves exactly what had been going on between Stanley and Barker.

Ernest peered into the small window of the workshop as Quinn tapped Ernest's shoulders, signifying he was aware of everything and his unique senses were fully prepared. Ernest meanwhile could see Stanley the Bassett hound had just entered the workshop, seemingly by pushing through a loose gap at the bottom of the big main doors.

"Oh, I see, so it's my fault, really, not the most secure structure we have been keeping our top secret in," he sadly admitted embarrassingly to Quinn, all the while concentrating on what Stanley would do next.

Barker, their amazing iron guardian, lay still and immobilised, completely shut down and in his dormant position. Stanley stood by the side of Barker's partly closed mouth and, after turning himself around, began wagging his tail furiously for what seemed like a full minute. Suddenly, Barker's eyes began to glow and before long, Ernest and Quinn had worked out that Stanley was fanning Barker's embers in an attempt to bring his friend out of his slumber.

All of a sudden, the whole building shook and rumbled as Barker sprang into life. Stanley nudged the giant mechanical Bulldog and, after doing so, ran towards the main doors. Barker, fully operational, stood up and followed Stanley. Once standing by the doors, used the bottom part of his massive jaw and lifted the door's heavy iron latch.

With the workshop doors fully open, Ernest and Quinn stood amazed as they witnessed the two dogs, mechanical and flesh and bones, trundle off and run into the grounds of the Big House.

For at least thirty minutes, Ernest and Quinn took in the magnificent sight of their mechanical marvel, along with Stanley, patrolling the estate's grounds, only stopping when they were alerted to what they believed was a suspicious sight or sound. Significantly, Ernest had noticed that when returning to the workshop, it was Barker who took the lead. A small but important sign to him and Quinn that in such a short time, it was now Barker who was the 'Top Dog' and not just a submissive pup.

Before the men returned to the house, they decided to stay for a bit longer and observe how this comical pair would cover their tracks. They did not have to wait long; peering and sensing by the small window, they observed Barker waiting patiently by the big double doors, whilst Stanley, outside, with a series of pushes, closed the doors just enough for Barker to nudge the heavy metal latch back into its secure locked position. Stanley, before leaving his mechanical friend, gave out a few affectionate whimpering yelps as, inside the workshop, Barker settled himself back into his correct 'immobilised' posture.

"Honestly," said Ernest to Quinn, "If we had slept through this night, I am convinced we would never have suspected any of what we have just witnessed had ever happened," said Ernest, as he put his arm around Quinn's shoulder and lead the way along the path back to The Big House.

As they walked, before they entered the building, Ernest became aware of disturbing sounds coming from Quinn's breathing and eating orifice in his neck.

Ernest began worryingly thinking to himself, hoping Quinn wouldn't 'pick up' on his concerns. 'This poor fellow can hardly breathe and is truly struggling with his health; the thing is, I don't think he is actually ill, but this unnatural way that he has to live is really beginning to take its toll. The more I've worked with this remarkable man, the more he has become like a brother to me; if there was anything I could do to help, I surely would.'

Suddenly, Ernest felt his thoughts being blocked by the familiar tingling sensation on the back of his neck, which he knew spelt that Quinn's voice would soon appear in his mind. Waiting a few seconds, surprisingly, there was no conversation this time. Ernest knew without a doubt that Quinn had felt his concerns but believing that on this occasion, Quinn had felt no words were needed between them, he realised that Ernest cared and that was enough.

Ernest made sure he kept his mind blank for the next few moments and once back inside The Big House, he bid his dear friend a good rest, as there were at least a couple of hours until sunrise.

"Quinn, you have a lay-in today; I will attend the meeting with the Police Inspector and his Constable alone," said Ernest, not really able to completely shake off his deep concern for his unique friend's health.

Sitting up in bed, unable to get the much-needed sleep for him to feel refreshed for his meeting, Ernest is kept awake, constantly thinking about what he could do to help his friend. His mind flashed back to the last time he was at The London Hospital.

I wonder, he thought, *If that book in Joseph's room would hold the key to what exactly makes up Quinn's physiology; hmm, I really don't think I have the authority to ask for the book and also my snooping around might alert that Bamforth character, that I know Quinn fears and doesn't trust. Anyway, I'm done with sneaking about that place. Ah, so he was correct; it looks like I Will be requiring his services again. As much as I am beginning to dislike Walter Sheridan, he is the one and only person I know who has the skill of obtaining a photographic copy of that intriguing book. Hmm, I am sure with all his detective skills, he will find a way of gaining access and leaving the hospital without arousing any suspicions.*

Attempting to relax his tense body and try to get at least a couple of hours of sleep, Ernest set his alarm clock for eight a.m. and let his thoughts diminish as he drifted off into a deep slumber.

Early that morning, standing at the front door, the guests arrived for their scheduled meeting.

"May I introduce myself? I am Inspector George Huxley and this is my finest law enforcer, Thomas Saunders, who insists you refer to him as all of us do, simply as Tom," said the smartly dressed bowler-hatted policeman in a deep but kind, authoritative voice.

Ernest looked towards the Inspector and, in an attempt to give the meeting an air of informality, joked, "I do believe if all your men are as formidable looking as this strapping fellow you have brought with you today, you probably wouldn't need my invention."

This remark caused an embarrassing look on the smart young police constable's face, along with an intrigued look on Inspector's face, at the mention of the word 'invention'.

"The reason I want you both to attend this meeting," continued Ernest, deciding to get down to the heart of the matter. "with your acceptance, I will be offering you exclusive and total ownership of my greatest invention to date. Now come along, gentlemen, follow me and I will brief you as we walk."

On the way to the workshop, Ernest explained to the Inspector and the police constable the basis of his Iron Guardian project and stipulated that he hoped that one day, very soon, if all goes well, his invention would be walking alongside PC Tom Saunders as his partner.

Opening the big main doors of the workshop, in front of them lay the dormant but truly impressive giant iron bulldog. The Inspector and Tom Saunders stood speechless until, breaking the silence, George Huxley, in a slightly angry tone, exclaimed,

"Is this a joke, sir? You may well be the great inventor of 'The Hand', but this iron statue looks to me as the work of a crackpot. I suppose the next thing you are about to tell me is that it can move!"

By now, as previously arranged, Samuel and Frederick arrived on the scene. After quickly introducing themselves, they both went through the much-practised 'firing up' sequence. Ernest knew there was indeed a risk factor in introducing Barker to unfamiliar faces and was glad he had the foresight to keep the emergency stop lever attached.

Frederick, keeping a firm footing this time, held both his hands tightly around the emergency device. At the side door of the workshop, suddenly, a tall figure appeared, wearing dark glasses, a fedora hat with the brim pulled down low and the collar of his long raincoat pulled up around his face.

Ernest's neck tingled as he heard Quinn say, "Don't be alarmed; this was the simplest plan I could think of. Just explain if they ask who I am that I'm your temporary assistant. Ernest, I have more than enough friends who really need to know the 'true me'; just ignore my actions and all will be revealed," said Quinn cryptically.

The Stroud brothers meticulously went through Barkers 'start-up' procedure. With the giant iron bulldog fully operational, emitting incredible heat from his mouth, in a steady and purposeful way Barker walked towards Ernest.

Not having the security of Stanley keeping Barker under control, I must admit, is a slight concern, Ernest worryingly thought to himself.

Peering over, he could see that Quinn had begun gently tapping the side of Barker's head and whilst doing so, the giant bulldog's eyes flickered as though it was being spoken to. Suddenly, the giant Bulldog came to an abrupt halt. Quinn began the strange tapping once more and seemingly understanding his command, his enormous body began vibrating and, with a series of thunderous steps, changed direction and headed towards the terrified-looking Tom Saunders.

Frederick prepared to pull the emergency stop lever and peered over to Ernest for guidance.

"Ernest, tell the policeman to stay calm." Ernest felt Quinn's voice enter his mind and, following his instructions in a loud and clear voice, said to the increasingly traumatised young police officer,

"Tom, be still; what I know is about to happen is the reason you are here today; now you must trust me. Walk away from us and the machine will follow you."

Tom Saunders, in a state of shock, obeyed the Professor's wish and walked out of the workshop onto the gravel driveway whilst Barker slowly followed the petrified young PC until eventually, when Tom stopped walking, Barker sat still by his side.

With his eyes glowing red and the hot coals in his mouth white hot, Barker sat poised, waiting for his 'new masters' command. Tom not quite prepared for the huge responsibility he had just been given, gave the only instruction he felt would make him feel truly safe.

In a meek voice, clearing his throat said, "Eh, hum, Barker, could you go back into the workshop, please."

Slowly and assertively, Barker stood up at his full six-foot height and turned his huge ten foot long four-ton bulk around, causing the ground to shudder until, eventually, he took back his position in the workshop.

Ernest, in awe of what he had just observed, thought proudly, *I am absolutely convinced it will only be a short matter of time before the whole of London will be able to witness the formidable partnership of PC Tom Saunders and our incredible mechanical Bulldog, Barker.*

Chapter Six

Revelation and Trickery

London 1888 was a foreboding place, but with the recent addition of the 'Iron Guardian Patrol Unit', all manner of street robberies and criminality had begun to decrease. Professor Ernest Postlewaite's latest invention, as he had always dreamed, made a great impact on his beloved city. PC Tom Saunders and Barker, having reached celebrity status in the daytime patrols, were frequently followed at a safe distance by hordes of admirers.

The Metropolitan Police Force headquarters had built a specialist annexe to house Barker. Frederick and Samuel Stroud, having recently moved back into their own home, had been given a new status as Barker's full-time mechanics and also as the Professor's Iron Guardian representatives. News reporters and the general press of the day, although one hundred per cent supportive of the professor's latest invention, continued their relentless pursuit of any information appertaining to any of his forthcoming projects and as time went by, this was proving to be a real distraction and began causing Ernest much distress. With this in mind, he arranged a press conference and announced that a law had been passed in parliament, forbidding any news reporters from attending his house without permission and that any questions pertaining to Barker should be addressed to the Stroud brothers Hampstead village.

Meanwhile, back at The Big House, Ernest felt compelled to ask his loyal friend a sensitive question, "Quinn, are you sure you are well enough to continue helping me?"

"Stop fretting; I'm fine," came the tingling reply in Ernest's head.

Heeding Quinn's warning, taking care not to fuss him any more, he changed the subject and once again spoke to his friend spoke, "I'm not sure if I have ever mentioned it, but in my mind, Barker is not the pinnacle of our Iron Guardian project; in fact, to me, it is just the beginning."

The strange tingling sensation began to creep up Ernest's neck, but this time, before Quinn's words had time to appear in a forceful manner, he projected his words into Quinn's mind. "Now, please don't interrupt and just listen; any questions or concerns you might have about my plans, you can put to me when I have finished explaining. You see, Quinn, dear fellow, Barker has always been a prototype for something far more advanced. As successful as he is, and going by the reports I am getting back from Samuel and Frederick, very reliable, our creation still does not possess the full potential of artificial intelligence. Your great success in building his command system is, I have to admit, a far superior unit than the crude version of a mechanical brain Wells and I developed. At first, I was happy with what we had achieved, albeit only possessing the intelligence and basic instincts of a dog, but that was before Wells proved it was far too easy to convert our creation into a killing machine. The next stage in the command systems development, if successful, will hopefully be something far more superior. My ultimate dream is to build an Iron Guardian with advanced artificial intelligence, but this time in the guise of a man. A mechanical being that will have the intellect and reasoning equal to any human and, who knows, eventually, with intense tuition, even superior to ours. There you have it; any thoughts? My mind is blank; fire ahead," said Ernest, waiting for the tingling reply to begin.

"Ernest, this is the best news I have had in ages; this is the kind of stimulation I need. You do realise that when we begin to undertake this work, I will require complete seclusion. You see, Ernest, together, our strengths are your ideas and enthusiasm and my ability to solve seemingly unfathomable mathematical equations. Now, please don't take this too hard, but It has become increasingly apparent to me, and when you think back, I am sure you will agree, that as the work reached the latter stages, you didn't actually help me develop Barker's command system, the truth of the matter is, in reality, you were merely a hindrance."

Before Ernest could interject, Quinn continued confidently, "The exclusive use of the workshop will be fine for my needs; when you next see them, would you please inform the Stroud boys that I will be requiring four large sheets of the light metal alloy we developed and also the use of their finest cutting torch."

Ernest, trying not to show he was hurt by his colleague's rebuff, bid his farewell and headed to his study. When a safe distance from Quinn, Ernest gathered his thoughts and pondered on how he was to proceed.

'*Hmm*, he might not want my help or hindrance, as he cheekily called it, but I will have plenty to do with the overall design of my proposed mechanical man. The thing I am worried about is if Quinn will be able to physically cope with the strenuous work. That rasping sound from his neck is getting louder, and I swear the poor fellow is struggling to breathe. I know Mrs Beddoes is just as concerned as me; what did she say the other day? he is not taking his gruel as he should. No, something has to be done; I cannot just sit back and let poor

Quinn suffer.'

Lying on his bed, unable to sleep the worrying over Quinn's health, Ernest's thoughts fleeted back to that disturbing book he had seen at the London Hospital, recalling in detail the horrific images the book contained. Suddenly, a disturbing notion formed in his mind, 'What if Quinn wasn't actually born the bizarre way he appears? What if, and God forbid I am correct, the poor soul as a baby had undergone nightmarish surgical procedures that had actually turned him into the freakish character he is today.'

As the unsettling thoughts swirled around Ernest's mind, he began to feel sick but knew the only way he could ever be sure that his disconcerting theory was correct would be to obtain that book with all its gruesome images. With that in mind, Ernest began to hatch a plan.

'I don't think I could take the actual book; that would arouse too much suspicion and if the owner, whatever monster that might be, notices that it is missing, then who knows what he would be capable of. No, what I need is a copy and there is only one person I know capable of achieving this, tut. I have really taken a dislike to that man, but just as he had predicted, it looks like I Will be needing his services again. Anyway, I must try and sleep now but first thing tomorrow, I will set out to visit him. I am sure I took note of his home address.'

With that, Ernest leant over and took his address book out from the bedside cabinet and flicking through, stopped when he found what he was looking for. "Ah yes, here it is, Walter Sheridan, 33 Electric Avenue, Brixton, SW9," he said quietly to himself as he dropped the address book onto the floor, exhausted but satisfied he had found a solution to help his poor, suffering friend. With that, Ernest let out a long yawn and rested his head on his pillow before gently drifting off to sleep.

*

After an uneventful journey travelling on 'The Hand' and after a short walk, Ernest arrived at Walter's House, immediately thinking to himself, 'If that 'cock sure' man is as perceptive as he believes, then he won't be too surprised in seeing me.'

Ernest's initial impression on Walter's abode was not quite what he had expected. *If he cannot afford a gardener, he could at least tend to this front garden himself; it is a disgrace,* thought Ernest as he looked around at the overgrown privet hedge and the weeds that had grown to the height of the terraced house front window sill.

Before having time to knock on the door, suddenly Walter's voice could be heard, which appeared to be transmitted from an approximately six-inch square metal box that was fixed high up in one corner of the small porch.

"Ah, Ernest, couldn't you wait for the shop to open? Visiting me on a Sunday must be very important."

Feeling slightly silly and not knowing what else to do, Ernest spoke his reply into thin air, "Walter, I am not sure what this trickery is, but could you come down, sir? I would like to continue this conversation face to face."

With that, a loud click could be heard coming from behind the front door, followed immediately after by a command from the talking box device. "Come in, man and close the door behind you."

Ernest, feeling increasingly uncomfortable about the whole situation, felt he had no choice and just did as he was told. Standing inside the small hallway, he became aware of a cacophony of very strange noises. Proceeding to walk along the corridor, Ernest pushed open the door in front of him and called out loudly, "Walter, stop playing games, your silly man. Now, where are you?"

With no immediate reply, Ernest waited patiently and, feeling very uneasy, thought to himself, *This is just this eccentric man's way of showing off. I will play along with it for a bit longer, but really, this is so childish.*

With no instruction from Walter, Ernest could wait no more and decided to enter the room and on doing so, with no warning, loud classical music filled the air. Ernest looked around and could see no sign of any musical device had no idea where the sound was coming from when, unexpectedly, all the curtains in the room closed on their own accord and threw him into complete darkness. Fully concentrating with his senses on full alert, Ernest could hear a distinct whirring sound when, amazingly, out of nowhere, vivid, moving images flashed onto the wall in front of him. Feeling somewhat disorientated, he fumbled around in the dark until he found what felt like a dining chair. Pulling it behind him, sat and watched transfixed at the astonishing moving images that were magically appearing on the wall.

Looking on, he saw a pride of full-sized lions begin to stalk a herd of antelopes. In the distance, he observed standing, wallowing in a water hole, a bloat of hippopotamuses whilst above them, high in the sky, huge birds circled. Enthralled with the fantastical picture show, Ernest became intensely gripped as he spotted running fast, as though about to pounce on the lions, an animal that instantly proved to him that the scene he was observing could only be a complete Walter Sheridan fabrication.

I am no zoologist but I am absolutely sure there are not any polar bears in Africa, he thought, feeling as though, at this moment in time, he was simply being toyed with.

With the picture show following a distinct pattern as though on a loop, all at once, the door burst open and letting out a loud laugh, Walter Sheridan, ever the showman, gave his grand entrance. "My dear fellow, I didn't frighten you, did I?" he said sarcastically.

Ernest, by this point, had made up his mind that Walter, in his home environment, was even more outlandish than he could ever have imagined. Taking time to study in detail his crazy-looking host, Ernest thought to himself, *Honestly, this man is losing his grip on reality; I mean, look at the state of his hair; it needs a good wash and a cut and capped off with that silk Chinese style headgear along with that harlequin patterned velvet jacket, this is not the garb of a sane man, in fact, I do believe he has gone mad.*

With the picture show having stopped and the curtains in their magical fashion fully opened, the low afternoon sun cast a dim light across Walter's face. Ernest glimpsed at his host's overgrown wild red mutton chop sideboards and noticed that one side of Walter's face was displaying a large scar, the type typically associated with an extreme burn. Not willing to comment on his observation at this time, Ernest decided he would wait to see if Walter felt he wanted to explain what had happened. He did, however, think he deserved an explanation on why he had staged such a dramatic presentation and said, "Was there any real point in you trying to scare me half to death?"

Not feeling the need to apologise, Walter proceeded to explain his dramatic presentation. "Ernest, you should actually feel privileged at seeing my 'Translite tape' picture show; you see, this is one of my latest inventions and something I am very proud of. This advanced moving photography has never before been given an audience, but I am hoping that one day this form of entertainment will be available for the masses," said Walter, extremely pleased with his display, adding cryptically in a menacing voice, "actually I am not quite ready to release any of my world-leading inventions onto the general public, as at the moment I just like the idea I have the power to shock at my disposal."

Walter turned his back on Ernest and walked out of the room and giving a nonchalant wave, he beckoned Ernest to follow. "This, sir, is my laboratory where it all happens," said Walter, loudly with his voice booming out as though on a stage.

Ernest couldn't help noticing that more than just showing off, Walter was actually acting as though mentally deranged and he began to worry if this obviously psychotic individual would be up to the job he was about to propose. With this in mind and needing answers, Ernest thought best he should address 'the elephant in the room'. "Walter, you must realise I have noticed that sore-looking scar on your face; what exactly happened, you, poor fellow? Have you seen a doctor about it?"

"Oh, that," replied Walter. "Don't worry, it's not anything for anyone to concern themselves with, but as you are here and you have mentioned it, I suppose I had better tell you exactly what happened. One of my, shall I say, more problematic devices was playing up. Come over here, and I will show you close up and personal the infernal contraption that I haven't quite got to grips with yet," said Walter sternly as he beckoned Ernest over to a large, unfamiliar-looking metal box sitting on one of the laboratories work surfaces.

"You see this," said Walter in an angry voice, as he gave the box a hard rap, "this is one of my most frustrating inventions. There are moments when it can fill me with joy on how it behaves, while at other times it is a complete mystery to me."

Walter proceeded to open the door of the intriguing three-foot square container and said, "Just a moment, let me get something so I can give you a quick demonstration."

Reaching down, he delved into a small wooden box by his feet and produced what looked to Ernest like thinly sliced bacon. Placing the plate of meat into the machine.

Walter closed the door and said, "OK, two minutes should be enough," as he confidently turned the switch on the machine.

Immediately, Ernest became aware above the humming of the machine a loud crackling sound and a distinct smell of bacon being cooked; as the two minutes were up, there was a loud audible ping.

"Well, thankfully, I think on this occasion, all went as it should," said Walter as he opened the door of the device and carefully removed the piping-hot plate of sizzling food.

Ernest sat stunned at this remarkable exhibition of a pioneering time-saving cooking machine, but as a fellow scientist was so intrigued at the complexities of this ingenious gadget, unable to keep quiet any longer asked, "As you well know, Walter, I am also an inventor and by the demonstration you have just given, you have definitely had a remarkable machine on your hands but if it's not too much of a secret, what is the strange power it uses?"

"Ah, I'm actually glad you asked, as this is one of the reasons it is not quite ready for the general public and for a moment there, I had almost forgotten why I wanted to give you this demonstration of my 'electromagnetic' cooking device," continued Walter as he went on to explain all the quirks and mishaps he had experienced during the many trials of his ingenious but unsatisfactory time-saving machine.

"I tried cooking eggs in it once but never again; it was quite scary actually as they all exploded like small bombs," he said, laughing maniacally as he continued. "Disturbingly, I have also come to discover that those electromagnetic waves are a very hard thing to contain; I suppose really, I should have warned you about this before my little demonstration," he said worryingly, causing Ernest to momentarily begin to stroke the side of his own face to check for any anomalies.

"You see, it was one day after a five-minute trial of cooking steaks that I must have opened the door too soon and as I bent down with my head almost inside the machine, I didn't realise until it was too late, it was still in its cooking cycle and before I could pull myself back far enough, I felt a searing pain as it went on to cook this side of my handsome mug," he said whilst rubbing frantically the heavy scarred tissue of his face.

Ernest, by now, was convinced that the man standing before him was not quite right in the head but could not ignore the fact that although Walter was 'as mad as a hatter' with all his ingenious contraptions was still the perfect choice for the mission he was about to spell out to him and swiftly went on to explain what he had planned for Walter.

"So, you have all the details you need," said Ernest to his eccentric scientist.

"Once you have gained access to the London hospital, you walk past the boiler room, down the short staircase and the room you need will be on the left. It is imperative that you take with you a map of the London sewer system, and some form of providing light for yourself; everything else I will leave in your capable hands," said Ernest as he waved goodbye to Walter and walked off towards the Brixton branch of the aerial railway, all the while not being able to stop thinking about a phrase he has possibly wrongly used. 'Capable hands,' I said. *Hmm, well, I'm not so sure after some of the things I have witnessed today if that is actually a true statement. It's sad thing, but I do think that fellow has begun to lose his grip on reality.*

*

Walter Sheridan, dressed on this occasion, not in his usual dandy garb, had disguised himself as a regular tradesman and waited for a short distance away from the entrance of the London hospital. By the front doors stood a burly-looking policeman.

Ernest was right, Walter thought to himself, having previously tried to open all the other doors around the building without success. *Oh well, at least it gives me time to try this little box of tricks,* he thought, happy he had found an opportunity to show off one of his greatest inventions.

In a secluded spot, away from the gaze of the police officer, Walter removed two small glass discs from his sturdy tool bag.

"So, which would be best to confuse that dim-looking oath," he whispered to himself in a cock sure voice. "Should it be, disc one 'the badly injured gentleman', or this one, 'deeply distressed woman'."

Deciding on the latter, he carefully placed the second glass disc into his 'Translite' projection device, closed the lid and turned the clockwork key, and when fully wound, removed the cover from the lens and released the on/off switch. On doing so, a piercingly bright light shone from Walter's contraption and with the machine's dynamo working perfectly, letting out a gentle hum, his portable 'Translite' projector, against the dark night air, projected a life-size moving image of a smartly dressed woman, running fast, closely followed by a stick-wielding street ruffian, as the images mysteriously vanish into the thick London fog.

Reaching for his truncheon, the completely bamboozled police officer left his post and cried out loudly, "Don't worry, madam, help is on its way!"

Walter quickly shut down his illusion projector and swiftly replaced it back into its container; holding firmly onto his heavy tool bag, he walked briskly unobserved through the front doors of the London hospital.

Following Ernest's directions, after walking a short distance, he became aware of the loud sound of clanking pipes.

Ah, I must be near the boiler room, he thought confidently. *What was it, Ernest said? Down the small staircase and it's the room on the left.*

Standing in front of the correct room's door, Walter bent down and peeped through the keyhole. After a couple of seconds, deeming it safe to enter, he turned the doorknob and tried to push open the door but quickly realised it was locked.

No problem for an adept private detective like me, he thought confidently as he skilfully picked the lock and gained entry. With no time to waste, Walter found the black book exactly where Ernest had said it would be. Taking out from his tool bag his 'high-definition multiple storage camera', focusing on the book, he proceeded to document the entire journal.

Using his finely-honed detective instincts, Walter noticed a thick layer of dust covering all the surfaces around him. Being very careful not to leave any incriminating prints, he began to take photographs of every page. Gradually beginning to relax as he realised no one had been alerted to his deceptive entrance, Walter began to feel ever more confident and took his time to study every page in detail.

My God, what sort of monster could do this to these tiny

children, he thought, feeling evermore disgusted as each page revealed disturbing images of different stages of extreme surgical procedures on babies, some Walter ascertained must only be a few weeks old. Some of the images were so graphic and bizarre he could barely bring himself to look at them, but he knew he had to continue as he went on to document every gruesome page.

Some of these pitiful children had been subjected to the most horrendous procedures imaginable, with their eyes removed and the sockets crudely stitched shut. Others had their limbs removed with what appeared to be skin grafted over the raw wounds, but worst of all; there were a couple of images that would forever burn into his mind. Shudders ran down his spine, and he could barely stop himself from vomiting as he observed the next image, which showed a sick experiment where two of these tragic babies had been given extra arms and legs surgically attached to their tiny bodies.

Feeling sick and nauseous, the only relief he felt was he knew there were only a few pages of the book left until he reached the end.

Chills came over Walter as he read the disturbing title of the last section of the book. *'My Living and growing success'*. Taking his 'multiple storage camera' from his bag, he began to document all the book's images, beginning with a picture of a normally featured baby boy. He tentatively turned the page over, dreading what atrocity he might see next. Shockingly, as he had expected, the following pages showed the same child having been subjected to evermore grotesque operations with its ears and eyes removed. As Walter, with his hands shaking, continued copying the book, he folded back the cover of the horrific journal and, on the last two pages, saw the same child but now as an older boy, perhaps two or three years of age, with lips his last natural feature to remain tightly stitched together but this time with what appeared to be a breathing vent crudely cut into the poor mite's neck. The final picture was so shocking Walter could not believe a human being could subject such atrocities to another human being as it showed the poor little boy mutilated to look like no other on earth, exhibiting a blank expanse of skin where all other human beings have their facial features. Feeling physically drained and emotional, Walter felt tears run down his face, as by now he had worked out that the last chapter of the book was a detailed chronicle of how Ernest's strange partner Quinn had been turned from a normal child into the freakish character he was now.

I had no right to judge that poor fellow so harshly; who could ever know what struggles and pain he had lived through during his unnatural upbringing and what he has to deal with on a daily basis, constantly having to prove appearance is not everything it's an energy-sapping situation and something I am regretfully finding out for myself these days, thought Walter to himself as he stroked the scarred side of his face and solemnly closed the gruesome book, being extra careful to leave no signs that it had been disturbed.

At that precise moment, worryingly, Walter heard the distinct sound of two male voices. Kneeling down and creeping as quietly as he could, he crawled over to the door and spied through the keyhole. With no means of escaping without being detected, he could do little but wait and watch to see what would happen next. Walter's heart began pounding loudly as he watched on as they began to approach the room, he was hiding in. It was then he recognised clearly that one of the men was Hubert Wells. The other, a slightly older man with his smartly groomed beard and confident stature, Walter, perceived to be a person of great authority.

"You did exceptionally well tonight, but you do realise that you still owe me," said the older man, answering in a defiant way.

Hubert Wells gave a forceful response, "To be honest, I do not care what you think any more; if I could turn the clock back to the first time we met and you enticed me to get involved in your sick practices, I truly believe it would have been better for me and all of London if, on that fateful day, I had shown the courage to kill you, but no, you saw my addiction and played on my weakness, now look at me, completely controlled by you. I have now become just as deeply involved in your perverse criminality and, in some ways, as guilty as you are."

Finishing his vitriolic statement in a loud, angry voice, Hubert shouted, "You, sir, have condemned both of us to Hell!"

Walter continued peering through the keyhole and observed that on the older man's shirt, there were heavy blood stains. He was shocked by what he had just heard and seen but felt a tinge of relief as finally, he saw the two men walk away and head towards the direction of the second room. When Walter heard the door close behind them, he felt it safe to escape his confinement.

Well, that's put paid to me leaving the hospital via the sewer works, he thought worryingly, creeping from the room, wasting no time. Walter silently tip-toed up the small staircase and, whilst doing so, pondered on how he could dupe the police guard at the entrance.

'*Hmm*, I suppose a simpler old-fashioned method will have to suffice.' Running as fast as he could carrying his heavy equipment, he sprinted past a stunned receptionist, all the while crying out at the top of his voice, "FIRE, FIRE!"

He burst through the hospital front doors, in doing so, almost flattening the police officer guarding the door while being closely followed by the frantic receptionist who, fearing for his life, was shouting, mimicking Walter, "FIRE, FIRE!"

Laughing out loud in a self-gratifying manner at the success of his escape, Walter continued running the full distance to the Whitechapel aerial station, the East London branch of 'The Hand'.

*

Arriving back at his house, Walter, in his dark room basement, began setting about developing the photographs he had taken using his high-definition multiple storage camera. Feeling proud at how well his mission had turned out, he was pleased as each image perfectly revealed itself. He began feeling nauseous and, having no choice but to look, was reminded of how abhorrent the surgical procedures were.

Walter hung the images up to dry and left his workspace. Tired out from his strenuous day's work, he climbed into his bed and tried to sleep, but it became impossible as his thoughts became a jumbled mess of what he had recently seen and heard. Restlessly tossing and turning with the burn scars on his face, still not fully healed and unable to get comfortable, nightmarish images and the worrying, controlling voices he had been experiencing since the time of his accident began to appear in his mind.

"Listen to us; we will show you the way," they chanted until eventually, managing to push the frightening, tormenting delusion to the back of his mind, suddenly more rational thoughts came to him.

As Ernest has employed me to do, I will deliver the evidence I have procured to him tomorrow, but no matter how he wants me to proceed, I am not letting this go away; whoever it was that carried out those obscene operations, I will make sure will never get away with the ungodly things they have done. I don't care what Ernest decides to do next, but I, for one, could never rest until that monster's day of reckoning comes, thought Walter sinisterly as he finally managed to fall to sleep.

The following morning, Walter dressed himself in his usual eighteenth-century dandy attire, but worryingly, his mental state was concerning him; the voices in his head were becoming more frequent and he had found a way to constantly pull away the reality of his surroundings. The monsters and ghouls' voices grew ever louder in his mind and fighting for his sanity felt a deep madness setting in.

"Why should I see a doctor? I am a strong person, I am sure I can sort this out for myself," he spoke out loud to himself in an attempt to block out the cacophony of controlling voices that were swirling around his mind.

Walking out of his front door and firmly closing it behind him, Walter walked the short distance along the road until he reached the Brixton aerial station. Placed his pass card into a slot in the door lock mechanism soon after the front gates opened and seeing his carriage already waiting, he rushed and, just in time before it departed, jumped aboard.

Sitting down and making himself comfortable, he noticed that all of his fellow passengers were staring at him. *Hmm, I could never be as boring as those dullards, absolutely no personality,* he thought, deluding himself that they were just staring at him in admiration.

Rubbing the scabs that had recently formed on the scared side of his face, he once again felt himself drift into madness. 'They all look so lost, but one day, with my help, I will show them the light.' His madman's mind was evermore filled with incomprehensible, outlandish notions.

Arriving at 'The Big House' after knocking loudly on the front door, as it opened Walter spoke excitedly, "Ah, Professor, sorry I didn't send a telegram, but I am assuming you were expecting me at some time or another."

Ernest shook his unconventionally dressed employee's hand and invited him in. Settled in the study, the pair spoke at length about how the mission had gone. All the while, Ernest scrutinised the pictorial evidence that Walter had procured. As he looked over the disturbing photographs, he increasingly began to feel deeply shocked at what he could see.

"What we have discovered here must stay between us two; now you must swear to me, Walter, you will never mention any of this to anybody," said Ernest forcefully.

Walter agreed to Ernest's wish and bid him a fond farewell but couldn't stop himself from adding in a cryptic way. "Yes, this is goodbye for now, but Quinn's your friend, not mine; you deal with the situation as you please but someone must be held accountable for this atrocity."

Taking in the air on this fine day, Walter decided he would walk the majority of the distance home when, after a while, feeling a little tired, he decided to hail a Hansom cab. Before entering the cab, he took time to look around his surroundings and observed a group of people going about their daily business. *Ah, it's so nice to see the minions at work and play,* he thought in a superior way.

Peering out of the Hansom cab window, suddenly, a sharp pain seared across Walter's brow; as the agony intensified, he began striking his head with the flat of his hand as the intrusive voices and bizarre thoughts began taking over his mind. Visions of him wearing a king's crown appeared and angelic music rushed between his ears.

This was the precise moment Walter knew, deep down, that he had lost control of his sanity.

'But how does a madman know he's mad,' he questioned himself, as he began twitching and the voices in his head grew ever louder.

"Here we are, sir, Electric Avenue. That will be one shilling," said the bemused cab driver as he watched on at his passenger, who was by now shaking his head violently whilst mumbling to himself.

Stirred by the cab driver's intervention, shaking himself out of his trance-like state, Walter took a florin from his coin purse and, drawling in a slurred voice, spoke.

"All of life is one big journey; but I believe the key to personal happiness is how big you want that journey to be." As he walked towards his house, he shouted out cryptically, "Keep the change, my good man; remember this day, things are about to change!"

*

Back at 'The Big House', Ernest, still in shock at the terrible photographs that he had in his possession, began thinking to himself.

'These really do explain what I have suspected for a long time now.' Trying not to break down in tears, he concentrated on the series of photographs that focused on Quinn.

He vowed to himself there and then that he would never divulge to Quinn that going on this evidence of the horrors that he had endured as a baby and a small child. Opening the bottom drawer of his bedside cabinet, Ernest pulled it out to reveal a secret compartment in which he placed all forty-four of the photographs. Pushing the drawer back inside the cabinet until it was fully closed, he cleared his head and tried to push the thoughts of the horrific journal to the back of his mind.

Walking along the corridor towards Quinn's room, standing outside, making sure his mind was clear of any dark thoughts, he focused his words on Quinn's mind.

"So, how are you today? Are you feeling any better? Do you want me to get you anything?"

Ernest's neck began to tingle as he knew Quinn was about to answer, "No, I am fine at the moment; now, could you leave me in peace."

Ernest obeyed Quinn's wishes but stood outside, eavesdropping for a few seconds, where alarmingly, he heard Quinn making a series of unsettling gurgling sounds as though struggling to breathe. Ernest had agreed to adhere to Quinn's wishes and reluctantly walked away and back into his study but promised himself he would do everything in his power to help his suffering friend.

As the weeks passed by, Quinn, whilst in the presence of Ernest, seemed to be dealing with his health issues, but Ernest was not fooled and knew that when Quinn was on his own, he continued with his struggles.

Quinn threw himself wholeheartedly into his solitary work and as he locked himself away for hours at a time, Ernest began to see less and less of him. On the few occasions Ernest tried to disturb him from his work, he would always give him the same answer and say, "Could you please go away? The only time I want to see you will be when I have completed the work."

*

The day had finally come and after one month of intense work, Quinn had decided it was time to show Ernest everything he had achieved.

Ernest entered Quinn's office come workshop and immediately was greeted by a baffling array of technical drawings and many 'super light metal' components littering the floor, as a worryingly tall structure that he assumed was the unfinished brain unit for their advanced Iron Guardian.

"Ernest," said Quinn, "I presume progress with our 'man's' body is nearing completion."

"Yes, we are getting there," answered Ernest confidently. "It's going great, guns. The Stroud boys are their usual efficient selves, but there is one thing they would like to know from you and that is, have you managed to finalise the dimensions of the brain unit?"

"Please, such trivialities, can you not perceive the complexity of the task I have been given? Everyone is concerned with how big they should build his head!" said Quinn abruptly.

"Well, you might say trivial," said Ernest, trying to assert himself as an equal status in their partnership, continued. "But it has to be proportionate. We both agreed that this guardian would be no more than ten feet tall, head to toe; Quinn, we will have to work together on this as I do not want our man to have a five-foot head," he concluded in an attempt to put a sense of fun into their discussion.

"Oh, well, I will work within those confines, but remember, no more interfering; the brain unit is all mine and you must promise me, no snooping around my room. All will be revealed in a couple of days. By the way, could you inform the Stroud boys that the neck and shoulder sections must be left completely clear and must be well insulated from any of the boiler's heat sources? The pipework from the brain unit and the fitting to all other drive systems will be my responsibility and will be assembled by me on-site. Now remember, Ernest, wait two days and I am confident you will see a mechanical device more amazing than you can ever imagine."

Chapter Seven

Iron Jack

The Stroud brothers had been hard at work building the body section for the new advanced Iron Guardian and Ernest, excited to see how far they had progressed, had strolled down to the workshop.

Samuel was engrossed in his work, his long hair ruffled and his boiler suit covered in oil and burn marks. Freddie was outside in the traction engine with the arms and legs and main boiler all finished on the trailer and ready for assembly.

"Nice to see you, Freddy; I won't hold you up too long. Is Samuel inside?" asked Ernest cheerfully.

"Yes, sir, hard at it as usual still; I'm sure he will be pleased to see you," answered Freddy, revving up the traction engine signifying how busy they were.

"Nice to see you getting involved," said Samuel to Ernest as his employer walked into the workshop. Finishing giving a large nut and bolt its final tighten, Samuel continued, "I'll tell you what, though, we won't be able to show you the completed body until all the parts are fully fabricated, which brings me onto the matter of the head section. You do know we haven't received a single drawing regarding that aspect of his structure. Still, there's nothing like leaving the hardest part till last," said Samuel sarcastically.

"Samuel, I realise your frustration, but on a good note, Quinn has informed me it will only be a matter of days until he has finalised the brain unit; rest assured, as soon as possible, I will get to you his working blueprints. Oh, by the way," Ernest continued, changing the subject asked the questions. "How are things in the city? Are Barker and Tom still working well together as a team? The newspaper's attentions seemed to have waned somewhat, so I suppose that's one good thing."

Samuel answered cheerfully, "Yes, we couldn't ask for better; Tom and Barker are quite the sensations, are the reports getting back to us. Oh, while you are here, I need to get something off my chest that has been bothering me."

Samuel nervously cleared his throat and lowered his voice in a guilty tone as he mumbled, "You see, what with the physical aspects of our fabrication work and the added responsibility as the Iron Guardian representatives, I am afraid it all became a bit too much for Freddy and myself and reluctantly, we have had to bring in an outsider."

Ernest's face turned red as he became enraged and shocked that the boys could do such a thing.

Not allowing Ernest time to speak, Samuel explained. "No, sir, not an outsider as such; I suppose I should have phrased it better; you see, the person we have enrolled is actually part of our family; it's our little sister Lilly. I know you have only met her a few times, but she has really come of age. The thing is, the attention Barker is attracting has become phenomenal, with many countries around the world showing an interest in acquiring a version of Barker for themselves. The correspondence we received daily regarding this has become far too much for Freddie and myself to handle. Lilly is already proving her worth and doing a sterling job and is only too pleased she is involved and helping out."

Ernest, at first, is stunned at this revelation but quickly accepted it was the perfect solution. "Samuel, when you next see Lilly, would you congratulate her from me and tell her I am only too pleased to have another Stroud on board? Oh, and you can also tell her she will receive her first wage packet next Friday," he said as he left the boys to get on with their important work and walked back to the 'Big House'.

On entering the house, Ernest remembered it was Quinn's meal time and a sly thought entered his head. 'Ah, so Quinn is downstairs in the kitchen being tended to by Mrs Beddoes. Maybe this is the perfect time for me to investigate what is causing that humming sound I can hear constantly coming from his room.'

Standing outside Quinn's workroom, Ernest remembered he had not long ago promised Quinn he wouldn't interfere in his work, but as though possessed and having a mind of its own, his hand gripped and turned the doorknob as he entered Quinn's sacred workspace.

The room appeared surprisingly tidy, with all the blueprints neatly stacked and the floor clear with none of the super light metal components strewn about.

All of a sudden, Ernest's eyes were drawn to a large, possibly two-foot tall pyramid-shaped contraption sitting ominously in the corner of the room. *That has to be it; I hope it works as good as it looks. It's absolutely brilliant.* he thought as he walked over.

The machine looked so delicate, with each element of this magnificent piece of engineering formed in intricate detail, some of the metal parts so thin they appeared as translucent as glass.

I dare not touch anything, but what harm can it be if I stay here for a bit longer and study in detail this phenomenal construction, Ernest thought to himself, itching to touch one of the tiny delicate cogs to feel if they were stronger than they look.

Like a naughty schoolboy, Ernest's temptation got the better of him and making contact with one of the larger components, instantaneously, the contraption burst into life.

Oh my god, what have I done? I'm sure to be found out now. What can I do? I haven't a clue how to stop it. Sweating and shaking, Ernest got himself into a panic as his worrying thoughts escalated. *What if it wasn't ready to be tested? If I have, god forbid, broken it with my stupid interfering, this could push our relationship to breaking point.*

By this time, feeling sick with worry and not really knowing what to do for the best, he could do nothing but watch on as the intricate machine continued changing into an array of wondrous shapes. Reaching what appeared to Ernest at its full speed the minute, pistons and gears moved in rhythmic patterns as though performing a hypnotic dance. Ernest was transfixed and stared on, amazed as suddenly the baffling array of moving parts reconfigured themselves and, with a loud bang, morphed into a large cube shape, causing Ernest to jump back. Stunned and looking on in disbelief, the centre of the cube began to slowly rise and in doing so its tiny cogs and pistons bloomed like little metal daggers and flowers.

Suddenly, the constant low humming sound of the fantastical machine dropped in volume until, eventually, it became silent.

Oh please, just go back to that original pyramid shape, Ernest agonised to himself. *At least if that happens, he might never discover my intrusion,* he worryingly thought, knowing in his heart Quinn, being so astute, would know that his unfathomable device had been disturbed.

With that, something so astonishing took place; Ernest knew he would never forget what happened till the day he died.

"Professor Ernest Postlewaite, I presume," said a voice in a loud, clear tone, inexplicably coming from somewhere inside the machine. "Quinn warned me this could possibly happen, so I prepared myself for any unscheduled test." The machine continued speaking as its metal 'trunk-like' appendage swayed slowly above the main structure.

"I have been told much about you, so for me, it's actually nice to finally make your acquaintance. Don't worry, I won't keep you long as I can tell you are beginning to get agitated and would prefer to leave, but have no fear. If all goes to plan, we will soon meet again. Quinn has informed me I have reached the required level of intelligence for me to be installed into my, hopefully expertly crafted head, something I am really excited about. Anyway, bye for now, don't worry, I won't mention this encounter," concluded the wondrous machine. Ernest looked on astonished as it gently rocked until the low humming sound ceased and, with a series of elaborate movements, perfectly configured itself back into its original pyramid shape.

Ernest's head was spinning in disbelief at what he had just experienced and he walked guiltily out of Quinn's room, knowing it would only be a short amount of time before his astute work colleague would summon him.

Standing outside, suddenly, with a hard thump on his brow, Ernest was brought to his knees. His head throbbed in excruciating pain as he experienced extreme pressure on both of his temples. Unable to move, his body became frozen to the spot, and expecting Quinn's angry words to rush into his head, he waited in trepidation until, as expected in a stern tone, like a parent telling off a naughty child, he heard, "Ernest, I am so disappointed with you! Tut, what are we to do? Trust me, WE WILL! Discuss this incident at length another time."

With one last intense throb, Ernest's head suddenly cleared, and the pain ceased. Feeling his punishment was over for now, he gained his balance and walked down the corridor in the opposite direction of Quinn's room, thinking to himself, 'I'll have a nice cup of tea with Mrs Beddoes,' believing this was the best thing to put the traumatic effects of the last hour behind him 'Ha, I am so British, a cup of tea sorts everything out,' he giggled to himself as he held his aching head and found his faithful housekeeper in the kitchen.

"Margaret," said Ernest, addressing Mrs Beddoes as he always did when in her domain.

"How did Quinn seem to you?" he asked in a concerned voice.

"Sir, I'm glad you asked me because I was at the point where I was so worried. I knew there would be an occasion when I would have to ask for some of your valuable time. You see, I know there is something desperately wrong with that boy," she continued with her voice quivering with emotion. "I can barely cope; his breathing seems a real effort these days. You know I love Quinn like a son, but feeding him has become very traumatic. I can hardly bear to look at that sore opening on his neck these days, as it is constantly weeping and I've watched him as he has to prise it open. To my eyes, it's like a cut that is trying to heal." Exhausted with her impassioned outburst, Mrs Beddoes waited for Ernest's reaction.

"There, there, Margaret, if Quinn allows me to, I will arrange for a doctor to visit," answered Ernest sympathetically, all the while thinking. *How can I really involve the medical profession once they become aware of Quinn's unique physiology they would want to take him away, possibly to experiment on him. No, I could never let that happen to him.* Keeping his worrying thoughts to himself, Ernest bid Mrs Beddoes goodbye, adding as he left the room.

"Now remember, don't you worry yourself any more; take the rest of the day off." As he reached for his coin purse and took out a half crown. Putting it tightly into Mrs Beddoes hand, Ernest, in a kind voice, said, "There you are, Margaret, treat yourself; you really deserve it." As he turned and walked out of the kitchen.

Two days had passed since Ernest had passed since Ernest had interfered with Quinn's work. *Oh well, I've got to face him sometime; perhaps a good discussion on the finer points of our guardian will put him in a good mood,* Ernest thought as he approached Quinn's room in apprehension.

Standing outside the room, unexpectedly, a feeling of warmth wafted over him, as Quinn's voice in a calm tone appeared in his mind. "Deep down, I knew your inquisitiveness would get the better of you. I am willing to put the incident behind me; just wait there. I'm coming out now; we need to see how the boys are getting on."

Quinn appeared outside his room and gave Ernest a comforting hug on his shoulder as they both walked together towards the workshop.

The Stroud brothers had made great advances in assembling the completed components of the Iron Guardian but were unable to progress any further.

"We still need the dimensions for the head section!" said Samuel to Ernest and Quinn in an urgent tone.

"I suppose, really, I should have warned you days ago,"

stated Ernest guiltily.

"You see, boys, I have seen Quinn's design of the brain section and it is a lot larger and delicate than I had imagined. The only solution I have is it should be housed inside a top hat section. I will supply details of the dimensions needed but for now, keep in mind this section, including the rim, must be made of double-reinforced iron, also incorporating a heat shield between the top hat and head section. Come on, boys, chins up. I know you can do it," he concluded, giving a thumbs-up sign.

*

Over the following days, in preparation for the completed head component, Quinn built a strong framework into the shoulder section of the Iron Guardian and, with the help of Ernest, carefully installed the impressive, delicate, super-light brain into Quinn's support construction.

Ernest and Quinn stood back and proudly looked at their achievement in all its glory. The huge structure, expertly manufactured and assembled by the Stroud brothers, was sitting on a great scaffold platform that had been constructed in the shape of a giant armchair. Incomplete but truly impressive, the imposing iron body with its arms and legs affixed was triumphantly capped off with Quinn's unfathomable glistening silver pyramid-shaped brain unit.

"Ernest, I will need to be left alone as it will take many hours connecting the thousands of our guardians essential, shall we call them 'nerve tubes' to his drive system. I will contact you when I am finished."

Quinn's words bore into Ernest's mind as he thought, *No more tampering from me after that last experience.*

Quinn continued, "Also, could you inform Mrs Beddoes I will be eating and sleeping down here for a few days, and would you apologise for me as I hope this will not be too much of an inconvenience for her," he said his usual considerate way.

As Ernest left the workshop, he could see that Quinn had already begun his work twisting and connecting the baffling array of tubes and levers to their iron guardian.

Back in the house, Ernest began wracking his brain, thinking how he could deal with Quinn's health problems; he was no further in finding a solution until, one day, an unexpected visitor to The Big House.

*

"Hello, professor. I hope you do not mind me turning up unannounced," said the timid-looking young woman. Quickly recognising her pretty face, he remembered that it was Miss Rose Morely, Walter Sheridan's maid.

"Oh, it's Rose, isn't it? Is everything OK? Anyway, I shouldn't keep you standing on the doorstep," asked Ernest, wondering what this impromptu visit was about.

Bursting into tears, Rose blubbered, "Sir, Walter, these days has become intolerable to work for. He has always had very eccentric ideas, but I have grown used to his unconventional ways." Seeing her obvious emotional distress, Ernest ushered Rose to the drawing room.

Having calmed down somewhat, she continued explaining why she had turned to Ernest for help. "You see, sir. It was when, one day, Walter suddenly announced he would be closing his shop and office full-time that I knew something was wrong. My first thought at that time was that he would terminate my employment but when I put my concerns to him, he said that would never be the case and gave me the opportunity to continue working for him but instead as a live-in housekeeper. I had to agree to his offer because I knew if I did not accept, I would have no income to pay for my rent."

Ernest sat back and thought to himself, *I have seen that nightmare of a house for myself with all of its peculiar contraptions; once was enough for me, let alone live there.* Picking up on the growing concern in Rose's voice, he continued to listen intently.

"The first night I stayed there was bad enough. I could not sleep a wink. Strange noises and lights were coming out of every room. He doesn't seem to ever rest, you know and is constantly talking to himself these days, anyway," she continued, "not really having any real choice, I stayed on. Today, he said something that actually scared me; I will never forget the words that he uttered as he stared at me with glazed eyes, saying. *'You do know we both love you, the good and the bad, Walter.'*

"Mr Postlewaite, sir."

Ernest stopped her there and then and insisted that from now on, she called him by his Christian name and agreeing, she continued, "I said to him, I didn't understand what he meant, when he replied, twitching his head and stroking that hideous scar on his face, *'This fellow wants to tell you he would like you to be his lover.'*

With such an inappropriate remark and not knowing how to react, I just ran out of his house, leaving all my possessions behind.

"Ernest," she continued, beginning to once again sob uncontrollably. "It was then I remembered that when you visited the shop, you had such a kind and friendly demeanour; you could possibly be my saviour. I know it is very forward of me, but do you think I could stay tonight and first thing tomorrow? I will seek employment. Perhaps I could revive my profession as a nurse," she concluded.

On hearing this, Ernest couldn't believe his good fortune. *This could be the answer to my prayers*, he thought. *Mrs Beddoes desperately needs help tending to Quinn's evermore challenging needs. What better than help from a trained nurse.*

"Eh *hmm*," Ernest cleared his throat and nervously proceeded to speak, "Rose, of course, you can stay the night, but I have just had a thought that would be beneficial for both of us. You see if you agree to my offer, then you won't have to look for work tomorrow, as I would like to employ you as a live-in assistant housekeeper."

"Oh, thank you, Ernest, you are so kind; I knew coming to you for help would turn out to be the right decision," she said, giving him a big hug.

"Eh *hmm*," clearing his throat once more, in his most authoritative manner, said, "Miss Morely, whilst you are in my employ, I think Professor would be the appropriate way to address me," said Ernest, not wanting to upset Mrs Beddoes in these early stages.

*

The two weeks that followed, it was as though Ernest, Quinn, Mrs Beddoes and Rose had been a team for years. Mrs Beddoes had taken to Rose instantly and soon as she was informed her new assistant was an experienced nurse, felt a great burden lift.

Ernest initially had concerns about how Rose would react to Quinn's unusual, most would think, frightening appearance but it turned out that his fears were to be wholly unfounded when Rose instantly put Ernest's mind to rest and informed him that she had seen far worse in her time nursing the unfortunate victims of war.

As the days and nights went by, Rose and Quinn grew ever closer, in fact, far more than Ernest had expected.

Hmm, I hope that boy doesn't get too distracted and remembers we still have our iron guardian to complete. Still, I am so happy he is finally looking and feeling much better, Ernest thought, giving himself a virtual pat on the back and settling down for the evening, vowing to himself, 'I will visit Samuel and Freddie tomorrow. It's all gone a bit quiet in the workshop; I hope those boys are not slacking.'

The final push from Ernest had done the trick when, two days later, the skilled mechanics arrived at the Big House by traction engine with a trailer attached carrying the sturdy reinforced shoulder, neck, head and top hat section of the iron guardian that had been securely covered in a tarpaulin so as to not draw too much attention as it proceeded through the village.

Ernest jumped back as unexpectedly Lily Stroud and Stanley the Bassett hound alighted from the back of the trailer, whereupon Samuel quickly reminded Ernest that his sister Lily and pet dog were, after all, very important members of the Iron Guardian Project team and it was only fitting that they should be present on this momentous occasion.

Today, if all goes to plan, thought Ernest, *we shall see the birth of an iron guardian possessing a level of true artificial intelligence that will give him the capability of patrolling unassisted without any intervention of any human being. If this trial, his wakening is successful, he will be able to serve the community as London's dedicated mechanical night watchman.*

Mrs Beddoes, Rose, Lily and Stanley stood and watched from afar as Samuel and Frederick, assisted by Quinn and Ernest, proceeded to raise the huge head section onto the Iron Guardian body.

"In this instance, I'm in charge; we don't want any accidents, do we," said Samuel in an authoritative, concerned voice.

"Freddie, you are sure you have done all the calculations correctly and are absolutely certain that when attached and he is in his standing position, he will definitely clear the roof," he continued, shouting over towards his brother.

Freddie answered in an annoyed tone, "Yes, I've measured three times now."

Irritated at his brother's questioning of his ability, adding, "I will say, though, that it will require the guardian to stoop as he exits the workshop. Still, this will be a good initial test of his intelligence because if he doesn't react sufficiently, then I am afraid Ernest, you will need new doors." Laughing to himself, hoping he wasn't being too flippant on such a grand occasion.

Quinn, at this time, was standing on one of the iron giant's legs and leaning into the body section, making absolutely certain he had not missed attaching any of the flimsy 'nerve tubes' whilst in such close proximity to the complex brain section, listened on as the remarkable machine began to communicate with him.

"Quinn, you must hurry up now; I can't risk any more contamination. I must say, though, those two boys have done a brilliant job in building me a handsome head."

Hmm, thought Quinn. *At least I know there is nothing wrong with the confidence settings.*

Quinn turned his strange, blank-looking head towards Ernest and nodded to signify all was fine. In doing so, they climbed down. Samuel and Frederick, outside the workshop, heaving and puffing, proceeded to manoeuvre the weighty head from the trailer onto a hoist platform and with Quinn and Ernest's assistance, after much struggling. Eventually, they raised the impressive head section until it was perfectly positioned above the delicate brain pyramid structure. Holding tightly to the winch handle, Frederick tentatively began to lower the mighty head structure onto the guardian's body.

"Clang! Screech!" The loud sounds echoed around the workshop as metal ground against metal until the two huge iron components finally made their perfect seal, encapsulating the delicate pyramid brain structure.

With the Iron Guardian fully assembled, even in its sitting position, it was a truly imposing, magnificent sight. Quinn began climbing the scaffold and when positioned next to the guardian's chest door, he reached over and opened it. At this point, the entire gathering had made their way into the workshop, and immediately, as though being summoned by an exterior force, all began to stroke the back of their necks. Even Stanley, the Bassett hound, twitched his head as though a fly had gone into one of his floppy ears. Instinctively, they all looked around at each other, knowing they were collectively experiencing a signal that Quinn was about to communicate to them in his unique way.

"I'm glad I have all your attention at once. It is something I haven't tried before on such a grand scale, but it seems to be working perfectly," said Quinn as he bent down and opened a small box that he had placed by his foot. Reaching inside, he lifted out a blue velvet-covered rugby ball-sized object.

"Before I unveil this most important component of our iron guardian, I must warn you, Ernest, that I purchased this particular object entirely using my own funds due to your generous wages and free bed and board. Anyway, enough of this waffling; here we have it," explained Quinn.

His captive audience watched on in awe as he ceremoniously dropped the velvet cloth to the floor to expose an impressive looking silver coloured object that glistened and twinkled as its thousands of dangling fine tubes began moving and wriggling, gravitating towards the open chest door as though magnetised, giving it an eerie appearance of a living, 'otherworldly' metal creature.

"Let me explain in more detail," continued Quinn. "This, my friends, is what you may perceive as our iron guardian heart, made mainly from the super light alloy I have developed. Its core is made from pure platinum and will serve as the purifying unit for all of his systems but equally important; once transplanted, it will become his soul."

Audible gasps could be heard from the enthralled gathering on this amazing revelation as Quinn carried on. "With this addition it will set him apart from any other mechanical device, Barker included. Astonishingly, if I say so myself, I have managed to contain in this precious device all of mankind's emotions, strength, fear, anger and love. Using these human traits, our iron guardian will be able to calculate and determine the best course of action to take in any given situation."

With that, Quinn carefully placed the precious platinum heart into the compartment, being careful not to snag any of the dancing trailing tentacles.

Once satisfied it was secured correctly, Quinn closed the compartment and focused his thoughts directly on Frederick. "Freddie, I have noticed the intense way you study everything I do. Don't worry; I'm not about to tell you off; I actually take this as a compliment. You see, I can sense you have great intelligence, and with your aptitude for this kind of work, I propose that on any of Ernest's and my up-and-coming projects, with the blessing of your brother, I would dearly love to have you as my apprentice. What do you say to that dear boy?"

Frederick, stunned at the master engineer's confidence in him, answered, "Sir, that would indeed be an honour; I am sure Sam will not stand in my way of bettering myself."

With that, Quinn switched his thoughts and, getting back to business said, "Samuel, as we rehearsed, could you double-check oil levels and prime all the iron guardians drive systems?"

Releasing his mind from everyone, Quinn climbed down the scaffold and walked towards his adoring friends, who, on greeting the amazing inventor, each in turn hugged and proudly patted him on his back.

Samuel signified with hand gestures that he had completed the 'start-up' sequence and with his finger hovering above the ignite button, in a dramatic, loud, clear voice, announced, "To all of us gathered here today, friends and relatives, may I present you with 'IRON JACK!' His words were barely heard as he pressed the start button and the thunderous boom of the guardian's mighty steam engine roared into life."

Only now could they all see the true magnificence of the mechanical creation before them. Iron Jack's large semi-circle eyes came alive as his steam engine reached full capacity. Peering just below the rim of his top hat as the heat transferred throughout his body, gradually his wide, oblong-shaped mouth vent began glowing an intense crimson red and his four armoured glass panels of the furnace door exposed behind them the glowing coals smouldering and intensifying until they burnt white hot. At his full capacity, Iron Jack gripped his huge metal hands firmly on the sides of the sturdy scaffold chair and, slightly spreading his massive legs, pushed down and began to slowly rise until moments later, he was standing proud and upright, his full height of ten feet. Lowering his great head, being extra careful not to hit any of the roof beams, with Quinn following close by, he manoeuvred his massive body towards the main doors of the workshop.

During this time, feeling it the safe thing to do, everybody in Iron Jack's trajectory had decided to run outside onto the grass and with their eyes struggling to adjust to the bright daylight, they all waited in great expectation and a sense of trepidation on what to expect next. Watching on in complete amazement and awe, they were amazed as they observed a series of complicated movements; Iron Jack twisted and turned until skilfully navigating the workshop doors, when finally, outside, he brushed himself down. Stretching back his shoulders, standing confidently upright, he dropped the intensity of his boiler and in doing so, his eyes and mouth began to take on a warm, comforting orange glow.

Shocking everyone, in a deep, booming synthesised voice, Iron Jack spoke, "You really are an easy crowd to please; if you think that me walking out of a workshop without hitting my head is impressive, then you will be amazed at some of the other tricks I have in store for you."

Purposely turning his huge 'top-hatted' head towards one of his creators, Iron Jack continued, "By the way, Quinn, just a minor criticism, but you will have to adjust this voice box because, at the moment, it's the only part of me that doesn't feel human."

For ease of discussion, Ernest called for Jack to sit down, after which they all gathered around him in a big circle, and each in turn began quizzing Jack on what he was feeling so soon after being activated. After a lengthy and informative discourse with

Iron Jack, giving an eloquent display of his intelligent and humorous personality, they all agreed to make a mental note of the time and date of this momentous occasion. Four thirty p.m. on the 15th of July 1888, Iron Jack's birthday.

Chapter Eight

Education, Love and Loss

In the days that followed Iron Jack's awakening, he had been given the important but rather simple task of patrolling the grounds of the 'Big House'. And as time went by, he would turn his skills to all sorts of maintenance work, fixing and painting anything he could see needed mending or renovating. Before long, this type of work proved to not be sufficiently stimulating for a being of Jack's high intelligence, and in fact, his work became sloppy; Ernest and Quinn began to feel their creation's frustration. Like a caged animal, Jack's attitude quickly began to change and in a very short time, his personality switched from someone that was enthusiastic to someone that was sullen and spoilt.

"That is, it!" exclaimed Ernest to Quinn. "You said it before and I agree, he is acting like a sulky child and this is the exact reason why I believe he is not ready to be enrolled into the Police Force. We need a solution fast, and what do we do with sulky children?"

In saying this, Ernest felt a stinging pain on the side of his head, that instantly caused him to point his finger at Quinn and said sharply, "No, not chastise them; you have to stimulate them. I'm telling you, Quinn, if we do not satisfy Jack's thirst for knowledge, I can see him sinking into a deep depression."

"Well, what do you suggest we do?" asked Quinn. "I won't be able to give him extra tutoring; I might as well tell you now I am still not fully fit. In fact, I am actually quite worried as these days I am constantly struggling to breathe. Thankfully, Rose has been brilliant; she is such a kind gentle woman and has never made me feel the freak of nature I know some people perceive me as. Ernest, I know it sounds dramatic, but honestly I don't think I'm long for this world."

Seeing Quinn was visibly upset, Ernest gave his long suffering friend a comforting big hug and said, "Don't you worry yourself, leave this with me, have a 'well deserved' rest and try to not exert yourself, forget about work, go and spend as much time as you wish with Rose, if you think that is the best thing for you right now," adding, "on a serious note, would you like a doctor's opinion on your state of health?"

"No!" said Quinn loudly, causing a sharp pain to press hard into Ernest's temples, as he continued firmly, "No more outsiders, especially in that profession, who knows they could be loyal to Bamforth and that is the one person, I NEVER want in my presence again."

Quinn's tone softened as he added, "Ernest I know you only want the best for me, so as a compromise, let's say you deal with the, Iron Jack, dilemma and with Rose and Mrs Beddoes assistance I will try to sort myself out."

Ernest agreed to his poorly friend's request and bid him farewell as they went their separate ways.

A short while later, sitting in his study Ernest had a 'eureka moment'. *Why didn't it come to me sooner,* he thought excitedly.

I will convert the workshop into a library. I'll give Iron Jack bored. I can stock it with every important book appertaining to the human existence, that should keep him busy for a while.

Immediately realising his plan had a fatal flaw he thought worryingly to himself. *With those massive iron hands, how can I expect him to read books? Never mind perhaps Quinn could think of a solution,* Ernest thought as he walked towards his friend's bedroom, quickly realising it was only minutes earlier he had advised his friend to rest.

Ernest, worried about his sudden intervention sheepishly knocked on Quinn's bedroom door and as soon as he entered knew Quinn was annoyed when his neck began to sting and Quinn's words rushed into his head.

"It was only ten minutes ago you suggested I should relax, now what is it?"

Ernest explained 'the reading books' and the Iron Jacks hands quandary, where instantly Quinn answered in a confident tone, "Oh, is that all? not a massive problem, this is what we will have to do. You will have to get the Stroud boys to remove his existing hands and in doing so explain to Jack this is for his long-term benefit and only a temporary measure. Instruct the boys to carefully disconnect and remove all of my complex tubing after which they should completely hollow out Jack's hands after which they will have to install them with a reinforced lining. In the meantime, I will set about forming new smaller highly sensitive hands. Once I have managed to satisfactorily fit them onto Jack his original newly hollowed out robust hands can be used as gloves for his more strenuous work. I know it sounds a lot for me to take on but actually it's only light work and could help me take my mind off my ailments."

"That's a brilliant idea Quinn, what would I do without you?" said Ernest, leaving his invaluable friend to set upon his work.

*

Two weeks later, the workshop had been converted into a fully stocked library and sitting in his huge scaffold formed armchair that had been expertly upholstered in the strongest dark green leather, sat a studious Iron Jack, skilfully using his new delicate hands arduously reading William Shakespeare's Macbeth. Jack, highly impressed by the play, began quietly speaking to himself.

"That man was a true literary genius; there is no doubt about that," Jack said to himself as he leant back contentedly. Putting the book to one side, feeling his furnace door had cooled, Jack remembered that it had been one month since his birth and although his boiler was far more efficient than any other similar drive system, worryingly, he could feel himself shutting down and knew it was time to top up his coals.

Stepping out of his library into the bright August sun, Jack spotted Quinn and Rose on one of their frequent strolls around the well-manicured grounds of the Big House.

"It's always in pairs, Quinn and Rose, Ernest and Mrs Beddoes, Samuel and Freddie and even Lilly and Stanley. This is why I am always feeling so sad; it's companionship that I am missing in my life!" Jack said loudly to himself, hoping that no one had heard him.

Feeling ever more morose, a coldness in his eyes set in and as they dropped to a deep blue colour. Walking slowly with his head down, he headed towards the coal store. *Ernest and Quinn built me encapsulating all human emotion. Did they not realise that by constructing a 'one of a kind' being, I would never be able to experience real companionship,* thought Jack sadly as he opened his furnace door and, pulling his robust hands from the newly formed holsters, placed them over his delicate hands and proceeded to fill his coal chamber. When satisfied it was at the correct level, he stoked up his firebox and, feeling reinvigorated, stared up at the glorious summer's bright blue sky. Lowering his great iron head, Jack began looking all around him, where he observed in fine detail his beautiful environment, the wonderful multi-coloured flowers in full bloom in their neat beds and the tall trees swaying gently in the light summer breeze.

Listening on, absorbing the delightful atmosphere, he could hear the sweet sound of bird songs and the distant laughing and chatting of the children from the nearby school as they enjoyed their playtime.

Straightening himself up to his full height, Jack thought to himself, *I may be alone, but I have to be truly grateful to be alive.* Whereupon he spotted not far away Rose and Quinn taking their usual afternoon stroll. As he watched how these two human beings interacted, constantly laughing, comfortable and relaxed with each other, he observed Rose affectionately brush against Quinn, causing him to give his girlfriend a gentle hug around her shoulders.

Jack, careful not to be seen, kept back for a while longer; fascinated at this wonderful display of human interaction, he let his gears and cogs and intricate metal nerves work at their full capacity until they dropped perfectly in place. It was at that pivotal moment Jack came to the conclusion Quinn and Rose were very much in love.

*

Fleet Street, six thirty p.m.

Tom Saunders and Barker are on a routine patrol of the area when suddenly they become alerted to a series of loud bangs coming from the direction of Goslings and Sharp's Bank.

"Barker, stop! Wait for me," cried out Tom to his increasingly independent partner.

The disobedient iron bulldog continued running until he found himself at the scene of the noisy disturbance, where he was confronted by a towering, immense metal giant that was unleashing powerful punches into the walls of the bank. Barker, using all of his primitive instincts, decided to attack the mechanical robber. Increasing the pressure in his boiler until it was at its optimum level, Barker leapt into the air in an attempt to topple the huge metal monster. Using unexpectedly quick reactions, the immense machine stopped punching the walls and turned his attention to the iron bulldog that was attacking him and, with an almighty thump, struck Barker full onto his jaw and, in doing so, completely dislodged it. Barker, in shock at what had just happened, began shaking his huge head, completely disorientated at the speed and intensity of his assailant's blow. Quickly realising he was in no fit state to continue the fight, Barker began to retreat. Dragging his jaw that was barely hanging on by a thread, he could feel all his vital water supply dispel from his boiler, whereupon his four legs collapsed beneath him and splayed out.

Unable to move, Barker's drive and command systems came to a halt. Sensing an easy victory, the huge metal robber began stamping on Barker's head and body until he was satisfied the giant iron bulldog was no more than a useless pile of scrap metal and nuts and bolts.

Tom Saunders, arriving on the scene, felt powerless to do anything but blow his whistle to try and alert his fellow officers as he had to watch on as the metal assailant callously kicked the pile of metal rubble that was once his loyal partner Barker into a recently formed huge pool of steaming oil and water.

Casually walking back to the virtually destroyed bank, ignoring the insignificant lone police officer, and skilfully locating all of the safes, the metal thief began to tear them open as easily as a human could peel an orange. Unlocking a door in its chest, the seemingly unstoppable machine began to fill its open locker with every last ounce of cash and jewellery.

*

Later that day, Tom Saunders gave his account of what had occurred to his inspector. "Sir, no one can be more upset than me. I have become so close to Barker, but he was no match for that thing. Where did it come from? It surely can't be anything to do with Professor Postlewaite," Tom asked in a concerned tone before concluding, "Anyway, when you do see the Professor, perhaps you could pass on these couple of details I can vividly remember. You see, sir, as that monstrous metal thing walked away, I could hear it making a deafening humming sound and also noticed that its eyes burnt a blinding white colour and shone two bright, piercing beams of light far into the distance. It was like nothing on earth I have ever witnessed."

Inspector Huxley thanked his diligent constable and bid him farewell, worryingly thinking to himself. 'I know what the Professor is capable of inventing; please, god, don't let him be mixed up in all this.'

*

The following morning, there was a loud knock on the front door of the Big House. Upon answering it, Ernest could see standing in front of him a distraught looking Lilly Stroud.

"Professor, it's a terrible thing," said Lilly, visibly shaking with emotion.

"Now, now Lilly, calm yourself; what is it?" said Ernest as he coaxed her into the hall and sat her down on the window seat.

Sniffling and trying to compose herself, Lilly answered Ernest, "He's gone, sir, smashed beyond repair."

Ernest asked Lilly to pull herself together and explain to him in full detail exactly what had happened to Barker.

"Thankfully, his partner, PC Tom Saunders, has not been injured at all but is in a terrible state, blaming himself. However, going by witness accounts, there was nothing he or anyone else could have done. It was around seven p.m. outside Goslings & Sharpe, the bank in Fleet Street; there was an incredible battle between Barker and a giant iron machine. Sir, they described it as a great metal man. Professor, was Iron Jack here at seven p.m. last night, we have to be sure."

Ernest could sense Lilly was getting quite upset and answered, "Definitely, it was only this morning I was thinking to myself, how nice it was to see last night Iron Jack join Quinn and Rose on their evening stroll. Whatever mechanical man committed this terrible act; it is most certainly not any of Iron Jack's doing."

Ernest's mind began to wonder. *Mechanical man? There is only one other person, apart from Quinn and myself, who has the engineering skills to build such a thing, hmm and that man is Hubert Wells. I was hoping the only time our paths would cross again would be in a divorce court, now I'm not so sure,* he pondered.

"Lilly, look, my dear girl, don't upset yourself too much about Barker; your brothers can easily repair his bodywork and as soon as we can, Quinn and I will rebuild his command system. Anyway, if you could come back here around this time tomorrow, I will tell you in detail who I think is behind the bank robberies and the mechanical man you described and what I am going to do about it. We can discuss it at length then on how I want to involve you in my plan," said Ernest to Lilly as he waved goodbye to his guest, who was scratching her head, not having a clue about what might be required of her.

Settling down in his study, Ernest opened up the cabinet drawer and took out a series of photographs that showed images of Hubert Wells and his then-wife Emily. Placing them on his desk, Ernest stared at the images and his first reaction was of great anger, which was quickly followed by an overwhelming feeling of sadness. Shaking his head slowly, Ernest whispered to himself, "If I could have turned the clock back, I would never have brought that man into my life." As he choked back his tears and put the damning photographs back into the cabinet.

Chapter Nine

Enrolment and Revelations

The meeting between Ernest and Lilly had taken place as planned. Lilly was given all the current information he had on Hubert Wells.

"Lilly, I would like you to work for me as a private detective. I realise this is a lot to take on for a young girl, but I have great faith in you and, of course, will pay you well, plus expenses for everything. The thing is, I would like you to try to find out where Hubert Wells is. I may add this man is extremely dangerous and under no circumstances must you approach him. If you agree to take on this work as soon as you feel you have any important information that I should know about, then don't hesitate to get back to me immediately," said Ernest, causing Lilly to gasp with a mixture of excitement and trepidation as she nodded her head, signifying she would accept the challenge.

*

Ernest, in concern for an 'unprotected' London, had contacted Inspector George Huxley, informing him a replacement for Barker had already been built and was ready for his first deployment.

Meanwhile, at the grounds of the Big House, Rose was on

her morning saunter. At the same time, Jack was taking a morning stroll and, spotting Rose from a distance, made his way to join her.

"Sorry, Rose, I hope I didn't startle you," said the massive iron man, stooping slightly so as not to look too intimidating.

"Oh, Jack, don't be silly, you don't frighten me, you know I love talking to you. Actually, my Quinn is not feeling well today; he told me not to fuss him. It's such a shame because it really is a beautiful day."

Jack had picked up on the phrase 'my Quinn' and thought, *I was correct; the emotion-detecting skills I used before were working perfectly, and now, having read many great plays and poetry on the subject of true love, I am absolutely convinced Quinn and Rose's relationship is far more than friendship. How exciting for them.* He thought, fighting hard not to let his newly found jealousy emotion get a grip.

"It's funny you know you couldn't be more different than Quinn and yet you remind me of him so much," said Rose, smiling affectionately as she looked up at Iron Jack.

Jack's eyes inadvertently brightened from a cool blue colour to a warm orange as he said, "Well, I suppose it's not really that funny, as it was solely Quinn that created the thinking, feeling part of me."

Finding a soft, dry mound of grass that had been created by Barker long ago, the pair of unlikely comrades sat down and chatted at length on all manner of subjects until, eventually, they came around to Iron Jack's personal thoughts on his very existence.

"I absolutely love my life and am truly grateful that I have been bought into this wonderful world. Of course, I can only comment from the perspective of a being with artificial intelligence, but it is only when I stop to feel the furnace burning inside of me and occasionally get a glimpse of myself reflected in the pond or the greenhouse windows that I realise I am actually a machine and not a human being. It's lucky for me I am part of such a kind and caring family," concluded Jack, as his giant eyes fluctuated between warm orange and cool blue, signifying his joy at being alive.

Feeling he had said enough on the subject and didn't want to start getting emotional, Jack changed the conversation to his current situation. "Anyway, my beautiful lady, we had better make the most of our little chat this glorious morning, as sadly, it could be our last for quite a while. You see, I have been informed that the crime levels in the city have increased significantly and that the terrible incident that destroyed Ernest's first iron guardian, Barker, has caused Ernest and Quinn to contact Inspector Huxley. It is such a pity I never met Barker; it would have been lovely for me to interact with a being that is virtually the same species as me. I bet I could have taught that dog a few 'mechanical' tricks humans could never do. It seems it was just not meant to be. They are not going to believe how advanced his replacement is when, in a matter of days, I am to be enrolled into the Metropolitan police force."

"Oh, Jack, you know I didn't expect you to be leaving us so soon, but don't you worry, I will visit you as much as I can; you would like that, wouldn't you?" asked Rose as she reached up to give Jack's huge back a friendly pat.

"Like it, I would absolutely love it," he answered, thinking all the while, 'Oh Quinn, why did you have to build so much of your personality into me.' As the coals in his chest increased in temperature and burnt a deep red. Trying hard to get his emotions in check before he felt he would burst, Jack had to accept the love he felt for Rose would be a love purely unrequited.

Standing up to his full height, as delicately as he could, he held Rose's hand and, in doing so, caught a glimpse of himself and his companion in the greenhouse window. It was at that moment he could truly see how different he was from any human and, for a fleeting moment, thought of himself as a freakish monster, merely a creation of someone's whimsical fantasy. Anger and sadness swirled around the cogs and gears of his complex command system until he managed to convert his negativity into thoughts of joy and gratitude at simply being alive.

I can never let myself feel that way again, Jack vowed sternly to himself as he quickly brought himself back to reality and pulled himself together.

"Come on, Rose, let me escort you back; it must almost be mealtime for you," he said as they continued to cheerfully chat and walked towards the big house.

*

Two days later, at 26 Old Jewry City of London police headquarters, having undergone extensive training, Iron Jack waited with his fellow officers for his first briefing on where and when he would start his duties.

"So that's enough about me. Would anyone like to ask me any questions?" asked Jack, waiting for a response as he peered down at the astonished ensemble of policemen who were all gawping in amazement at the ten-foot iron man that had been 'holding court' for the last ten minutes.

"Oh, well, if that's it, then what time do I start work? And while I am on the subject, why am I the only one without a moustache," asked Iron Jack cheekily showing off his sense of humour, when at that moment, his senior officer walked in, causing all to stop laughing as they stood to attention and waited for the inspector to speak. Addressing his rookie constable first, he said.

"Iron Jack, as your senior officer, your duties will be to patrol and protect the City of London. You will be on twenty-four-hour alert, so I trust you will keep yourself fully prepared for call out at any given time. I have been briefed by the professor, who has assured me that you do not need to sleep in the conventional way."

Iron Jack and his fellow policemen listened intently to the inspector as he continued, "Police constable Tom Saunders has requested that he would like to formally congratulate you on your recruitment. Go ahead, Tom, have your say."

Tom Saunders stood in awe of the giant mechanical law enforcer and staring up at Jack, spoke, "I had the great pleasure of working alongside the professor's previous iron guardian. Jack, correct me if I am wrong, but as far as I am aware, you never met Barker, but if you ever feel the need to ask anything about him, it will be my privilege to tell you everything we did in our short time together. He was a really remarkable machine with a brilliant personality. I truly hope that one day the professor can find time to repair him so he can join me again on my beat." Jack felt Tom's sincerity and summoned a quick burst of heat from his furnace to his mouth. A warm orange glow flickered across his mouth, signifying a smile as he tipped his head towards his human comrade.

With the briefing over, the inspector dismissed his team but asked Iron Jack to stay. As the pair walked across the courtyard, the inspector proceeded to show Jack where he would be staying at his time at the police station.

"We have gone to a lot of expense," said the inspector as he lent backwards and stared up into Jack's intense glowing red eyes.

"When Barker stayed here, we had built him a very basic unit, more like a giant kennel, but since then, we have gone to a lot of trouble in preparation for your stay and have built you this," said the proud officer as he pointed towards a magnificent large brick-built building.

Leading the way, the inspector pushed open the twelve-foot tall doors of the impressive abode, where it revealed a plush, fully kitted-out living space that included a huge coal bunker and a plumbed-in water supply along with a massive leather chair and an enormous re-enforced couch/bed. Most importantly, an entire side wall had been built as a fully stocked library with a dazzling array of books on every subject.

"Thank you, sir. I can see you have given my needs much thought; I can see I will be very happy here," said Jack gratefully.

"Don't get too comfortable yet; here you are, my man," said the inspector as he stretched up to reach Jack's hand.

"This is a map of your work route; I will leave you now to allow you to familiarise yourself with it, as you start work in fifteen minutes," said the inspector in an authoritative tone as he walked outside and left Jack deep in study preparing for his first patrol.

*

In no time at all, the citizens of London gave their hearts to Iron Jack. Crime levels dropped dramatically as the criminals realised Jack could be on the scene in a matter of minutes. He soon gained a reputation as a strict officer who is not to be messed about with and patrolling the streets all hours in his self-assured manner. The 'mug hunters' and vagabonds quickly learnt he was no soft touch.

Another of his qualities was his superior vision; night or daytime, he could spot any disturbance in his vicinity. Jack had also learnt that by opening his furnace door, he could project a condensed blast of heat that would stun the fleeing law-breakers. Thankfully, it was never fatal, but sometimes it would cause very serious burns. When questioned if he might consider his actions too harsh, in response Jack would always give the same brief answer, "Well, they won't do it again." A saying that circulated amongst the criminal fraternity and bolstered his image as London's most feared law enforcer.

The thoughts of love and poetry he had let consume him during his time at the big house had virtually disappeared and in his new threatening environment, Jack had quickly settled in as an integral part of the metropolitan police force and proved to all that London's second iron guardian was just as formidable as the much-revered Barker.

*

A few days had passed and at the big house, Ernest sat and read the latest glowing newspaper reports on Iron Jack. Eager to share these latest revelations, he headed for Quinn's room.

Suddenly, Ernest felt a thud, as though he had been punched in his forehead, that caused him to stop in his tracks. Instantly, he knew it was Quinn's doing but was shocked at the severity of the punishment that had been delivered. As the pain began to dull, Ernest heard Quinn's voice in his mind, "Do not under any circumstances enter. I don't know how long I will need to be alone, but you will have to tell everyone that I need to be on my own," cryptically adding, "that's if I manage to survive, I will make sure you all know when I am fit enough for anyone to visit me, until then I hope that you can all respect my wishes. I am sorry if I am coming across as a bit harsh, but there is nothing anyone can do to help me."

Feeling shocked at Quinn's request, Ernest walked back towards his study, worrying all the while about how he was going to break the news to Rose and Mrs Beddoes.

*

The following days at the big house proved to be very traumatic. Early one morning, Mrs Beddoes approached Ernest as he was about to visit the village shops. "Sir, you might be able to carry on as though there is nothing wrong, but I cannot. I am at my wits end with worry."

Ernest could see his faithful housekeeper was visibly upset and settling her down, he allowed her to carry on expressing her concerns.

"That boy cannot carry on like this; he has stopped eating and drinking. Every day, it's the same thing; I have made his gruel in the same way, delivered it to his room and left it outside as you have asked me to do. Not one of those meals had been touched, in-fact the last time I was there, I was so concerned I stayed and eavesdropped for a while and could hear him moving around and making all sorts of strange gurgling sounds. I know you forbade me to, but I couldn't help myself. I knocked on his door and waited for his words to come into my mind, but he didn't reply. Sir, you know him better than anyone. Please make him see sense," she concluded, shaking with emotion.

"Please don't distress yourself any more; leave it with me, Margaret and thank you for this latest information. I didn't want to worry you, but since you brought it up, Rose had similar concerns and what she heard was similar to your description."

"I'm so glad it's all come to the surface; oh, I might as well tell you there was a lot more going on, other sounds, as though he was fidgeting about like he was itching and scratching. Even before he decided to lock himself away, I noticed he was constantly rubbing an area above his chin, sometimes causing it to bleed. I just thought it was a habit he'd picked up, but the poor thing with all his physical deformities, who knows how much he is suffering," answered Mrs Beddoes, who by now was getting in a terrible state.

"Don't worry; this has gone too far and has to stop. No matter how he responds to me, I am going to his room right now!"

As Ernest approached the corridor leading to Quinn's room, he instinctively held his hand onto his forehead as he waited in dread for what he thought would be the inevitable virtual punch in his head. When, thankfully, it never happened, he waited in trepidation outside Quinn's bedroom door, as he was determined on this occasion he was not going to be put off.

"Quinn, I'm coming in!" he yelled as he pushed the door open.

Surprisingly, there was still no response from Quinn and standing still for a moment in the pitch-black room, Ernest focused hard and listened for any sounds or signs of life.

'Please, god no... Is he dead? I will never forgive myself. I can't hear him breathing at all.'

Stumbling about in the dark, Ernest felt his way towards Quinn's bed, where, almost tripping up on something, he stopped abruptly and bent down to feel what his foot had caught on.

Ernest recoiled back in horror as what he touched felt slimy and cold.

"Quinn, Quinn, what has been going on?" he called out desperately, hoping his long-suffering friend would respond.

The sinister silence, together with the peculiar object he had just touched, forced Ernest to try to locate the gas lamp and the vesta box that was kept nearby. Striking a match and turning the gas knob, he lit the lamp, and the room became illuminated in a soft glow. As he looked down, he saw Quinn with his back towards him, laying perfectly still and was convinced his friend had sadly passed away. About to reach over to feel Quinn's pulse, Ernest became distracted and glanced at the strange object he had tripped. At first, thinking the light was playing tricks with him, what he saw made him begin to feel physically sick. Daring to pick it up, he could now see clearly that what he had in his hand was undoubtedly human skin. Holding the gruesome napkin-sized object directly in front of the gas lamp, it was evident that it was in two sections. Feeling bold, Ernest placed his hand inside as though putting on a huge mitten, and as he moved his fingers slowly around, the sticky substance made him feel nauseated, and sharply, he pulled his hand out and dropped the disgusting object to the floor.

As he did so, unexpectedly, Quinn began to move and slowly rolled onto his back. With that, a gentle tingling appeared at the back of Ernest's neck as Quinn's words in an exhausted tone appeared in his mind.

"Don't be shocked, old friend. I know what you have just held and discarded must feel abhorrent to you, but although it's been a part of me for much of my life, I have come to believe it was given to me unnaturally, and for a long time now, I have worked out that it was this part of me that was making me so ill and knew it had to go. So, as snakes do in the wild, I had to shed the old skin. I must admit, there were times I thought I would not survive this ordeal, but although I am very tired, thankfully, at long last, I am free from pain."

Ernest stared affectionately at his unique friend; nothing else mattered as, at this moment in time, he was just grateful that Quinn was alive. What he saw next would burn into his memory forever. Between the pus-like discharge and dried blood all over Quinn's head, he could see where a mouth should be there was now a perfectly formed pair of lips. It was then Quinn pushed his tongue through a set of pristine teeth and as he moistened the raw-looking orifice, amazingly he spoke, but surprisingly not in his unique telepathic way but this time with a croaky voice using audible speech the same as most humans do.

"I have always suspected I was not born the way I appeared," he said, struggling as though his throat was sore and continuing.

"I will discuss this matter with you at length at a later date, but for now, could You, Not Mrs Beddoes, bring me a bowl of hot water and some soap? I will need to clean myself up a bit before anyone else sees me," concluded the amazing, ever perplexing Quinn.

Ernest did as his friend asked and after a short discussion on how they were to proceed, they both came to the same conclusion that a gathering of all their closest friends in the sitting room for a group meeting would be the best course of action.

"Ernest," said Quinn, slightly slurring as he tried to ease his barely used jaw muscles. "If possible, I would like to see Rose in private before we go ahead with the meeting, if you wouldn't mind."

Accepting that only Quinn knew what was best for himself, Ernest agreed to his request and answered, "Not at all; I can appreciate revealing yourself to all of us in one big gathering might be too much for you."

Quinn let out a strange-sounding, unpractised laugh before he replied, "No, it's not that at all, Ernest; look, you are an intelligent, perceptive man and you must have noticed how close I have become to Rose. I could be deluding myself, but it's a risk I'm willing to take. You see, I honestly believe she is not bothered at all by the way I look, and now, with, shall I say, my more acceptable appearance, I feel this is the perfect time to tell Rose how I really feel about her. You see, Ernest, for my heart to settle, I seriously have to know if she also thinks of me as more than just a friend," said Quinn, projecting his new voice as skilfully as he could, concluding, "Ernest, I have never felt this way before, but I truly believe I am in love."

Ernest gave Quinn a comforting hug and a quick succession of friendly pats on his back but couldn't help worryingly thinking, 'Oh, I do hope Quinn's assumptions are correct. There is no doubt he is the kindest, most thoughtful man I have ever met, but even in this, shall I say, 'more human' guise, he is still a very bizarre-looking fellow.'

Ernest felt his neck tingle, but this time, there were no words that followed or no pain in his temples; it was as though his grateful friend had felt his concern and just wanted to show him, he should stop fretting and put any negative thoughts to one side.

Ernest could see Quinn needed to rest and felt it was time to leave, walking away.

"Don't worry, I haven't forgotten. I will go and bring you the soap and water you have asked for straight away." As he closed the bedroom door to leave his exhausted friend in peace.

One hour later, Ernest returned and knocked on Quinn's door. Instantly, he was taken aback when he heard Quinn, using his new voice, ask him to enter.

Quinn stood before him, fully dressed in daywear. Never had his guest looked sharper, wearing his best smart blue serge suit along with a freshly laundered and ironed crisp white ruffled shirt.

"My word, man, you look the perfect gentleman about town," said Ernest

"Oh, such flattery will get you everywhere," joked Quinn, confidently using his new voice loud and clear.

Ernest noticed that Quinn, for the first time ever, had completely covered his original eating/breathing orifice with a crisp silk cravat but, on this occasion, decided not to pry and just let his friend revel in his new appearance.

*

That afternoon in the main dining room, around the impressive oak dining table, sat all of Ernest and Quinn's closest friends, waiting in joyful anticipation at the happy news they had been promised they would be getting very soon.

'I'm glad you could all make it here at such short notice, as this is a momentous occasion for Quinn and he has categorically told me that if any of you, his dearest friends, had not been able to attend, then I was to cancel this gathering. Thankfully, you are all here, so the meeting will go ahead as promised," said Ernest as he gazed over at the group's eager faces.

"Excuse me, sir. Do you not think we should wait for Rose before you carry on with the proceedings?" blurted out Mrs Beddoes, who knew it was above her station to interrupt but couldn't stop herself.

"Ah, don't worry, you didn't surely think I would have

forgotten to invite Quinn's most dear friend, do you? Just relax and all will be revealed presently," answered Ernest, trying not to sound as though he was telling off his faithful housekeeper.

Samuel, Frederick and Lilly Stroud, along with Mrs Beddoes, sat and listened on as Ernest shouted out, "Quinn, they are all here; you may come in now; this is your time!"

Unexpectedly, Rose appeared alone and, looking over at all her friends, made an announcement, "Ernest and I have had the benefit of being with Quinn these last few hours, where fortunately, we have been able to get accustomise ourselves to the 'new Quinn'. Please don't be alarmed by my words; this is purely my way of preparing you. I hope mine and Quinn's actions will show you all much more than any words can say."

Rose walked out of the room, where, moments later, she re-entered, but this time arm-in-arm with Quinn. Before anyone had time to notice and comprehend the massive change to Quinn's appearance, Rose turned her head towards her partner and, staring lovingly at her dashing companion, passionately kissed Quinn on his newly formed lips.

Actions, not words, had indeed portrayed to all that Rose and Quinn were in love.

Rose stated that Quinn had more revelations to convey and made her way over to the other guests. "Quinn over to you now," shouted Rose as she sat down.

"I really hope you all like the look of the 'new me'. Now I have a little experiment I would like to try," said Quinn, shocking those who had not heard him speak in the conventional way.

All of a sudden, the guest's faces glazed over as though they were in a trance, where simultaneously, they all reached for the back of their necks. Stanley, the Bassett hound, came running in, sat himself next to Lilly and began twitching his large floppy ears as though someone was calling him from afar.

"I was hoping this wouldn't alarm you," said Quinn, as his telepathic voice appeared in everyone's head at the same time. "Anyway, to the point, the reason I have connected with you all in my old way is that in the future, I have decided that it will only be you, my dearest friends, that I will communicate like this with ever again. Unfortunately, in the past, I have come to realise that some minds I have entered have felt so belligerent and aggressive that I would never wish to connect with them again. Two of these individuals, some of you have met before. I am talking about Hubert Wells and Walter Sheridan. There is, however, one other person that bothers me that none of you have met, a man who passes himself off as a respectable surgeon at The London Hospital and I believe is the personification of pure evil. His name is Leopold Bamforth, an imposter who posed himself as a father figure to me, but I have now discovered by delving back into my blocked, suppressed traumatic memories, that in fact, he was the sick monster that had, god only knows why disfigured me from birth."

The entire audience at this time sat emotionally drained and transfixed at Quinn's every word as he continued, "From this day forth, you, the only people I can truly trust, can think of yourselves as my 'chosen few' and working as a team, I believe we will be able to prove there is a collusion between Wells and Bamforth and hopefully bring both of them to justice."

Before anyone could respond, Quinn added, "I will conclude this discussion by stating that I haven't forgotten about involving our newest and very important member, Iron Jack, but due to his sheer size and his gruelling workload, he could not attend but believe me when I tell you my telepathic powers are far stronger than any of you could imagine and Iron Jack has heard every word I've divulged at this meeting."

Over the next few hours, all congratulated Quinn and Rose on their relationship and chatted about the exciting times that lay ahead of them. Finding the opportune moment, Lilly, spotting Ernest alone, approached him and said, "Ernest, I didn't want to steal Quinn's moment, but I can tell you I have brought all my reports on Hubert Wells with me today."

"That is great, Lilly, but be careful what you say. I don't want Quinn fully involved at this stage, especially so soon after his traumatic transformation. I think he deserves a convalescent period in peace. Come with me; I am sure we won't be missed for a short while," said Ernest as he led the way towards his study.

Ernest stared admiringly at his stunning companion, with her short black bob hairstyle cut in such a way as one side obliterated one of her dazzling green eyes. It certainly was a unique look. Dressed in her immaculate attire, her perfectly tailored tweed suit showed off every curve of her trim figure.

'Phew, I must say she is one stunning woman.' Gasped Ernest to himself as he put his distracting thoughts to one side and asked her to go ahead and show him all the evidence she had gathered.

"The photographs you gave me were absolutely brilliant; in fact, they proved invaluable. Once I had identified Wells, I stalked him from a distance for quite a few days and found out by talking to a few locals found out he is quite a notorious character around certain parts of London."

With that, Lilly took a notepad out of her clutch bag and produced detailed sketches containing notes and times of all the recent places Wells had been frequenting.

"So, he's always alone, never with the woman I gave you photographs of?" asked Ernest, with a lump in his throat, surprised at how much concern he still felt for his ex-wife.

"Yes, that is correct, sir, but that doesn't surprise me because, as you can see, the places he visits are not suitable for a true lady," answered Lilly as she ran her finger over the detailed map she had drawn, stopping her finger at strategic points.

"For instance, this place is a notorious harlots lodge used by highly paid prostitutes. I will add, though, it's not only top-class whores that he is interested in because, on other occasions, I have followed him to the slum streets of Whitechapel and Spitalfields, where he engages with the lowly streetwalkers. It's here where a few times, I've watched on as and after procuring the attention of one of the whores he will wait with her until he is met by an older distinguished looking gentleman. They will usually talk for about five minutes maximum; after that, Wells leaves while the older man walks off in a different direction with the prostitute. One particular foggy evening, I stalked him from a safe distance until we reached a big Georgian house in Stepney, where I waited and waited until when dawn came, and he still hadn't appeared; I assumed I had found his permanent residence. It transpired I was very wrong when, on further investigation, I discovered that, in fact, the building was a notorious opium den. Arriving at the same house at dawn on another occasion, I found out that it was around six a.m. when he eventually left and would wait for the first Hansom cab available. Where he goes after that, I haven't been able to ascertain yet," concluded Lilly proudly.

"Good heavens, what a marvellous job you have done so far, way beyond my expectations. I do think, though, we have seemed to reached an impasse because I can't think of a way you could possibly follow the trace any further," said Ernest as he scratched his head.

"Don't worry, sir. I have been giving this some thought

myself and have decided the next time he takes a cab, I will use my bicycle to follow him," said Lilly in a confident voice.

Ernest, stunned and shocked at her solution, began laughing and said to her, "Lilly, I have got to say this is a preposterous idea. For one thing, a bicycle is not a suitable contraption for a lady and secondly, even if you do indeed own one of these boneshakers, then how do you suppose riding along the cobbled streets of London, you could keep pace?"

Not impressed with Ernest's sudden lack of faith in her abilities, she answered in a confident voice. "There are two things to note about what you have just said, sir; for one thing, my bicycle is no ordinary bone shaker but is, in fact, a 'state of the art' sophisticated chain-driven machine fitted with the latest pneumatic air-filled tyres and secondly, and most importantly you have suddenly forgotten I am no ordinary lady," said Lilly as she stared at Ernest with the one exposed piercing green eye. She fluttered her extra-long eyelashes as she cheekily gave him a couple of gentle pats on his shoulders.

I have to admit Lilly Stroud is more skilled and adept at this kind of work than most men I know, thought Ernest, as he guided her out of the study by her slim waist to re-join the other guests.

Before they reached the main party, Lilly added, "Please, Ernest, don't let this investigation make you completely forget about Barker; after all, he was your first iron guardian.

"Of course not, you silly girl. It's just with all the worry over Quinn's state of health and the investigation, I'd rather put poor old Barker on the 'back burner'. You leave it with me; I have many ideas. Now come along the others will wonder where we've been," said Ernest cheerfully as they re-entered the dining room.

Leaving Lilly to mingle, with his head having cleared

somewhat, Ernest suddenly had an idea.

"Freddy, could I please have a word with you in my study!" said Ernest in a loud voice towards the bemused, slightly worried-looking mechanic. Making his nervous guest feel at ease, Ernest got straight to the point and said, "Freddy, do you remember when I told you Quinn had you in mind as his apprentice? Well, I am sorry..."

Frederick's face dropped dramatically and before Ernest could finish explaining, he interrupted, "Oh, dear, I'm guessing with Quinn's relationship with Rose, he won't be able to find time to tutor me," said Frederick, always believing that a lowly mechanic being taught by a true genius was always a 'far-fetched' concept.

Frederick, "If you hadn't interrupted and let me finish, then I could have wiped that sulky look off your face. How about, as an alternative, you have an Oxford University graduate and fully-fledged professor as your tutor."

Frederick's face lit up as he gave his answer. "Ernest, I really am humbled. You're not teasing me, are you, sir? The inventor of the world's most advanced aerial rail system and, Barker, London's first iron guardian and not forgetting Iron Jack, the most incredible machine to ever walk the earth. What made you believe I could ever think of you as second best? Of course, I will accept your offer; it would be a great honour for me to be your student," answered Frederick.

Ernest, taking the opportunity while he had the young mechanic's attention, continued, "While we are on the subject of Barker, I haven't forgotten him, you know and as soon as I can, I will drop off at your workshop all of Quinn's original blueprints pertaining to Barker's command system. You will have to study them long and hard, but I am confident that a clever boy like yourself will quickly fathom the complexities and concept of what it takes to build a machine capable of artificial intelligence."

Ernest's thoughts suddenly darkened as they shifted back to the original unthinking killing machine that Wells had turned Barker into. Trying to lift his mood, he looked towards the enthusiastic, honourable boy who he had just taken on as his apprentice and was confident he was leaving the fate of the 'new Barker' in safe hands. Proudly patting Frederick's shoulder, Ernest ushered him out of the study to re-join the other guests.

*

One week had passed since Quinn's remarkable transformation and by this time, he had become full of confidence and had decided that, at long last, he was ready for an excursion to any part of London of Rose's choosing.

Rose, approaching Ernest in the hall, said in a cheerful tone, "Sir, being that it is such a lovely day, Quinn and I were thinking this would be the perfect time for us to venture out."

Ernest, trying not to show any concerns, answered, "Rose, I can see as the days have gone by that you have grown ever closer to Quinn, so if that is what you both want, then it is not really for me to interfere and I will have to trust your instincts."

Adding in a concerned tone. "I do think it best on Quinn's first trip out that maybe myself and the Stroud boys accompany you. You see, I am not being rude about your boyfriend, but we have all had quite a bit of time acclimatising ourselves to Quinn's appearance, and even with him sporting a regular mouth, you have to admit, Rosie, to some, shall I say, less liberal-minded people he will still look rather frightening," said Ernest, hoping he hadn't upset his sensitive guest.

"Ernest, I completely agree and thank you for being so thoughtful, but I may add I do believe this excursion into town could be the best thing to happen to Quinn in a long while. We should all go there with him and hold our heads up high; it is about time my man came out of hiding and showed the world what a great man he is, regardless of how he looks," said Rose, fully supporting the man she loved.

Chapter Ten

Acceptance the Quinn Way

Ernest helped Quinn adjust the buckle of his smart grey paisley patterned silk-lined waistcoat. "OK, old friend, we've come a long way since I first met you at the London Hospital and I am so proud of you. What a smart fellow you have become, now just as we rehearsed," said Ernest with his voice full of positivity.

Quinn questioned, "OK, then, but just one more time, then can we actually set off for the real thing before it gets too dark for normal-sighted people."

He jokingly remarked, "Now, please stop worrying; I've got this," Quinn continued. "Rose and myself will walk arm in arm whilst you walk alongside me kerb side. Ten paces behind, Samuel and Frederick will follow us. Our group will promenade along Regent Street until we reach the Dickens and Jones store. After that, we will take a gentle stroll, only stopping to chat with anyone if they show interest in us and are inquisitive about our appearance. If all goes well, we will stop and rest outside The Liberty Store, where after, we will re-group and saunter along to Claridge's in Brook Street, Mayfair, for a spot of lunch. Now, the only thing that can go wrong is if you have forgotten to tell the Stroud boys the time and place we are meeting them."

Ernest applauded his friend and, speaking in a positive tone, said, "Very good, Quinn, that was Perfect."

Continuing, putting his friend at ease. "And don't you worry yourself; you can be confident we will all be there for you."

Helping Quinn button up his crisp white ruffled shirt, Ernest could see that beads of sweat were beginning to form on his friend's bizarre head. '*Hmm*, we all love Quinn, but I'm not absolutely sure society is quite ready for him yet. Will they accept his strange appearance as readily as we have? I don't know. Let's hope they don't just see him as some sort of circus freak,' Ernest worryingly asked himself.

Pushing all negative thoughts away before Quinn telepathically picked up on them, in a loud, clear voice, Ernest said, "Come on, my man, it's time to go; you have made a supreme effort and have never looked smarter, let's go and impress the public at large," he said loudly, trying desperately to hide his true concerns.

*

Rose Quinn and Ernest waited in the main road, not far away from the 'Big House'. Today was to be a landmark occasion for all of them, none more so than for Quinn, as in all his life, he had never tried or had the opportunity to show himself to many people at one time. As they had all meticulously planned, today they would make the landmark journey to Piccadilly, but all agreed that travelling with the commuters on 'The Hand' could prove too traumatic, so instead, they would wait for the next Hansom cab.

"Quickly, Ernest put your arm out! We don't want to miss this cab; the next one could be up to an hour away," said Rose urgently.

As the cab neared them, the horse pulled up sharply and

began shaking its head violently. Rearing back, it lifted its front legs high into the air and began to loudly neigh and whinny.

"Whoa!" cried out the driver, trying to calm his horse as he clung tightly to the reins and jumped down from the cab. Desperately struggling to get his horse under control, suddenly, it gave the unsuspecting driver a glancing kick, causing him to fall to the ground and let go of the reins. The horse, at this time, was leaning back with its front legs high in the air, flying around in a panicked fashion. Before anyone noticed, Quinn calmly walked directly in front of the frantic animal as if about to commit an act of suicide when suddenly the horse, magically somehow managing to keep balance, moved back on its rear legs, just far enough away from Quinn so as not to crush him. As the horse stood still on all fours, its loud, agitated whinnies gave way to a calm snuffling sound as it gently breathed out through its nostrils.

The driver, visibly shaken but showing no sign of injury, pulled himself up from the floor and angrily pointed his finger towards Quinn and shouted out, "It's that, that thing, that caused this. I've always suspected there were funny goings on behind the great walls of your house, but making monsters, urgh, Professor, what have you done?" cried out the cab driver as he walked aggressively towards Quinn.

"It's fine, Rose and Ernest, please don't get upset," said Quinn, trying hard to get used to speaking in a normal way.

"Oh, it's fine, is it!" shouted the cab driver as he raised a clenched fist, about to strike Quinn.

Suddenly, the driver became inexplicably frozen to the spot and lowered his arm, becoming composed with a tranquil expression on his face as, all the while, he began to gently rub the back of his neck. As Rose and Ernest looked on, they both recognised the strange, serene expression on the driver's face as something they had experienced. It became obvious to them that Quinn was communicating with the driver in his unique way. This time, however, it seemed more; it was as though the driver's mind had been cleared of any aggression.

Hmm, I'm not sure I like this, thought Ernest worryingly, *It's as though he has 'brainwashed' that man. Quinn's powers even bamboozle me at times; oh well, I suppose on this occasion, he thought it was the only course of action he could take. Anyway, as long as he doesn't try it on me, I'm all right with it.*

Quinn continued projecting his words into the hypnotised driver's mind. "I have accepted I look different to everyone else, but having an odd appearance does not imply I am a monster. You see myself along with my beautiful lady and my small group of friends intend to visit the city on a regular basis. Think of it this way, Harold, you are my first 'outsider' acquaintance, so, sir, would you do me the honour of conveying to all of your future passengers that the great professor Ernest Postlewaite's co-builder of Iron Jack, although he looks rather peculiar, he is in fact a congenial, pleasant fellow and simply likes to be known as Quinn." With that, the driver's eyes blinked and with a twitch of his head, he opened the side of his cab and gently ushered in his passengers.

Quinn, with an urgent tone, shouted out to the driver. "Hurry up, Harold. I would like to get to Regent Street before all the shops close."

Before setting off, the driver slowly turned his head towards Ernest and asked, "I must say your friend is very assertive and anyway, how does he know my name is Harold?" All the while scratching his head as he gave his horse a gentle whip.

*

"Oh, you finally made it then; it is very unlike you to be late, Professor. Anyway, not to worry, we are all here now," said Samuel Stroud as he continued, "Go ahead now; Freddy and I will be just behind and will come to your assistance at the slightest hint of any trouble."

The first excursion into town Rose and Quinn had thought was a perfect success, but in reality, it was quite an ordeal as on numerous times Samuel and Frederick constantly had to fend off certain gawping, aggressive members of the public. Although they believed they had done a fine job in keeping this unwanted, unacceptable behaviour from Quinn, Ernest knew in his heart that nothing had escaped that remarkable man's mind.

The following day, Ernest decided to take a morning stroll into Hampstead village. As he approached the corner shop newsagents, he was suddenly stopped in his tracks as he noticed The Morning Post's newsstand disturbing advertising sheet.

IRON JACK'S CREATOR
EXPOSED AS UNWORLDLY
FREAK

Ernest entered the shop and could see the proprietor, George Marems, stacking shelves; before he had time to speak to him, Ernest watched on as he saw him quickly disappear into the back room, whereupon, immediately after, a young shop assistant appeared.

Hmm, that was a strange, thought, Ernest, *old George is definitely trying to avoid me.*

Perusing through the daily newspapers, Ernest picked up his

usual copies, paid the young assistant, and left the shop and went back home to his study. He began to read all the newspaper headlines, beginning with the Illustrated London News. Suddenly, Ernest's mood lifted, as emblazoned across the front page, above an extremely good artist's impression of Quinn, in bold lettering was the headline.

IRON JACK'S HANDICAPPED CREATOR CHARMS THE TOURISTS AND GENERAL PUBLIC OF PICCADILLY

Hmm, differing opinions by the press. Well, that's nothing new. Anyway, there is still much work to do because little do, they know Quinn is far from handicapped. Also, I didn't like the assumption that Quinn was Iron Jack's sole creator. That's something I will have to 'nip in the bud' as soon as I find the opportunity, thought Ernest jealously.

As he continued reading all of the other newspapers. The Morning Chronicle, Lloyd's Weekly and The Pall Mall Gazette had all written similar glowing reports on how Quinn had presented himself. Reading the articles in more detail, Ernest's eyes kept being drawn to certain words. Monster, Freak, Bizarre and Peculiar.

It's going to be a hard slog, but in some ways, it couldn't have gone better because, on that day, that remarkable man managed to charm virtually everyone he came into contact with. I really hope in my lifetime that all negative attitudes based purely on appearance become a thing of the past, Ernest pondered.

Due to some of the derogatory words that had been used, he made sure Rose or Mrs Beddoes would not stumble on the newspapers and hid them under the sofa.

Feeling as though he needed to clear his head, Ernest had made his mind up that another trip to see Samuel and Frederick would do him a power of good. "Mrs Beddoes, no lunch for me today; I am going to visit the Stroud's," he said cheerfully to his loyal housekeeper, all the while thinking to himself, 'I need to thank Samuel and Freddy for their support yesterday; I wonder if they have also read some of the newspaper articles on Quinn's excursion into town."

*

The Stroud family Home, Finchley Road.

"Well, yes, Freddie and I agree that, thankfully, the reports all seemed to be favourable, but I've discussed it with my brother, and he is in agreement. Ernest, we can both see a big backlash coming from this and mark my words, the press is never going to leave you alone," said Samuel in a concerned tone. Ernest stayed chatting with the Stroud boys and eventually left on an upbeat note when Samuel stated he had managed to repair the bodywork of Barker and had installed extra reinforcing to his jaw. Bidding his farewell, they all agreed to keep each other informed on any reports of Quinn they heard.

The following days at the 'Big House', Hampstead were hectic beyond belief, with the newspaper press gathering outside the 'Big House' at all hours. In the end, Ernest decided that the only way to deal with the unwanted attention would be to arrange for a press conference at Iron Jack's residence, where photographs would be allowed, and any questions pertaining to Quinn's role in the construction of Iron Jack would be answered.

*

The Courtyard, Metropolitan Police Station. 4 Whitehall Place.

Two days later, Ernest, Rose and Quinn arrived, as arranged, at Iron Jack's abode.

"It looks like you have really settled in nicely," said Ernest as he stared up at Iron Jack, who, although seated, still towered above him.

"Oh, it is such a treat having three of my favourite people in the world all visit me at the same time," answered Jack as he sat back and relaxed in his enormous armchair.

"In a short while, outside in the courtyard, you will meet all of London's press," Ernest continued, addressing Jack in his most authoritative tone, "on this occasion, I will deal with any questions relating to any technical issues. Rose and Quinn have decided they will answer any queries on their relationship, and Jack, you can talk about all your experiences since your time of employment with the Metropolitan Police Force," concluded Ernest firmly.

Jack stood up his full ten feet with his eyes flickering between cool blue and warm orange. He proceeded to unclip his large armour-plated right hand and placed it into the metal holster on his right hip. With his delicate, nimble 'superlight' metal hand exposed, he went around in turn, shaking his friend's hands. Holding onto Rose's hand longer than he should, his eyes intensified to a bright red, causing him to quickly let go of the beautiful lady's hand as he felt his furnace had risen above a safe level for close contact with humans.

Damn that Quinn, if he is so clever, then why on earth did he give a metal being such as me the ability to fall in love with a woman made from flesh and blood, thought Jack solemnly as he discretely moved his sensitive hand up to his platinum heart in an attempt to calm himself down.

All of a sudden, Quinn's words appeared in Jack's mind. "You are older now and hopefully much wiser, so you must have worked out by now that true love has to be reciprocated. You see, I built your artificial intelligence unit to be ever-evolving, learning, rationalising, equating and expanding. Use the depth of this knowledge you possess and work out once and for all that Rose loves me and not you," adding, "If there is a time where I feel it necessary to adjust any part of your artificial intelligence unit, have no fear, it will not be the 'emotion of love' section that I tamper with. Trust me, when I find the jealousy section that is festering and spoiling and taking over your mind, then that will be the part I will remove," concluding on a positive note, "Jack, remember, you are your own man now and really there is no need for me to interfere with any part of you again, although we are deeply connected we are two different people."

Heeding the wise 'life lesson' he had just been given, Iron Jack clicked his armoured hand back on, and with every ounce of emotion he possessed in his body, in a loud voice, blurted out, "Tis better to have loved and lost than to never have loved at all."

Taking Rose and Ernest by surprise at his seemingly random outburst, causing them to lean back in shock, Jack turned away from his friends and lunged his giant body towards the doors of his abode, and in his most cheerful voice, said, "Shall we go outside? I don't know about you, but I've had enough of this chit-chat; I can hear the Press getting a bit restless out there; we'd better not keep them waiting any longer."

Once outside, Jack took his place at the centre of the group, towering above Ernest to his right and Rose and Quinn, arm in arm to his left. Raising his fire box to a crackling white hot and then letting the temperature quickly drop, the bright red coals began to glow intensely behind his furnace door; at his optimum capacity, he tipped his head forward in preparation to address his enthusiastic audience.

With his huge semi-circular eyes peering below his top hat, when glowing at their most intense red, he focused his gaze firmly on his enthralled, mesmerised spectators and announced, "It's nice to see some familiar faces, but for those who haven't met me before, I am assuming you must know I am the creation of the great Professor Ernest Postlewaite."

At the same time, he placed his massive hand on Ernest's shoulder and nodded his head admiringly, he continued, "These lovely people with me today are the most important people in my life." And as he turned to face Rose and Quinn, he tilted his head slightly and in a display of recognition, Jack skilfully lowered the heat behind his right eye until it turned pitch black and gradually increasing the heat turned his eye a warm orange until it reached an intense bright crimson red. It was apparent to all that Iron Jack had just 'winked' at the handsome pair by his side.

Jack, with his huge finger pointing at Quinn, continued to speak, "This wonderful man is the person responsible for making me who I am today; in fact, he has been like a father to me."

Placing his other giant hand as gently as he could onto Quinn's shoulder, Jack then focused his attention on Rose and continued, "And this wonderful woman, the beautiful Miss Rose Morely, Quinn's fiancé, has taught me so much." Jack struggled to lift his left arm up and felt the gears and leavers in his mind grind, causing him to feel a stiffening to the back of his neck. Jack could see his words had made Rose blush and had made Quinn angry because he knew he had said too much.

"Jack, thank you. Yes, you are correct in your assumption that one day I will ask Rose to be my wife, but I am very sure she would like to hear my proposal from me, not you. Fiancé, now I have some explaining to do." Quinn scolded Jack telepathically, causing his iron-creation metal brain to almost seize up.

*

The press conference was deemed a great success and over the following days and weeks, there were many newspaper reports that now accurately stated that, in fact, it was Professor Ernest Postlewaite and Quinn in a joint venture that had created Iron Jack. There were also many articles on the relationship between Rose and Quinn and none thankfully highlighting Quinn's physical deformity in a negative way. It seemed that Ernest's stipulation to the press that words such as freak, monster, or any other derogatory adjectives relating to Quinn's physical appearance should never be written and published had worked.

Quinn, however, was still sceptical that he would be accepted by all of London's citizens as he had noticed that on the one occasion, he had found the courage to show himself to the general public; he could clearly sense that certain individuals had turned away from him, as though in disgust.

In the sitting room, Quinn began to chat with Ernest. "Ernest, I have thought long and hard on the subject of my acceptance into society, and I will never be happy until I take what I think would be the 'next step'. You see, the next time I travel outside the confines of the big house, it will not be to see how Samuel and Freddy are getting on. I will take another trip into the city, but this time, I have made my mind up; I will go completely alone," said Quinn, massaging his jaw still not used to speaking in the normal fashion.

"My dear boy," said Ernest in a jolly voice, trying not to

sound condescending, continued, "Why put yourself at such risk? You know, not everyone will be easy to convince that although you look different, you are still a perfect gentleman. Surely it would be much easier to just wait for the occasions when we all feel like a trip into town, because, and please don't take this the wrong way, and don't be hurt when I say that even though you are now in possession of the god given mouth and lips you were born with, you will just have to accept that with no eyes or nose and ears, too many people you are still very frightening to look at."

Quinn slowly lowered his head, and Ernest could tell he had deeply upset his sensitive friend. Not wanting to leave Quinn with negative thoughts, Ernest continued cheerfully, "Look, if you are adamant and must travel out alone, then why don't you let me, with Rose's help, devise some form of disguise for you."

"No! Never!" said Quinn angrily.

"I've made up my mind; I will use all my charm and hope that that's enough to convince the bigots to accept me as I am. Tomorrow morning, I'm travelling to Piccadilly alone, and there is no one that will be able to stop me!" he shouted as he stormed out, slamming the door behind him.

The following morning, as he had promised himself, Quinn had left the confines of the 'Big House' and had made his way to the main road, where he stood and waited for a Hansom cab.

Letting the first cab pass, having sensed it was driven by someone he didn't recognise, he thought to himself, *I don't mind waiting a bit longer for Harold; no point putting myself under unnecessary stress before I even get to Claridge's.*

"Oh, Mr Quinn," said Harold, trying to act as normally as he could as he spoke to his strange-looking passenger. "On your own today, then? Where would you like to go? The usual

Hampstead Village, or maybe a bit further, perhaps the Stroud garage."

"No, not today; this is a big day for me; take me to Claridge's in Mayfair, my good man," said Quinn, trying to sound as confident as possible.

*

Quinn entered the foyer of Claridge's and immediately experienced hostility as the footman and concierge attempted to bundle Quinn out of the front door.

"It's OK; this man is here at my request," lied the manager, trying not to let the uncomfortable scene escalate.

"Ah, Mr Quinn, let me take you to your table," he said, continuing his deceit with his calming subterfuge.

"Now look here, Quinn, if that is how you like to be referred to, as I have read. Well respected, you may be, but to me, your looks will always abhor me. I will let you eat here today, but this will be the last time I ever want you in my restaurant; I cannot take the risk of you upsetting my regular customers. It might have been a different matter if you had made a reservation and came along with the Professor and some of your, shall we say, 'normal' friends. I suppose that could have been a great publicity stunt for my restaurant. You have really put me on the spot today, so just this once I will let you stay. Just eat your food and refrain from any interaction with any of my other customers," concluded the rude manager in a snarling, sinister voice, adding an extra insult, "This is a respectable restaurant, not a circus."

Quinn was so shocked and traumatised at what he had just experienced at such an early stage of his social experiment; feeling hurt and humiliated, he just did as he was told. Having chosen what, he wanted to eat and drink, Quinn sat at his table alone and upset.

I should have listened to Ernest; he was right. Why am I putting myself through this, he thought sadly, as he could sense the uncomfortable murmurs and fidgeting amongst the other diners.

Quinn ate his food in his most dignified manner; with every forkful he delicately lifted to his lips, he would dab the corners of his mouth while uncomfortably sipping a glass of water between each slow and arduous bite.

Quinn sensed some of the diners leave their tables mid-meal, as they seemed to purposely raise their voice, demanding they would like their money back. One particular hurtful remark bore into Quinn's mind as one of the diners blurted out, "I don't care if he is one of Iron Jack's creators. To be honest, I would have tolerated the company of the great metal man, but I cannot endure another moment in this establishment while that thing is sitting there."

As the spiteful comment seared into Quinn's mind, he experienced something that had only happened on a few occasions in his life. His chest began to thump so hard it caused him to breathe rapidly. *I don't know what's happening to my body; I can't release my emotions; it is as though my head is about to burst. I have felt Rose's tears when she gets upset; is that what's happening to me? Perhaps I am crying inside,* he thought sadly to himself.

Standing up and brushing himself down, Quinn, leaving most of his food untouched, prepared to leave the restaurant. Removing his coin purse from his waistcoat pocket, he placed ten shillings on the table and, with his shoulders back and his head held high, walked towards the exit, purposely barging his shoulder against the rude concierge as he stepped into the busy street. Pulling his coat collar up as high as possible, for the first time ever, he made an attempt to hide his appearance from any passers-by.

As the cool September evening began to draw in, Quinn thought worryingly, *After that rather unsettling experience, I'm not risking walking along Regent Street, with its busy throng of commuters and tourists. I will navigate myself around the back streets; I'm bound to come across a Hansom cab somewhere or another.*

Pulling up his collar even higher, he set off and as the thick London fog set in when, after a short while, Quinn uncharacteristically found himself lost. Strangely, a strong sensation of warmth came over him, and after standing still for a while, his senses picked up on a group of people chatting.

"What's that?" Quinn heard in his mind, establishing the voice was coming from someone standing barely a few feet away.

Quinn had inadvertently stumbled upon a group of ten or more tramps who were drinking strong alcohol and sitting around a raging coal brazier.

"You ain't from around 'ere; find your own patch!" shouted out a particularly scruffy, dirty vagabond.

"Bill, take a closer look; he's a toff, well it ain't his lucky day, is it!" exclaimed an equally wretched vagrant as he picked up a large piece of wood that lay next to the fire. Waving it angrily, he lunged towards Quinn.

At the same time, two other 'down and out' men began talking loudly to each other.

"Bert, look at his mush; it ain't right," said the ne'er-do-well to his filthy companion.

"Yeah, I saw that ugly mug; it's that thing that's been on the front of all the papers, something to do with Iron Jack; mark my words, that great hulking lump of metal will be here soon, come on Sid, we'd better scarper," shouted out the fleeing drifter, as his mate quickly joined him and they both swiftly ran away.

Alerted by the commotion, a second group of tramps appeared on the scene and Quinn, in desperation, anticipating in dread the assault he thought was imminent, in his most humble voice, began pleading for mercy. Sadly, for him, it was to be of no avail, as at this time, the rest of the angry group, taking advantage of the opportunity to steal Quinn's expensive clothes, money and jewellery, ran at Quinn and began punching and kicking him. Showing hardly any means of self-defence, the best Quinn could do was tense up in an attempt to alleviate some of the pain as a vicious procession of thumps and boots struck his tortured body. Feeling weak and in extreme agony, two of the younger ruffians took advantage of their victim's lack of resistance, grabbed him around his neck and wrestled him to the ground.

With his fine overcoat viciously pulled from him, laying in a deep puddle of filthy water, broken and near to collapse, a further succession of increasingly ferocious blows rained down on Quinn's battered body, and he began to feel himself beginning to pass out. It was then something very strange began to happen. Quinn, not really knowing how he did it, used every bit of his telepathic power to project a blinding white light into his attacker's eyes and, at the same time, mustering every last ounce of his being, filled their minds with a deafening, ringing sound causing a searing pain inside their heads, as though their brains were being squeezed and twisted.

As the tramps, one at a time, fell to the soaking wet

cobblestones, writhing and wriggling in intense pain, they squirmed and groaned in agony. The commotion they made caused such a racket that it alerted a group of revellers from a nearby public house, and shortly after, they arrived on the confusing scene of agonised muggers and their seemingly barely alive victim.

Quinn, just managing to stay conscious, by now realised that in his desperation, he had somehow summoned from his mind a form of a 'defence mechanism', an 'extra sensory power', that even he didn't know he possessed.

I have to get away; I'm not sure I can hold them at bay much longer, Quinn thought; ignoring the inquisitive revellers, he continued projecting the piercing light and deafening noise towards his aggressors, rendering them paralysed.

Feeling himself about to pass out and desperately wanting to escape, Quinn made a decision that he knew later on he would regret forever. Not really sure if the revellers would help him, or much worse, join in with the assault, with no easy alternative solution, he began to reluctantly project his newfound 'mind stunning' tool towards the possibly innocent group of inquisitive pub-goers. Instantly experiencing the excruciating painful sensations, they all began to grab their heads in intense agony and also fell to the cold, wet pavement.

Eventually, when getting to what he felt was at least a quarter of a mile away, Quinn began to release his 'mind grip' and found a dry, secluded area between two houses to lay down.

I didn't honestly think my last days on earth would end like this, thought Quinn as he felt his life ebbing away. He placed his hand over a huge patch of blood on his trouser leg that was growing larger by the second, eventually turning into a steady stream of blood that congealed into a thick puddle around his feet.

Before completely blacking out, Quinn experienced an intense burning sensation at the top of his leg and felt that somehow, miraculously, his life-threatening wound had been cauterised. Feeling disorientated but gradually gaining full consciousness as a strong pressure on the back of his head and under the back of his knees appeared, Quinn felt the distinct sensation of being lifted. Suddenly, his head became filled with the comforting voice of Iron Jack.

When the hurly-burly's done,
When the battle's lost and won.

Said Jack, quoting a short passage from William Shakespeare's Henry VI, continued, "Quinn, oh thank god you are alive; I could sense you were in extreme distress from a good three miles away. Sorry about my dramatic recital, but I have been chanting the great Bard of Avon works over and over as I ran as fast as I could to your assistance. I thought it would let you know I would soon be here to save you."

Jack then turned his head towards where he believed Quinn had been assaulted and bellowed out, "Don't worry, you'll not get away with this attack; as long as I have fire in my body, I will seek to find every single one of you that has done this to my father and bring you to justice!"

Taking massive strides, seeing that Quinn was beginning to recover, Jack spoke, "Quinn, the bleeding has stopped. I will be as gentle as I can, but you need proper medical care, so hold on tight, my brave man, and I'll soon have you back home in a jiffy where your darling Rose and Mrs Beddoes can tend to your wounds." As he sped off, double-checking Quinn was sitting safely on his holster, Jack skilfully navigated London's maze of back streets and alleys.

Arriving at the 'Big House' around two a.m. Iron Jack peered over the tall iron gates and spotted Ernest running up the gravel drive with his forefinger placed vertically in front of his lips, signifying to all they should be as quiet as possible.

"Oh my god, what has happened?" said Ernest as he looked over at the heavy, blood-stained Quinn, cradled in Jack's arm.

In a weak voice, Quinn answered, "Ernest, whatever happens, you cannot let Rose and Mrs Beddoes see me like this. Jack has done a fine job stopping the bleeding, so if you could get me to my room and assist in cleaning me up, I will tell you all about my ordeal in more detail. Oh, by the way..."

Quinn paused for a bit, then asked, "Ernest, Jack was as quiet as possible when we first arrived; how did you know we were here?"

"Well, I'm not one hundred per cent sure myself, but about one hour ago, I remember waking up with swirling stinging pains in my head, causing me to sit bolt upright. No matter how hard I tried, I could not go back to sleep. Oddly, all I could hear were William Shakespeare quotes, and at first, I just thought I was having a nightmare, but there was something at the back of my mind that told me you were in deep trouble. It appears that the three of us have formed a far stronger bond than any of us could have imagined," said Ernest as he bid Jack a safe journey home, adding.

"Jack, you mustn't overdo it, and please put any thoughts of vengeance to the back of your mind. Even metal men need to rest sometimes," he called out as he proudly watched his iron guardian disappear into the distance.

With Quinn propped up with his arm around Ernest's shoulder, they walked as quietly as they could along the 'Big House' gravel path and once safely inside, Ernest assisted his wounded friend to his bedroom, thinking to himself. 'I'm not going to lecture Quinn now, but hopefully, this ordeal has made him come to his senses; London is far too dangerous a place for anyone to walk about alone, especially for someone with his physical deformities.'

Quinn instantly 'picked up' on all of Ernest's concerns and thought to himself, *I won't mention it now, but little does he know I have found out I am more than equipped to walk anywhere alone. Hmm, I don't like keeping secrets from Ernest, but this latest skill I have of being able to incapacitate one or more people just with the power of my mind is so 'freakish' and unworldly, I don't think I should ever divulge it to anyone, not even Rose. I can't take the chance of alienating myself from anyone else, especially my one true love.*

The following morning, after getting a few hours of much-deserved sleep, Ernest went to Quinn's room to check on how he was after his traumatic ordeal. On entering, Ernest saw Quinn was fully dressed, and before he had a chance to ask how his friend felt, Quinn spoke in a tone as though nothing had happened. "Do you know what, Ernest? I think I will go and visit the Stroud boys today and see what progress they have made with Barker."

Ernest, glad Quinn was in such high spirits so soon after his assault, respected his friend's wishes and made his way to his sitting room to read the daily newspapers. Tucked away, a few pages inside the London Pictorial, his eye was drawn to a short article on an incident that had occurred in Claridge's restaurant.

Hmm, not too much detail, but if Rose or Mrs Morely see it, they are not silly. Let's not take any chances, he thought to himself as he prepared to hide the newspapers under the settee. Before doing so, he spotted a headline that intrigued him so much it stopped him in his tracks.

London residents give accounts of strange apparitions hovering above them whilst out walking.

As Ernest continued to read the article in depth, suddenly, he was disturbed by a loud knock on the front door. Hiding the newspapers under the sofa, Ernest got up and went to see who it was and was and, opening the door, was pleasantly surprised to see Lilly Stroud standing there.

"Hello, Lilly. It's lovely to see you as always. Anyway, don't just stand there. You know you don't have to be invited to come inside," said Ernest to his striking private detective, adding.

"I suppose you are here as you have found out more on the Wells/Bamforth collusion. Am I correct," said Ernest, confident in his beautiful detective abilities?

"Yes, Ernest, you are correct, and you will love all the juicy information I have got for you," answered Lilly as she stared at her employer with her one exposed piercing green eye.

"Come on, Lilly, we had better continue this discussion in my study," whispered Ernest, not wanting to disturb any others in the household.

"You see, sir, that Bamforth character is turning out to be as much of a mystery as Wells. Apparently, he just left his position as top surgeon at the London hospital without saying a word to anyone or leaving any forwarding address or clues on how he could be contacted. Anyway, let me continue; one evening, I saw Wells approach a prostitute, whereupon the pair of them walked off. To be honest, sir, I just thought he was going to take her down some grubby back alley and do his business with her er-h'r'm said Lilly clearing her throat feeling embarrassed at her slang phrase continuing if you know what I mean."

Ernest looked shocked for a moment that his young detective

was so candid in her speech but, not wanting to show his prudishness, let his young detective carry on giving her account. "But you see, sir, that never happened, so I stealthily followed them and, and to my surprise, he took her to meet Bamforth. It was then Bamforth and the prostitute went one way, and Wells went the other. I followed Wells because that is who you employed me to investigate, but that proved to be a fruitless exercise because that night, he made his way to the nearest tavern and stayed there all night until annoyingly, when he did appear, he was so drunk he was helped by a couple who lived next door to the public house who must have let him stay for the night. I was really tired by that time and needed to get home myself.

"Ernest, I have been back there on two more occasions, and it's the same scenario every time. All this strange activity got me wondering why Bamforth uses Wells to pick up the prostitutes, so I started talking to the street harlots myself. It was then one of them told me that recently, some of her friends had gone missing. I took my time and found out more information on the last whore Wells had 'picked up'; you see, her name was Mary Kelly. Ernest, you must have seen this," said Lilly in an alarmed tone as she took out from the inside pocket of her jacket a torn page from a newspaper. Unfolding it, she pointed to the headline.

The latest victim of 'Jack the Ripper' is identified as local harlot Mary Kelly.

Ernest had been so keen to read the press reports on Quinn's visit to Claridge's that, in his set ways, he had failed to even notice the headlines. With his mind racing on how best to proceed, he began to worry he was putting his young detective at too much risk. Suddenly, an idea occurred to him that could be the solution.

"Lilly, how would you like the prospect of working with a

partner?" asked Ernest

"What with you, sir? answered Lilly in a shocked voice.

"No, not me; I would just get in the way; someone as high profile as me snooping around would draw far too much attention," answered Ernest.

"What with my brothers then?" questioned Lilly.

"No, now stop interrupting and listen; how would you feel about having Rose Morely as your assistant?"

The tenacious Lilly Stroud, completely unphased, answered. "Ernest, that's a wonderful idea, two respectable women working as detectives who would ever suspect; it is the perfect cover, although I am a bit worried because as much as I love Rose, she will need a lot of toughening up," she concluded with a smile on her face, tapping her strong brogue shoes together.

Ernest, knowing that Lilly was fully committed to continuing with the investigation, felt it was time to show her everything he knew.

"Lilly, these photographs you are about to see are truly horrific."

Laying the images across his desk, Lilly studied them one by one, each one grislier than the other; as she studied all the gory details of the surgical procedures Bamforth had performed on those unfortunate tiny babies, tears began trickling down Lilly's cheek.

"Lilly, I know this will be hard to accept, but this last selection of photographs I have come to believe are all focused on Quinn. Beginning with him as a perfectly formed baby boy, the perverted operations he endured seem to have been performed over a three-year period. I know it is hard to take in, but look at this last picture. It shows a young Quinn with all his natural features covered in a thick layer of skin, and with that eating, breathing orifice he has surgically formed on his throat."

Lilly had come over queasy but soon pulled herself together and, in a voice full of rage, said, "Ernest, if Rose is to work with me, then you do know she will have to know all the facts, and I do not envy you, but you do realise she will also have to see these harrowing images."

Ernest didn't answer Lilly; instead, he just held his head in his hands, knowing that the pictorial evidence of what her loved one endured could push Rose over the edge. Lilly, seeing Ernest's distress, said in a confident tone. "Sir, after the things you have just shown me, no matter how Rose responds, have no fear. I am even more determined to bring Bamforth and Wells to justice! Even on my own if needs be!" said the courageous detective as she stamped her foot on the floor. Showing her rarely seen feminine side, Lilly, sobbing and choking back her tears, stood up and, shaking with emotion, fell into Ernest's arms in a short while; when finally able to compose herself, Ernest walked Lilly to the front door and wished his brave young detective a safe journey home.

Ernest, exhausted by the whole traumatic ordeal but knowing he had to show his strength, went back into the living room and pulled out the newspapers he had hidden under the settee, where he began to read in full detail everything, he could see relating to the Ripper murders. Satisfied he was fully informed of that situation, he took his time scouring the papers for any more accounts of the ghostly apparition's article he had read earlier.

Hmm, interesting, similar incidents, but in four different London locations, witnesses all stating the same thing that they had seen strange creatures hovering in the night sky. The thing is, with Lilly and Rose heavily involved in the Wells/Bamforth case, there is nothing else for it; I will have to get off my backside and investigate these strange sightings on my own, Ernest pondered as he settled down for the evening.

*

The following day, in mid-morning, Mrs Beddoes gave Ernest an official-looking envelope.

Ernest opened it up and saw it contained a beautifully gold-edged, handwritten card.

Professor Ernest Postlewaite and Mr Quinn are cordially invited by Prime Minister Robert Cecil to join him for a formal dinner and award ceremony in recognition of exceptional services to the Metropolitan Police Force.

Eight p.m. Friday 17th October 1888

The Holborn Casino, Drury Lane, London.

Formal dress is required.

RSVP

Oh, this is marvellous! Hmm, I hope one week is long enough for Quinn to get over the last ordeal he endured in public. Oh well, he told me to stop worrying and Mollycoddling him, thought Ernest to himself as he laughed. *Ha, and it must be a coincidence, but they have chosen the award ceremony on the same day as my birthday. And just to think I'd decided this would be the year I didn't want any fuss.* He chuckled to himself as he prepared to tell Quinn the good news about their award.

*

The big day had arrived. Rose gave Quinn a farewell kiss as Ernest and his brave companion shut the main gates of the 'Big

House' behind them.

Rose waved excitedly until her two favourite men in the world disappeared from her sight, worryingly thinking to herself. 'Oh, I do hope Quinn doesn't get harassed. I'm not sure everyone has accepted him yet. Still, at least he liked the suggestion I gave of him to wear a hat. I don't know why I didn't think of it before; it really gives him an air of authority, fitting Iron Jack's co-inventor.

Approaching the main road, Ernest asked Quinn if he preferred to travel on 'The Hand' or Hansom cab.

"I might as well start as I mean to go on. Come on, Ernest, it is time for me to once again face the public. I think we should use 'The Hand' I don't care how many commuters are on there," answered Quinn, mustering up as much courage as he could.

Ernest and Quinn sat pensively, the only two passengers, in the eight-seat carriage as it proceeded on its controlled descent towards the aerial railways Covent Garden Station. Slowing slightly at the inter-change stations to allow passengers to get on or off, as the carriage approached the Kentish Town platform, Ernest saw three individuals waiting in the exact spot he anticipated their carriage would stop.

Immediately, as the three commuters alighted, he watched on as one of them, a burly-looking workman, sat as far away from them as he could while the others, two women, sat directly opposite. Immediately, the older, smaller, rather plump-looking woman began speaking.

"Sir, may I introduce myself? I am Mabel, and this is my friend, Mary," said the jolly passenger, not giving Ernest time to react continued speaking.

"We have always said to each other we might be lucky enough to meet you on 'The Hand' one day and now it has actually happened and to be honest, sir, it has left me all in a tizzy," she concluded with glee as she settled herself into her seat.

Not feeling as confident as he initially thought he would, Quinn sank his strange head into the collar of his overcoat as much as possible, at the same time pulling the peak of his Homburg hat down as low as he could.

"And you, sir! must be the brilliant Mr Quinn, who I've read so much about," shouted out the bespectacled younger looking of the two women companions as she leant forward and tilted her head to one side and, leaning slightly, began peering under Quinn's hat and, in her most gentle soothing voice, whispered, "Mr Quinn, I don't know why you are hiding yourself from me. I am a great admirer of yours, and this experience of meeting you here is something I will never forget."

Continuing as she leant back. "Mr Quinn, if I could be so bold, I would like to shake your hand," she concluded and waited in high anticipation for Quinn's response.

Quinn, by this time, had begun to relax and, leaning forward, held out his arm and shook the hand of the smiling, friendly woman sitting opposite, all the while sensing that the burly-looking builder had started fidgeting uncomfortably.

"Come on, Mary, leave Mr Quinn in peace. He doesn't want you chatting to him all day, and by the way, this is our stop," adding. "You wait till I tell my grandson I met the great professor Postlewaite and my friend Mary actually got to shake the hand of Iron Jack's inventor, anyway have a nice rest of your journey." Shouted out the elated woman as she waved goodbye, causing Ernest to wince that she had given Quinn all the credit as Iron Jack's creator.

Thank god, it's only two more stops, thought Quinn, as he could feel the thick-set builder getting ever more agitated.

Worryingly, he had shuffled his way along the bench seat to where the two women had previously been sitting and sat directly opposite Quinn.

Ernest, believing it best that he should intervene in an attempt to 'break the ice', began to make small talk to the grim-faced construction worker. "Ah, by your attire, a builder, I presume. I have to say I admire people who possess practical skills more than anything."

Waiting for a reply, Ernest didn't get the response he had hoped for as the builder stood bolt upright and, seething in anger, lowered his head and stared imposingly at Quinn. With a loud snorting sound, the antagonistic builder brought phlegm up from the back of his throat and spat it out over Quinn's shiny black dress shoes. Turning his attention towards Ernest, he snarled, "What are you doing bringing that thing out with you?"

As the increasingly aggressive man continued pouring out vitriol towards Quinn. "What's that smell? There's a real stench of the zoo in here; it must be that animal. Huh, the inventor of Iron Jack, I don't think so, more like one of your creations that went wrong," he continued aggressively as he clenched his fist and lifted his arm, preparing to throw a punch at Quinn.

Ernest, using his quickest reactions, quickly pulled his friend out of harm's way when suddenly, inexplicably, as though a different person was standing before them, the raging builder's face took on a serene look and, in a soft tone, said, "I didn't like to interrupt earlier whilst you were chatting to those two ladies, but I'm getting off at the next stop, sir. Could I shake your hands? Just to think, I have travelled in the same carriage as London's two finest inventors. They will never believe me back at the building site." He said as if all the previous hostility he had shown towards Quinn had never happened.

Shaking Quinn's hand first and then Ernest's, he continued, "I'm humbled to be in your presence; this has been a really great day for me," he concluded as his words tailed off, and he shut the carriage door behind him.

"What on earth happened there? It was as though he was two different people?" asked Ernest as he took out his handkerchief and wiped the disgusting spit from Quinn's shoe.

Quinn, clearing his throat, spoke, "Trust me, I will never take a beating again like the vicious assault I suffered a few days ago. Ernest, my dearest friend, if I have to resort to, shall I call it 'my mind lesson', then so be it."

"Look, the main thing is you got through this unpleasant episode without being struck, and the lord only knows what I could have done to help; I never was much good at fisticuffs, you know. Anyway, I digress; from what I could see, you actually 'brainwashed' him, and that is the second time I've seen you do that; remember the Handsome cab driver incident? Quinn if you are going to resort to that 'mind trick' every time you are shown any hostility, then quite frankly, my man, I don't think you should ever use it again. If there had been witnesses today, the word would soon get around that you are not 'normal' and you don't want that to happen because before long, you would be back at square one, hiding yourself from the world. There, I have had my say," said Ernest emotionally, really just glad his friend had not suffered any physical injuries.

'Mind trick', They are your words, not mine, but I have to admit it is a very apt description," said Quinn, continuing. "Rest assured, it is not something I will be using on a regular basis, as it's a procedure that really drains me." Adding in a more serious tone, "Ernest, you know you are my dearest friend and if you were honest, you see yourself as my protector, but you see, over the last few days, I have come to find out things about myself I haven't told anyone about, not even Rose. The power I have discovered I possess is so extraordinary that even I am shocked by its intensity. Let's just say you will never have to worry about protecting me again; I really can look after myself," said the amazing Quinn confidently, adding in an upbeat tone, "Now, enough of all this 'mind trick' talk, come along, this feels like it's our stop." The genius pair of inventors stood up and, with conviction and purpose, walked towards the doors of the 'Hand's' carriage and waited as the ever-dependable aerial train steadily approached the Holborn interchange station.

Chapter Eleven

Mirages and Mayhem

Upstairs, in the dining area of the Holborn casino, on a table for three sat Ernest, Quinn, and Prime Minister Robert Cecil.

"This award, gentleman, is, I believe, just the start of great things for you two. Also, you might like to know I have put you both forward for the new year's honours list. There are whispers the king is a great admirer of your work. I don't know if it's true, but there is a rumour that he commissioned a one-quarter scale model of Iron Jack, which he displays in his study. Anyway, enough chit-chat; what say we eat first, maybe a couple of drinks, and then afterwards join the rest of the guests in the casino," said the prime minister, trying his hardest not to stare at Quinn.

Suddenly, interrupting the congenial atmosphere, a loud scream was heard, followed by an almighty commotion emanating from the hubbub of revellers who were in the gaming area below them. Looking down, Ernest could see the casino patrons, who only seconds before were laughing and gambling were now running frantically towards the exit, almost trampling over each other as they attempted to escape the high flames and thick black smoke, which by now had completely enveloped the downstairs area.

"Come on, you two, the award can wait; let's get out while we can!" cried out the prime minister, pushing Ernest and Quinn out of his way.

With the prime minister gone, Quinn, instead of following, held Ernest back and spoke. "Ernest, sit," he said in a calm voice, a request that alarmed Ernest as he could clearly see and hear the crackling flames only a few feet away from them. Quinn, having sensed Ernest's fear, explained why he was being so calm.

"Ernest, I believe you when you say you see and hear this raging fire because I can sense this myself, but ask yourself this: can you smell the smoke or feel the heat?" asked Quinn in a 'zen-like' fashion.

Ernest, trusting his extraordinary friend completely, belying the pandemonium below and all around them, sat calmly and listened as Quinn went on to explain his theory in more detail.

"This, albeit a convincing display of a raging fire, is nothing more than a grand illusion; try and relax, breathe in deeply and let all your trusted senses take over, then admit to me there is no smoke smell or any extreme heat at all," stated Quinn confidently.

Ernest sat transfixed with the sudden realisation that everything Quinn had told him was true and instantly began to form a theory on who he thought could be responsible for this ingenious mirage.

"Quinn, you have only been in his company once, but I remember you remarking to me at the time that you didn't trust him. Remember Walter Sheridan Rose's previous employer? Well, by you convincing me this is one big illusion, I believe he is the only man I know who could pull this off. He came to my mind a couple of days ago when I read in the newspapers reports of strange unearthly apparitions popping up all over London and I already had my suspicions that man could possibly be behind them. Wait here, Quinn, let me try to get a better look," said

Ernest as he walked over to the balustrade of the balcony and fearlessly put his head straight into the convincing-looking flames. Peering down as hard as he could, Ernest tried to focus through the projected smoke until he could just make out an individual wearing what appeared to be a metal helmet that was bending down, scooping up cash, and stuffing it into a large bag. Ernest squinted his eyes together and stared harder, recognising the nasty scaring on the side of the robber's face and catching a glimpse of bright ginger hair protruding from the helmet. He had seen enough to convince him that this ingenious thief was indeed Walter Sheridan.

Ernest made his way back to Quinn and, breathing heavily in excitement, said, "Come on, man, ours and everyone's evening has been ruined; there is no more we can do here; let's get out. I will tell you more about Sheridan on our journey to Jack's place at the police station."

Ernest pulled out his fob watch and could see the time was eleven thirty-five p.m. and continued, "I'm sure Jack said he had a break at midnight; if we hurry, we should just catch him before he starts his second shift."

Ernest and Quinn emerged from the mayhem in the casino into the usual thick London fog and fought their way past confused firemen and newspaper photographers; Ernest felt compelled to stare up, where he instantly noticed that all was not as it should be. The dark evening sky had taken on an eerie purple hue, and as the warm glow of 'The Hands' gas lights filtered through the strange atmosphere every now and again, they would highlight what appeared to be a group of large black shadowy creatures, not unlike the models of flying dinosaurs he had seen in the natural history museum. As they swooped dramatically, they caused the ever-growing audience to scream in fear at the unworldly sight unfolding above them.

Attempting to attract a Hansom cab, the driver struggled to stop as his horse, spooked by the mayhem, continued running and rearing up in panic.

"Quinn, it's only a couple of miles to the police station; there is no chance of getting a Hansom cab in this pandemonium. There's nothing for it; we will just have to walk."

"Don't worry yourself, Ernest, we won't have to resort to that; I can sense Jack is on his way," said Quinn, causing a puzzled look to appear on Ernest's face.

Moments later, feeling a sudden rush of warmth, the professor looked to his side, where he could see the unmistakable figure of Iron Jack. As Jack's eyes took on a warm orange glow, he peered down at Ernest and, in his most comforting voice, said, "It appears that, indeed, all that glitters is not gold, to quote the great Bard of Avon. It is such a shame yours and Quinn's award celebration didn't go to plan, but anyway, as some small consolation, let me wish you a happy birthday."

As the chimes of Big Ben began to strike midnight, Jack added, "It looks like I've just made it in time; another moment and your birthday would have been over."

"Jack, what do you make of all this," asked Ernest, keen to get the opinion of his and Quinn's metal genius.

"Well, you see, as soon as I got here, I had already ascertained that this fire was just a fanciful illusion and merely a clever distraction for a robbery. You must have seen the reports, but I can tell you first-hand that lately, while on duty, I've noticed this type of activity before and have come to the conclusion that these unworldly mirages are becoming increasingly sophisticated. I mean, just look at that sky; we are all intelligent enough to know this can only be an optical illusion. The thing is, not everyone is as practical in their thinking as we are. More worryingly, I am beginning to notice that there are small factions forming of people who are convinced the strange apparitions are not illusions and actually think they are the work of a higher entity. Although we three learned gentlemen know this is not the case, my worry is these rumours could quickly escalate, and before we know it, the whole of London is thrown into chaos as more and more of the usually rational thinking citizens are swayed and cajoled into joining the ever-growing groups of deluded gullible fools."

Ernest, wanting to make haste, said it urgently, "Come on, Quinn, we have our suspect; we are accompanied by an officer of the law; now let's go after him; strike while the fire is hot, or in this case, cold." He cleverly joked as he and Quinn climbed onto Jack's holsters.

"Jack, head for Brixton Station Road. I think we should look there first; it's a good possibility he could be in his studio. It's only a hunch, but he could be projecting his illusions from there," shouted Ernest above the sound of Iron Jack's boiler as the astute iron policeman built up his pressure, preparing for full steam ahead.

Taking massive strides, Jack ran towards their destination, occasionally urging his friends to hold on tight, and covered the five-mile journey in what seemed minutes.

Bellowing above the roar of Jack's engine, Ernest shouted out, "That's it over there, slow down!" He pointed over to what he recognised as Sheridan's shop but now appeared shut down with a boarded-up front.

Coming to a halt, Jack carefully lowered Quinn and Ernest to the pavement and with the three of them standing outside, they began to realise the place was not as derelict as they first suspected when they noticed signs of activity in the dimly lit rooms above the shop.

"Quinn, I know you don't like doing this, but before we perform any drastic action, we should all make sure if it is indeed Sheridan that is inside," said Ernest.

Knowing full well what Ernest wanted him to do, Quinn put his index finger vertically in front of his lips, signifying to all he wanted them to keep silent and rocking his head slowly from side to side; after about thirty seconds of this action suddenly in a quiet voice, Quinn spoke, "Actually, it is a good thing we didn't just go barging in, as I cannot sense any sign of Sheridan. I can tell you, though, that the activity is caused by a middle-aged woman with her two children, a three-year-old girl and her baby brother, oh, not forgetting their pet tabby cat."

Ernest and Jack were left speechless at Quinn's concise description, but not wanting to comment and waste any more time, Ernest turned his attention towards Jack, and once again, he and Quinn climbed onto their iron guardian holster's. "Jack, set your co-ordinates. Our next port of call is 33 Electric Avenue; let's see if we can catch him at his home," said Ernest urgently. Jack's eyes glowed a crimson red as in a jolting leap forward, almost throwing his friends to the ground; he darted around a series of back streets at top speed and, in less than one minute, arrived outside Sheridan's home address.

"OK, Quinn, you know what to do," whispered Ernest.

All stood silent while Quinn scanned the property, and after a few minutes and sensing no sign of life, Ernest had his own theory on what could be going on and spoke, "Quinn, do you remember back at the casino? I told you Sheridan was wearing a strange-looking helmet? Well, do you think that mad inventor could have devised a contraption that could block you, obstructing you from getting into his head?"

"*Hmm*, when I come to think of it, you could be right. I can remember now the only time I did try to enter his mind. It was a very uncomfortable experience and I felt a stronger resistance than ever before. It was as if there was no way he would accept I could communicate telepathically," answered Quinn.

"Eh, Hum, I hope you two are not forgetting I'm here. Personally, I've had enough of this telepathy stuff for today. If he is in there, could you both stand back? I'll show you a unique way I could help flush him out," said Iron Jack, as his eyes flickered in excitement.

Before Jack could show off his idea, they all became distracted by loud, unfamiliar, howling sounds coming from afar. Feeling compelled to look up, the three companions were astounded as a fantastical light show began to play out above them.

Fierce fork lightning bolts began piercing the unearthly purple sky, creating 'The Hands' carriages to be intermittently illuminated by the unearthly display.

"Jack, you take over, whatever your plan is, if he is in there, we have to stop this now. If this illusion continues any longer, I feel the whole city will be filled with hysteria," said Ernest urgently.

Iron Jack bent down, and with his huge head barely fitting into the porch, he signalled to his friends to stand back. Building up the pressure in his boiler to its highest level, Jack's body began to rock violently and to release the pressure before he caused any significant damage to himself, he let out a huge blast of heat, dispelling it into every nook and cranny of the house. Jack continued this impressive activity for about one minute until, eventually, he stopped and spoke.

"Well, that should have done it; those blasts of one hundred and fifty degrees hot air are enough to flush out any living creature. Give it a little while and it will be safe to enter," said Jack, proud of his actions.

Thinking the time was right, warning his friends to stand aside, Jack, with one of his huge fingers, pushed the door and, with a show of his immense strength, effortlessly snapped the lock. As the door swung open, a blast of heat rushed into the cold, foggy night air, causing an impressive plume of hot steaming vapour to fill the street. Once cleared, Jack signalled to Ernest and Quinn that it was safe for them to enter and explained that, sadly, he wouldn't be joining them as he was too big to follow.

"Ernest! Stop. I can sense there is a strange, unfamiliar object not that far ahead," said Quinn to Ernest telepathically, having picked up on a ticking sound coming from the end of the corridor.

"Yes, I can hear it now. Quinn, we had better get out of here because I do believe it could be a bomb," said Ernest, urgently projecting his theory into Quinn's mind.

"No, we are safe as far as that is concerned. I have already ascertained it doesn't contain any explosives, but I may add, it is a very sophisticated piece of machinery," answered Quinn confidently.

Feeling it safe to do so, they walked along the corridor until they reached the steadily ticking box. Ernest could now see that at the side of the strange object, there was a flashing green light that illuminated a small black button. Feeling compelled and drawn in, Ernest let his reckless, inquisitive nature take over, and without consulting Quinn, he pressed the button. Suddenly, the machine began emitting a low humming sound, and after only a few seconds, Ernest and Quinn were startled as Walter

Sheridan's voice filled the air.

"Ah, Ernest Postlewaite, I presume. I knew it wouldn't take someone as intelligent as you long to work out that it is me who is responsible for all the illusions that are appearing in our capital. Don't waste your time looking around the house because I am not here in person, but I will take this opportunity to give you some very important information with this recorded facsimile of me.

Now I want you to listen good and hard. First of all, I have chosen my moment well as I could see the police were already at breaking point with the Whitechapel murders and the banks being destroyed by a mysterious giant. That metal thing, I can assure you, has nothing to do with me, but I did wonder for a while if it was you're doing. That was until I pulled myself together and realised no one as virtuous as the great Ernest Postlewaite would do such a thing. Anyway, I digress; what I have shown London so far is just a taster of far bigger things to come. You can prepare Iron Jack and the entire Metropolitan police force or involve the army for all I care because trust me when I tell you, nothing will be any use at all in stopping the next phase of my master plan, what I am calling my 'Illusionary Wave of Terror'.

Think of me as a magician on a grand scale. Ernest, you are intelligent enough to realise there is always a strong contingent of a magician's audience that believes what they are seeing is real and not a trick. It is this gullible majority that will become my power. Mark my words. You have not seen anything yet."

After a one-second pause, there was a loud click from the talking machine, followed by a short, abrupt message. "This 'Translite' tape and mechanism will self-destruct in five seconds."

Suddenly, as the message declared, the amazing talking box began making a loud fizzing sound as thick black toxic smoke poured out and eventually, the contraption disintegrated into a pile of acrid-smelling smouldering wood and melted 'Translite' tape. Ernest and Quinn, for once, both speechless, stood silently frozen to the spot, stunned at what they had both heard and witnessed.

"That Sheridan is insane but extremely dangerous, a lethal combination, I fear. I have to admit, even when I first tried to connect with him, I instantly took a dislike to the man and could sense he was very devious," said Quinn, worrying about how they should proceed.

"*Hmm*, and that speech was rather ominous. Sheridan had mentioned the metal bank robber and worryingly, this has highlighted to me that he is not the only mad genius active at the moment. Anyway, I will give you my theories on that subject later on," said Ernest, as at the same time his head suddenly filled with disturbing notions on what the devious Hubert Wells could be up to these days.

"Come on, Quinn, old fellow, let's tell Jack everything that just happened and get off home," continued Ernest as he walked outside as he and Quinn casually climbed up onto Jack's holsters as he instructed his remarkable iron guardian to take them back to the 'Big House'.

"Quinn, do your best. I am convinced he is blocking you, but he could possibly drop his guard, so keep trying to track him on our way home," said Ernest telepathically to Quinn, and hanging on tightly as they could, the miles flew by as Jack sprinted towards the 'Big House' through Stockwell and Clapham before crossing Vauxhall bridge. Along the journey, all three could sense and see that the entire south London sky was continuing to put on its spectacular, unworldly light show, and more alarmingly, it was now accompanied by frantic screaming sounds that filled the air that were even audible above the loud roar of Jack's steam engine.

God only knows what nightmarish visions Sheridan is subjecting them to at ground level, thought Ernest, concerned for the innocent, impressionable general public that could not work out that what they were experiencing was nothing but a complete sham.

Quinn, unsuccessful in tracking Sheridan after a fast and rather uncomfortable eight-mile journey, eventually gave up trying. As they all finally arrive outside the 'Big House' gates, before Ernest and Quinn could let Jack get back to his duties, they decided it would be a good idea to form a plan of action.

"Jack, you work in the heart of the city and come in contact with many people. What I suggest is that, amongst your daily duties, you could promote the idea that these fantastical apparitions are nothing more than illusions created for the sole purpose of causing hysteria. I trust you, Jack and have complete faith that you will be able to use more than just your fear factor to persuade the people. The public trusts you, Jack," said Ernest, so proud of his and Quinn's creation.

Jack agreed it was a good idea and bid his friends farewell as he quickly increased his boiler pressure and furnace and, in no time at all, disappeared into the distance.

"Quinn, you and I will have to put our thinking caps on; this Sheridan has to be stopped before I fear he will send the entire London population as insane as he is," said Ernest with his voice full of concern as he escorted his friend down the gravel path towards the 'Big House'.

*

Over the following days, heeding Ernest's words, Iron Jack came up with what he believed would be a great plan.

I have to start somewhere, so why not with the 'little 'ns'. I must convince the children it is just purely a harmless moving picture show and let them be the teachers this time. Hopefully, they can convince their parents that what they are experiencing is nothing more than a sophisticated form of trickery, Jack thought to himself, proud of his ingenuity.

Keeping to his plan, whilst patrolling the streets, in the beginning, he would seek out the street urchins and gipsy kids, and with their permission, he would take them to where they said they had seen the ghouls, werewolves or whatever other scary apparitions Sheridan had dreamt up. On a few of these excursions, when the illusions were in full flight, feeling safe in Iron Jack's arms, the excited children would ask him to take them directly into the heart of the illusion. At first, they would scream uncontrollably, but very soon, they thought of the whole experience as though they were being treated to a fairground ride.

"More, more!" cried out the scruffy eight-year-old girl, cradled in Iron Jack's left arm, sitting next to her queasy-looking friend.

"Come on, Mary!" shouted out her older brother, who was sitting comfortably in the bend of Jack's right arm. "Jack cannot spend all day with us; he said the next time we see the monsters and things to bring all of our mates along and give them a go," continued the older boy as he patted Jack's chest and smiled, signifying that he wanted him to stop.

"So, you see, kids, it's all just a picture show," said Jack as he punched the air theatrically around the faked werewolf's head.

"I'm off to the school now, something you should try one day," he joked as he winked his enormous right eye, red through to orange, then back to black. Carefully lowering his young passengers to the ground and waving goodbye, Jack made his way to the prestigious Westminster private school.

*

With the teacher's permission, Jack carefully lifted the school's four most respected pupils onto his holsters and took them to an area that was renowned for showing scary mirages. Going through the same procedure, he had subjected the street urchins to, the privileged children hung on tight as Jack confidently ran in and out of the harmless, terrifying visions.

"Now, after I have dropped you back, remember, as we discussed with your teachers, it is you four who are allowed to take half an hour off from your studies each day to explain to your fellow pupils exactly what the ghouls and monsters really are," said Jack as he carefully unclipped his right-hand glove section and placed it in his holster, and continued, "Louis, could I have your notebook and pencil." Whereupon he began to draw a diagram on how to build a simple 'Muto-scope' explaining as he did, that the machine responsible for projecting the frightening day and night time moving picture show, was in fact nothing more than a bigger, more elaborate version of this simple devise.

Taking his excited pupils safely back to their school, as he left, Jack had the worrying thought that although those astute children had trusted and accepted his explanation of what the strange apparitions actually were, would they be able to convince the adults, teachers, parents and relatives of the truth.

It wouldn't be long before his fears were realised as during his journey returning to the police station, as he cut through Hyde Park, he observed a large gathering at 'speakers' corner', many carrying placards with simply the one word, 'BELIEVE' painted in bold letters on them.

Jack stopped for a while to watch the attentive crowd. Standing tucked away behind a tall tree, from a distance far enough to hear, he listened to everything the main speaker was broadcasting to the growing crowd.

"It is the coming of a new dawn as prophesized. Cronus will be overthrown and our god Hades, along with his queen Persephone and their guard Cerberus, will lead us to a new beginning. I was chosen in a heavenly vision to show you the way, but you must believe what your eyes see is the truth. Only then will you be able to call yourself a true 'Disciple of Hades," concluding in a loud voice. "Be confident and firm, disperse now, and go forth and spread the message 'Believe' to all you know!"

Jack watched on worryingly as the frenzied crowd, with glazed expressions on their faces, ran in all directions, approaching all in their wake, screaming out the prophecy they had just been told.

Phew, this is incredible. This cult is escalating faster than even I had expected. I will have to ask Inspector Huxley to invite Ernest and Quinn to my place tomorrow. With what I've just seen, this needs a crisis meeting to work out how we should proceed, thought Jack, full of concern as he headed back to his abode at the police station.

*

The following day at one p.m., Ernest, Quinn and Iron Jack met Inspector Huxley at Jack's place to discuss the next best plan of action.

"So, if what you have discovered about this Sheridan fellow is correct, then all we have to do is find and apprehend him, and this will be the end of the chaos our city has been thrown into," said the inspector to Ernest, trying hard to convince himself this would be the simple answer to bringing London back to some form of normality.

"*Hmm*, not quite as easy as you assume," replied Ernest, trying not to sound too condescending. "You see, George, worryingly, Jack has informed me there is a group of extremely deluded 'disciples' that are beginning to use other more violent methods of recruiting members, resorting to using 'press gangs' to viciously enrol them into their cult. Mark my words; I predict it will only be a short while before we see this unacceptable bloodshed escalate to murder on our streets."

"I have also discovered something I haven't told anyone yet," the inspector interrupted.

"I received a telegram from the Liverpool City Police last night that had really puzzled me, now it seems to make perfect sense. It said Liverpool had also been experiencing strange illusions day and night and expected an influx of their citizens who seemed obsessed with having to get to London. It seems my dear fellows, somehow, this Sheridan character has managed to spread his net far and wide. Trying to put an upbeat spin on his grim prediction," he added, "It's not all doom and gloom though because Jack has informed me that in his spare time, he has been doing sterling work educating all those who are willing to listen."

"Everything my inspector just said is correct, but we will all have to work fast because no matter how hard I try, there are always some that just cannot accept the truth," said Jack with his eyes flickering with extreme intensity. And suddenly, he stood up from his leather-bound scaffold armchair and walked over to his extensive collection of books. Pulling out a large leather-bound book using the index finger of his smaller, delicate right hand to find the page he was looking for, Jack gave out a small cough and, in a clear voice, delivered the rousing speech from the prologue of William Shakespeare's great work, Henry V Act One.

"O, for a muse of fire that would ascend the brightest heaven of invention, a kingdom for a stage, princes to act, and monarchs to behold the swelling scene."

Ernest, Quinn and the inspector stood stunned in silence as Jack finished his soliloquy. Giving a foppish wave, proceeded to sit back down in his great reinforced armchair.

"Jack, your ever more frequent Shakespeare quotes are beginning to grate on me; please try and grasp the seriousness of the situation or believe me, the next time we meet, I will make sure I have my toolkit with me," said Quinn, angrily pointing and shaking his finger as he scolded his metal prodigy.

"Oh, Quinn, please don't get upset, my good man," said Jack, thinking he had not really done anything wrong.

"It's not my fault I have this constant thirst for culture and knowledge because that blame lies solely on one person, and that person is you. After all, it was you that built my brain?" Jack said in a cocky tone, as though he had just performed 'checkmate' in a grand game of chess.

"All right, I take your point, but flippant, random Shakespeare quotes will not win us this fight," rebuffed Quinn, all the while reluctantly accepting to himself, he had in some ways created an uncontrollable 'monster'.

Jack, choosing his moment and letting Quinn feel exonerated for telling him off, spoke once again, "All right, Quinn, you do have a point, and really, I should have told this straight away; a trustworthy source has informed me that very soon there is to be a great display in Hyde Park where the 'Disciples of Hades' have been asked by their fanatical leaders to congregate. Apparently, their 'god' has informed them this is a very important day and will be known as the 'final coming'."

Standing up as straight and proud in a booming voice added, "Little do they know that this is also the day that Iron Jack will expose their 'god' as a fraud," adding in a quieter tone, "However, for my plan to succeed, I will need assistance and I think I have come up with the perfect solution. You see, I have perused every article pertaining to London's first iron guardian 'Barker' and by all accounts, before his early demise, had put up a sterling fight against some mysterious iron bank robber. I worry if that thing appears again, along with the threat of Sheridan's grand illusion, I would never be able to cope on my own. So, could you two fellows hurry up in getting Barker fully operational, as I could seriously do with some help," concluded Jack abruptly as he lifted his hand to his chin and intensely stared at Quinn and Ernest, waiting for their response.

Ernest, feeling Jack's concern, answered, "I will do my best, and rest assured, I have been informed that the Stroud boys have been working hard on repairing Barker and will check their progress as soon as I can."

Suddenly, Ernest felt his neck tingle as Quinn's words formed in Ernest's mind. "Ernest, I can feel you are as proud of Jack as I am, but sometimes I am sure he thinks he is our boss and I worry he is getting too big for his giant iron boots."

"Eh hum, if you must talk about me, could you either say it to my face or, at the very least, make sure you are a lot further away from me? Tut, are you both forgetting our connection? It is so great. I can hear everything you are telepathically saying to each other," said Jack out loud, leaving George Huxley scratching his head, not having a clue what he was talking about.

Walking out into the courtyard, the inspector addressed Jack and, bringing his mechanical police officer abruptly back to earth, said, "Come on man, that's enough talking for one day; you're on duty in ten minutes."

Quinn and Ernest bid George Huxley and Jack farewell and assured both of them that repairing Barker would be their number one priority and that they would keep them both updated on when he would be ready to resume service.

*

After interrogating some of the weaker 'disciples', Jack found out that the mass congregation of Sheridan's followers in Hyde Park was to be in two days. While out patrolling a slum area of Camden Town, Jack's mind began working overtime, trying to fathom out a way he could get one step ahead of Sheridan.

If I stand here on this spot, right, it's 1.58 p.m., that means in only a couple of minutes, his daily picture show will appear, thought Jack to himself as he stood in anticipation.

As he had predicted, at precisely two p.m. the usual cacophony of howling, roaring sounds appeared; at the same time, scores of terrifying ghostly apparitions began to swoop down from the sky.

Standing bolt upright directly in the centre of the illusion, the fearless iron guardian began to work on a plan. *So, let me see if I am correct,* thought Jack to himself as the fantastical light show intensified. 'In thirty seconds, time, the werewolves will appear from the west, followed ten seconds later by an attack of the skeleton army from the east.'

As the scary mirage continued swirling in a clockwise frenzy, with the roaring banshee sounds reaching fever pitch, Jack, confident they could do him no harm, fearlessly stayed put and, turning slowly, ignoring the ghoulish images, walked casually away from the din, and finding a quieter spot, stood still to gather his thoughts.

Just as I had suspected, it follows the same pattern every time, thought Jack, as he peered across London and could see that in every direction, the mirage had spread far and wide, all the while performing its astonishing, mind-boggling set routine.

Suddenly, Jack's eyes began to glow and flicker as he came up with what he believed would be one of his greatest ideas. *Why wait for Sheridan to perform his 'big moment' in Hyde Park? If I can work out the central position of these illusions, I should be able to catch that sneaky madman red-handed.*

Jack quickly switched his thought pattern to his mathematical equation mode and, setting off at speed, headed towards the Whitechapel illusion. Upon arrival, deep in concentration, he began speaking to himself quietly, "So I've just covered five and a half miles from the Camden town illusion; if I use Pythagoras's theorem, I should be able to decipher the epicentre and source of the four major, regular picture shows."

Using the trusted mathematical hypothesis, Jack ascertained where he believed Sheridan was projecting the phantasmagoria and, using his extensive map database, quickly calculated it was coming from a sewage work near Finsbury Circus Gardens. Setting off at speed, Jack reached his destination in ten minutes and without hesitation, after snapping the lock of the sewage work gates, he began to make his finite calculations. Heading towards where he had worked out the projector and, hopefully, its operator were, as he approached the area, the light show appeared to condense and intensify in brightness, preparing to pounce and apprehend Sheridan. Jack felt a waft of sadness as he stared at the fantastical projection machine and could see it had no human operator.

As the ingenious glistening machine continued its eerie picture show, Jack shielded the blinding light from his eyes and, trying hard to focus, could see the projector was actually a large, possibly two-foot square faceted glass prism. As it proceeded to throw out its array of spectral visions high into the sky, the hypnotising prism rotated slowly, reflecting and refracting the light into thousands of fine multi-coloured beams.

Damn it, I should have realised, someone with the devious qualities of Sheridan would not allow himself to be found this easily. Hmm, very clever, it looks like it works with a timer and is fully automated, thought Jack as he bent down and picked up the machine to stop it from emitting any more illusions.

As Jack lifted the object, there was a loud bang, as the glass prism, without warning, shattered in Jack's hand.

As the remnants fell to the ground, Jack watched on as the hundreds of broken fragments disintegrated and melted before his eyes.

True to form, that man will not allow any part of his inventions to be scrutinised, oh well at least I've stopped his picture show for today, and perhaps I have done enough for the city to have a quiet night, thought Jack, not convinced that what he had just done would entirely stop Sheridan's brainwashing hallucinations.

As Jack walked back to his police headquarters, he scrutinised the beauty around him, and with the disruptive daytime illusions brought to a halt, it gave him time to reflect on what a glorious winter's day it was in London and began thinking.

'Normality and calmness are a rare thing these days' something that megalomaniac Sheridan has unquestionably put paid to'. Suddenly, Jack's mood changed to urgency, as he quickly reminded himself that Sheridan's 'Believers', the rapidly growing cult 'The Disciples of Hades' were at this very moment spreading their divisive message across London and as his inspector had predicted with large crowds of 'Believers' arriving from outside the city.

Continuing his journey to his headquarters, Jack suddenly stopped as he was alerted to a scene of pure mayhem. Groups of dishevelled women were walking and bumping into each other as though drunk. On closer inspection, he noticed that one of them was talking loudly to herself while foaming at the mouth.

In an attempt to help the distraught individual, Jack approached her and said in a concerned tone, "Madam, what is the problem? Is there anything I can do to help?" The obviously deeply disturbed woman continued to sway uncontrollably and suddenly, with a series of grunting sounds coming from deep down inside her, she spat out a huge ball of phlegm and saliva, causing Jack to recoil in horror.

Realising there was nothing he could do for the severely troubled women, Jack's eyes became drawn towards a different group that were also acting erratically. In disbelief, he watched on as they began tearing their clothes off, and one of them, when naked below the waist, in an act of pure depravity, began defecating in the street, whilst at the same time another bent down and began smearing her face with the faeces. Jack, not knowing what to do, could only look on as the mentally deranged women continued displaying ever more outrageous actions.

As others began to perform sexual acts on themselves, Jack decided he could watch no more and thought to himself, *I may be many things, but I am not a doctor. These poor souls need urgent medical attention.* Leaving the sorrowful scene, he quickly ran towards the Bethlem hospital for the insane. *Surely that's where those wretched souls must have come from, and if they haven't, then I'm sorry to say, that is where they should be,* thought Jack, as his human emotions at their full capacity, felt a trickle of warm water flow from his huge metal eyes.

Upon arriving at the hospital, Jack was greeted by a sight that would burn into his memory forever. With the main gates of the asylum strewn open, he watched on as a horde of screaming, manic people emerged and, with their glazed, frenzied, looking eyes, spurted out loud guttural noises and gibberish as they dispersed into all directions.

Jack, amongst all the mayhem, could see discarded on the floor near the gates, a massive opened padlock. Walking over to pick it up, he instantly noticed that it was not as he had expected; it had been unlocked and not forced or snapped.

Jack pondered to himself. *Hmm, it seems the gates were deliberately left open; that man is a genius; he knew that while I was disarming his projection device, I was miles away and took the opportunity to cause this physical distraction. It seems he's hellbent on destroying the fabric of this city by any means possible. Sheridan, you are not the only cunning genius in this town and your day of reckoning is coming very soon. If only you knew, you will never outwit me, the great Iron Jack,* thought London's trusted protector, as he felt a sharp pain in his platinum heart and recalled the insane actions of the pitiful, mentally disturbed women, he could do nothing to help.

So, Hyde Park, Monday evening 22nd October it will be. You *might be hiding now, but I'll get you then, Sheridan,* thought Jack as he set off determinedly towards his home.

The following day, newspapers were alarming, all with the same headlines stating that London was out of control and on the verge of pure anarchy. Sporadic illusions continued to appear all across the capital, as the cult of the 'Disciples of Hades' had by now grown to tens of thousands. As the alarming situation escalated, further mental institutions and prisons were deliberately broken into, allowing the troubled inmates to disperse into society, striking fear in all in their vicinity. Violence across the city escalated as the cult followers clashed with the few 'non-believers' who had tried in vain to escape the metropolis.

*

Hyde Park, late afternoon, 22nd October.

Just before sunset, Ernest and Quinn, along with Iron Jack and Rose, met up with Lilly Stroud and her two brothers, Samuel and Frederick and grouped together in the park. Standing well away from a large gathering crowd, they all waited in trepidation, not sure how the night's activities would unfold. Iron Jack, in an effort to comfort his friends, assured them that he had already formed a plan on exposing and hopefully capturing Sheridan, but admitted that controlling the huge ever-growing cult of 'Disciples' could prove an impossible task, as by now, they had greatly outnumbered his fellow police officers.

"Jack, don't be silly; how can you say that? It looks to me as though the entire metropolitan police force are out there patrolling the park," said Lilly, trying hard to convince herself that all would be fine.

"Lilly, my dear girl, I wish I shared your confidence, but it transpires that the devious Sheridan has found a weapon that physical strength is completely useless against. With his cunning ways and ingenious inventions, he has created a level of 'mind control' previously unheard of. Brainwashing any potential foe into joining your cause must surely be the most effective tool in any war. You see, what I have overheard and seen over these last few days, I have to say, is giving me much concern. I have noticed that, lately, a lot of my fellow officers at the police station, no matter how I try to dissuade them, are beginning to 'turn' and have themselves become 'Believers'. Sadly, even, Tom Saunders, Barker's old handler, has been 'got at'. I can hear his words now. *Jack, there are things out there beyond man and machine. Accept it; Hades is coming, and he will show us the righteous path.*"

Jack continued, "As hard as I tried, I could not change his opinion. I even sank to asking my inspector to stand him down and suspend him from his duties, but when he refused my request, his answer and the reasoning behind his decision chilled my furnace. I can hear it now. *You never know, Jack; he could be right; we will have to see what unfolds at the gathering in the park.*"

Adding worryingly, "I think even the head of the metropolitan police force is on the verge of becoming a 'Believer'," concluding in an upbeat tone. "The one good thing on our side tonight is that at least we have become a solid group, and together, we will be victorious."

With Jack's rousing call to arms, Quinn, in a normal voice began speaking, "I have given you all the ability to telepathically connect with me, but we have never tried long distance and on mass, so this is the perfect opportunity to try it out."

In a large circle, standing one yard apart from each other, Quinn connected to all of his colleagues and they instinctively placed their left palm on the back of their tingling necks. Emptying their minds of any distracting thoughts, the group allowed Quinn's words to enter their minds.

"Keeping the circular shape, I would like you all to steadily walk backwards until we are at least twenty feet away from each other."

When the intrepid group were satisfied, they had successfully carried out Quinn's request, it wasn't long before they heard his next instruction.

"If all is going to plan, you should be so far apart you can barely see each other, but you should still be able to hear my voice in your head. If this is the case, I want you to all lift your left arm to signify you have just heard what I said."

All at once, the group did as Quinn asked and looking over at each other, they could see they all had their left arm raised.

"Now, the hard part! I am going to concentrate on one single, different word for all of you individually. I want whoever at the time hears my words to concentrate hard and think back to me. If this exercise is a complete success, I will relay the complete sentence the words make up back to you.

Ernest, here is your word **'Together'**.

Jack now over to you, **'We'**.

Rose, **'Are'**.

Lilly, **'One'**.

Samuel, **'Amazing'**.

Last but not least, Freddy, here is your word. **'Team'**."

Confused at what sentence they had just made, as Quinn relayed it back to them, they all excitedly ran towards their amazing tutor to give him a hug.

Iron Jack, at this time, had become somewhat distracted, as he noticed appearing approximately four hundred feet in the sky, completely blocking out 'The Hand's' track and carriages Sheridan's 'show of his life' had begun.

Suddenly, the whole of London was thrown into complete darkness, and moments later, piercing through the pitch black, crimson red flashes of light appeared, highlighting the houses of parliament, giving the impression it was being consumed by a raging fire. The deafening sound of the screaming terrified citizens was accompanied by the eerie wailing disciples of Hades.

Adding to the unworldly scene, Sheridan introduced the full inventory of his terrifying illusions. Lions, tigers, ghosts, werewolves and the skeleton army darted around the park; all the while, his army of disciples press-ganged and bludgeoned anyone reluctant to join their cult. Jack and his band of friends at this time could do nothing but watch on as alarmingly numerous policemen began tearing off their uniforms and eagerly ran to join the ever-growing horde of fanatical 'Believers'.

At the centre of the frantic crowd, elevated by a massive scaffold platform, sat the top disciple flanked by a group of giant tigers and lions. In an authoritative voice, he ordered his cult following to be silent and as the sky turned to an eerie violet colour, changing every few seconds to a dark emerald green, it pulsated rhythmically in the otherworldly colour pattern as the frenzied crowd, unable to stop themselves in their trance like state began chanting the word 'Believe'.

Trying to penetrate the deafening cacophony of sound, Quinn, using all of his immense mind power, endeavoured to locate the source of Sheridan's disruptive projections. Sadly, Quinn, after many unsuccessful attempts, eventually had to admit defeat, as it became clear to him that Sheridan had as suspected devised a method of blocking his thoughts.

As the wailing and frenzied screams intensified, to everyone's amazement, appearing majestically high in the sky, a forty-foot vision of Walter Sheridan's face materialised directly above the park.

Wearing his deep blue tinted large round spectacles, with his flame red hair poking out from the sides and back of a strange-looking metal helmet, and his badly scared face framed with impressive ginger mutton chop sideboards, he looked so outlandish it was as though he was a being from another world.

Turning the scarred side of his head slowly and menacingly towards his baying audience, he shouted in a loud booming voice, "Killing 'non-believers' is the only way. Disciples disperse, hunt down your prey!"

Seconds later, obeying their master's wishes, a crowd of disciples ran out of the group towards Ernest and his tightly grouped gang. Catching Jack off guard, four men, two on each side carrying a huge metal chain, ran past Jack and purposely caught the middle section of the chain behind his knees; whilst continuing to run, they tugged with all their might until the four fanatical cult members managed to topple Jack over.

At the same time, two other manic 'Believers' whisked Rose off her feet and dragged her away deep into the throng of the deluded, baying crowd.

"All try and concentrate your thoughts towards Rose!" shouted Quinn in an attempt to locate her location.

Iron Jack, with his pride somewhat dented, had by this time managed to stand upright and had joined his friends to 'telepathically' find their abducted friend, but It was to be of no avail. Quinn explained the only explanation could be that, somehow, Sheridan was shielding Rose's mind.

"Quinn, you have made a noble attempt using your unique skills, but I think I should take it from here; there's no time to waste, and it's time to test out my plan," said Iron Jack confidently.

Standing bolt upright and stretching himself to his maximum ten feet, stooping slightly so that his chimney perfectly lined up with the terrifying projection of Sheridan's head that appeared in the eerie pulsating violet sky, building up the pressure in his boiler, the coals in Jack's firebox began to glow white hot, and his whole body began to shake uncontrollably as if about to explode. At the peak of this crescendo, Jack, in extreme danger to himself, allowed a stream of water to enter his firebox, whereupon instantly a deafening hissing sound could be heard as boiling hot steam gushed from every joint of his body, causing Jack's body to rock violently as if about to explode.

Jack then inexplicably began emptying virtually all of his water supply into his system and as his eyes dimmed and went inky black, he stopped moving. Using all of his remaining power with his chimney perfectly focused on his target, Jack dispersed a massive plume of thick black smoke.

Watching on as the sky began to be filled with a thick fog, the image of Sheridan's face gradually disappeared, and as Jack's chimney continued to disperse every last ounce of smoke, it gradually penetrated and filtered into the illusion light source and became trapped shining a path down to ground level.

Jack focused his eyes towards the lowest part of the smoke-filled pinpoint of light and shouted out loudly so that he could be heard above the roar of his engine, bellowed, "You must all wait here because it is far too dangerous for you to follow me, but I do believe I've located the scoundrel." Using all of his skill, he brought his furnace up to full power and, breaking into a series of massive strides, ran towards where he thought Sheridan was hiding, unashamedly knocking over anyone who dared to try to get in his way.

Quickly arriving at the projection source, he could see it was coming from what appeared to be a builder's small work tent, and wasting no time, Jack aggressively ripped it open to expose a petrified, quivering Walter Sheridan and, with a small, controlled blast of heat, stunned the shocked maniac detective, upon where he immediately fell to the ground.

"Where's Rose? Tell me now! I swear if I find out she has come to any harm; I Will kill you," shouted Jack as he picked up Sheridan and shook him like a rag doll.

"We are going to end this sham right now, so sit up and face the projector and tell everyone you are not a god and that you are no more than a human being, a pathetic one at that. If you can successfully stop this madness, I might spare you and give you the chance to plead insanity," said Jack as he knocked off Sheridan's metal helmet and with a skilfully controlled flick, he sent the terrified trickster's spectacles flying to the ground.

Firmly grabbing hold of Sheridan's head, Jack pushed it towards the projector's mirror. With the thick smoke having cleared, a perfect image of a shaking, sobbing Walter Sheridan appeared high in the night sky and in a weak, pathetic voice, he repeated exactly what Jack had told him to say.

"If you truly are my disciples, then you will obey all my commands. Do not harm anyone; all violence must stop. I have hoodwinked you all. Everything you have witnessed tonight is nothing more than a deceptive illusion."

With that, stunning the crowd below, Iron Jack's massive hand appeared in the sky; with his huge metal fingers gripped around the top of Sheridan's head, Jack pulled him up and showed the stunned, silent crowd; what a pitiful feeble man their so-called god really was.

Jack, after dropping the humiliated Sheridan, posed himself in front of the mirror and, when satisfied, the image of his face was projected bright and clear, in a booming voice, proclaimed, "This is the end; this is the final coming. You should have listened to your children and 'Believed' there is only non-human you can truly believe in is me, Iron Jack."

Jack went on delivering his speech to the deluded followers and gave his ultimatum, "There is a woman amongst you that is very dear to me; she will announce herself as Miss Rose Morely and you must release her now. If I discover she has come to any harm, or god forbid worse, then mark my words; the gallows will be full tomorrow. This fanatical worshipping of a false god has to stop right now. In the future, anyone that is heard talking about Hades or calling themselves 'Believers' will be severely dealt with by me. Now all go home, police 'Believers' included; we will discuss your position tomorrow."

Moving back from the mirror, Jack grabbed Sheridan by the scruff of his neck and, with his other hand, picked up the projection device and, in a quiet, understanding voice, said to the snivelling maniac. "Walter, I know it's a mental illness that has brought you to this, so I will do all I can to give you a second chance. If you agree to make available all of your genius inventions to the general public, I will do all in my power to save you from the gallows. I believe with medical help; your skills could be a real benefit to the entire world. Come on, I'm locking you up at my place tonight; I will see who I can trust to deal with you tomorrow," Jack concluded.

Firmly holding on to his prisoner, Jack began walking over

to a space in the park that only had a few people, it was there where he spotted Rose running towards him.

"Oh, Jack, thank you. I truly believe you have saved my life tonight," said Rose as she gave a fierce kick to Sheridan's leg.

"Walter, why all this? You used to be such a good man," she continued, trying not to cry. She suddenly felt a wave of sympathy for her old employer rush over her.

Turning the horrifically scared side of his face away from Rose, Sheridan stared at her and spoke' at long last having the courage to show his real feelings towards her.

"I have not been right for a long while; it's those voices in my head that tell me to do things I don't want to do. There is also jealousy of the relationship you have formed with Quinn. Rose, if I'd have had the confidence to tell you about the love I felt for you when I was a sane, rational person, then who knows, our lives could have taken a different path. Anyway, it is far too late for that now. You have found your soulmate, and I wish you and Quinn all the best in the future." Sheridan fell silent but, for some perverse reason that only he knew why, couldn't resist turning the mutilated side of his face towards Rose. Cupping her hand over her eyes, Rose whimpered in a mix of pity and disgust and quickly ran away.

Keeping track of her journey, Jack could see in the distance Rose being held tightly in Quinn's arms. 'Love, such a powerful human emotion, does it really have a place in this iron body.' The profound thought echoed in his mind when suddenly a massive jolt rocked the left-hand side of his chest and a rush of sadness wafted over him. Unable to avert his eyes from Quinn and Rose, Jack fought hard not to picture himself in Quinn's position, embracing the woman he loved, the woman who had broken his platinum heart.

*

Walter Sheridan was initially sentenced to death by hanging, but due to an intervention by Ernest and Iron Jack, his sentence was reduced to life imprisonment on the strict condition that he would divulge all of his inventions and would agree to work alongside fellow scientists to build prototypes that could be released into the public domain and would spend his entire term incarcerated in a specially adapted wing of Newgate prison.

Iron Jack, believing he was the only police officer who was not brainwashed by Sheridan's cult, breaking all usual protocol, was given permission by the government to personally interrogate all of his Metropolitan Police Force comrades, including his Inspector. Any of them showing signs of strange subversive behaviour were suspended from duty and would be tried in court, and if found guilty, were imprisoned.

Over the next few weeks, due to these severe measures, it was a slow affair bringing London back to a state of normality. Ernest agreed with Iron Jack that as an extra safeguard in the near future, partnering with him with Barker was the way forward and as a formidable duo of iron guardians, they would prove to be great assets in maintaining London's welfare. Quinn suggested that to speed up Barker's repair and have him back up and running, it would be beneficial if he stayed at the Stroud's home and worked alongside Samuel and Frederick to rebuild the virtually destroyed Barker.

Chapter Twelve

Dark Discoveries

With Quinn away from the 'Big House', Ernest's thoughts strayed towards the mysterious connection between Hubert Wells and the surgeon Bamforth.

It's no good; I can't avoid it any longer; if I expect Rose to work alongside Lilly Stroud, then she deserves to know everything, thought Ernest as he scrutinised the images of the poor mutilated babies, focusing on the series of pictures and diagrams that he believed was Quinn. Ernest made up his mind there and then that as harrowing as it would be for Rose to see these photographs, he was sure she would agree that Quinn one day would be ready to know the truth of how he became the bizarre, unique human being they both loved.

Arranging a meeting with Rose in his study, Ernest proceeded to show his housemaid the disturbing photographs.

"Rose, calm yourself, please; I want you to be strong for Quinn," said Ernest as he gave his distraught housemaid his handkerchief to wipe her eyes. When satisfied Rose had settled down, Ernest put forward his proposal that he wanted her to assist Lilly in the Wells/Bamforth investigation.

"Oh, Ernest, do you really have the confidence in me? What experience do I have?" asked Rose timidly.

"Rose, you shouldn't put yourself down; you have a lot of good attributes that are sadly lacking in many people. For one thing, I have noticed you have great astuteness and show deep empathy for others, which, along with Lilly's tenacity and courage, I believe will make you two the perfect team. Remember, I will be at the helm guiding you and between all three of us, I am convinced we can ensure Wells and Bamforth days of freedom are numbered." Rose sat quietly and took in the enormity of the task she had been given. She gave Ernest a confident nod of acceptance, looking drained, sat quietly as she recalled the horrible pictures she had just seen.

"Rose I can think you've seen and heard quite enough for one day; take the rest of the day off and have a lie-down; I will tell Mrs Beddoes you are not feeling well. Make sure you have a good sleep tonight and tomorrow; when you are refreshed, I will arrange a time for Lilly to meet us here," said Ernest confidently as he escorted Rose to her room.

*

Brmm. Brmmm. Pop. Pop... Pop. Pop! Loud engine sounds came from the direction of the main gates. "What on earth is that noise thought Ernest, barely able to think straight over the racket outside his house." Deciding to go outside to investigate, Ernest was confronted by Lilly Stroud astride what appeared to be a large motorised bicycle.

"Not too early, I hope," shouted the leather-clad Private Detective, straddling the clanking, roaring, unfamiliar two-wheeled contraption.

"I'll spin it around and park it near the workshop. I won't be a minute," said Lilly as she sped off, causing the throaty growl of the two-wheeled vehicle to almost deafen Ernest.

He watched on as Lilly skilfully parked the powerful

machine and started walking towards him.

"I am glad you have called for me today because there have been a couple of developments that I am very sure you will be interested to hear," said the beguiling young detective as she lowered the leather-framed glass goggles from her eyes and let them loosely droop around her neck.

A truly remarkable young woman, thought Ernest, as he studied her every move, as she removed her bowler hat and ran her fingers through her jet-black tousled locks, shaking her head and causing her immaculately cut short bob hairstyle to fall on one side, covering one eye. With the other dazzling green eye focusing intensely on Ernest, he had to admit to himself Lilly Stroud was an undeniably beautiful woman. Suddenly, Ernest realised he had been gawping at his stylish guest a bit too much and, breaking the silence said, "A truly impressive machine, Lilly, but you couldn't exactly call it stealth-like."

"Ah, but it is very fast and can cover all sorts of terrain. It's a gift from Samuel and Frederick, of which I must admit I am very grateful. I didn't want to spoil the moment when they gave it to me, but basically, I think I am a guinea pig for their motorised bicycle prototype," replied Lilly as she held on to Ernest's arm as they entered the 'Big House'.

In the comfortable drawing room, Lilly sat down and proceeded to give her rather thorough and police-like account of her latest investigation on Wells and Bamforth.

"On their last meeting in Whitechapel, I stealthily followed Bamforth through the fog, whereupon he entered the basement steps of a derelict building and mysteriously disappeared. Later on, when I felt it safe, I observed that the basement door was boarded up, but noticed that a manhole cover had been disturbed and it was obvious to me this was the only place he could have escaped."

Standing up and taking a stance as though to demonstrate something, Lilly began to undo the buttons of her black leather jacket and continued speaking. "I might be brave, Ernest, but I was not going down there unassisted and unarmed, which leads me to this," said Lilly as she flung open one side of her coat and revealed to Ernest what alarmingly looked like a small double-barrelled shotgun.

"I have a licence, you know, so I am not stepping outside of the law," she concluded, hoping she hadn't shocked her employer too much.

Ernest, captivated by his dauntless guest, also noticed that the shotgun's holster strap was adorned with ten red and gold objects he instantly recognised as shotgun cartridges.

"Lilly, you may have a licence, but I'm guessing it only allows you to shoot rabbits and vermin and does not warrant you to go toting a shotgun around the streets of London like one of those cowboys in the wild west of America; I have read accounts of in the penny dreadfuls!" Ernest exclaimed, exasperated.

"Really, as if I would, but you would have to admit it could be a very effective tool in an emergency," answered Lilly, attempting to put Ernest's mind at rest.

Ernest, feeling after Lilly's last remark it was a good time for a break in proceedings, rang the bell that adjoined the kitchen and drawing room and, speaking into the wall trumpet intercommunication device said, "Mrs Beddows, could we have a pot of tea for three and some cake? Oh, and would you find Rose and ask her to join us."

Rose entered and made herself comfortable sitting next to Lilly. She listened as Ernest began to lay out his plans.

"Rose, Lilly will go over the finer details later, but basically, the investigation I assigned for her has escalated rapidly. I still do not want to involve the police at this stage as I am convinced their heavy-handed approach would blow our cover and send Wells and Bamforth into hiding; I will, however, get word to Iron Jack and bring him up to speed. After all, we all witnessed the impressive way Jack quickly devised a plan to foil Walter Sheridan and as he is family, he deserves to know everything."

Mrs Beddows entered the room and placed the tea and cake on the table. "Oh, sir, if I could be of any assistance," said Mrs Beddows, unable to be 'just the housekeeper'.

"Margaret, that will be all for now," said Ernest bluntly, all the while thinking, 'If she really knew what had happened to Quinn from birth, she would be out hunting Bamforth with a shotgun herself.' "Perhaps you can get a bit of village gossip on how people are coping after Sheridan's assault on London," continued Ernest in an attempt to make his invaluable housekeeper feel extra important.

After the short break for tea, Lilly asked Ernest and Rose to accompany her outside, explaining on the way to the demure housemaid it would be the perfect opportunity for her to get acclimatised as a motorcycle passenger.

"Rose, honestly, you cannot sit on it 'side saddle'. If you are to accompany me on my missions, I am afraid full-length dresses will just not do. Anyway, hoist it up for now, cock your leg over the saddle, put your arms firmly around my waist and hold on tight," said the feisty young detective.

There was a loud roar as Lilly kicked down hard on the pedal of the powerful machine, causing the massive combustion engine of the motorcycle to burst into life.

"Tuck your head into my shoulder if it's more comfortable," yelled the young motorcyclist over the roar of the engine as she turned her head and winked one of her beautiful green eyes, fluttering her long eyelashes at Rose, the petrified, refined passenger.

"Oh, yes, I can feel it in my bones; we really will be the perfect team," shouted Lilly as they sped off around the grounds of the 'Big House'.

After a few laps, Lilly skilfully pulled up alongside Ernest, where she asked him if he would help Rose dismount. With the engine still running, she expertly pulled back the heavy machine onto its stand, got off, and walked over to give the trembling housemaid/apprentice private detective a big reassuring hug.

"Now you are sure you will be all right," said Lilly, hoping she hadn't frightened her newly recruited timid partner too much, continuing, "Rose, I'll pick you up tomorrow, say about eight a.m. Oh, before I forget, you will need to pack some clothes, as I think it is best to stay at my house for a while. Quinn and the boys will be working hard on Barker, but take note that it is very important that whilst you are in Quinn's company, you must do your utmost not to let your thoughts drift onto anything regarding our investigation. I'm sure if he picks up on it, he would never agree or allow you to assist me. Maybe just say Ernest wants us to do some public relations work, promoting the forthcoming partnership of the two iron guardians, Iron Jack and Barker. Remember eight a.m. by the main gate. I will bring a spare pair of goggles. You might want to wear a…" Lilly paused for a bit as she looked over at her very ladylike partner, knowing she could never convince her to dress any different, continued, "and a nice thick overcoat. It will keep your good clothes clean." Whereupon Lilly jumped on her motorcycle, revved up the engine and sped off into the distance.

Yes, and I will wear my headscarf tightly wrapped around

my ears. I do not know what is worse, the deafening roar of that machine or Lilly's insistent, youthful, exuberant chatter, thought Rose, smiling to herself, apprehensive but extremely excited about the prospect of her new venture.

*

Whitechapel, Tuesday 20th November

Lilly with Rose clutching on tightly, parked the motorcycle at the spot of wasteland where she had observed Bamforth and Wells meet up before. The two intrepid detectives hid out of view around a corner of a candlemaker shop and waited patiently, hoping to spot either Wells or Bamforth going about their suspicious, seedy business.

After waiting all night with no sight of either suspect, feeling despondent, they decided to try again the following evening. This pattern continued for two more nights, and on the verge of giving up, Lilly began to worry that on the last time she had stumbled on them, the devious pair had realised they were being followed. Just before they prepared to go back home and devise a different plan at long last at around eight p.m. their diligence paid off as Wells and Bamforth arrived on the scene.

Rose got as close as she could and, being careful to stay out of sight, tried to eavesdrop on what they were saying, but sadly, they continued their meeting in silence. After roughly five minutes, Bamforth gave Wells what appeared to be a large amount of money before going their separate ways. Rose crept back to Lilly, where they observed Wells disappear into Brick Lane, a road notorious for prostitution and illegal opium dens. Bamforth, however, entered the derelict house and climbed down the basement steps, the exact place she had lost him last time.

Giving him a few minutes, Lilly and Rose proceeded to walk down the steps, and as before, Bamforth had mysteriously vanished.

"Lilly, I realise I am only the junior partner in this team, but I am older and less impulsive than you. If we are to follow him down there..." said Rose, pausing and pointing towards the manhole cover.

"I think we should wait a while before we continue our pursuit," concluded Rose in an authoritative manner.

"Yes, and it will also give me enough time to load my shotgun," said Lilly, causing Rose to almost faint.

"Now come on, I hope you bought the motorcycle lamp with you as I had asked," she exclaimed in a firm manner.

Struggling at first to open the manhole cover, after finding a sturdy piece of wood in the debris, the brave pair managed to prize it open. Dimming the lamp to its bare minimum so as not to alert Bamforth of their presence, the intrepid pair of detectives entered the dark, foul-smelling sewer that lay below them.

"Rose, are you absolutely sure you can do this," asked the fearless Lilly as she lowered herself down the metal ladder.

"If you have fully prepared your shotgun and are as fully proficient in its use as you proclaimed, then the answer to your question is quite categorically: yes, I can definitely do this," answered Rose, evermore determined to apprehend the monster who had so severely abused her darling Quinn.

Both standing in their dark domain, the brave investigators stood straddling the steady stream of rancid water that trickled steadily along the sewer. Lilly passed the motorcycle lamp to Rose and proceeded to unbutton her leather jacket and remove the shotgun from its Holster. Breaking it open, she took out two cartridges from her shoulder strap and firmly pushed them into the barrels. Carefully slipping the fully loaded shotgun into her belt, Lilly took out a map of the London sewage works from her jacket pocket and whispered to Rose, "This map will serve us as a means of escape if we get lost, but for now, we can only use our detective instincts to guess which direction Bamforth would take from here."

Rose pointed the lamp all around them, highlighting the two main sewer tunnels, one to the west and a larger tunnel to the east.

"I don't think it will be the big tunnel, look," said Lilly pointing to the map.

"That one leads towards Kings Cross. Why would he come down here when he could have easily slipped through the backstreets to get there? My gut feeling is this one," she continued as her index finger touched the map, moving it slowly, showed Rose that particular tunnel led towards the London Hospital.

The fearless duo proceeded cautiously along their chosen tunnel, making sure they kept the lamp as dim as possible so as not to be spotted from afar. Steadfastly continuing their uncomfortable pursuit, the only sound they could hear was the occasional plip plop of water as it dripped from the ceiling of the sewer into the foul-smelling stream below their feet.

"Shush, turn the lamp down to a flicker, and hold onto my jacket," commanded Lilly, having just heard what sounded like a human's muffled groan.

Lilly could feel Rose trembling behind her and giving her a quick reassuring squeeze to her hand; as she let go, she proceeded to carefully and quietly as possible cock the shotgun and hover her index finger above the weapon's trigger.

Suddenly, they both became aware of a loud splashing

sound, as though someone was running along the tunnel. As the noise gradually disappeared into the distance, Rose turned the lamp up to its full brightness and, taking the lead, ran towards where they had heard the disturbance. Focusing the bright lamp ahead of them, they spotted what they both ascertained was a door projecting from the side of the tunnel. Approaching cautiously, Lilly, with the shotgun in full readiness, stood next to the door and could distinctly hear disturbing sounds of what could only be a person in deep distress. Lilly tapped Rose's shoulder and placed her left index finger vertically between her lips. Lowering her hand slowly and steadily, she held it under the shotgun barrels and with the weapon stock pressed firmly against her right shoulder, Lilly pointed the shotgun in front of her and with a quick burst of speed, they both burst into the concealed room.

Rose immediately began to projectile vomit as she focused on the horrific sight before her. Completely shocked at what she could see, she fainted and dropped the lamp, causing it to go out. The chamber took on an eerie glow as six strategically placed candles barely illuminated the room. Lilly, with her senses on overload, didn't know what to do first, but with her distressed friend foremost on her mind, tore her eyes away from the gruesome scene before her and, taking one of the candles off the shelf, held it in front of Rose, where she saw her partner was groggy but fully conscious.

"Rose, take this candle and wait outside; I will deal with this in here," said Lilly sympathetically as she helped her distraught partner to her feet.

"No, I have to find the strength. I am a trained nurse, and I am ashamed of how I reacted; I should have been prepared for anything. Lilly, there has to be something I can do to help this poor woman," said Rose as she shook herself down and pulled herself together.

Lilly and Rose stood transfixed for a brief moment, their eyes gawping in horror at the unspeakable sight before them. Lying on a blood-soaked couch was a young woman barely alive and writhing in pain. Her face was covered with deep gaping slash wounds, with her nose and ears having been severed and worse of all, both of her eyes had been gouged out. Her breasts had been hacked off and there were two massive incisions on her torso, one vertically and the other horizontally, in the shape of a large cross where her vicious assailant had folded the four sections of her skin back, exposing all of her internal organs. The barely alive woman's heart was fully visible, barely pumping, floating in a mass of congealed blood. The scene of carnage was completed with the victim's intestines removed and draped outside of her body. Rose, although still deeply traumatised by what she and Lilly had stumbled on using all of her medical knowledge, had suddenly come to an alarming conclusion.

"Lilly, as hideous and savage this attempted murder is, I can tell you one thing for sure: this heinous act has not been committed by an opportunist maniac but, I believe, by a skilled surgeon who wanted to keep this poor unfortunate woman alive for as long as possible."

Rose slowly waved the candle around the chamber, illuminating the floor and exposing in the sea of blood an array of body parts. Amongst the fingers, toes and all that had been dismembered, even more disturbing, they both spotted what was undoubtedly an umbilical cord and placenta.

Rose and Lilly, suddenly alerted by a quiet whisper, listened on as the horrifically mutilated woman tried to say something to them.

"My baby, is my baby alive?"

Then, suddenly, with a long, horrible, gurgling sound from the pitiful victim's mouth, they watched on as her heart gave out its final beat. The pair of detectives, completely overwhelmed and shocked at what they had just heard, stood stunned until, after a brief moment, Lilly spoke, "Rose, I think Ernest's assumptions were correct. Bamforth must be Quinn's and those other poor babies' torturer, and going on this gruesome evidence, he must surely be responsible for the spate of Whitechapel ripper murders. Sadly, there is nothing we can do for this poor soul, but I am sure if we are quick, we still have time to catch this monster," said Lilly to her increasingly brave partner. Somehow, with her hands trembling in anger, Rose managed to reignite the oil lamp and turn it up to the full beam; they both ran out of the scene of torture with Rose waving the lamp, directing a beam of light to both sides of the channel and the stream of water below their feet.

"Look, there is a trail of blood that hasn't washed away yet; he can't be far ahead of us. Let's just hope that lunatic hasn't managed to escape," shouted out Lilly as she sprinted ahead with her fully loaded shotgun in hand.

"Stop! Believe me, you will get both barrels; your time is up, Bamforth!" yelled Lilly as she spotted a shadowy figure about fifty feet in front of them.

Suddenly, the figure stopped and slowly began to turn.

"Hands up in the air, trust me, I will shoot," cried out Lilly.

Standing alongside Rose, the pair were now approximately twenty feet away from Bamforth.

"If I do as you ask, then I will have to drop this!" yelled the murderer, as a slapping noise could be heard, followed a split second later by the unmistakable sound of a crying baby. Turning very slowly towards Rose and Lilly, Bamforth squeezed the infant, causing it to scream in agony, whereupon he lifted his hand to expose what appeared to be a scalpel-type knife.

"Now, it is my turn to make the demands. First of all, you must not make any attempt to follow me; if I can hear or sense you behind me, I will not hesitate in cutting this baby's throat. You have both seen what I am capable of and know I am not making an idle threat," continuing, "you will stay where you are until this watch chimes."

With that, the demented killer took out his fob watch and carefully laid it on a dry section of the sewer path. "There, I have set it to chime in twenty minutes. Let's hope for your sake that your lamp holds out," said Bamforth sinisterly, and firm in the belief they had taken his threat seriously, he confidently walked away, occasionally squeezing the baby hard, causing it to scream as he made his escape.

As predicted, twenty minutes later, the fob watch rang out its gentle alarm and not a moment too soon, as the oil lamp dimmed and threw them into darkness. Without the insight of bringing a candle, the two brave detectives blindly made their way along the putrid-smelling sewer path. Rose stopped momentarily when she felt her foot almost trip on an object. Bending down, squinting and focusing her eyes as well as possible; she could see it was the discarded watch. Putting it in her overcoat pocket, thinking it could be incriminating evidence, she ran and caught up with Lilly.

"Rose, my eyes are adjusting slightly to this darkness and a little way ahead that looks to me like a set of metal steps," said Lilly as she broke into a sprint and, once there, proceeded to climb the sturdy ladder. Reaching the top, she tried to push open what appeared to be a heavy metal cover, but when it proved too heavy for her to dislodge on her own, she called for Rose to help her. As they both pushed, and it still wouldn't budge, they began worrying Bamforth weighted the cover down to trap them inside.

"Lilly, are you all right?" said Rose as she saw Lilly's foot slip.

"Sorry, Rose, I came over a bit faint; look, I know I give out a tough persona, but this experience has really got to me. I just can't seem to get the image of that brutally murdered mother out of my mind," answered Lilly, sobbing, showing a vulnerable side of her character Rose had not seen before.

Before Rose had time to comfort her friend, suddenly, inexplicably, the heavy cover began to rise on its own accord. As the soft moonlight light filtered into the chasm, Rose and Lilly, shocked and frightened of what might be above them, instinctively jumped to the floor, whereupon Lilly, showing her usual tenacious self, pointed her shotgun up towards the opening and, in preparation to defend them both gently began to squeeze the firearms trigger.

Loud, crunching sounds and a muffled explosion could be heard as the shotgun was ripped from Lilly's hand and crushed to a pulp, causing thick smoke to fill the sewer. The terrified private detectives, not knowing what to expect next in fear for their lives, froze to the spot. It was then, through the haze of shotgun smoke, that they saw something they both instantly recognised and gave them a feeling of calm and relief. Rose gave Lilly a reassuring pat on her shoulder, signifying she could go first, and Lilly, completely unafraid, walked towards the fumbling giant iron hand and allowed herself to be gripped and lifted up. Moments later, Rose waited patiently for the comforting huge iron hand to lift her to safety.

Both shaken but relieved, the intrepid detectives stood firm-footed on the wet grass and both stared up at the imposing sight of their metal friend Iron Jack.

"How did you know where we were?" asked Lilly in a tone of a mixture of confusion and pure relief.

"It was about half an hour ago when I first knew there was something not quite right. I could sense Rose in a distressed state, but the telepathic messages were different. It felt muffled and I don't know how I do it myself sometimes, but I quickly worked out that the feeling I was getting was transmitted from underground. Once that fact was established, I just honed in on Rose's thoughts and that eventually led me here. You see, there have been occasions in the past when I could feel Quinn needed help, but even I was amazed this time that I could sense Rose was in danger. I suppose it goes to show what a powerful bond Rose has with Quinn. Anyway, enough of my idle ramblings; you can tell me exactly what's been going on the way home. The first thing we all need to do right now is to take care of this little mite," continued Jack as he held a tiny baby as close to his furnace door as he dared and skilfully adjusted his temperature to its optimum comfort level. Rose and Lilly both gave out audible gasps of relief, but before they could say anything, Jack, giving out a quick flick of one of his huge boots, accurately kicked the manhole lid into place. Stooping down, he carefully lifted the girls one at a time until he felt sure they were comfortably sitting on his holsters.

"Hold on tight, you two. I promise I won't go too fast, but we need to get this baby medical attention as quickly as possible; after all, there's only so much an iron man can do for a human child," said Iron Jack in an urgent tone as he took a series of massive strides towards Christ's Foundling Hospital Bloomsbury WC1.

Chapter Thirteen

The Lair of the Night-Drone

As soon as he could, Iron Jack informed Inspector George Huxley that another vicious ripper murder had been committed. He suggested to his superior office that as this particular murder had taken place in such an inaccessible area, perhaps the general public should not know of the incident, especially as they were still in a vulnerable state after Sheridan's recent wave of illusionary terror. The inspector agreed with Jack and assured him he would sympathetically deal with the poor victim's body and remove all evidence of the heinous crime. Also, as added reassurance, he said he would only speak to the press once he was satisfied that Leopold Bamforth and Hubert Wells were finally apprehended and caught, dead or alive.

*

Two weeks had passed since Rose and Lilly's dangerous subterranean investigation had led them to discover that the London ripper was, without doubt, the eminent surgeon Leopold Bamforth. Inspector Huxley issued the entire police force with images of Bamforth and Wells and proclaimed that tracking down their whereabouts and apprehending them should be their number one priority.

Ernest, with his suspicion of a Bamforth and Wells collusion being proved beyond doubt, made the decision that it was now the time to tell Quinn everything he knew about Bamforth's criminal activity.

Ernest began to feel sick with worry as he knew by doing this, he would have to let Quinn 'see in his own unique way' the images of the torturous surgery that he had been so cruelly subjected to. Finding Quinn relaxing in the library, Ernest entered and joined his friend.

"Quinn, I am sure you have been aware that I have employed Lilly Stroud as a detective. Well, I hope you can forgive me, but it is my duty to inform you I have also enrolled Rose to be her assistant."

Feeling the tension building up in Ernest, not letting him continue, Quinn interrupted, "Ernest, before we carry on, let me spare you the pain of explaining all the recent decisions you took upon yourself to make without my approval. More importantly, old friend, I won't let you upset yourself by telling me of your findings on my traumatic upbringing. You see, I have known about them for quite some time. Don't think for one second you are not the only person who can sneak around the house. I have to admit, the evidence you have obtained is so graphic it did upset me for a while and stirred up memories I have been suppressing my entire life. Also, my dear Rose could never conceal her concerns for my welfare and as much as I didn't like doing it, I had to delve deeper into her thoughts. You, however, have become quite adept at hiding your emotions from me, but not always successfully." Quinn, not wanting to seem as though he was scolding his friend, went on to say.

"Oh, Ernest, really old pal, I love the fact you have put so much time and effort into proving the heinous surgical experiments Bamforth committed, but getting back to the original question you asked, Yes, Rose has my blessing to carry on the investigation with Lilly, I think we have both found out that lovely woman is a lot stronger than either of us first thought," concluded Quinn.

Ernest left feeling stunned at Quinn's astuteness burying his notion as deep as possible thought, *I'm not sure I like the way he's been delving into my inner feelings, but I suppose it's just something I will have to get used to. Anyway, I'm glad he likes how things are going and I have his approval.*

Giving his unique friend a big hug, Ernest signified that no more words on the upsetting subject were needed. Thinking it best to move on, stood up, rang the wall bell and spoke loudly into the intercommunication funnel.

"Mrs Beddoes, tea for two in the library, please."

Later that day, Ernest informed Inspector Huxley that he had officially employed two private detectives who would be working with Iron Jack on the Wells / Bamforth case and, at first, would concentrate all their efforts on finding the whereabouts of Hubert Wells. He also suggested to the inspector that due to the known aggressive behaviour of Leopold Bamforth, it would be best that the Metropolitan Police, with their extensive workforce trained in using firearms, would be better prepared to locate and apprehend that particular homicidal maniac.

*

A few days later, on a particularly crisp December morning, Lilly, with Rose in tow, trod a path through the back streets of Whitechapel, checking on all the usual haunts of Hubert Wells. Approaching Nell, a known prostitute and opium den user, they showed her a photographic image of Wells and an artist's impression of Bamforth and asked her if she had seen either of them around the area in the last few days. Recognising one of the suspects, Nell said to Lilly,

"I know that one, Wells did yer say, I've seen 'im, 'ere, before," she said, causing Rose to lunge back as the hard-working whores foul-smelling breath forced its way through the gaps between her rotten black teeth

"I didn't approach 'im. There's something about 'im I don't trust; besides, I ain't gonna cause a scare with me mates. I 'ave to say though it's funny 'ow all the girls 'e goes orf wiv, I never see again."

Lilly stared at Rose knowingly and gave Nell a half crown for her information, then grabbing her partner by her arm, the intrepid pair ran back to the wasteland where Lilly had parked her motorcycle. Helping Rose to get comfortable on the back of the saddle, the skilful motorcyclist jumped on her powerful machine and checking her new gun was fully in its holster and fully concealed under her leather jacket, kicked down hard on the start peddle and revved the engine while expertly steering out of the wasteland onto the Whitechapel Road.

"Brrr, not exactly the weather for investigating!" shouted Lilly as she pointed to the sky, showing Rose it had just begun to snow.

Thinking it a good place to start their investigation, Lilly, barely keeping balance skidding, eventually got to a secluded part of Graham Street and parked up. Knowing the area pretty well, she confidently spoke to Rose, "Just around the corner is where the Regents canal starts. Ever since the first time I came here, I have thought it's a great way in and out of London for all sorts of activities. You never know, we might find someone, as

Nell described, 'mooching about', possibly looking for punters."

Rose stared at the images of Wells and Bamforth. "On the face of it, these two look like a perfect pair of gentlemen that could easily fit in around here without rousing any suspicion. Having said that, if they were after picking up 'ladies of the night' in this more refined area, I don't think they would ever encounter the likes of Nell," said Rose as she tried to erase the smell of the prostitute's breath from her mind and gently patted her pretty nose with the bottom of her royal blue headscarf. Distracted by her thoughts, she hadn't noticed at first that Lilly had already begun walking towards the manmade waterway and putting a spurt on; she ran to catch up with her young, enthusiastic friend.

Leaving a trail behind them in the freshly settled snow, the bold detectives continued their journey until they found themselves at the edge of the canal.

"Let's just stroll along here for a while; we might see some local residents, perhaps out walking their dogs. It's worth a try before it gets dark," said Lilly, shivering, wishing she had decided to put on a big overcoat just like the one Rose was wearing.

The brave women walked along the canal edge for about one mile, and after not seeing a single person, both agreed that the recent snow flurry was probably keeping everyone indoors.

"Look, Lilly," said Rose excitedly, pointing towards a set of massive indentations that were perfectly highlighted by a ridge of newly settled snow.

Lilly stared at the anomaly and said. "As massive as they are, weirdly, they look like giant footprints. Look you can see by the walking pattern they have left. My first thought was that they were made by Jack, but look at the enormous size of them! They are even bigger than Jack's feet," exclaimed Lilly as she jumped inside one of the giant hollows and began running around it excitedly. After a while, Lilly suddenly stopped her childish 'messing around' and, in an exaggerated adult tone, said to Rose, "Are you thinking what I'm thinking? These can only be the footprints of that giant that destroyed Barker. If I am correct, surely this was the place he disembarked. Rose, I am feeling it in my bones; these giant indentations are of great significance to our investigation. Come on, Rosie, hurry up. I'm freezing. Let's get back to the 'Big House' and tell Ernest of our discovery," said Lilly sharply as she jumped out of the huge hole and ran towards her partner, being extra careful not to slip on the snow-covered canal path.

*

Arriving back at the 'Big House' just before dusk, Lilly and Rose relayed all their latest information to Ernest and Quinn. When satisfied he had heard enough, Ernest suggested that as his hard-working detectives had had such a long, fruitful day, and as it was getting quite late, perhaps Lilly should stay the night.

"Lilly, I will get Mrs Beddoes to run you a nice warm bath," said Ernest, adding cheekily. "And Rose, I'm sure you and Quinn have a lot of catching up to do. Quinn, why don't you run Rose a bath in the big washroom? I'm not sure where she will be sleeping tonight; I will just leave that up to you two."

Suddenly, Ernest felt a quick, sharp, stinging pain in his temples, followed quickly by an itching, tingling sensation on the back of his neck. Feeling he had just been chastised by Quinn, Ernest made his excuses to his friends and left the room.

As Ernest walked towards his bedroom, he began thinking about the giant footprints the girls had described. Worryingly, a thought that had been persistently nagging him resurfaced. 'I bet it's that Wells at it again. Only he could have built that monster that destroyed Barker. *Hmm*, if I am correct, he must have had helpers, but I vow now I will make sure everyone who colluded with him will eventually be brought to justice. I suppose deep down, I'd always had this feeling he would go on to build his own mechanical man, but I know he doesn't have the skill to build something as intelligent as Iron Jack.

Ernest began to let his imagination run wild and visualised an army of unthinking killing machines rampaging across London. *No, we can never let this happen. Going by the evidence the girls described to me, at least we know where the metal giant disembarks, and I am certain Wells could only take him back via the Thames. Rose and Lilly will have to start somewhere, so I will prepare them a map of the canals and tributaries of the direction I believe Wells would travel and give it to them first thing tomorrow morning,* thought Ernest confidently as he entered his Library and set about his work

After a refreshing sleep and a cordial chat over breakfast, Rose and Lilly, with a firm plan in mind, bid their farewells to Ernest, Quinn and Mrs Beddoes and set off towards The Stroud family home.

"If we are to continue this investigation properly, then we must prepare for some long days and nights. I will ask Samuel and Frederick to quickly rig up some panniers for the motorcycle. Also, we will need some sleeping bags and camping equipment. Oh, and Rose, I am not just asking; this is an order! You will Have to wear a pair of my thick tweed trousers. I appreciate you are not a 'Tomboy' like me, but the adventure we are about to embark on is usually men's work. I also think that for your protection, you should carry a small handgun," said Lilly firmly to her increasingly worried-looking partner whilst roughly hoisting her onto the motorcycle passenger seat. After making sure Rose was comfortable and had got over her domineering outburst, Lilly proceeded to start up her trusty machine and, finding first gear, roared off towards her family home.

*

The Stroud House 17th December 1888

Making the most of a comfortable night's sleep in a proper bed the Stroud family and Rose met up in the dining room for a hearty breakfast of porridge, toast and tea. Rose and Lilly peered out of the window and could see that it had snowed overnight but had virtually melted and appeared to have refroze, leaving a treacherously slippery road surface. Waving goodbye to Samuel, Frederick escorted his sister and her colleague outside.

"Are you sure the motorcycle is safe in these conditions? Would you like me to take you in the traction engine?" asked Frederick kindly, concerned for their safety, as he looked on at Lilly and Rose perched precariously on the fully laden motorcycle.

"Don't be silly, Freddy, travelling in that decrepit old bone-shaker, it would take us a week to get there. You just concentrate on getting Barker ready for action," cried out Lilly as she skidded away, just managing to keep her balance as she and Rose sped off into the distance.

"Hold on tight, Rose; I'm going to test out the new knobbly tyres Sam has fitted," she yelled, hoping Rose had heard her over the roar of the engine.

Half an hour later, the audacious detectives arrived at a footpath that led to the canal edge and seeing a way through for the motorcycle, Lilly drove off the road over a bumpy grass track where suddenly they both spotted a small boy hiding behind an overgrown private bush. Accelerating slightly, Lilly skilfully headed towards the boy, who by now was preparing to make a run for it. Braking hard, with a long skid, Lilly blocked the boy's path where Rose, more agile than usual wearing her new trousers, jumped off the back and, mindful to not frighten the little boy too much, grabbed hold of the terrified youngster.

"It's all right; we're not kidnappers; we just want to ask you a few questions," said Rose in a comforting tone.

"It's about 'im, ain't it? This is where 'e gets off the big boat, yer know," said the scruffy young urchin.

"Yer see them big pools." As he pointed to the six massive footprints that had completely filled with melted snow water, continued, "'e's much bigger than Iron Jack yer know, and 'e makes a really funny noise like no engine I've ever 'eard before, It's more like a swarm o' bees. I got so near to 'im last time the bloomin' racket nearly blew me ears orf."

"Weren't you worried the thing would see you?" asked Lilly, taken back by how brave the young guttersnipe was.

"Nah, I just told yer, he ain't nuffink like Jack, this one's face looks 'alf dead, like he aint got no brains. I had to watch out a bit, though, cos he might be dopey, but he uses 'is eyes like torch lights, pointing them the way 'e's walking. I keep out of the way of 'em cos they are so bright I weren't 'avin him lighting me up," said the boy with his bright blue eyes staring out of his grimed in dirty face, glad the two nosey women seemed to be believing him.

"So why have you come back here now?" asked Lilly, prying a bit more.

"Oh, it's like me 'obby now, much better than watching the

trains. I still ain't found out where 'e disappears to, but when I do know, I'll tell me mates and get 'em to help me. Don't you worry, I'll be 'ere ready, and next time 'e does a bank smash, we'll try and follow 'im," said the enthusiastic ragamuffin, sniffing and using his cuff to wipe his snotty nose as he spoke.

"Well, we are really glad we found you here today. You are like a proper little detective. You take this and run off now, oh, and what is your name," said Rose as she gave the helpful little scruff a shiny florin.

"Fankyou missus, really all that I've never 'ad so much. Oh, my name, I've only got one. It's Teddy," said the bright youngster, gripping his two shilling piece tightly.

"That's OK, Teddy. Now try and find Iron Jack and when you find him, do tell him you saw Lilly and Rose and explain everything you've just told us. Oh, and Teddy, if you find out any more about this iron giant, remember to tell Jack first and I will make sure there will be more money for you where this has come from; you might even get a half-crown," said Lilly as she rubbed her finger and thumb together.

"You've got 'o be kidding me, 'alf a crown, I'de be blinking rich," said Teddy as he ran off into the distance to look for Iron Jack.

"Come on, Rose, we've got work to do," said Lilly, not giving her friend time to prepare herself. She almost threw Rose onto the passenger seat. Revving up the engine on one wheel, they sped up the grass bank towards the main road.

"Hold on tight, Rose, we're off to the Limehouse Basin Lock; that's where this canal ends," cried out Lilly, somehow managing to hang on and read her map while skilfully driving her motorcycle.

*

Approximately half an hour later, Rose and Lilly arrived at their destination and, dismounting, began surveying the area.

"This is far too built up; look, there are cottages everywhere, although this looks more promising," said Lilly as she laid out her map and pointed to the small hamlet of Latchingdon.

"What's the time now?" asked Lilly.

Rose pulled out the expensive fob watch that Bamforth had left in the sewer. "Twelve thirty," answered Rose, shuddering as she held on tightly to the timepiece, she had vowed she would keep on her until the day Quinn's abuser was finally brought to justice.

Seeing her friend was becoming distressed, Lilly thought it best to make a move. "Come on, Rose, it's going to be a bit bumpy, but I am afraid we have to go off-road again," she shouted above the din of the engine as the pair mounted their trusty machine and hurtled across the bumpy grass field. Eventually, Lilly brought their trusty machine to a halt, stopping a short walk from the canal's edge.

Dismounting the motorcycle, the two detectives peered towards a distant stretch of water, which, by checking their map, was known as the river Blackwater.

"Rose, you see these small tributaries, well, this one looks promising," said Lilly, running her finger along the map to highlight the river Chelmer.

"This one will take us right into the village of Latchingdon," adding, "I'm not sure what the terrain is, and I'm not even confident the motorcycle would have enough petrol to get us there and back, let alone get us back home. Rose, I'm sorry, but there is nothing else for it; I'm afraid we will have to get all of our equipment out of the panniers and continue on foot. I'll go and find some old twigs and branches to cover the motorcycle. Oh, and while I am gone, could you take note of where we are? I suggest we use a landmark like those two big conifers on either side of that village pub. See, we are directly in line with them." Pointed out Lilly, showing she was in full control of the situation.

"Fourteen miles! That's a bit of a trek," said Rose, looking at the map. Continuing to speak in a weary tone added.

"Shall we just go halfway and then, if we feel we are on the right track, maybe re-evaluate the situation? After all, we are only going on a bit of a hunch," said Rose, confirming Lilly's fears that her partner was not really an outdoors type of woman.

"Rose, please remember you have a job to do, and you have been enrolled as a fully-fledged detective. As the senior detective in this partnership what I feel is this is more than a hunch. We have already worked out that travelling by water is the only practical way Wells could transport his iron giant in and out of London. These waterways ahead of us lead to the only village for miles, and you don't need much brains to know he needs a land base, so I suggest the next time you feel this lackadaisical attitude come over you, you should think of your darling Quinn and how we are trying to bring his perpetrator to justice. Now, please keep your detective nose twitching because I'm not going to let you spoil my unbroken run of going back to Ernest with important information." Looking over at her embarrassed-looking friend, she concluded.

"Now, make yourself useful and fetch the binoculars. We are looking for a house, presumably a rather large one," ordered Lilly, feeling a twinge of guilt that she might have been a bit too harsh.

The two courageous women trudged along the river bank for

what felt forever but disappointedly still had not had sight or sound of anything relative to their search when, on the verge of turning back, a distant noise disturbed them.

"Shush, can you hear that," said Lilly whilst grabbing hold of Rose and pulling her behind a bush a few feet away from the river's edge.

"Yes, I can hear something; it sounds like the chugging of an engine to me," answered Rose, feeling apprehensive as she snuggled up to Lilly.

"Rose, please try to calm yourself; you need to be one hundred per cent focused; you never know. You might even have to use the gun I gave you. Remember your Deringer is a small calibre weapon, which is only effective at close range, so don't go and waste any ammunition, whereas mine," continued Lilly when, after a short pause, removed from a concealed holster a most fearsome looking gun.

"According to Samuel you know, this is the most advanced revolver available in the world. The Enfield No. 2. Sam assured me it is capable of eighteen rounds per minute and effective up to one hundred feet away. Rose, I know I only gave you a little one, but you never need to worry whilst I'm by your side; trust me, I will always have you covered," said Lilly, knowing deep down she shouldn't tease Rose, who was, after all, a perfect example of womankind that, unlike her, had never shown any need for danger and this type of work. Giving her prim friend a comforting hug and an affectionate peck on the cheek, the diligent pair, making themselves as small as possible, continued hiding behind the bush. Still not sure what was heading towards them, they listened on pensively as the chugging engine sound grew ever louder and peering over to the river, they both noticed small waves forming and, in the distance, a large river barge approaching.

Moments later, with the barge parallel to them, Lilly recognised the man at the helm was none other than Hubert Wells. Holding her powerful gun at arm's length and focusing down its sight, Lilly whispered to Rose, "I'm quite capable of shooting him from this distance, but where would that get us? Are we one hundred per cent sure Wells and the bank-smashing iron giant' are a connection? At this stage, it is nothing more than conjecture?"

"Correct, said Rose, adding, but let's look at all the positives; our hunch of his route into London is proving to be correct and look, the barge is pulling a trailer, and I am betting that under that big tarpaulin, you will find the metal man exactly as young Teddy described. I think we should go straight back to London and inform Iron Jack of the imminent attack," concluded Rose, hoping her impetuous partner would agree.

Lilly, showing her skills as a senior detective, put her thoughts to Rose. "It has taken us two hours to get this far and the majority of time was taken up by driving at an average of forty miles per hour. That barge I am estimating is travelling at around five miles per hour, so I am guessing, as a rough estimate, that Wells will not arrive in London before ten p.m. Rose, if we are quick about it, we will still have time to briefly explore his house and make an exact record of its coordinates."

Rose, as usual, gave in to Lilly's suggestion but had a sick feeling in her stomach that, this time, Lilly's insistence on taking control could prove to be a bad decision. Reluctantly, she tagged behind her dogmatic partner and continued to trudge along the river bank in the complete opposite direction of Wells and his mysterious cargo.

"Lilly, could we turn around now? That Wells house could

be miles away," said Rose.

"Ye of little faith," cried out Lilly as she held her binoculars to her face.

"I can see it; that has to be his house, it's the only building in the area. I reckon about another ten minutes at a fast pace and we'll be there." As she gave her binoculars to Rose and burst into a fast sprint.

"There it is; it's absolutely massive. Rose, what do you think, an old mill or something at one time and look at those big open doors near the water wheel? This must be where he moors the barge."

"Lilly, honestly, I don't know if I'm up for this I am really feeling quite sick," answered Rose, feeling the whole adventure was beginning to be too much for her.

"Look, you just sit here and make sure the Deringers safety catch is off. When you're feeling a bit better, mark down our co-ordinates on the map. If I am longer than ten minutes, you will have to come looking for me," ordered Lilly as she leapt from the river bank and clung onto one of the big gates, causing it to slowly swing shut.

Phew! Rose could be right; this place is already giving me the creeps, thought Lilly as she peered around the cavernous shed and watched on as the huge water wheel grabbed gallons of loud, rushing water. It was then she had to make a crucial decision, whether to go back to Rose or enter the pitch-black tunnel entrance before her; eventually, letting her detective instincts override any fears and doubts, she pensively stepped into the foreboding dark opening.

'If I can go on just a few more feet, there's a glimmer of light just ahead, thought Lilly as she forced herself to continue. A short while later, reaching the end of the oppressive tunnel, she

found herself standing in front of a wooden door. Spying through one of its small windows, Lilly saw something that made her wish she had one of Walter Sheridan's advanced compact cameras. Trying to take in as much visual information as possible, she observed a woman on the floor, similar to how Ernest had described his wife, Emily Postlewaite.

Well, I don't think she is dead. I can see her stirring, but honestly, you wouldn't leave an animal in such a state, thought Lilly as she stared at the wretched woman lying in a fetal position on the hard-stone floor. Taking in more detail, she noticed the woman had a tourniquet tied tightly around her left arm and her dress was hitched up almost to her waist, exposing her soiled undergarments as a trail of urine trickled down to her feet. Averting her eyes from the pitiful woman, Lilly could take in the vast dimensions, unlike any room she had seen before with a ceiling at least twenty feet high. Letting her eyes trail down towards the floor, Lilly spotted all types of tools hanging on the wall; some she recognised were the same as her brothers used and some were not so familiar.

Gotcha, Ernest's hunch has proved correct, thought Lilly, as she saw leaning against one of the walls what could only be described as a huge pair of iron legs.

'They look much bigger than Iron Jack's; it seems Teddy's description of the giant he had seen must be accurate. Going on the size of these appendages, proportionately, the mechanical monster Wells has built must be pushing twenty feet tall. No wonder he finished off poor Barker so easily.'

Lilly knew she had to make haste, so she began running back as fast as she could to where she had left Rose. After running only a few yards suddenly she stopped herself and for a split second worried about the poor woman she had deserted. Holding her head in her hands she knew deep down there was just no time to attend to her and regretfully took flight once again.

"ROSE IT'S ME!" screamed Lilly as she flew through the air rugby, tackling her petrified-looking partner to the ground, at the same time skilfully grappling Rose's Derringer pistol out of her hand.

"Rose, that's the spirit and I'm glad you found the courage to come looking for me, but perhaps a little more caution next time before you aim to shoot. Anyway, no harm done, and it's nice to see you are feeling better. I'll tell you about everything I have just seen on the way back to the motorcycle, but we'll have to hurry as we must warn Jack what he could be up against. Wells is definitely building more of his metal monsters; in a massive room, I just saw a spare pair of huge legs and going by the proportion of them, heaven only knows what size his fists would be," joked Lilly, trying to make light of the situation.

Rose gave out a sigh of relief at the news; they were finally heading back home and eventually reaching the landmark of tall conifer trees; they found their perfectly hidden motorcycle. In less than a minute, they had removed all the twigs and branches and stood the trusty machine up. With Lilly her hands gripping tightly to the handlebars started the engine up and, in her haste, almost rode off, leaving Rose behind.

"I have to admit, Rose, you seem to be getting the hang of this detective business, a far cry from when you tried to ride side saddle in your flowing dress," said Lilly in a playful, sarcastic tone to her rather reserved friend.

"Hang on tight, Rosie; it's going to be a speedy ride; we are off to find Iron Jack. I'm hoping we either see him on our way or he will be at the police station," yelled Lilly over the roar of the powerful machine's engine as she sped off full throttle towards

London.

*

Stopping a young police constable doing his rounds, they asked if he knew where they might find Iron Jack, whereupon he informed them they had just missed him, but this was his usual time for a break before his night-time patrol. Arriving at Jack's police station abode, they were relieved they had caught Jack just before he resumed his work. Straight away, Lilly gave a quick and concise update informing Jack that, worryingly, an attack by Well's mysterious iron giant was imminent.

"Great work, girls; I will get on it straight away. You two look like you need to rest, but if you could, can you go to the 'Big House first and bring Ernest up to speed." Appreciating there was no time to waste, Jack bid farewell to his friends and headed straight to the spot Rose and Lilly had told him he would more than likely find their little informant, Teddy. Arriving at his destination, Jack spotted the scruffy street urchin hiding behind a large bush.

"Blimey! Didn't expect you 'ere, the famous Iron Jack. I've always wanted to meet you up close, but I ain't in trouble, am I," said the bright little ragamuffin, completely unfazed at the sight of the huge metal policeman standing before him.

"I am assuming you must be Teddy; my two lady acquaintances have told me a lot of good things about you. Now tell me all you know about this 'metal imposter' you have seen around this area," said Jack as he gently picked up his excited informant, placed him comfortably onto one of his holsters, and walked in the direction Teddy guided him.

"I was a bit late getting 'ere tonight, but look at those

whoppers. I must 'ave just missed 'im cos there's new ones. See, the grass is all squidgy!" cried out Teddy as he jumped off Jack's holster straight into one of the enormous footprint impressions and tried in vain to stretched his short legs to reach the next crater.

Suddenly, in the far distance there was a series of loud bangs as Jack quickly deduced that the loud noise, they had just heard was the sound of another bank being broken into.

Realising time was of the essence, Jack stooped down to Teddy's level and said, "Look here, my boy, I cannot allow you to put yourself in so much danger with that thing on the prowl. Now make haste and make your way home."

Lowering his booming voice to a whisper, continued, "Tell no one of our meetings; from now on, you can be mine and my detective lady friend's secret spy. Now be off with you." He concluded, raising his voice as he gave out one of his famous winks and waved his hand forward, sending the brave young ragamuffin on his way.

Hmm, it's all gone a bit quiet. I'm guessing he will be long gone by now and heading towards his escape point. It's obvious he will go back via the river but exactly where is another thing. Let's think about this: I'm at the start of the lock, and It's approximately five miles from here to the Strand and all the banks. Once that thing finishes its criminal deeds, I bet Wells would pick it up at the Limehouse lock, thought Jack as he hurriedly made his way along the canal path.

Reaching his destination, with all his senses to the maximum, Jack stood silently at the canal edge when, after only a few minutes, he could hear a distant chugging sound. Taking cover, Jack knelt down and with his huge metal knees, sinking snuggly into the grass, he lowered the heat in his firebox until his intense red eyes and mouth softened to a warm orange glow.

That's him. It has to be Wells, thought Jack as he peered around, expecting to see the giant metal monster appear at any moment. Suddenly, Jack could make out a human voice shouting in the distance and as he had expected, with a series of thunderous strides, the massive bank robber came into view.

"Faster next time, or believe me, I will dismantle you and leave you to rot in the Thames." Jack heard as he watched on as the large barge and trailer aligned itself to the edge of the canal. Wells proceeded to remove a large tarpaulin and as the metal giant lumbered towards the trailer section, Jack struggled to stop his furnace from increasing in power because, in clear view and only a few feet away from him, it became very clear just how enormous his soon to be foe actually was.

Jack, up until now, had rarely used his 'fear emotion', but all of a sudden, his mechanical brain began to rattle as never before, as his eyes fixated on the immense iron giant, almost twice his size, was apparently distracted by something. Igniting its two dazzling white eyes, it began sending blinding beams of light into the distance, turning its head slowly as it scaled the terrain.

Jack worryingly got the unnerving feeling his whereabouts had been discovered and, at that moment, began to hear, just as Teddy had described, a deafening buzzing sound. As the ear-splitting racket increased, Jack, at this point, knew it was futile to try and hide and, as it wasn't in his nature to run away, stood bolt upright, making himself as big as possible. Flexing all his joints, Jack increased his furnace to its maximum, and with his eyes and mouth, at the most intense crimson red, hoping to catch his fearsome foe off guard, he took a massive lunge forward.

This was Jack's first mistake; as the buzzing sound increased to what seemed like a thousand swarm of bees, Iron Jack's nemesis took one of its huge strides and, with a swiping blow to Jack's head, completely buckled and bent Jack's mouth. Falling back, Jack somehow managed to keep balance, quickly bending his mouth back into shape, shaking himself and thinking. 'The only real advantage I have over this thing is my intelligence. My smoke plan worked against Sheridan, so let's try it again.'

As before, increasing the intensity of his furnace while at the same time closing all his steam valves, as the pressure in his boiler reached a critical level, Jack purposely began to spill the boiling water into his firebox. Seeing his foe preparing to release another punch at him this time, Jack quickly ducked down and, taking his chance, released a massive plume of thick black smoke. At the same time, turning his chimney, he fired the smoke straight into his opponent's eyes.

Having the desired effect of blinding his foe, Jack heard a series of swishes as his metal antagonist began wildly punching into the smoky, thick black air. Keeping as low as he could to avoid the vicious blows, Jack focused on the deafening buzzing sound and, when satisfied he was right next to his adversary, leapt into the air and, with both his fists, struck his enemy square in the chest. In the darkness of the cloud of smoke, Jack sensed his opponent begin to topple, but alarmingly, at the same time, felt a strong grip on his right shoulder.

Suddenly, Jack felt his body become weak as gushing steam and oil spurted from his shoulder. He looked at his injured body, causing his fear emotion to intensify as he could clearly see his right arm had been dismembered. Feeling ever weaker, he waited for his iron assailant to finish him off, but instead felt surprised and relieved as the metal giant, presumably thinking he had fatally injured Jack, changed direction and walked towards the barge. Fearful for his life, Jack, in a vain attempt to save himself using his one remaining hand, began squeezing the dangling, gushing pipes and pinching them as hard as he could managed to create a temporary seal. Satisfied he had stopped the main flow, he twisted his head and could see his enemy standing at the water's edge, dismayed and confused as it watched Wells and the transporter barge disappeared into the distance, leaving it stranded. Jack, by this time, having lost so much of his essential fluids, began to feel his life ebbing away and falling to the ground, knowing he only had seconds to live. Using all his remaining strength, he flicked off his armoured glove and, with his smaller, delicate hand, began twisting and pulling at his platinum heart until once dislodged from its housing, he held it in front of his dying furnace. Looking down at his remarkable lifeforce, he observed the tens of thousands of minute tentacles as they slithered and squeezed in behind his firebox door, attaching themselves to every last barely glowing burning coal.

Quinn, please hurry. I truly feel this is the last of me, repeated in his mind as he struggled to telepathically project his last conscious thought. Laying helpless, barely alive in the sticky mix of boiling oil, water and mud, desperately trying to make the strong mind connection he had with his creator, moments later, Jack became rigid and still as he completely shut down.

*

Meanwhile, at the edge of the canal, a separate scene of despair was unfolding, as Iron Jack's nemesis stood confused, deserted and lost. The metal colossus, with his buzzing sound intermittently stopping and starting, attempted to twist the gears of his feeble mind, trying to form a thought. Facing his huge head towards where his basic senses told him was home, the brainless mechanical man slowly stepped into the murky water. Instantly, there was a series of loud fizzing crackling sounds and uncontrollably, the mindless monster began to flay its arms around as the entire top half of its enormous body began emitting a series of flashing beams like small lightning bolts increasing in intensity until a plume of white smoke began pouring out the top of its head.

Straining every cog in its feeble mind, the slow-witted mechanical man found enough intelligence to work out that water and his drive system were not compatible and if it were to survive this ordeal, it had to get back to dry land.

Standing on the edge of the canal, the pitiful machine mustered up the one instinct built into it that was stronger than anything else it possessed: the will to survive. As the gears crunched in its primitive mechanical brain, it surmised it would have to find the way to get back home, but worn out and damaged with its puny command system working overtime, it knew the first thing was to hide and rest and somehow forming a simple sentence the words rattled around its feeble mind.

'I need to find my master so that he can help me.' With that, the dim-witted colossus took a series of massive strides and began walking across the grass field until it found itself standing on the main road of the village. Aware that if it didn't hide quickly, it would cause a commotion, metal monster spotted a ten-foot-high brick wall, which it effortlessly stepped over and immediately found itself on the grounds of a grand Georgian house. The fight and the 'double punch' it had sustained had done much more damage than it at first had realised and unable to take another step, the critically injured iron giant, completely exhausted, carefully laid itself down on the wet grass. 'Master, why did you leave me?' The question repeated in its inferior mind until the buzzing sound of its drive system gradually dropped to a barely audible low hum on the very verge of shutting down.

*

Eight a.m. the following morning, Miss Grace Ellerton was in her garden, chasing 'Blue' her Persian cat. Running excitedly towards the further reaches of her long well, well-maintained, secluded garden, Grace constantly shouted out to her pet to stop chasing a mouse as it frantically tried to escape. The exuberant six-year-old, unable to keep pace with her cat for a split second, thought she had lost her 'Bluey' until, from the corner of her eye, she noticed her disobedient pet dart into the shade of the great willow tree.

This was Grace's favourite part of her garden, the place where sometimes, for hours on end she would let her young girl's imagination take her away into a magical fairyland where she became its ruler, the exceptionally beautiful Princess Grace. Suddenly, with all kinds of stories flashing through her young mind, Grace stopped in her tracks as on the grass, only a few feet in front of her, she saw laying down an enormous metal giant.

In this six-year-old innocent, overactive imagination, what she could actually see was just a massive iron man having a rest, having no idea; in reality, it was a fearsome machine programmed to kill and destroy.

Showing no fear at all, Grace tapped the giant's huge metal cheek with her tiny knuckle and said, "Eh, excuse me, are you Iron Jack? You are just like how my Daddy says you look. I have heard you before you know when you walk past my house. I wanted to say hello to you but my Daddy says it's far too late for me to be awake, but my Daddy and Mummy say it's good you are outside as it means we can all sleep safely."

With its last ounce of brain power, the metal giant sensed it had been discovered and with a faint buzzing sound, its massive eyes gave out a dull flicker.

"Oh, that's good you are awake now. Can I get you some breakfast?" said the playful little girl as she continued giggling to herself. "My daddy says Iron Jack likes to eat coal; oh, you are such a funny metal man."

It was at this moment that Grace, the ruler of her magical land of dragons, fairies and pixies, decided in her playful imagination that, in fact, this was not Iron Jack, but was actually her own metal giant that she 'remembered' had Always lived in her enchanted garden.

Using all its remaining energy, the injured and confused iron monster sat up, towering a good ten feet above Grace. Its buzzing sound intensified as it tilted its fearsome-looking head down towards the innocent-looking little girl and igniting its bright white eye beams illuminated the entire space of the willow tree canopy.

Grace was not in the slightest bit frightened because, in her mind, she could come to no harm; it was Her magical kingdom, and after all, she was Princess Grace.

Suddenly, completely drained of power, the giant's buzzing sound stopped and as it slumped to one side, just about managing to steady itself, its eyes gave out a weak flicker as something in its bare instinct of survival told it to open its small furnace door before it collapsed.

Lying on his side with his dying furnace fully exposed, the pitiful giant waited in desperation hoping his small human friend would be able to help him.

"Ha ha, you are like Iron Jack. You funny thing, you eat coal as well," said Grace as she stared down at the barely alight firebox. The dying metal giant, confused and utterly helpless, could not move an inch as it felt his life force ebb away.

Grace, seeing her new friend, was 'hungry' but still had a bit of 'food' in its belly looked around for a fallen branch. She had often watched Lucy the maid poke dying fires to make them glow.

"I'm sure this won't hurt you, but it might tickle," she said playfully as she proceeded to poke the branch into the iron giant's small furnace. Remembering something else Lucy had done to bring the fire alight, she took off her cardigan and, flicking it up and down, fanned the dying coals and watched on gleefully as they sparked into life and began glowing crimson red.

As the iron giant's power increased, with its newfound energy, it stood bolt upright its full eighteen feet. Lightning energy ran through its body as the buzzing; droning noise increased to a fever pitch. Lowering its huge head and focussing its eyes on its tiny human helper, its first instinct, the thing that had been programmed into it, was to grab and crush this tiny human being.

This morning, however, something in its primitive, feeble mechanical brain had significantly changed. Pushing its buckled chest section with all its might the bent metal screeched as it stretched it into place. Standing still and passive the metal giants white eyebeams intensified in readiness as it waited for Princess Grace, it's new master first command.

This small girl, who had shown no fear, had managed to save this thing's life and taught the fearsome iron giant in the short time it had been with her more of human nature and kindness than Hubert Wells had shown the entire time he had been its master. This gigantic metal monster had learnt from the six-year-old Grace Ellerton that not all humans were bad, just to be crushed and killed.

The towering giant, feeling the new human emotions of remorse and compassion, dimmed its eye beams and lowered its head as though in shame.

"My metal friend," said Grace, still pretending to be a princess.

"You will always be welcome in my magical palace, but I am a bit sad," she snivelled, continuing, "I don't want anyone else to find you in my kingdom so you will have to leave now. Maybe you could go and play with your friend Iron Jack." Concluded the innocent little girl, completely unaware that Iron Jack was, in fact, her metal friend's staunch enemy.

Her iron giant stooped and proceeded to kneel down and, bringing his enormous head as near to the level of Grace's eyes as possible, outstretched its arm and, with one of its massive metal hands, gently stroked the small girl's face. Unable to form a sentence and proclaim its gratitude, the metal simpleton stood up and slowly walked away. Carefully stepping over the boundary wall, it instinctively turned its enormous head and could see Princess Grace smiling and waving excitedly. Feeling more and more human traits flood into his primitive mechanical brain, no longer feeling an 'it', the remorseful iron giant focused on 'his' positive future and strode into the distance.

It was on that morning Hubert Wells's metal creation, previously an unthinking monster, had changed beyond recognition. Full of deep regret for the carnage he had previously inflicted on London and its citizens, with his newfound ability to reason and think for himself, the gears in his brain began to form a basic thought. *No more killing, no more destruction and maybe one day all the citizens of London could forgive me and be as nice as my Princess Grace,* he thought as he put one giant foot in front of the other and walked purposely to where he had last seen his previous master to find his way back to the only place he knew as home.

*

Meanwhile, in an area of wasteland near the Limehouse Loch, Iron Jack lay motionless, with his platinum heart exposed and barely beating with its myriad of tentacles struggling to find a source of heat. Jack was moments away from death.

"It's a good job you knew he was in danger; the remarkable connection you have formed with Jack is stronger than ever. Oh Quinn, look at the terrible state he is in, do you think we will ever be able to get our Iron Jack back from this?" said Ernest, fighting back tears, convinced their 'one of a kind' metal man had been destroyed beyond repair.

Quinn instructed Ernest to keep strong and careful not to burn his hands pushed Jack's platinum heart deep into the last remaining smouldering embers of his furnace while Ernest frantically fanned the firebox. Moments later, they both watched on as, amazingly, finding their correct connections with their newfound source of heat, the thousands of fine tentacles, one by one, began to bond onto Jack's internal drive system. Ernest and Quinn waited nervously for any signs of life in Jack's body and after what felt to them like hours, almost giving up hope that Jack would live the remarkable iron guardian's eyes began to flicker and in a feeble voice, he finally spoke.

"When the hurly-burly's done, when the battles lost and won," said the one and only Iron Jack, randomly quoting

Shakespeare.

"What is he going on about?" asked Ernest, convinced Jack's brain had taken a mighty blow and had become faulty when, without warning, sitting up straight and using his one remaining arm, Jack wrapped it around his two creators and gently pulled them towards him, looking down at them and spoke again.

'There are few die well that die in battle.' Anyway, you had better get and fix me up and I don't know where the other one is, probably in the canal, but I definitely need two arms." In saying that, he gave out a raucous laugh at the same time, letting one eye go pitch black and instantly glowing bright again, gave one of his famous winks to his friends.

Ernest still confused about what Jack had said earlier, said to Quinn, "Are you sure he is all right? He's not delirious, is he? I mean, he is coming out with some very strange sentences."

"Yes, nothing a few minor adjustments couldn't sort out because, honestly, we can't have him quoting Shakespeare day and night; that would be far too much to endure," answered Quinn seriously, but deep down, very proud of how educated and sophisticated their creation had become.

Jack, suddenly distracted, feeling it not the best time to give one of his witty retorts. He saw in the distance walking towards him his police inspector flanked by two of his fellow officers. Arriving on the scene and sadly looking at their badly injured work colleague they were quickly reassured, by Quinn and Ernest that apart from talking too much, they were sure with a major overall he would soon be back ready for duty.

"Ah, George, you've found us then. Mechanically, Jack has sustained so much damage; I cannot allow him to walk anywhere, so could you send one of your officers to the Stroud garage and ask them to bring the traction engine and trailer to take him back for repairs," asked Ernest, glad for any help at all. Inspector Huxley agreed to the professor's request and as one of his police constables disappeared into the distance, he took the opportunity to express other rather worrying developments he had read about.

"Ernest, could you follow me here," said the inspector, wanting to be out of Jack's earshot as he continued. "With all this going on, I don't suppose you have seen today's newspapers, but there are full of witness accounts of this incident and it seems that although Jack had put up a good fight, he was no real match for the thing all the newspapers are calling The Night-Drone."

"Apparently, this monster makes a constant buzzing sound, similar to the sound of a swarm of bees but far louder. Anyway, seemingly, during the fight, everyone was too frightened to go outside and help Jack and could do nothing but watch on helplessly as the metal giant almost twice Jack's size walked away, crushing everything in its path, but somehow managed to disappear without a trace. Although I must add speaking to a few villagers on the way here, they all said they heard the same deafening noise again around ten a.m. this morning. Thank God, with such a vicious attack, there have been no reported injuries of any human beings."

It was at this point that Ernest began to worry he hadn't heard back from Rose and Lilly, but putting his fears behind him, having complete confidence in his intrepid detectives, he thought it the perfect time to tell the inspector of his hunch on where the Night-Drone as it was now called would be heading. "George, we are not completely clueless regarding this incident; you see, I have employed two private detectives who are on this case as we speak. With a bit of luck, they have obtained all the trying vital information about Wells and the Night-Drone we need to bring this case to an end," said Ernest confidently as he added.

"Anyway, George, I will tell you more on the matter later; most importantly, with the situation getting so serious, you will be pleased to know we are hoping by tomorrow evening at the latest, Iron Jack will be back in action," concluded Ernest, worried he hadn't even consulted Quinn or the Stroud brothers if this promise was even achievable.

"Ernest, to be absolutely candid with you, do you honestly believe that even with Iron Jack in full tip-top mechanical order, he could defeat this 'Night-Drone' monster," said the inspector as he pointed over to Iron Jack, sitting up but with his dismembered arm looking rather forlorn.

Ernest, being as honest as he could, replied, "George, the simple answer is No, but to give you a degree of confidence, if we all work hard over the next few days on Jack's next encounter, he will not be alone. Let me explain; it was only early this morning I was given the great news by the Stroud brothers that Barker had been fully repaired."

Ernest felt a small sharp pain in his temples as Quinn telepathically scolded him for making rash promises. At the same time, he was shocked as he felt a physical sharp kick in the back of his leg. Where instinctively turning around, he saw Samuel Stroud standing, fists clenched with an angry look on his face.

"Did I hear you say Barker And Iron Jack will be fully operational by tomorrow evening? well, if that's the case, you had better make yourself useful and help Freddy and Quinn strap Jack down onto the trailer; after all, we can't have him falling off on the way to the workshop, creating even more work for us," shouted Samuel at Ernest, satisfied he had thoroughly chastised his employer.

*

Midnight, 18th December, Hampstead Village. The Stroud Brothers workshop.

"Ernest, we did all we could; if I'd have known it would have come to this, I would have shot Wells when I had the chance," said Lilly as she broke down, sobbing uncontrollably, completely distraught at what had happened to Iron Jack.

"Lilly, please don't blame yourself; you and Rose have done marvellously; why don't you go and have a laydown and let the rest of us get on with the repairs," said Ernest.

Making sure Lilly was comfortable on the large Chesterfield sofa, he covered her with a blanket and went outside to help get the immobilised Iron Jack onto the workshop's big trolley cart.

"Quinn, tell me when you have straightened up the internal components in his shoulder and I will help you re-attach his arm!" shouted out Samuel as, in a quieter voice, he began speaking to his brother.

"Oh, and Freddy, I think we only need two of us to work on Jack, so it might be a good opportunity for you to take Ernest to and show him the progress you and Quinn have made with Barker," concluded the confident mechanic, throwing orders around and showing exactly who was in control in this, his domain.

Rose, finding Lilly asleep on the big sofa, also totally exhausted from their recent ordeal, made her excuses and made her way to the adjoining cottage to rest while Frederick Stroud, accompanied by Ernest, took the short walk to the end of the garden and entered the large detached garage.

"I really think you will love the way the new Barker looks. Samuel has done an immense amount of bodywork repairs plus adding many reinforced head and body panels, especially to his jaw where we found a distinct weakness that needed to be addressed," said Freddy proudly as he whipped the tarpaulin off the huge mound in the centre of the garage.

Ernest on his initial sight of his first iron guardian, became quite emotional, as a plethora of good and bad memories flooded his mind. Trying hard not to get too emotional, he watched on and listened as Freddy continued describing all of Barker's new additions and improvements.

"Obviously, with all of this extra protection, he now weighs considerably more, but to compensate for any loss of power and speed, myself and I have compensated this issue by increasing the capacity of his steam engine," stated the young mechanic proudly.

Ernest, scrutinising every nut and bolt of his impressive first iron guardian, had to ask a question that had begun to bother him.

"I see his cranium section is especially heavily armoured. But it is what's inside that I'm particularly interested in. How did you and Quinn get on with building him a new mechanical brain?"

"Ernest, I have to confess and please don't be too alarmed at what I am about to tell you, but you see, Quinn showing so much faith in me basically gave me a pile of his old drawings and some of that super light metal and more a less told me to get on with it. You see, we all thought that Iron Jack was coping so well; we never dreamt the new Barker would be called for action before we had given him a proper trial. Anyway, sir, I am confident I have built the best 'command unit' I was capable of. The thing is, because his brain is totally my creation, it will contain traits of my own personality and whether this will be up to yours and Quinn's standards, we can never know until he is 'fired up'," answered Frederick, hoping his employer and mentor were not too shocked by this revelation.

Stepping out of the garage, the pair of inventors walked towards the main workshop and both decided it would be best to wait until Iron Jack had been repaired before they awakened the new Barker. Meeting up with Samuel and Quinn, they were all of the same minds. They agreed they had done enough for the night and went their separate ways to get some well-earned sleep.

The following morning, Ernest realised with all that had been going on, he had almost forgotten that in only a few days, it would be Christmas Eve and felt a great responsibility knowing the threat the London citizens were unprotected from an attack by Wells and his destructive machine a pang of fear and apprehension rushed through his body as he remembered the rash promise he had given to Inspector Huxley, that Iron Jack along with Barker would definitely be fully operational by this very day.

Ernest determined to make his pledge come true, entered the big workshop and could see Quinn standing alone in one corner of the space with his hands working frantically on Jack's brain whilst Freddy and Samuel were diligently going about their work, giving all Iron Jacks nuts and bolts a final twist making sure they had cleaned off any residue of oil and hydraulic fluid from the impressive guardians, re-attached arm.

"Is he ready to be woken up yet?" shouted out Ernest in a cautious tone, hopeful there would be no setbacks.

"Well, we've done all we can here, but I'm not sure what Quinn's been doing to his brain; you'd better go and see what he's up to, as he won't let me and Freddy anywhere near it," said Samuel as he pointed over to Quinn, who was deep in concentration with his hands a blur delved deep into Iron Jack's brain mechanism.

"Give me another five minutes," said Quinn sharply as he simultaneously telepathically projected his words into Ernest, Samuel and Fredericks's minds, causing them to rub the back of their necks as they began tingling. "Right, Freddy," Quinn shouted, this time deciding to air his vocal chords.

"If you come over here and help me carry this, perhaps Sam and Ernest could give Jack's neck and shoulder housing a final check, making sure there are no obstructions. As soon as you have brought Jack's firebox up to its full power and his boiler to its optimum level, as a precaution, I have added a ten-minute delay function before his brain becomes fully operational; this will give us ample time to securely bolt down the head section. After that, if my upgrade has been successful, hopefully, the result will be as though our old metal friend had never left us."

Samuel and Frederick began to manoeuvre Jack's heavy head onto the steam hoist when, suddenly, the morning light flooded the workshop as Lilly and Rose, dressed in their practical work clothes, entered via the side door. Excited at the prospect of Jack's reawakening, they watched on as Samuel signified, he had tightened the last bolt.

Ernest looked down at his watch and seeing there was one-minute left before the brain mechanism ignited, he got into a perfect position to greet Jack as he woke up. As Quinn had predicted exactly on time, Iron Jack sprang into life, standing bolt upright with his crimson red eyes glowing more intense than ever. Jack slowly walked over to all of his friends and suddenly, as though he had never gone, spoke.

"Quinn, I know you have done something, but I can't quite put my finger on it yet. Not too much messing about with my brain, I hope, because personally, I was very happy with the way

I was. Anyway, enough about me. Whilst we are here, where is this Barker I have heard so much about? If he is as strong as I am left to believe, then he could be the extra help I need to defeat Wells's monster. Believe me, I have felt it's sheer brute strength," said Jack as he flexed his new arm, double-checking that it wasn't about to fall off.

Frederick, wanting to give Barker a final check before his awakening, ran out of the workshop and, as doing so, shouted out to his friends and siblings to meet him at the garage in a few minutes.

Frederick had factored into Barker, a strong loyalty bond to himself, but was slightly apprehensive about how his version of Barker might react to everyone else, at least not to Iron Jack.

Freddy stood back as Barker's huge steam engine roared into life, and with a deafening sound, like a huge metallic yawn, he opened his great iron jaws and fully exposed the crackling, popping coals of his furnace.

Frederick released all the steam valves on the Barkers drive system and gave the first iron guardian a basic instruction.

"Now, wait here until I call for you," said Frederick in a firm tone as he watched as Barker's enormous four-ton body began to shake with excitement. Confident the giant metal bulldog was acting obediently, Frederick walked outside the garage, where he found his friends and family and Iron Jack waiting patiently.

"It is imperative at this stage of 'my' Barkers life, that he is introduced to all of you at the same time. If have done my job properly in a few minutes we should have a new, indispensable member of our team."

With that, Fredrick shouted out his short, concise instruction loud and clear. "Barker, come here, boy."

Everyone, apart from Iron Jack, stood back in apprehension,

not really knowing how the 'new' Barker might react. Frederick stood behind the great metal Bulldog, with his hands poised, ready to pull the newly fitted, temporary emergency stop lever.

Iron Jack, showing no fear, walked slowly towards Barker and, in doing so, caused the giant bulldog to show off his programmed guardian instincts. Suddenly opening wide his huge jaw, he tilted his massive metal head back, exposed his two shiny rows of sharp metal teeth and in a show of just how fearsome he could be, Barker intensified the fire in his furnace and gave out an ear-splitting growl.

Iron Jack, taken by surprise by this seemingly hostile reaction, quickly stepped back and prepared to defend himself, and Frederick, in a panic, grabbed hold of Barker's emergency lever. Suddenly, unexpectedly out of nowhere, alerted by all the commotion, Stanley, the Bassett hound ran between Iron Jack and Barker.

As the metal bulldogs furnace began to soften, Frederick took the decision to not shut Barker down and letting go of the emergency lever, watched on in amazement, as Stanley nuzzled up to Iron Jack's leg and, after doing so, ran over to Barker, where he began making calming whimpering doggy sounds, as though speaking to his long lost old mechanical pal.

Stanley, leading the way, turned his head and, when satisfied his huge metal friend was following, obediently walked over to Iron Jack.

Quickly repositioning himself behind Barker using his snout and with a couple of pushes, Stanley coaxed his giant bulldog companion to sit obediently by Iron Jack's side and proud of himself with his tail wagging, he gave out a series of his best loudest barks.

"Oh, this is brilliant; you didn't tell me I was going to have two dog partners," said Iron Jack as he gently patted both Barker and Stanley's heads and stood waiting to hear the next part of the plan.

"It's now or never, gang; we know where the scoundrel lives and we can give him no time to launch an attack. Jack, you run alongside Barker and Lilly. You know the quickest route, so I want you to lay down on Barker's neck and give him the directions as we go."

With no time to waste, Ernest gave his remarkable team a few final instructions and once the trailer was securely attached to Barker the rest of the fearless band all climbed in and made themselves comfortable in the long bench seats, making sure Stanley was sitting safely at their feet.

Lilly hung on tightly to one of Barkers metal collar studs and shouted to Jack to keep as close to Barker as he could, whereupon the entire party sped off towards the village of Latchingdon and Wells house, the lair of the Night-Drone.

With Barker at full steam and Jack barely able to keep up, they soon reached their destination and all gathered together, the astounding group of detectives began discussing how they should proceed.

"Go on, girls, you two take the lead; you are the only ones here who really know this place," said Ernest, confident in his prodigies.

"See that big old mill over there? well, that's where we saw those giant metal legs and that poor woman," said Lilly as she suddenly had a worrying thought, *Oh dear, if that poor wretch I saw laying on the floor is Emily, then maybe I should have warned him of the terrible state she was in.*

Thinking it best to say nothing at this moment in time, Lilly joined the rest of the group, who were by now standing a few feet from the back door of the mill, waiting while they contemplated their next move.

As the water wheel noisily scooped up gallons of water, Ernest could faintly hear in the background what appeared to be a loud thumping, accompanied by the buzzing and humming sound associated with the Night-Drone. As the incessant noise grew ever louder, until it reached fever pitch, everyone, including Iron Jack and Barker, hastily retreated as alarmingly they watched on in fear as two giant iron fists burst through the side wall of the mill.

Holding their hands above their heads to protect themselves from the flying debris, the humans of the party froze to the spot, gawping as eventually they saw a massive pair of arms appear and begin flying about wildly, smashing and punching its way out of the mill. This was followed by a series of thunderous kicks, releasing the metal giant into the outside area, showing itself in all its terrifying glory. Standing what appeared to be well over twice the height of Iron Jack, the thing must have been a good thirty feet tall. Unlike Iron Jack or even the Night-Drone, for that matter, this iron monster hardly bore any resemblance to a human being. Its extra-long arms had no visible joints and were more like octopus tentacles with huge claw-like appendages on each end. Running the full width of its shoulders instead of a head, it had four massive ball-like structures that were constantly twisting and turning in every direction, shining powerful beams of blinding white light in every direction.

"This is definitely not the same mechanical man I fought," said Jack loudly, remembering his recent encounter, reassuringly rubbed the shoulder of his newly attached arm.

"Quinn, I know you never built cowardice into me, but I am sure if Barker wasn't here, you wouldn't see my iron legs for dust," joked Jack, quickly realising this wasn't actually the time for frivolity.

He instantly formed a plan and shouted out. "Barker! Run behind that thing and try to topple it over. As the old saying goes, 'the bigger they are, the harder they fall'."

Before Barker even had the chance to move one of his giant paws, with an almighty kick, the crackling, buzzing-sounding monster struck the metal bulldog clean on the jaw and began wrapping one of its tentacle arms around the stunned iron bulldog. Dazed but not immobilised, Barker somehow broke free and, shaking his slightly buckled jaw back into place, took the opportunity and, with one almighty leap, belying his enormous bulk with his mouth fully open, managed to clamp his jaws around one of the freakish monsters massive 'eye' structures. Using his four-ton weight to his advantage, fully attached to his foe, Barker began to shake side to side violently as Iron Jack, with the next part of his plan already formed, stole the opportunity and, with a flying lunging dropkick to one of the legs of the struggling giant sent his enemy crashing to the ground. As the thing lay on the floor, in some ways, it was just as dangerous because with its long-reaching snake-like arms free, it managed to wrap them around Jack and Barker simultaneously and began squeezing tightly.

"Barker, whatever way I move, walk and pull as hard as you can in the opposite direction," cried out Jack urgently, as he felt his insides being viciously crushed. With the things arms at full stretch, Jack, with what felt like his last breath, shouted, "Barker, old boy, I know you have it in you; now run with all you're might." At the same time, Jack, with the last ounce of his power, began pulling in the opposite direction when suddenly, as though the centre of a massive tug-of-war, the things tentacle arms snapped off and, at the same time, released their grip on Jack and Barker.

In a show of what appeared to be pure vengeance, Iron Jack stooped down and, staring directly at the remains of his unearthly foe, shouted out, "It's a pity I can't let you live because I would have loved you to be able to tell your little brother exactly what it feels like having your arm ripped off."

Watching the thing writhe and convulse on the ground, turning his attention to his brave partner in a relieved tone, Jack added, "Come on, old pal, we've done it; let's push this abomination into the drink!" Suddenly, everyone had to duck a huge wave as the thing hit the water and the surface of the canal lit up with what looked like a series of small lightning bolts with gushes of steam spitting out everywhere. When at long last fully submerged, the monster sank to the depths and let out one final long, shrill ear, piercing buzz.

The fight to the end was over and the group, feeling it safe to do so, ran over and began frantically checking over Jack and Barker, making sure they were both fine.

"Quinn, after witnessing that battle royal with that atrocity, my deepest fears have just been confirmed. Wells has never intended to build any of his automatons with a degree of real intelligence; it seems his simple answer was to be bigger is better. My god, if he unleashed an army of those things, London or the rest of the country for that matter, I am afraid to say we were completely unprepared," said Ernest worryingly to Quinn.

Once satisfied the two iron guardians were fit enough and their water supply had been replenished, everybody began surveying the carnage around them and deciding it was time to proceed. They all walked cautiously through the massive hole in the side of the mill. Jack and Barker took the lead, pulling away any dangerous parts of the structure and clearing a path for their human and canine friends.

"Stanley, I think the best job for you will be to run back to the trailer and keep guard. Remember, be a good boy and give out one of your biggest barks if you hear anyone approaching," said Lilly as she patted Stanley's back legs with her hand, gently pushing him on his way.

Ernest, once again, taking control of the situation, began to speak.

"The one thing I am hoping is that we haven't missed Wells. After all, for all we know, he could have set off again with the Night-Drone or, worse still, with one like the terrifying metal gargantuan Jack and Barker had just defeated. In hindsight, perhaps it would have been a better idea if some of us had taken the canal path to get here." Suddenly, everyone focused on Quinn as he looked agitated.

"Shush, all of you, I am trying to concentrate. Wells is here somewhere, but I can't lock in his thoughts. You know, I've always suspected he had learnt how to do that," said Quinn, pointing ahead to a big corridor that looked as though it would lead to the other rooms of the mill.

"Leave him to us; me and Rose can handle him," said Lilly as she impetuously pulled her gun from its holster.

As they all ran ahead, it soon became obvious the corridor was far too narrow for Barker to proceed and as the others caught up, they had to tell their sad looking iron guardian that although they would never have got this far without him, the only job he could do for now was to wait and guard the entrance.

Iron Jack, distracted saying goodbye to his new partner, felt ashamed he had let his human friends go in front but it was too late as, by now, everyone had already gathered in the large living area of the mill house.

Samuel, Frederick, Rose and Lilly all stood with their guns at the ready as Quinn put his index finger vertically in front of his lips, signifying all to be quiet and in deep concentration, and began rocking his head side to side at the same time Jack turned his head slowly shining light all around the massive room as everyone searched every nook and cranny until they were satisfied that no one else in that part of the house.

As they all prepared to go upstairs, Quinn lifted his hand and held back everyone as he telepathically sent his thoughts to his companions.

"I am getting nothing from upstairs; if anything, it's down there," he said as he pointed his finger to the floor.

With no visible means of getting below, feeling a strange magnetic force, Quinn instinctively began rubbing the stone-built internal walls and signified for Jack to do the same when, after a few moments, one of Jack's massive iron hands became stuck.

"Jack, this was what I was hoping for. Now pull hard," said Quinn urgently.

Everyone watched on as Jack began twisting and wriggling his wrist until he gradually eased the magnetic 'stone' out of the wall.

Suddenly, as a loud rumbling began to fill the air, everyone, Jack included, prepared to run, as a large section of the wall began pivoting and eventually opened like a massive stone door.

"Jack, could you need to brighten your eyes," said Quinn, almost forgetting mere mortals needed the chasm illuminated before entering the dark, dank, musky-smelling tunnel that presented itself before them.

With the tunnel bathed in a warm glow, the immense dimensions of the long underground path became apparent and with Iron Jack taking the lead, Ernest, Quinn along with, Rose, and the Stroud family cautiously began their descent into the unknown.

Jack intensified his eye beams, giving the eerie ravine a deep red hue. Suddenly, emerging into a cavernous room, bolt upright in one of the corners stood the awesome figure of the Night-Drone.

Jack, initially shocked at the sight of his nemesis, threw his arms out wide to stop his friends from proceeding and building up a head of steam prepared himself for battle. Pulling the huge lead truncheon from his belt, Jack got ready to give the Night-Drone a hefty clout but held himself back as he realised the motionless iron giant did not attempt to make the slightest movement and was clearly immobilised and no threat.

Suddenly, everyone's attention was drawn towards a shuffling sound coming from a far corner of the room. Jack swung his head in the direction of the sound and brightly lit up the area. Everyone looked on, shocked at the pitiful sight before them. Slumped on a filthy, blood-splattered couch were the unmistakable figures of Hubert Wells and Emily, Ernest's former wife.

Wells appeared to be holding tightly the ends of two bandages, one tightly wrapped around his arm, the other around Emily's.

The comatose woman's head was slumped on Wells's shoulder, hardly moving as she breathed and distressingly, she was foaming at the mouth, showing the whites of her eyes as they rolled sporadically to the back of her head and, at the same time, giving out the odd grunt and groan, as though in a mix of pain and pleasure.

Wells suddenly spoke. "I realise your first instinct would be to shoot me and save Emily. Don't even try," he sneered, continuing, "any attempts at saving her will be futile. You see, I have injected both of us with enough pure heroin to kill an army of men. It is only these tourniquets that are preventing the drugs from rushing into our veins. I, for one, am glad it will end like this."

Snarled Wells at Ernest as he continued. "All of this, including building my destructive inventions, along with the affair with your wife, you see, Ernest, is actually your fault. Why didn't you just forget about me? The Dons at Oxford University had long ago worked out my real character; they knew, why do you think they asked me to leave? Ernest, my dear fellow, you should have left me working there at the London Hospital, then you would have never been caught up in my criminal activities. Bamforth latched onto my weakness straight away. He knew I was easily led and drew me into his web of depravity at the earliest opportunity. It was different for you; you had everything: a respected figure in society and a beautiful wife who loved you. What else did you really need? As soon as I agreed to come to your house to 'help' you, I knew your life was about to change for the worse as my true character took over and I proceeded to poison your world.

Anyway, you have proved beyond doubt that you have always really known that out of the two of us, you are the true genius. OK, until you discovered my whereabouts, I admit I was on the verge of building an army of my metal monsters, but they actually frightened me as I could never fully control them. I mean, there is no comparison; look at what you've built," he said as he pointed towards Iron Jack.

"He's probably the most intelligent being out of all of us. No, defeat is a bitter pill to swallow, but I knew I was ultimately beaten when my bank-robbing giant found its way back and wouldn't do anything I asked. That's why I eventually had to shut it down. Ernest, you see, my greatest weapon is control and once I knew I had lost that, I had nothing. Believe me, though, when I tell you at this moment in time, I am the one who is fully in control of Emily's and my life." Sneered Wells as he glared at Ernest and sharply gave the two tourniquet cords a quick tug, releasing the lethal drug into their bodies, causing him and his stupefied captive to instantly slump to the floor.

"Do something quickly," cried out Ernest, knowing deep down it was too late as Hubert Wells and Emily's bodies began to convulse and writhe uncontrollably until, after only a few seconds, they both let out their last dying breath.

Everyone watched on in sadness as Ernest crumpled to a heap onto the hard-stone floor, shaking with emotion inconsolably, having just witnessed his former wife being murdered before his very eyes.

"Rose and Lilly, could you take Ernest back? Don't worry; he can't hear me at the moment," said Quinn, focusing his words simultaneously into the two brave detectives' minds continued "It's best you two comfort him at this traumatic time, so if you don't mind, I will stay here with Jack and the boys and try and fathom out what we are to do about this terrible situation. Let us do all we can for now, and we will meet you outside in about half an hour."

Quinn asked Jack to assist him in looking over the dormant Night-Drone and suggested it would be a good idea if Samuel and Frederick, if they didn't mind, could go and tend to the bodies of Hubert Wells and Emily.

"Quinn, there is no more we can do for them at this time; we will have to come back at a later date and collect them after we have arranged the funeral details," said Samuel solemnly as he and his brother bid their farewells and left Jack and Quinn to work out what to do with the dormant Night-Drone.

Towering over them with its massive head bowed low, Jack stared into the enormous pitch-black dead eyes of the Night-Drone when once again he felt the stirring emotion of fear as he reluctantly admitted to himself that in these close quarters and without the help of Barker, he would be no match for the fearsome foe standing before him.

Suddenly, startling them both, they began to hear a low buzzing sound, causing Jack to quickly position his hands, poised, ready to scoop Quinn up and whisk him away from danger,

Quinn and Jack noticed the Night-Drones head had lifted and his eyes had lit up, but curiously, the iron colossus's arms had stayed limp at his side and, feeling they were in no imminent danger, watched on and waited to see what might happen next. After only waiting a few seconds, suddenly, a booming voice echoed out from the giant metal man. "I do not fight; I do not kill."

Jack, in an attempt to engage with his old enemy, asked, "Do you need us to help you? You need not fear us. We can be your friends."

After waiting for what felt like a full minute, with still no response, Jack, perplexed at the situation, spoke to Quinn.

"What do you think is going on here?" he said as he scratched the side of his massive head with his huge metal hand.

"Really, at this stage, I am not sure. I have tried to connect with him, but his brain is so feeble I cannot latch onto any thought patterns. Jack, why don't you try to speak to him again?"

"Eh, hum. Why do you feel this way?" asked Jack, keeping

his questions short and to the point for his dim-witted adversary to understand.

"I was taught this lesson by Princess Grace," answered the huge, at very least twenty-foot-tall Night-Drone.

"Quinn, you and Freddy will have to work your magic with this one. He is definitely brain damaged and delirious," said Jack, convinced he had done more damage in his battle with the Night-Drone than he had previously thought.

"If he really has become this pacifist, I think it might be safe for you to try and find out exactly what it is that drives him. I mean, what is that buzzing noise?" asked Jack as he pointed up at a relatively small door at one side of the Night-Drones huge body.

Quinn asked Jack to lift him up parallel to the door and once in a position, not really knowing what was inside, he hesitantly twisted the large metal knob and pulled the heavy iron door until it was fully open. The low hum of the Night-Drone instantly increased to a deafening buzzing sound.

Quinn, sensing his life could be in danger if he delved too far into the unfamiliar machinery, instead ran his fingers over a sign he felt on the inside of the door and over the din of the mechanism telepathically told Jack what it said.

{Electrical Storage Units only to be charged when at ten per cent power. Failure to comply with this instruction will result in a critical overload}

"Aha, and just to think you thought I only read the works of Shakespeare, well you see, Quinn, old fellow, it all makes perfect sense to me as I have studied many books and articles relating to the pioneering work of Nikola Tesla. A brilliant Austrian inventor who specialises in the field of electricity. If I remember his thesis correctly, he has for a long time been working on how he could harness and store electrical energy. It looks like Wells had also been studying Tesla's work and had managed to build an advanced version of this pioneering power supply," said Jack, glad on this particular occasion he had shown Quinn his superior knowledge.

"It's such a shame Wells's undoubtable genius was not accompanied by a good moral code because the super advanced hybrid drive system he built for the Night-Drone is such a remarkable invention it could have applications that would radically advance all forms of transportation," said Quinn, as he asked Jack to lower him down to ground level, whereupon Jack decided before they completely shut the Night-Drone down, it would be a good idea to speak to him again.

"Going on the little you have told me today; I believe your attitude has changed beyond recognition. You have shown us that you do have the ability to learn. You do know we will have to immobilise your drive system, but I want you to trust us and know we will come back for you and give you the life you deserve." Hoping his message had got through loud and clear, Jack opened the Night-Drone's firebox door and said to Quinn.

"I know you have worked out like me, that he still needs a small steam supply to fully function, so we are going to have to extinguish his fire." With that, Jack fearlessly put his hand inside the iron giant firebox and pushed down hard on the coals, pinching out every last ember. When satisfied the fire was completely suffocated, he walked away and, turning his head back to take one last look at the completely silent giant, Jack's body gave out an involuntary shudder as he recalled the day that fearsome Night-Drone had viciously pulled his arm off and left him for dead.

With the entire group gathered outside the mill house, Ernest was standing with his arm around Lillie's shoulder. The traumatic experience of the sad demise of his estranged wife, Emily, had left him a broken man. Full of guilt of not protecting his one true love, Ernest had visibly aged, something Iron Jack instantly noticed.

Quietly speaking to Quinn, Jack said, "Have you all realised in only five more days, it will be Christmas Eve? We all need to make this Ernest's best Christmas ever and do everything in our power to help the poor professor put this dreadful experience behind him." Quinn agreed and helped his friend and Lilly onto the trailer; everyone took their positions and let Iron Jack take the lead as they all headed off towards the 'Big House' Hampstead.

*

The following day, back at work, Jack gave his inspector all relevant information on Wells and Emily's deaths and also mentioned the Night-Drone and any other mechanical antagonists were no longer a threat as they had either been destroyed or immobilised. On a better note, he would also inform him that in one day's time, London's much loved first iron guardian, Barker, would be ready to join him as his new partner.

With Ernest still in a seriously depressed state, it became clear he was blaming himself for Emily's death and when anyone tried to help in an aggressive voice, he would say, "It is true what Wells said. It was my fault; I should never have brought him into my life. We could have sorted out our problems, but instead, she latched onto him. I should have been stronger." With no one making any headway in lifting Ernest out of his deep depression, Quinn, Rose, Lilly and Mrs Beddoes agreed a huge Christmas celebration would be the only chance they had to raise their friend's spirits.

Samuel and Frederick, on Quinn's request, were asked to arrange Emily's funeral and accepted this would entail them going back to the mill house and performing the horrible but necessary task of moving the two bodies. They were also asked to take along a supply of building materials as they would have to fully secure the secret entrance to where the dormant Night-Drone was being kept.

*

One cold and bleak winter morning, the industrious brothers made their return to the mill house and, after respectfully removing Wells and Emily's bodies, made their way back down to the secret chamber to scrutinise the fully immobilised Night-Drone before they set about sealing him in.

"Of course, he does possess a rather primitive command system, if I say so myself, although I do believe my Barker is far more intelligent. In fact, I was tempted to add a voice box to Barker, but in the end, I just thought it wouldn't be appropriate. Anyway, if nothing else, you have to admire the workmanship and ingenuity of that thing's engine. I have never seen anything like it," said Frederick, not really thinking of the significance of what he had just said.

"I think you have really hit on something there, Freddy. Maybe one day, when the professor allows us to, we can 'copy' that drive system. I don't suppose Wells was the kind of man that would bother patenting his inventions." Also, said Samuel, continuing, "Wells could never have built such a complex thing without the help of some very skilled people. When we get back,

I suggest the first thing we should do is to tell Inspector Huxley we suspect the entire occupants of the village of Latchingdon should be investigated."

It was at that moment the Stroud brothers spotted something in the room they had not seen before. In the far corner of the basement floor, they noticed what looked like a trap door. Inquisitive at what was below it, Samuel walked over and cautiously lifted up the wooden hatch.

"Freddy, light up the lantern and give it to me here," said Samuel, as he started to climb down the small wooden staircase that lay beneath. As Samuel descended, closely followed by his brother, they soon found themselves in a large underground room.

"Unbelievable!" said Samuel loudly, as his eyes fixated on what appeared to be the spoils of all the Night-Drone's bank robberies.

"Huxley will have to know about this," he continued as, for a split second, he had contemplated saying nothing and making his brother and himself the richest mechanics in town.

"Sam, I can see where you are going by the look on your face, but we have to do the right thing," said Frederick as they looked on in awe at the huge stash of gold bars, jewellery and cash before them.

"You know we are not criminals, but why does anyone else have to know about this?" asked Freddy excitedly, as he pointed towards a desk that was stacked high with what appeared to be highly detailed blueprints.

"Freddy, you know all this stuff is above me, but I'm sure you, Quinn and Ernest would love to study them," said Samuel as he flicked through the intriguing drawings; even with his limited knowledge of such complexities could see it showed the intricate workings of Wells complicated hybrid drive system.

"Of course you are right, there are certain things old Huxley doesn't have to know about," said Samuel slyly, adding, "Come over here, Freddy and give me a hand to carry them. Ernest, Quinn and you can wrap your brains around them back at our place."

"That's a good idea, but we better hurry now because don't forget we promised Ernest we would brick in the Night-Drone and I've just realised that would entail us sealing in all the loot. There's nothing else for it; we will just have to tell Huxley about our find and he will have to retrieve it at a later date," replied Frederick as he picked up a big pile of the important drawings and, following his brother, climbed out of the secret basement to start their building work.

Chapter Fourteen

Celebrations and Retribution

Over the coming days, Scotland Yard became a hive of activity as Iron Jack and Barker smoothly settled into their duties. Their very first patrols were quite a sensation, with everyone from far and wide flocking to see them with huge crowds gathering outside their living quarters, waiting eagerly for their metal heroes to emerge.

Iron Jack quickly realised the public's show of affection, sometimes bordering on hysteria, could present a problem but hoped it would be a passing phase and a novelty that would soon wear off. Over the coming days, with Christmas just around the corner, as the crowds continued to get even bigger, Jack knew he had to do something and quickly came up with a plan at the first opportunity and spoke to his Inspector.

"Sir, with Christmas only days away and the mayhem Sheridan inflicted on our beloved city still fresh in the public minds, do you think, as a gesture of goodwill tomorrow morning before our shift, we could throw a little street party to show off mine and Barker's skills."

With the Inspector agreeing it was a great idea, as word quickly travelled as the queue began blocking off the entrance to the police station Iron Jack and Barker re-directed their show to an area of wasteland a short distance from Scotland Yard.

"Jack, Jack, can Henry sit on Barker while I have a go at riding on your holster?" cried out an excited red-faced boy as he tugged on the arm of his less confident friend who had been hiding behind his back. Jack lifted the boys into position and gave them an exhilarating ride, only to come back to a queue of parents and children that would have taken them a week to fulfil all their needs. It was at that moment Jack had a bright idea that deep down he knew he should have consulted Ernest about but seizing the moment, in his most authoritative voice, he shouted out to his hoard of admirers.

"Thank you so much for coming here today. I can truly say on behalf of Barker and myself that we have really enjoyed meeting all of you lovely people. I can tell you one thing: it's made me realise that if we lived in much safer times, we would love to dedicate all our time to being children's entertainers. The problem I have today is Barker and I need to start work very soon; therefore, sadly, the next ten children in the queue will have to be the last ones today we can take for a ride. I can see the rest of you getting upset, but it is not all bad news though, as I have decided that all those who have queued patiently today are invited to the 'Big House' Hampstead on December 26th for Professor Ernest Postlewaite's grand Boxing day party. Please wait for your official invitation cards, which PC Tom Saunders will hand out to you shortly."

Tom Saunders scratched his head and, taking out his notebook using his initiative, began quickly jotting out and signing his makeshift invitations as he made his way along the queue.

"Could the first ten children go over there by the hedge and wait for the trailer? I have something special in mind for you. How do you like the sound of a fast ride to Piccadilly Circus and back," said Iron Jack as he put on an impromptu strength exhibition, effortlessly picking up the traction engine and lifting it above his head. With a series of 'traction engine' push-ups for full effect, he gave out a few short bursts of thick black smoke from his chimney, at the same time making sure his eyes glowed at their most intense, occasionally tilting his head back, spitting out streams of fire high into the sky showing everyone what he was really capable of if they dared to get on the wrong side of him.

*

Ernest, on his first opportunity to meet up with Jack, scolded him for his rash promise but, secretly admiring Jack's resourcefulness, resolved himself to the fact he was committed to hosting an extravagant Boxing Day party.

However, Christmas day 1888 at the 'Big House' would be a different matter as Ernest wanted it to be the perfect family affair surrounded only by his dearest loyal friends.

Quinn, Rose and Lilly were happily playing parlour games whilst Frederick and Samuel Stroud chatted to their host, trying hard to keep the delicate balance of respect for his recent loss and the good times that lay ahead. As they all gathered around the blazing log fire, they began gratefully exchanging their presents.

Lilly's gift to Rose was a leather skull cap and a pair of leather-clad motorcycle goggles, giving her Tomboy friend a grateful hug, telling her in a not entirely truthful way that 'they were something she had always wanted' she was urged by the rest of the group to try them on causing everyone to laugh and giggle at the usually demure woman looking so out of character in her protective attire. Rose almost jumped out of her skin when

Stanley the Bassett hound, not liking what he saw, gave out one of his loudest barks and began growling at Rose until she decided to take off her wonderful new present. All are feeling content and full from the wonderful Christmas dinner Mrs Beddoes had cooked for them, they reminisced about the recent exciting times that they, as a group, had spent together. Mrs Beddoes, as busy as usual, began diligently clearing the mess of wrapping paper strewn around the room, telling anyone off in her vicinity about the dangers of throwing paper around so near the candles on the magnificent Christmas tree. Eventually, beginning to relax, she took full advantage of being treated as one of the family and showing no sense of her social standing in society. Mrs Beddoes made herself comfortable and had a quick doze in Ernest's favourite armchair.

Samuel, Frederick and Quinn huddled around Ernest and began discussing all the great times they had when working on Barker and Iron Jack. Ernest, being a modest man and feeling as though he was being given extra attention, began to feel uncomfortable and out of the blue, a pang of sadness wafted over him. After putting on a brave face for the next half hour, not wanting to cast a glum atmosphere over the party, Ernest announced to his adopted family that as much as he enjoyed their company, he felt exhausted and bid goodnight to his beloved friends.

As he stood alone in the hall, he suddenly realised what it was that had made his mood dip, thinking to himself. 'This truly is a most wonderful day but not all my friends and family are here. What about Iron Jack and Barker? OK, they are mechanical and made of metal but are such an integral part of my life I really should have made an effort to at the very least visit them on such an important day.'

Suddenly, hearing a commotion and taking Ernest by surprise, all the guests ran into the hall as Quinn excitedly announced. "Ernest, I try not to do it very often, but I read your mind a while ago and knew instantly what was upsetting you. Old Huxley has given them both the time off, so if you open the front door, there is a pleasant surprise waiting to greet you."

Doing as Quinn asked, as promised, standing resplendent in all their glory stood his two greatest inventions. Before Ernest had the time to run and give his two iron guardians a massive hug, Barker threw out a blast of heat and stood obediently next to his partner as Jack took centre stage and put on his most theatrical stance with his eyes glowing a burning red intensity quoted in his most booming theatrical voice a line from William Shakespeare's celebrated play Love's Labour's Lost.

"At Christmas, I no more desire a rose Than wish a snow in May's new-fangled mirth." Taking a bow, Iron Jack patted Barker on his back as they both looked lovingly towards their creator.

Exasperated and truly happy that his family Christmas day celebrations were complete, Ernest expressed his regrets that it was a pity because of their sheer size and stature; Iron Jack and Barker couldn't come into the house and join the party.

"Oh, don't you worry yourself about that, said Jack as he continued. Barker is quite content because I've told him everything I can recall about your wonderful home."

Ernest began scratching his head, not quite knowing what his puzzling metal 'son' was going on about; when seeing his 'father's' confused look, Jack explained himself, "Don't look so shocked, Ernest. I have been to your house before, as you well know. All right, granted, I wasn't fully assembled, and it was only a part of me, my brain, to be exact. Anyway, you must remember you got a good telling off by Quinn for talking to me."

With the witty retort from the one and only mechanical 'human being' on the entire planet being taken in good humour, the happy group of partygoers, in a display of love and affection for one another, began chatting, keeping warm as they all huddled up close to Barker as Ernest ran to the Christmas tree and picked up the present with Iron Jack's name on it. Running back and thrusting the parcel into Jack's hands, he said, "You can open it later when you get back home, but I know you will love it. Well, I hope you do. It cost me a fortune and it's a first edition you know." He concluded that he was unable to keep a secret due to his overwhelming joy of having everyone he loved at his Christmas day party.

Suddenly, everyone heard Stanley's pitter-patting feet on the hardwood floor, along with the distinctive sound of a leather ball bouncing down the hall. As the ball landed at Barker's feet, it was apparent to all that Stanley, not allowing his friend to be left out, had gifted his giant iron bulldog companion with his favourite well-worn toy.

After a short while accepting it was getting late and time to say goodbye, the extraordinary team walked towards the gates of the 'Big House' where Ernest, Quinn, Rose and Mrs Beddoes waved goodbye to the Stroud family along with Stanley the Bassett hound and the two remarkable iron guardians Iron Jack and Barker.

Back inside the house, Ernest suggested to everyone that as tomorrow was such a big day, they should all retire to bed, thinking to himself along the way.

When Quinn built Jack's brain, did he really have to factor into it such a will of its own? I mean, really, it was lovely seeing Jack tonight, but at times, he can be so annoying. I mean the audacity of him. 'Professor Postlewaites grand Boxing Day party', without a single consultation. Hmmph and Rose and Mrs Beddoes are getting as bad; sometimes I wonder if they think they own this house. I'm guessing between them, they have invited the entire village. Oh well, there are plenty of 'Nosey Parkers' itching to get behind the 'Big House' walls. Well, what do I care? Let them see for once and for all that we are just like everyone else, thought Ernest, forgetting for a moment that in reality, his group of friends, consisting of a mind-reading superhuman, a giant iron man and his mechanical dog, were, in fact, the polar opposite of an ordinary family unit.

*

The 'Big House', December 26th. The Grand Boxing Day Garden Party.

It was a glorious winter day at the grounds of the 'Big House'. Ernest had called in a local company to erect an impressive marquee and as what appeared to be the entire village mingling and chatting with each other, the 'Big House' had never been more lively, with different groups of happy partygoers gathering at the garden tables and chairs and tucking into the neatly cut sandwiches whilst being served drinks by Mrs Beddoes.

Iron Jack peered all around him until he saw Barker, unusually keeping still. Suddenly, Jack noticed Stanley the Basset hound leading a small group towards the magnificent mechanical bulldog and, when satisfied his job was done, ran away and began barking at the feet of a different group of merrymakers.

Barker, surrounded by the curious attentive revellers,

became animated, shaking his body side to side as a display for all the fuss and attention he was getting and very soon, full of confidence and showing no fear, the happy crowd huddled up to the giant mechanical bulldog, rubbing their hands together as close as they dare in front of his firebox to warm themselves up. Within moments, drawn towards the sight of Barker, small children appeared on the scene and began climbing all over him where Jack was pleased to see the adults acting responsibly and gesturing to them to be careful and not burn themselves.

Eventually, as the night began to draw in, virtually everyone who had stayed formed a big circle around Barker and sat quietly drinking their mulled wine, reflecting on what a lovely day it had been as they watched their children gradually fall asleep. Jack stood back on the edge of the grounds to have a short rest, exhausted with dealing with the pure scale of people who had wanted his attention, when all of a sudden, he could see he was being approached by one of the village's more prominent residents.

"Ah, I've heard so many good things about your kind self," said the smart-looking elderly woman who had made her way over and planted herself firmly next to Iron Jack.

"She's beautiful, and therefore to be wooed; She is woman, and therefore to be won," said Iron Jack, confusingly in a loud and clear theatrical tone, baffling the stunned-looking corner shop owner.

Stooping slightly so as not to intimidate Mrs Marems, Jack continued. "Oh, Just a few lines from the great Bard's Henry VI part one. I am sorry if I made you think you were listening to a babbling idiot, but once I saw you standing here beside me looking so lovely, I felt that particular quote very appropriate. Anyway, enough of my ramblings, but while you are here, can I just say..." continued Jack as he couldn't help noticing the portly shopkeeper begin to blush. "that was it down to your instant acceptance of Quinn's unique appearance that he eventually found the confidence to venture further than Hampstead village. Honestly, I don't know where that fella would have been today without you. We all know there are many small-minded people who cast judgement just by how someone looks. Thankfully, you were a better woman than that. Worryingly, though, I have heard from reliable sources there has been quite a bit of tittle-tattling about the recent bank smashes. You know, the sort of thing, did the Professor build that metal monster? Was it one of his creations that escaped?"

Mrs Marems looked a bit taken aback and embarrassed, as though she had just been accused of something. Before she had time to react, Jack lowered his huge metal head until his mouth almost touched Mabel Marems ear; being extra careful, his glowing embers did not burn her, whispered, "To be absolutely honest, Mrs Marems, you should just come to me if you want to know the truth about anything regarding Professor Postlewaite and his associates. As a much-respected influential woman in this area, you have to realise that careless talk can prove to be very costly."

Mrs Marems, feeling guilty, knowing that in the past, on many occasions, she had spread many speculative rumours, lowered her head in shame and not wanting to admit guilt and defend herself, gave out a small cough and said, "Iron Jack, it has been a pleasure talking to you today, but I won't take up any more of your time; I am sure there are many people here far more interesting than me that you would like to talk to." With that, she gave the very astute iron guardian a friendly pat on his back as she left him to mingle with the other guests.

Iron Jack kept focus on the busybody shopkeeper and watched her lips intently, seeing if she was slipping into her gossiping ways, but was pleasantly surprised when all he could make out as she pointed her finger towards him was. "He is so articulate and nothing like I expected. I must say he is very handsome and charming for an iron man, especially when he quoted a short passage from Shakespeare to me," she said, giggling as she put her hand to her mouth and walked away. Turning her head, she looked straight over towards Iron Jack and thought to herself, *I am not quite sure what happened earlier. I still can't work out whether I had been complimented by Iron Jack or he had told me off?*

As the evening's party drew to a close, it began getting dark, deeming it a great success. Virtually everyone, as they left, told the professor they couldn't wait for next year's celebration and, if he didn't mind, could they bring their relatives along next time? Ernest held his head in his hands and thought, *Oh, why do I let him do this to me?* as he chuckled to himself, deep down, appreciative at what a great success Jack's inspired idea had turned out.

*

Meanwhile, on Boxing Day at ten thirty p.m. at Newgate Prison at the Walter Sheridan high-security annexe, a different story was unfolding. Bert Cooper and Frank Harris had been given the responsibility of keeping the highly dangerous criminal Walter Sheridan well and truly locked up.

"Bert, how's that nutcase been today?" shouted out Walter Sheridan, pretending to be Frank Harris, the night-shift guard. Bert Cooper, the day-shift guard, on hearing the usual banter from who he believed was his work colleague, had no reason to be suspicious or think anything was any different from all their previous changeovers.

"Bert, look at the pattern, that's it, stare at it... Be still, be very still. Soon you will start to feel sleepy, very, very, sleepy, sleep, sleep... Sleep," said the heavily disguised Walter Sheridan, continuing to repeat the word 'sleep' in a barely audible whisper at the same time slowly waving a spinning black and white spiral-patterned disc in front of the dozing Bert Cooper.

As the duped, hypnotised warden eventually fell into a deep slumber, Walter Sheridan removed his set of cell keys and propped and posed his victim behind his desk as though fully alert.

Right, that's got both of those idiots out of the way, ha; I don't know who was easier to hypnotise, that dopey guard well tucked up in my cell or this numbskull here. Anyway, the first bit of my plan worked. Now all I have to do is get myself out of this hell-hole, thought Sheridan, laughing to himself as he began testing the keys one by one until he eventually unlocked the annexe door. He made his way into the main prison block.

'Hmm, if I can pull off this next bit, this escape will have to go down as one of my greatest deceptions, thought Sheridan slyly to himself.

Once inside the main block, the master of trickery ran swiftly down the corridor at the same time, throwing away his guard cap, exposing his shock of flame-red hair and turning his prison warden jacket inside out, proceeding to open every cell door along the way. In no time at all, Sheridan had released every high-security convict until, eventually, the marauding horde of criminals noisily spilt out into the concourse of the imposing prison.

Sheridan hid out of sight as he watched a group of escapees brutally attack the terrified front entrance guard and, after kicking him senseless, steal his keys and unlock the massive prison gates. As the dangerous gang split up and headed into all corners four of London, Sheridan, feeling it safe to emerge, calmly removed the comatose front gate guard overcoat and putting it on, pulling the collar up as high as he could to obscure his badly scarred face he began the long four-mile walk to 2 Eaton Place Belgravia. Speaking to himself loudly along the way, he said to himself.

"It's important. I am absolutely certain I've got this right. What was it that snitch said? Ah, that's it... When you get to the address, go to the tradesman's entrance, give two sharp knocks, then three taps one second apart."

After sneaking around the backstreets, Sheridan eventually found himself at his destination. Standing silently outside in the dark area by the tradesmen's door, he couldn't help thinking to himself. *Funny how it could turn out if the police do their job properly, they would have the opportunity of catching London's two most notorious fugitives in one go. Still, I needn't worry about that; those dopey Peelers haven't got a clue and, in a way, what I am about to do is all their fault. They could have done away with me a long time ago, but stupidly, they let me off the death penalty. I'll show them how to administer real justice; wait till they see what's going to happen to that twisted bastard,* thought Sheridan, as the dominant side of his personality took over him and began spreading horrific images into his brain.

'Do you know what? I can almost feel and taste his warm blood as it splatters around the room. Can we keep him alive for a while as I cut his eyes out?' Asked the bad vicious side of Sheridan's split personality. Trying hard to focus on the job at hand, the completely insane escapee gave the secret knock and waited when, after a few seconds, the door slowly opened. Sheridan, with frightening speed, lunged at Bamforth and, with one almighty vicious bite, sank his teeth deep into the shocked surgeon's face. Thrusting his head violently back, he laughed out loud to himself as he fully ripped off one of his victims' cheeks and watched, cackling maniacally as the gaping wound gushed out a stream of blood.

Spitting out the large portion of muscle and skin he had just bitten off, Sheridan watched Bamforth writhe on the floor in agony and proceeded to violently kick his victim in a hate-filled frenzy. Stamping his foot onto the corrupted surgeon's mouth, he began grinding his heel in a circular motion until his victim's cries became muffled. Then, using his full body weight, he began pushing his foot down harder and harder until he felt Bamforth's teeth break and snap one by one, and with two final hard-hitting stomps, the groaning and gurgling stopped as his traumatised victim finally passed out.

With the mass murderer at long last 'getting a taste of his own medicine, blacked out in pain, Sheridan dragged the unconscious surgeon by the hair across the cold basement floor and, tearing a table cloth into shreds, tied his prisoner's hands and feet together. Plunging his hand fully into Bamforth's mouth, not wanting his victim to choke and die too soon, he proceeded to pull out and throw on the floor a disgusting mix of congealed blood and broken teeth and filled a nearby glass with tap water.

He proceeded to viciously pour it down Bamforth throat. "Those poor women and the unspeakable things you did to Quinn and those helpless babies. Bamforth... This is retribution!" yelled Sheridan as he intensified his vicious attack.

As the mortally wounded surgeon gradually came around,

groggy and in intense pain, Sheridan spotted what he had been looking for; in the corner of the room, on a small wooden table, he could see glistening in pristine condition Bamforth's 'work tools', his dependable surgical instruments.

What Sheridan proceeded to do next was fully justified in his warped mind. Slowly torturing Bamforth until eventually, he died, he left the body in the same state the psychopathic surgeon had 'posed' his numerous victims with body parts and entrails strewn around the room and in a gruesome statement of vengeance for what Bamforth had done to Quinn, Sheridan had completely cut off demented surgeons face and pushed the shredded flesh deep into the orifice where his victim's mouth had once been.

"Gone! There will be no more killing or twisted surgical experiments from that filth any more," he screamed out. "We have finally rid London of the Ripper!" Hallucinating and shouting out to what he could see was a captivated audience.

(Worryingly, with his split personality fully in control, the completely insane Sheridan had now begun thinking of himself as two entities) Continuing in a calmer tone, he concluded, "I know you good people could never find it in your hearts to forgive us for the terrible things we have previously put you through, but at least you can sleep soundly in your beds, safe in the knowledge the London ripper will never murder again. We have finally rid you of that wicked, evil maniac."

Leaving the terrible scene of horror behind him, Sheridan, deranged and in a 'trance-like' state, looked to the sky and said in a timid voice, "God, it is up to you what you want to do with us. Strike us down now if you must and we will take our punishment with dignity but if you let us proceed with our mission, we will take it as a sign and when it finally is our time,

Heaven or Hell we will accept your divine judgement. Oh Lord, in your great wisdom, will you please forgive our act of retribution? Surely, it was nothing compared to the heinous atrocities committed by Bamforth that sadistic fiend." Sheridan, the demented, psychotic former private detective, concluded his prayer and solemnly left the scene of horror, firmly closing the basement door behind him.

Trying as hard as he could to get back to a state of reality, Sheridan managed to snap himself out of his split personality delusion and somehow, finally gripping onto the rational side of his personality, began working out how to proceed with his 'master plan'.

'Hmm, now there is something I need to do back home if I am going to make it possible for Bamforth's body to be discovered without incriminating himself.

*

At the 'Big House' the morning after the grand Boxing Day garden party, Ernest was awoken by Mrs Beddoes, who immediately informed her employer that Inspector George Huxley was in the sitting room waiting to speak to him.

"Ernest, it's Sheridan; he's escaped," said the inspector in a worried, excited tone to his concerned-looking host, who replied.

"I don't believe it, or maybe I should correct myself and say, I do believe it. We should have all guessed it would take more than bricks and mortar to keep that egotistical maniac confined."

"I will, of course, keep it as 'hush, hush' as possible," continued the inspector, adding. "We both know there is no way we can let this sensitive information get out to the general public. I mean, the last thing we need after everything London has been through recently is another uprising of Sheridan's fanatical followers. Thankfully, we have rounded up most of the prisoners he had released. But Ernest, we can't take any more chances with that megalomaniac, so I have ordered all my officers, if they discover his whereabouts, to not approach him and to shoot to kill. Look, Ernest continued the Inspector, I know in the past, you have used your own private detectives and I have suspected there have been occasions that you withheld possible vital information from me but please, in the future, I must insist for us to have mutual trust in each other, that any information you have on Bamforth, the 'Ripper' you must share it with me."

Ernest felt a pang of guilt as he admitted to himself that, in the past, he should have been more forthright to the Inspector and in an effort to make himself feel better, he divulged everything he knew about Bamforth, even telling the inspector that on one occasion his private detectives had almost caught the twisted surgeon in the act of one of his brutal killings.

"George, we know for sure Bamforth is the Ripper, but even with the stalwart work of my detectives Rose and Lilly, the simple fact of the matter is, sadly, we are still no nearer to finding out his whereabouts. We have discovered he left his practice at the hospital, giving no notice, so I am presuming he knows he is a wanted man and has gone into hiding."

It was at that moment that Ernest had an epiphany. "That's it… It's all making sense; Sheridan has escaped for more than just the reason of freedom. I believe that, somehow, in prison, he has found out a lot about Bamforth and his criminal ways. Think about it: Bamforth, being a dishonest practitioner, must have many criminal connections to whom he supplies his illegal drugs to. I believe over the weeks Sheridan has spent in jail, he has discovered who has been hiding that deranged surgeon and has found out where he is staying," said Ernest, satisfied the key to capturing both fugitives Bamforth and Sheridan lay somewhere in Newgate Prison, continuing.

"George, you know what you have to do next; you will have to interrogate all of Sheridan's inmates you manage to capture, and also, don't forget the guards; they could have information on Bamforth as well. You've got your work cut out, as have you have told me on many occasions; the criminal code of honour is virtually impossible to be to break," he concluded with his voice in a sinister tone.

Not wanting the Inspector to leave stressed and overwhelmed, he added on a good note, "Oh, and George, don't you worry yourself. We are one big team now. I will keep my promise and make sure I inform you of any breakthroughs at my end."

The inspector left the 'Big House', feeling relieved that, at long last, they would all be working towards the same goal.

*

December 28[th,] at three a.m. after his long walk, Walter Sheridan eventually arrives at his old house at 33 Electric Avenue Brixton. As he made his way along the muddy alley that led to the rear garden of his terraced house, carefully climbing two fences as quietly as possible, hiding and checking from time to time his movements hadn't alerted anyone, he eventually found himself at the rear of his former home. Knowing the exact place to look, he cleared a pile of leaves and, as silently as possible, kicked the partially mulched foliage away, revealing a concealed hatch.

Prising the small door open, he made his way down the short wooden staircase and, when at the bottom, fumbled around in the dark until he found the door that would lead him into his laboratory. Gripping and twisting the stiff handle at the same time, he gave the barely used door a firm shoulder barge, and as it swung open, he found himself in complete darkness. Tracing the walls of the pitch-black room, he eventually found the cupboard he recognised as the one he always kept his oil lamp and vesta stick.

With the room fully illuminating his familiar surroundings, the exhausted madman slumped into his comfortable old Chesterfield armchair. The good side of Sheridan, full of remorse at the violent act of murder he had just committed, twitched his head uncontrollably and, ripping at his horrific scar in a mad, frenzied crescendo of intense self-harm, began ripping off huge shreds of skin from his face.

Suddenly, the rational good side of Sheridan took over his mind and as a way of stopping his self-harm compulsion, the tortured soul spoke to himself, "I hate this side of me! No More, never again."

In one final desperate act of exorcising the bad side of his personality, he pushed his fingers straight through his mutilated cheek and with a series of almighty gut-wrenching tugs, crying in agony, Sheridan attempted to rip off the entire side of his face.

Ribbons of blood-soaked muscle and sinew hung down from his maimed cheek and crying and sobbing at what he had just done to himself, the tormented, mentally ill wreck collapsed in pure agony.

After what seemed hours of restless slumber, Sheridan finally managed to pull himself out of the armchair. Suddenly, he felt a surge of intense pain and became aware of the sounds he was making as he breathed. Shocked, realising the enormity of what he'd done to himself, he moved his fingers around the gaping hole that was once his cheek and for the first time in such a long while, the tormenting voice he expected to appear did not materialise. The relief he felt that he had finally got rid of his demons was so strong he felt shudders and tingles consume his body as he knew whatever the outcome he faced as a consequence of his murderous deeds; he at last felt happy he had regained his sanity.

With a newfound determination, Sheridan walked up the basement staircase and emerged into his old living room, where instantly bright sunlight filled his eyes as it filtered through the gaps of the external wooden boards that had been crudely nailed over the windows.

Are they really that dumb? Did they honestly think a few planks of wood would keep me out of my house? Well, how wrong They were; I'm here now, so let's get to work, thought Sheridan, blocking out the pain of his self-inflicted wound as he began to locate all the vital components, he needed to assemble one of his 'Translite' voice recording' machines.

I hope history will show that my killing of Bamforth was justified; after all, it was for the benefit of London. Anyway, I digress; old Postlewaite and Quinn deserve to know the truth; it's up to them what they do with the information, he thought as he tightened up the last screw of his ingenious device and switched it on.

As it whirred into life, he began recording all the important details and information he had torturously extracted from the deviant surgeon Bamforth and waiting for the cover of darkness, carrying his bulky 'Translite' tape recorder in a canvas bag, the heavily disguised, hooded, Walter Sheridan set off towards the 'Big House'.

*

28th December eleven thirty p.m. outside the grounds of the 'Big House'

Walter Sheridan made his way to a secluded spot of the boundary wall, and, gripping the top railing, he pulled himself up and climbed over into a secluded corner of the impressive garden. Hidden by the darkness of night, Sheridan crept up to the porch area and, as quietly as possible, placed his 'Translite' machine near the front door; checking everything was set as it should be, he peered around and noticed that bathed by the dim light of a street gas lamp a grass mound banked up against the wall. Effortlessly climbing the small grass hill, balancing precariously on top of the wall, Sheridan jumped to the outside pavement.

Walking away from the 'Big House' he stopped for a moment and stared up at the winter evening massive full moon and bathed in its cold light. He had an overwhelming feeling of being small and insignificant. Casting his mind back, he began remembering his happy days as a small child and later on as an ambitious young photographer, the days before he had become the bitter, deformed criminal he now was. In this quiet moment, he suddenly became aware of a putrid smell of rotting flesh that jolted him back to his surroundings. It was then he worryingly realised that the putrid odour was actually coming from his own body.

Allowing the intense throbbing pain he had for so long managed to suppress take over him, Sheridan instinctively touched the foul-smelling strands of skin and sinew that hung from his face; moving his fingers all around them, he touched a mass of congealed blood that had formed into the gaping hole on the side of his cheek and as he pushed it, droplets of clotted blood fell into his throat, causing him to gag.

In intense pain, disgusted at what he had done to himself, he ran towards Hampstead village and arrived at his destination. In a vain effort of what he believed would make him more presentable, Sheridan combed his fingers through his matted fiery red hair and, with his blooded head held high, strolled casually into the local police station.

"I believe you are looking for me," he said to the shocked-looking front desk sergeant, who had begun to involuntarily vomit as he stared at the hideously deformed figure standing before him.

*

29th December, Saturday morning at eight a.m. the 'Big House'

Shall I touch it? Oh dear, I'm not sure; I've never seen the likes of it, thought Mrs Beddoes as she stood back, gawping at the one-foot square box that lay on the porch floor.

Appearing on the scene, wondering why the front door was open, Ernest said to his confused-looking housekeeper. "Don't worry, Margaret. I've seen one of these before; I will take care of it from here. Oh, by the way, I'll have my breakfast in the study this morning," he concluded as he carefully picked up the black wooden box.

What has that 'man of mystery' been up to now, thought Ernest, knowing that such a device was only ever used by Walter Sheridan.

As Ernest looked over the contraption, trying to remember how to bring it to life, before he even had time to fiddle about with it, he became aware of a ticking sound.

Dammit, I'm not ready yet. I must have disturbed something, he thought when, without warning, Sheridan's voice began emitting magically from within the black box, whereupon Ernest made himself comfortable on the hall bench seat and sat back and listened to the message.

"Ernest, long ago, when you first brought me into your life, I was so completely in awe of you I was actually surprised you thought me worthy of your attention. Oh, my dear fellow, if only I could turn the clock back, there are so many things I would have changed, not least my disdainful attitude towards your friend and colleague Quinn. Of late, I myself have come to realise the struggles of living with a deformity, but instead of dealing with it in a dignified fashion as Quinn has his entire life, I allowed my disfigurement to escalate my delusions and before I knew it, I had become a virtual law unto myself. Anyway, I digress; with all the extra time on my hands incarcerated in prison, I began thinking back to the images of the surgical journal that I presented to you. Those terrible pictures of those poor mutilated babies have never left me. Bamforth's ungodly experiments, as heinous as they were, did, however, result in one superhuman survivor, your friend and colleague, the extraordinary Quinn.

I am sure you have wondered as many times as I have how it was that Quinn actually ended up in the London hospital under Bamforth's 'care' and control. Well, you see, Ernest, through means of torture, I have extruded some very important information and you, sir, and your amazing friend Quinn should waste no time and take a trip to the Hanwell Pauper and Lunatic Asylum, Southall, West London. Unfortunately, that was all I could extract from that degenerate before he had the audacity to die on me, but I am sure you will both be able to find all the missing pieces to the puzzle you need when you visit the mental institution."

With that, after a short pause, came the final message, "This 'Translite' tape will self-destruct in five seconds."

Fumbling about for a pencil and a scrap of paper, Ernest, making sure to remember what he had just been told, repeated the address over and over in his mind as he jotted it down.

I do hope that was correct, Ernest worryingly thought to himself, when suddenly, as predicted, there was a loud click, followed by a fizzing sound and a strong acrid smell. As the 'Translite' tape machine erupted into flames, Ernest panicked and, in an attempt, to put the fire out, he threw the hall rug over it. When thinking it was safe enough, he pulled the rug back and could see a pile of smouldering ashes where once there had been the amazing speaking machine. All the evidence that Sheridan had ever been in contact with Bamforth had been completely destroyed, and at that moment, Ernest had to admire the thoroughness of his former private detective plan.

Hmm, completely deranged but undoubtedly a genius, thought Ernest as he walked to his study, where he spent virtually the entire rest of the day pondering on how and when he should tell Quinn the cryptic information Sheridan's machine had given him. Eventually, letting his head clear, he thought it best to sleep on it.

*

The following morning at nine a.m. Iron Jack stood on the gravel drive of the 'Big House' and, letting his body cool for a few seconds, knocked on the front door.

"I thought I heard you open the main gate, and to what do I owe this pleasure of your company this fine morning?" asked Ernest as he stared proudly at his creation, the impressive ten-foot-tall iron guardian.

"I just wanted you to know before the press get hold of it that Sheridan has handed himself in," answered Jack, still puffing small plumes of smoke after his speedy journey.

A short moment later, Quinn arrived on the scene, but Ernest, not believing it was the appropriate time to mention the 'Translite' tape message he had listened to the previous morning, let Jack continue speaking.

"Yes, apparently, he was in a terrible state and didn't say much to the desk sergeant, only that he had important information he would only divulge to a superior officer. As soon as Huxley got the message that Sheridan was at the local police station, the first thing he did was to send a Bobby to summon me. Once I spoke with my inspector, he got me up to speed with all the relevant details and said before I meet him at the address, I should go and fetch you two. So, Ernest and Quinn, could you put a spurt on, please as I don't want to keep old Huxley waiting too long," conclude Jack, fidgeting, wanting to get going.

"Mrs Beddoes," shouted out Ernest, "Myself and Quinn will be out for the day, so don't bother cooking anything for us." As he closed the front door and allowed Jack to lift him and Quinn onto his holsters.

"I said I would meet him in Belgravia in one hour's time. It's only about twenty minutes away so we will definitely get there in time," said Jack as he ran up the gravel drive towards the 'Big House' gates, leaving a trail of dust behind him. As the coals in his firebox began to glow white hot, Jack shouted out urgently to his passengers.

"Hang on tight, you two and keep your hands covered. You won't want to burn them. I'll show you how fast I can really go," cried out Jack as the loud hissing of his steam boiler increased in volume as he sprinted down the main road towards 2 Eaton Place Belgravia, SW1.

*

"Good man, Jack. Glad you got them both here safely," said Inspector Huxley to his reliable iron policeman.

Quinn and Ernest carefully dismounted Jack and immediately stood back and let Huxley assume full control as he spoke to Tom Saunders.

"Tom, would you and Barker scour the area within one mile of here?" asked Inspector Huxley, watching on as the old partnership walked off into the distance. Asserting himself as the chief investigator in the case, the Inspector once again spoke.

"According to the information given to me by Sheridan, this is actually the residence of Ambassador Alexander Ivanovic, an important dignitary that for a long time has had strong connections with Bamforth. Actually, he is quite the crook, supplying massive amounts of illegal heroin into the country, although I don't expect to find him here today. If the Russians are true to form once they get wind of what he has been up he is bound to be replaced and that will be the last of him in this country." Changing the subject, Huxley turned his attention to his mechanical police officer.

"Jack, I know you will want to use your extensive array of detective skills today, but regretfully, I am sorry to say your pure stature has made it impossible to let you investigate inside the house with the rest of us. As I told you earlier, Sheridan is not admitting any involvement with anything we might find inside this address, so I want you to scour the road thoroughly and try to find any leads or physical evidence that could link Sheridan to this address," concluded the Inspector as he carefully removed his gun from the holster and, with much trepidation, led Ernest and Quinn down the basement steps to the tradesman's entrance.

Suddenly, they all became aware of a loud buzzing sound coming from behind the basement door.

"Don't worry, that noise has nothing to do with the Night-Drone on this occasion," said Quinn confidently as he put both palms of his hands onto the wooden door, knowing his actions would cause the swarm of flies he had detected inside to die. Immediately, inexplicably to his comrades, the buzzing sound stopped.

"There you go, that should make it a little more comfortable in there," said Quinn, leaving the inspector scratching his head, not quite sure what exactly had just happened.

Quinn, taking the lead, gave the door a sharp kick and as the morning daylight flooded into the basement, a scene of pure horror confronted them. With the dim light filtering around the room, Quinn pushed Ernest and the inspector back and said. "I am not sure you are really prepared for this." As his superior senses, fully alert, absorbed the scene of carnage surrounding them. Walking into the foul-smelling area, it was then Ernest began retching and heaving.

"Come on, man, pull yourself together; we are all big boys here," said the Inspector sternly, kidding himself he was the toughest person out of all of them. As Huxley scoured the scene, he suddenly felt weak, but knowing he had to be strong, he slowly walked across the sticky floor that was completely covered in a disgusting mix of dead flies, maggots, congealed blood and human skin. Worst of all, as they began to take in the full horror of the scene, they spotted numerous dismembered body parts that had been strewn around the small room.

Ernest could take no more as the enormity of the fact dawned on him that he was the one person here who definitely knew it was Sheridan who had committed this savage murder. Sheridan, a man, a fellow scientist and someone that he had once admired and respected, he could not believe was capable of such an act of unadulterated carnage. Making his excuses, trying hard not to vomit, he left Quinn and the Inspector to carry on the investigation at the murder scene while he quickly ran up the basement steps to grab some fresh air and join Iron Jack outside.

"Quinn, you possess powers a simple man like me could never really comprehend. So, tell me, what do you deduce from this frenzied scene? Is it just a copycat Ripper killing, or is there more to it? If it was Sheridan that performed this act of savagery, then tell me what possible advantage was it for him?" asked the inspector, feeling uncharacteristically flummoxed.

Quinn, having already made up his mind, answered, "George, I have experienced the depths of depravity human beings can inflict on each other from the day I was born. There is nothing in this world I can ever sense that will shock me, but I will tell you here and now, this was not a killing purely for recreation or blood lust; it was, I believe, a murder committed as an act of revenge and retribution."

Once outside and the team all gathered together, the Inspector assigned Barker with the duty of guarding the crime scene and informed the others that he would prefer to walk back to the Police Station alone. PC Tom Saunders reminded him not to forget that tomorrow would be New Year's Eve, always an extra busy time for the Police Force.

"*Hmm*, let's end this year on a positive note. It's not far to Fleet Street from here. Come on, Tom, let's inform the press the Ripper is dead. That should give everyone something to celebrate," continuing as he walked away, "Jack, you take the rest of the evening off, but make sure you are back on duty early tomorrow. I think when the news of the Ripper's death filters through the community, the ringing in of 1889 will be a more raucous affair than usual, especially in Whitechapel. Those working girls with the threat of the Ripper attacking again lifted, will be out in force. Oh, and Jack, just ignore them tomorrow." Adding in a kind tone, "Let them and their punters have a good time; they all deserve a bit of freedom after everything they have been through this year," concluded Chief Inspector Huxley as he briskly walked off towards Fleet Street.

*

As they all arrived back at the 'Big House', Ernest felt mentally exhausted as the entire way home, he couldn't stop thinking about the address he was given by Sheridan. As the sides of his temples had been stinging on the entire journey, he knew that his efforts of concealing anything of any importance from Quinn had been futile and standing at the 'Big House' front door, Iron Jack lifted Ernest and Quinn from his holsters.

Jack had also felt there was a strong tension in the air, but deep down, he knew whatever was bothering his two human friends, he had to leave them in peace and said, "I think you two had better sort it out between yourselves. You do know that these days, I think of myself as an equally important part of this family, so when you both feel the time is right, I would eventually like you to confide in me."

Before Quinn and Ernest had time to respond, Jack, standing as tall and straight as he could, with his head tilted slightly back and his eyes burning their most smouldering red, in a loud booming voice, said, "I count myself in nothing else so happy as in a soul remembering my good friends."

Quoting a line from Shakespeare's Richard II, he left Quinn and Ernest exasperated and shaking their heads in disbelief at the latest theatrical outburst from their amazing mechanical 'son' as he disappeared into the distance to resume his stalwart work as London's iron guardian.

The two weary companions entered the 'Big House' where Ernest asked Quinn to join him in his office. Once both seated at his desk, he went on to tell Quinn everything Sheridan's 'Translite' tape machine message had said. Quinn, shaking with emotion on hearing the ominous mental asylum address, eventually spoke, "Ernest, this is almost too much for me to take in, so a madhouse is possibly my heritage. Why did that insane idiot Sheridan let Bamforth die before he got all the facts?" asked the perplexed superhuman in a tone expressing more raw emotion than Ernest had ever heard before.

Feeling Quinn's pain, Ernest gave his distraught companion a comforting hug and as he stared up at the strange, virtually blank head of his friend rocking back and forth, it was at this moment Ernest began to wonder if this meeting between his highly deformed friend and his possibly insane relative could ever be of any benefit for either of them. Quinn picked up on Ernest's concerns and said.

"Ernest, actually, I suppose I should be happy that Sheridan, a person who once hated me so much, had felt the need to help me find out more about myself. There was no real reason he had to concern himself with my affairs apart from maybe a semblance of guilt at the way he treated me with such disdain in the past. Also, I should be grateful for how much time and effort you, the girls and Iron Jack have put into investigating who and why made me the way I am. So, with that all said, I have decided I will go to the asylum and try and get some answers on why I was given up to be raised by that perverted maniac," said Quinn as his voice began shaking with emotion, adding in a softer tone.

"Oh, and by the way, I must insist that Rose comes along with us. I mean, she has agreed to be my wife and if I am carrying a strain of mental illness in my genes, then she deserves to know," concluded Quinn as he sat in silence with his strange head in his hands, not wanting to say another word on the subject.

"Come on; this has been a stressful day for both of us. Let's get a good night's sleep and I will meet you and Rose in the drawing room at about eight a.m. We'll just have a light breakfast and set off around nine a.m. It shouldn't take us long to get there; we can go most of the way by 'The Hand'," said Ernest in an upbeat tone, adding.

"Quinn, you mustn't upset yourself; no one on earth has been braver than you, and this next step should be the final piece of learning of your birthright, something you fully deserve to know," said Ernest as he hugged his poor, tormented friend, and they both headed up the stairs to their respective bedrooms.

Chapter Fifteen

New Beginnings

Ten a.m. New Year's Eve, Outside the Hanwell Pauper and Lunatic Asylum.

Ernest paid the Hansom cab driver and joined Quinn and Rose, who discussed how they should proceed with their delicate investigation.

"I don't know about you two, but I'm aching all over; that last couple of miles in that rickety cab has ruined my back; it's a pity the 'Hand' doesn't come out this far," said Quinn, not noticing that his fiancé had walked away to look for somewhere to rest.

"I agree and just hope I haven't done any permanent damage to myself," said Ernest as he twisted and stretched his aching body and, with his face grimacing in agreement, added.

"As for the 'Hand' not coming out this far, it's something I've been thinking about for quite some time, but that's a project for another time. Anyway, let's get on with what we came here for," he concluded as they both walked over to Rose, who was trying to look comfortable sitting on a rather rough-looking garden bench.

Entering the imposing-looking brick-built building, the three companions had formed a plan, but before they had time to find a senior doctor, they spotted a nurse who had obviously recognised the striking trio and was running towards them.

"I knew you would come here one day," said the excited young carer, adding, "She has done nothing but go on about you for the last few months, ever since you became famous."

Ernest began scratching his head, perplexed by what the carer had just said. Just as he was about to ask what she meant, the nurse spoke again. "No, I am not talking about you, professor; I'm talking about the extraordinary Quinn. Ever since he has been in the newspapers, Mary has kept everything he has appeared in," concluded the plump nurse in a rather crazed tone.

Quinn, visibly affected by what he had just heard, looked even more bizarre as all his blood began draining from his strange head when suddenly, unexpectedly, everyone but Quinn became frozen to the spot. As they all tried to move, they realised it was to no avail. The more they struggled to move, the louder the ringing sound that permeated through their minds became. It became obvious to Ernest and Rose, who were used to their friend's extraordinary powers, that whatever it was restricting their movement was all Quinn's doing.

As the ringing sound gradually quietened down, Quinn's voice entered their minds, "Don't worry, the nurse will be fine; unlike you two, I've put her into a deep hypnotic state and when we all eventually walk out of her sight, she will remember nothing about our visit. You see, Rose and Ernest, someone here is drawing me towards them and I know whoever it is emitting this strong force, it is someone I need to deal with on my own. Even as I speak to you, my mind is full of jumbled words and messages rattling around my head, a feeling I have never experienced before, but the lure is so compelling I am unable to resist. All I know for sure is there is someone in that room that is very important to me. Please forgive me for what I am putting you both through and I promise as soon as I get some answers, I will release my 'grip' and give you both my decision if it's best we leave and never speak of this place again or you, my two dearest friends come and join me and experience this new vital part of my life with me."

With that, Quinn walked purposely towards the room he was drawn to ready to confront the ominous entity that was causing him so much distress. As the jumbled words reached a fever-pitched crescendo, Quinn tentatively entered the small, dimly lit room and, using all his superhuman powers to keep the confusing messages at bay; he focused his unique senses where he visualised a demure-looking woman sitting down, completely unfazed by her new strange looking companion. He quickly deduced the slim lady, although having a youthful middle-aged complexion, going by her hands, was probably more in her late sixties. The ravages of her harsh environment had obviously taken their toll as her eyes were sunken with dark circles as though she carried the worries of the world on her hunched shoulders, but underneath her broken demeanour, her long wavy silver hair and prominent cheekbones showed she was still a very beautiful woman.

"From the very first day I saw your name emblazoned across the headlines, I knew it couldn't just be a coincidence and from that day on, I convinced myself that you were my long-lost son. Do you know your full name is…?"

Quinn stopped her from saying what subconsciously he had always known and in a quiet voice, he whispered his full name, "It's Michael Quinn, isn't it?"

Mary Quinn broke down and began crying at the realisation that the son she had for years presumed either lost or, worse still, dead was well and truly alive and was actually standing there talking to her. Quinn suddenly felt a twinge of compassion for the tragic woman sobbing uncontrollably, but instead of letting her absorb the enormity of the moment, he suddenly felt a wave of rage waft over him and yelled.

"But why! Why, out of all the people in London, did you have to leave me with that monster? Was I so deformed you felt you couldn't cope any more? Whatever reason you abandoned me, you had better have a good excuse, or I might as well leave now," shouted Quinn in anger until, without warning, he felt a huge flow of love waft into his mind, and as the strong bond between mother and son firmly cemented itself into his brain, he gradually calmed down. Making himself comfortable, he sat on the edge of the hard, basic bed and asked Mary Quinn to tell him all she could remember about the time she had with him as a tiny baby.

"Of course, I will; you deserve to know," she answered, continuing. "First of all, I should explain to you that I am not in this asylum because of a mental illness. I never really was mad, but sadly, being a single mother with no income, this is how our cruel system deals with women in that situation. The real shame is I have been held prisoner in this horrible place for so long it has begun to take its toll on me and at times, I lose touch with reality. I see things the doctors insist are not real and that gives them a reason to perform some terrible so-called 'cures' on me, such as ice-cold baths and sleep deprivation. I try to make out their 'cures' have worked, but it's not before my visions appear again. They actually deemed me a bad influence on the other patients and eventually segregated me and gave me my own room. Anyway, enough about my troubles, it is time that you for you to know everything.

I will start by saying that whatever made you as you are

today, it was none of my doing because from your moment of birth until that fateful day, you were forcibly taken from me; you were a perfectly healthy baby boy."

"Mary, said Quinn, not feeling comfortable enough yet to address her as mum or mother. There are two other people with me today who are very dear to me and I think they deserve to hear all you are about to say first hand."

With that, Mary Quinn nodded her agreement and waited silently as she watched her son sit still and rigid as he focused his thoughts, releasing his mind 'grip' he had put on his two closest friends and telepathically guided his adoptive father and his future wife into the room he and his mother were sitting in. After an emotional greeting, they all sat comfortably and waited for Mary Quinn to speak.

"Michael, I know some of the things I am going to divulge will, at times, enrage you, but I'm begging from the bottom of my heart that when you accept the sad chain of events that led me here, were completely out of my control, you might feel it in your heart to forgive me. Before I continue, I insist you all sit in silence with no interruptions until my unfortunate tale is told," Mary Quinn cleared her throat and, composing herself, began her tale.

"Michael, I realise you have already experienced much heartache in your life and hate that I have to start on such a negative note, but we mustn't wash over the fact your actual birth father was not a very noble man. Nothing he ever did was carried out in the correct fashion. He never held down any job for more than a couple of weeks at a time and even in the early days of our relationship, life was really hard. We both lived in the same workhouse but were kept apart for most of the time, so on the few occasions we managed to find some privacy, they, shall I say, became rather passionate. When I eventually fell pregnant with you, he immediately told me his real duty was for his country and that he had enrolled in the army to fight in the Crimean War. His actual words were along the lines of, 'You will be all right; the workhouse won't put you on the street' as if that was some sort of consolation. Of course, I never really believed he would join the army; he just wasn't that sort of honourable fellow it was all one big excuse so he could abandon us; needless to say, that was the last I ever saw of him.

As soon as you were born, although living a pauper life, I always held onto the hope I would be able to keep you. I had spoken to other mothers who lived in my workhouse and could see their children had been schooled and put to work, so the idea the same could happen to me didn't seem that inconceivable. Sadly, that option never materialised, as one day, I was told by the manager of the workhouse that my baby would have to be put up for adoption. I will never forget that horrible day when they asked me to bring you, a barely one-month-old baby, to attend a meeting with someone they told me was a much-respected physician. Apparently, he had 'fortuitously' singled me out and said I had the perfectly healthy child he would like to adopt. What could I do? They told me how could a lowly workhouse resident protest after being given this rare opportunity to give her son such a privileged start in life.

Oh, Michael, my dear boy, if I had even an inkling your prospective parent was the perverted monster, he turned out to be, I would have run out of that building with you in my arms as fast as I could. As he took you away on that fateful day, I was so inconsolable. It wasn't until sometime later that I knew all was not as it should be when I realised, I had not been left with a single trace of you and never received any proper adoption papers. One thing is sure, though, I will never forget his smarmy face as he walked out of the door carrying you in his arms or his name it is etched on my mind; it was Leopold Bamforth," she concluded as she let out a loud sigh as, at long last, she was able to tell the truth to her son. Feeling the weight of guilt, she had carried for so many years finally lift, closing her eyes, exhausted with emotion, she bowed her head and waited for a response.

"Mary, I promise you here and now you I will get you out of this asylum. With my high standing in society and, shall I say, your son's unorthodox persuasive ways, we will take this to the highest authority. Mark my words; you will not spend one day of 1889 in this cruel archaic establishment," said Ernest in his most authoritative tone as he led Rose out of the room to leave Michael Quinn with his mother for a few more precious moments.

Sitting outside the asylum on the rickety bench after a good few minutes, Quinn joined his companions and the team together, began chatting about the enormity of what Mary Quinn had told them. All agreed there and then it was best for as long as they could to conceal the fact to her that Bamforth, Michael Quinn's abductor, would also go on to become the Ripper, London's most notorious killer.

"It's obvious she will find out herself very soon because we know she has access to the newspapers, and another thing, Ernest, that was a rather rash statement, wasn't it, 'you will not spend one single day of 1889 in here', that means we only have ten hours to arrange for my mother to get out of this place before new year's eve which is in case you forgot is tonight," said Quinn angrily, inexplicably knowing the asylum clock was about to strike two o'clock, he continued. "And another thing, we are basically stuck here. I don't know about you two, but I do not fancy walking two miles to the main road and the prospect of another long, uncomfortable Hansom cab journey is too much to comprehend." He concluded as he rubbed his back, reminding his colleagues of the uncomfortable journey they had experienced early this morning.

As they all sat pondering on what to do next, Ernest had an idea. "Quinn, why don't you summon Jack? Hopefully, he won't be too busy and if possible, maybe he could bring Barker as well, so we won't have to be too cramped," said Ernest as he stared at Rose, fidgeting on the cold hard bench.

In less than half an hour from when Quinn sent his telepathic request, Iron Jack and Barker arrived on the scene and with barely time to let their engines cool down for their passengers to board them, Jack spoke to Quinn in a stern tone, "I thought this 'mind bond' thing we have was to be used only in emergencies, not for a bloody cab service."

Before Quinn and Ernest had time to reprimand Jack about his use of bad language in front of Rose, Jack continued speaking. "Anyway, my apologies for being so rude in front of such a beautiful woman," causing Rose to blush, he went on, "perhaps Quinn can tell me on the journey home why you were all here. Before that, though, I have some important, slightly disturbing news. I have to warn you all that Sheridan is on the run again. It almost beggar's belief how sly and conniving that man can be; it transpires while he was being treated for his terrible self-inflicted facial injuries. Whether by his unparalleled power of pure persuasion or his more favoured means of late hypnosis, he has apparently absconded with his entire medical team. One theory is they could be dedicated 'Believers' from his disbanded cult, but if we are to trust him by the note he left behind, it went something along the lines of. 'If I survive my skin graft operations, I will never do wrong again. The thing is, I cannot stand being locked away and feel I still have much more to give.' To be honest, it sounds like the same old, insincere drivel to me, but let's hope and pray that for once he tries to stick to his word.

Myself and the rest of the police force will do our utmost to hunt him down, but with his unparalleled trickery, he could already be out of the country. Anyway, hey, let's try and all look on the bright side," said Jack as he watched on as Quinn and Ernest climbed on Barker and Rose looking slightly dishevelled but as beautiful as ever walked over to Jack and waited for him to lift her onto his holster.

Oh no, there go my emotions again, thought Jack as he pondered. *When Quinn had had the opportunity to adjust my brain, he should have taken the time to make me less sentimental because, if I'm honest, I feel I am getting even worse. The entire works of William Shakespeare could not express the love I have for that woman, and I daren't let Quinn know I still have feelings for his fiancé; that would be the 'the last straw that breaks the camel's back', and he would be well within his rights to dismantle me once and for all.* As Iron Jack gently lifted onto his side holster the beautiful Rose Morely, the subject of his unrequited love.

*

Two thirty p.m. New Year's Eve, 'The Big House' Hampstead.

"Jack, when you and Barker get back to the police station, would you ask your inspector that I need him to do me a big favour? If you just wait a couple of minutes, I will draft a quick letter that I want you to give to him. It is imperative you tell him the letter Must be delivered to the prime minister at ten p.m. this evening if I have any chance of keeping my promise," said Ernest in his most official-sounding voice, adding in a quieter tone. "Oh, and tell old Huxley he and his wife are officially invited to my New Year's party I am having here tonight." Thinking proudly to himself, *That's more like it. At last, a party at my house under my terms.*

Quinn had 'picked up' on Ernest's urgency and had read his mind as he wrote the letter for the inspector. "Ernest, you never cease to amaze me; yet again, you have gone way out of your way to help me. With your influence and a declaration from the prime minister, it surely will be enough for my mother's release from that horrible place. Honestly, I don't think I could ever repay you for your kind offer of letting my mother stay here," said Quinn, full of gratitude.

Hmm, let's hope she hasn't become too institutionalised and will be willing to leave that terrible place at such short notice, thought Ernest, hoping Quinn hadn't 'picked up' on his concerns as he said. "Quinn, I am going to be 'tied up' here helping Mrs Beddoes prepare tonight's 'shindig', so would you mind terribly going over to the Stroud's and inviting them," said, Ernest

Quinn lowered his head slightly and Ernest watched on as his friend's body began to tense up. Guessing what his unique friend was about to do, Ernest quickly interrupted.

"I can see you are in the process of summoning them all telepathically; well, for one thing, I am not sure that is a good idea because I can see the visible strain it puts on you; also, don't you think it would be nice to tell them personally about the good news of you being reunited with your mother. You can also use the time to bring them all up to speed on Sheridan's latest escapade. So, with all that said, off you go," said Ernest firmly, adding in an upbeat tone.

"I am really excited having all our friends and family here tonight. We will ring in this new year like no other." Quinn brushed himself down, gave a couple of affectionate pats on Ernest's shoulder and said goodbye as he prepared himself for the thankfully short Hansom cab journey to the Stroud's home.

*

Four p.m. New Year's Eve, The Stroud's Family Home

"Hello Quinn, we don't usually get a visit from you this late," said Lilly as she stared at her unusual-looking visitor, still taken aback at times by how bizarre her friend actually looked.

"Oh, Lilly, have I got news for you but I think it best you go and get your brothers so I can tell you altogether."

With them all settled down in the Stroud's comfortable but cluttered living room, Quinn spent the next half hour telling them all the good and bad news of the day's events and, as Ernest had asked, invited them all to the New Year's celebration at the 'Big House'.

"Samuel and Freddy, have you thought any more on when you might be able to collect Wells Night-Drone and bring it here to start his much-needed adaptations," enquired Quinn, itching to get involved with another Iron Guardian project.

"The Stroud's don't 'let the grass grow under their feet', you know!" exclaimed Samuel as he roughly pulled his brother out of his comfortable armchair.

"Come on, Quinn … Oh, sorry, or do you prefer Michael?" Abruptly stopping himself, feeling embarrassed as he now knew Quinn's full name.

"Samuel, whatever you feel comfortable with. Now, what was it you were about to tell me just after you ruffled up your brother? The way you were carrying on it must be something very exciting," said Quinn, dying to know what Samuel had to say.

"Quinn, we can do better than tell you. Go on, Freddy, you lead the way. He's more your 'baby'," said the fidgety mechanic as they all, Lilly included, headed towards the big garage come workshop.

"I don't really like the dark. Could you leave the light on next time, please?" Came a booming electronic-sounding voice emanating from the once fearsome Night-Drone sitting looking forlorn, taking up a whole corner of the spacious garage.

"Sorry, everyone, I'm still working on his volume control," said Frederick, turning towards a shocked-looking Quinn. Proceeding to walk over to his sad-looking iron giant, Frederick leant back and stretched and looking at his huge mechanical baby square in his eyes he said.

"There-there. What are we going to do with you? OK, I promise I will leave the light on next time, and if you like, I will get you some new books, but I will make sure they have more words in them," said Frederick, comforting his dim-witted pupil.

"It's early days yet and I'm not sure he could ever be as learned as Jack, but I am very happy with his progress so far. Do you know it was only two days ago he couldn't read at all?" asked Frederick, extremely proud of how his new advanced brain mechanism seemed to be performing.

Turning his attention once more to his childlike iron giant, Frederick said, "Come on then, don't be shy; hold your head up. I want to introduce you to the amazing Michael Quinn, a man who I can quite categorically say if he hadn't taken me under his wing, you would not even exist. I know this is all a bit confusing for you, but when I feel you have developed enough, I will tell you everything about your past life and introduce you to others just like you."

Frederick, seeing his creation was becoming a bit overwhelmed, ushered Samuel, Lilly and Quinn out of the workshop and, giving his rather pitiful-looking iron creation a friendly pat on his massive shoulder, waved a friendly goodbye.

"I have to say, Freddy, you have done a marvellous job with him; what do you think? Early next year, we might be able to put him to some sort of use," enquired Quinn, with his voice full of admiration for his young apprentice.

"I would say very early next year; I can't quite believe it myself; it's unbelievable the astonishing rate he is evolving, but Quinn, I mustn't take all the credit for his development. Did you not sense how silent he was? No more of that incessant deafening buzzing? In fact, I think we will have to think up a new name for him. You see, his drive system is all down to Samuel. He has managed to refine Wells's old hybrid Steam-Battery engine to such a high degree it's basically a completely different machine. Its applications could be very extensive: Trains, motorcars, who knows, even 'The Hand'? In fact, he has already converted one of Lillie's motorcycles. Anyway, enough technical chat for now; I am sure he would like to explain everything to you in more detail at a later date," Frederick concluded as he and Quinn joined Samuel and Lilly outside to help finish loading up the traction engine trailer

"Freddy, make sure your 'baby' is comfortable and tell him we won't be back until tomorrow morning. Don't forget to explain and warn him about the fireworks. If you are not confident, he will be able to cope; then you might have to put him to sleep and shut him down. Talking of fireworks just reminded me of someone who loves making a lot of noise this time of year.

Lilly, you know who we are talking about? Where's Stanley? We can't possibly leave that dog behind. He will keep the whole neighbourhood awake, and anyway, how could we not take him with us? He has been such an important integral part of the Iron Guardian project."

Lilly ran off to fetch here faithful pet, and as Frederick quickly returned from locking up the workshop, he helped his sister and Stanley to jump on the trailer and waited as his brother, confident in the driver's seat, let out a loud toot of the traction Engine's whistle. Engaging the gear lever and thrusting it forward, the trusty, rather slow, old, antiquated machine jolted into action. Samuel turned his head briefly to check all his passengers were safe and sound and spun the driving wheel while focusing on the road ahead, shouting out at the same time, "All aboard... Next stop, the 'Big House' Hampstead." As they all sat holding on tightly as the noisy, clanking, puffing traction engine chugged up the short drive to join the main road.

*

The 'Big House' six p.m. New Year's Eve

"Quinn, I actually think I've done it; Huxley sent around one of his Bobby's earlier on and has told me all is in place for your mother to be released from the asylum. There are still a couple of hurdles before I am hundred per cent confident she will be here tonight and I have to admit one of them is quite concerning. The thing is, your mother has been incarcerated in that horrible place for so long she may have become institutionalised. The other problem, admittingly not so worrying but nevertheless something of concern, is I am sure your mother has never met Iron Jack before. We can assume she must have seen pictures of him in the newspapers, but in real life, in all his glory, he does strike a rather daunting figure. Anyway, I don't know why I'm letting it get to me because we both know Jack is clever and charming enough to convince her he can be trusted and is nothing to worry about. I'm telling you, Quinn, that this whole situation with your mother has made me seriously think about getting into politics. Being incarcerated in a mental institution for having a baby out of wedlock is not on. Something has to change."

"Ernest, what you have already done is absolutely brilliant. Look, if the worst comes to the worst and she doesn't want to leave, at least I have found out where she lives and I can always visit. Now, what is it we say to each other in uncertain times, onwards and upwards, so please stop worrying and fretting and start relaxing. Whatever the outcome, it will make tonight the perfect New Year's celebration. Can you see over there? I think Samuel and Freddy have already primed Barker with some fireworks; that must be what they meant on the way here when they said they had something special planned for him?" asked Quinn, full of anticipation about what great things the night might hold.

Mrs Beddoes and Rose called everyone over to help set the main dining table they had temporarily set up in the hall in front of a blazing log fire.

"I hope you don't mind, professor. I thought it would feel less formal and people can help themselves to food and drink and go in and out as they please. I've heard from the usual gossip there is a big party planned in Trafalgar Square this year and with a bit of luck, we will be able to see the fireworks display from here," said Mrs Beddoes, full of enthusiasm.

"With the amount of incendiary devices, I've seen the Stroud brothers load onto Barker, I think it will be the other way around.

Everyone in London will be able to hear and see My firework display, now the boy's; please keep him well away from that open door; one spark from that fire and we will blow up the house," said Ernest laughing his head off at his own joke while Samuel and Frederick steered the giant metal bulldog as far from the front of the house as they could.

*

Hanwell Lunatic Asylum, eight p.m. New Year's Eve

Mary Quinn stood with a small brown suitcase by her side, holding hands with one of the asylum's nurses.

"I said that Peeler was telling the truth. My word, he's even more impressive than I imagined he would be," said the jolly, rather plump nurse as she spotted Iron Jack walking along the drive to greet them.

"Mary, you have to be excited that, at long last, you have been set free. Of course, I have known for years there is nothing really wrong with you, but at least I persuaded them to give you your own room. I tell you, the goings on in that big communal ward almost drove Me mad. Sorry if I didn't take you seriously at first when you said the 'famous Quinn' was your son but you surely have proved me wrong. And look, you have your son's invention, the one and only Iron Jack, waiting to collect you. Oh, Mary, it's hard to believe this is the last time I will ever see you, but I can't imagine you would ever want to come back to this horrible place again," said the caring nurse, Mary Quinn's closest friend, as she pulled a small handkerchief from her sleeve and wiped a tear from her eyes.

"Would one of you two young beauties mind going to collect Mary Quinn and tell her that Iron Jack's personal cab service is waiting outside for her?" asked Jack, jokingly, managing to make light of the situation and be his most charming self at the same time.

"You silly thing' I am Mary Quinn," said the blushing elderly woman, playing along with Jack's obvious charm offensive, continuing. "We can leave straight away if that's all right with you. I am all packed and just have to say goodbye to these lovely people before we set off."

Jack felt slightly confused at what Mary had just said as he could definitely only see one other person apart from Quinn's mother, but not wanting to dwell on it, he carefully lifted his frail passenger onto his holster and tucked her suitcase securely into his chain belt. Looking over towards the nurse, he could see she was smiling at what she had just heard Mary say. Jack turned his body, making sure Mary could not hear what he was about to say and whispered in the nurse's ear, "I hope it's not this place that's getting to me, but please tell me I'm not going mad and there are definitely only three of us here."

"Oh, I see what's bothering you; how would you know? The thing is, Mary often sees things no one else can see. Personally, I think her visions are very real and she has a gift. She has played them down of late because she knows if the doctors saw her 'talking to herself', they would start experimenting on her again," answered the kind, sympathetic nurse.

Phew, I think just for now I had better keep this information 'under my hat'. Quinn is so looking forward to being reunited with his mother I don't want to put a damper on it and tell him his mother is probably 'non-compos mentis'. Hmm, seeing things that aren't there. Until someone shows me undeniable proof that ghosts exist, I will stick to the notion that the only things alive on earth that are non-human are Barker and me, thought Jack, shaking his head slowly in disbelief at what he had just been told.

"Iron Jack, would you mind if I leave Mary in your safe hands now," said the plump nurse, continuing. "I have to get back to my ward, and by the way, it was lovely actually meeting you in person. The first thing I'm going to do is tell all my colleagues you are just as charming as the newspapers say you are," said the nurse, causing Jack's head to swell with pride.

Jack suddenly thought that he could seize the moment and use his intimidating presence to frighten the cruel doctors and nurses who had been abusing their positions and had basically tortured one of their patients. Carefully lifting Mary off his holster, Jack explained to his elderly companion that although he quite rightly expected it would be her son that she would want to spend most of her time with later on, as he had never had a mother of his own would she mind if the pair of them took the opportunity and spent a bit of 'quality time' together now.

"Iron Jack, it would be my privilege. Where do you want to sit? Personally, I think you are too big to go inside and to be honest, I wouldn't feel comfortable talking in there. That's the one place I never want to set foot in again."

"Sorry, Mary, but will you trust me and wait over by the bench for a moment? I won't be long and when I'm back, I'll find a spot really cosy for us; there is something I forgot to tell the nurse," said Jack as they quickly ran over to catch the carer before she went back into the asylum.

"Joyce," said Jack, noticing the plump nurse's name embroidered on her apron, continued, "Would you do me a big favour when you go back inside? Could you 'play down' how charming I've been? Oh, and if you see me acting strange later, remember none of what I will be doing will be aimed at you because, going by what you have told me, it seems you are the only decent member of staff working here. Also, all the time you continue to work here, I want you to be my 'eyes and ears' and report back to me if you see or hear of anything untoward going on." Joyce gave Jack a knowing wink and waved goodbye, giggling to herself nervously, knowing she was to be an integral part of the famous iron guardian's plan.

As Jack re-joined Mary Quinn, looking at the frail woman sitting subserviently, waiting patiently to be told what to do next, it filled him with a waft of sadness. This poor woman who had been so cruelly incarcerated against her will had, in a perverse way, been protected from the horrors of the outside world. Looking at his battle-worn hands made him think how much of late he had spent either fighting or being involved in terrible murders.

Jack sat down on a high grass ridge surrounded by perfectly manicured privet hedges and satisfied they would be sheltered from the cold winter's evening wind, he turned up his heat, casing the ground all around him to dry out. When happy it was comfortable enough, Jack beckoned Mary over to sit down beside him.

"Look at the size of the moon; it looks like it's falling out of the sky. Have you ever seen it more impressive and beautiful?" asked Jack, feeling completely overwhelmed, as it was the first time in a very long while he felt he could relax and soak up the wonder of his surroundings.

"I know it's an amazing, extraordinary place. I've been there, you know," answered Mary, shocking Jack to his core by his elderly companion's response; it was at that moment he was absolutely convinced Quinn's mother was far more ill than she realised.

"Oh, yes, and I've also been to the bottom of the sea; I had a wonderful time speaking to the king of the ocean. He is a giant clam, you know."

Jack felt an immense pang of pity and, at first not knowing how to react, eventually removed one of his armoured 'gloves' and put it carefully into its holster and with his small 'book reading' hand fully exposed, he held out his arm and gestured for Mary to put her withered hand into his. It was then Jack felt the true sensation of what it must be like to have a mother. Mary began singing in a lovely, quiet, self-conscious voice an old lullaby Jack had seen written in one of his books.

"I see the moon, and the moon sees me, God bless the moon, and God bless me..." She went on singing in a crystal clear but shaky voice until the entire song had finished.

"It was a favourite of mine. I used to sing it to Michael in the few precious months I was able to spend with him," said Mary.

As without warning; she let go of Jack's hand as though snapping herself out of a trance and, in an excited tone, said. "Iron Jack, it is getting late now and I am beginning to feel a bit tired, so if you wouldn't mind, could you take me to see Michael now, please."

Jack, delving into his mechanical brain, realised he had been at the asylum for almost two hours and, bringing himself back down to earth, put his armoured glove back on. "Mary, I promise I will be as quick as I can, but could you just wait here for a bit? I just want to do one lap around the asylum and get a good look at the place before we leave. I don't think either of us will ever want to come back here, so I might as well take advantage of this opportunity," said Jack, as on his quick tour, he stopped at every ground-level window and pushed his massive head as close to the glass as he could without breaking it, making sure every time he could see a doctor or nurse to put on his most fearsome expression and make his eyes glow in intensity as if to say 'I AM WATCHING YOU!'

Once back at the side of his elderly companion, Jack carefully lifted the slender old lady onto his holster 'seat'. When satisfied she was sitting safe and comfortably, Jack tensed up his massive iron body and cried out, "Hold on tight, Mary, next stop, the 'Big House' Hampstead, your new home. You will absolutely love it there." As he put on a burst of speed and sprinted down the main road.

*

'The Big House', ten thirty p.m. New Year's Eve

Jack carefully lifted his wind-swept passenger from his holster and helped Mary Quinn compose herself.

"To be honest, Mary, I can't see Michael anywhere. I'm sure if I had tried to contact him, he would be waiting here with open arms to greet you," said Jack, feeling rather agitated as it was not the grand welcome he expected for his rather important guest.

"Oh, that's good. I've seen the professor and you have already met him, so it's not like I'm deserting you. Anyway, I suppose you must be fed up with me by now, so hold onto my hand and I will take you to him," said Jack, jokingly, relieved that he could leave Mary in Ernest's good company.

"Thank you, Jack; I will look after Mary now. I'm not sure where Michael has gone; maybe he is in the house, but if you want to, you can go and join all the other guests. Go on, relax. You deserve it; you've done quite enough work this evening," said Ernest, glad that everything seemed to be going to plan and, at long last, Quinn's mother was free from that terrible mental asylum.

"Mary, I am so glad you have decided to take up my offer. We will do everything we can to make this a fresh start for you," said Ernest, excited at the prospect of this new phase in Quinn and his mother's life.

"Oh, there's Michael over there; I'll take you over to him. I'm sure you two will have a lot of catching up to do instead of talking to this old fuddy-duddy," said Ernest as he escorted his rather overwhelmed looking guest to meet her son.

Ernest felt a waft of exhaustion as the whole of the day's events had finally caught up with him, and feeling like a bit of 'alone time', he walked to the back of the 'Big House' and sneakily avoiding everyone along the way he entered his home through the back door. Climbing the stairs in due course, he found himself standing in his massive library and gazing through the large circular window. He looked down below at the hustle and bustle of his human and mechanical friends as they all happily chatted and went about their business as the night drew in towards the start of the new year.

It really is something to behold, thought Ernest as he pulled up his leather captain's chair, sat comfortably and began to soak up the party atmosphere from afar. *It's unbelievable, really, but there is nowhere else in the world quite like this and when I really think about it, it's all down to me,* he pondered as he began to reflect on his life, especially the enormity of some of the recent events.

'Every action has an equal and opposite reaction' that's what Newton wrote. That Wells was up to no good even before I brought him into my life and it wasn't long before Emily showed her true character. I am absolutely convinced she would have left me for someone else anyway. If I am to be honest, living with me wasn't the life she really wanted and how was I to know that once

I brought that blaggard into our life, he was the perfect catalyst she was waiting for.

As for Sheridan, that man with his brilliant mind and his constant need to experiment and invent things, by the time I had got heavily involved with him, he had already had that horrific accident and begun his descent into madness. I really have to stop blaming myself for things that were way beyond my control.'

Ernest began to relax and felt as though a great weight had been lifted from his shoulders. He sank back into his cosy chair. Watching on from his perfect vantage point, he could see his amazing family sing and dance happily together as they all waited eagerly for Barker his first iron guardian to put on the highly anticipated midnight firework display.

In less than an hour, it will be 1889 and I already know what my new year's resolution will be: 'no more negative thoughts'. From now on, I will focus on what a privileged life I have and do my utmost to help all my loved ones to lead happy and prosperous lives. Staring upwards, Ernest's eyes were drawn to one of 'The 'Hands' carriages as its dull lights from within threw a gentle glow into the perfectly still pitch-black sky. *Surely a thing of practicality and beauty that anyone would be proud of*, he thought, full of self-admiration, when suddenly a thunderous laugh distracted him and caused him to peer down where he could see Iron Jack being the life and soul of the party as all around him burst into fits of laughter at his antics; Jack took on a series of theatrical poses probably quoting Shakespeare at every given opportunity.

Who would have thought it? Surely not Quinn or myself. From our initial conception to this magical moment, Jack has developed into someone far more independent than we could ever have believed, thought Ernest, pinching himself, that he and

Quinn had actually created the impressive ten-foot-tall iron mechanical policeman.

Ernest turned his attention to a different part of his impressive garden where he saw the Stroud family, Barker and Rose all gathered together. Samuel and Frederick fussed over the impressive iron bulldog as Rose and Lilly stood back and hugged and chatted with each other. Ernest smiled to himself, knowing that all these people who were getting along so famously, tending to his first iron guardian, would never have met if it were not for him. Taking a deep breath, Ernest continued observing from afar, looking over at Mrs Beddoes, his loyal 'rock' of a housekeeper keeping old Huxley's children occupied as they played with Stanley, the basset hound, while the 'annoying at times' police officer danced with his wife.

Peering all around, Ernest suddenly felt quite emotional as he focused his attention on the astonishing Michael Quinn, who was holding his mother's hand as he introduced her to all the other guests. This truly unique man was his best friend and brilliant work colleague. A man who had faced more adversity, physically and mentally than anyone else on the planet, had somehow found enough self-belief and determination to come through it all and find not only the love of his mother but also the love of Rose Morely, his future wife, such a beautiful woman inside and out.

None of these wonderful, good, positive things could ever have happened if his lifelong vision of living, breathing, self-thinking mechanical beings had not been persevered and seen through to the end.

Ernest, in his relaxed reflective view of his life, had lost all concept of time and, pulling his fob watch from his waistcoat, saw that he had actually been in his library for almost one hour and realised if he didn't join the party his guests would start to worry where he had disappeared to. Feeling refreshed with his mind clear and full of positive thoughts, Ernest made his way down to join his friends and the people he had come to think of as his adoptive family.

As Jack synchronised the bells of Big Ben and rang out twelve loud chimes, the entire party stood as far away from Barker as to be safe when suddenly a huge explosion was heard. They all tried as hard as possible without being blinded to focus on the mechanical bulldog that appeared to be on fire in a dazzling white ball of flame. Deafening blasts erupted from Barker as jets of coloured sparks shot in every direction high into the pitch-black sky, lighting up the 'Hands' huge dome structure as they intermittently flew past. Watching on in awe and at the impressive display, soon it seemed as though the entire village had come out to observe the wondrous spectacle, either standing in the street or looking out of their windows, clapping and cheering at a firework display the likes of what they had never seen before while in the grounds the entire party, human and mechanical gathered together and holding hands in a massive circle danced around Barker while they sang 'Auld Lang Syne'. As the final flurry of fireworks shot upwards and rained down, a glistening shower of pure white balls of light disintegrating into thin air before they reached the ground, Ernest noticed Quinn stand back to have a rest and thinking it the perfect opportunity to get his friend all alone, he walked over to him and tapped him on his shoulder and said.

"Quinn, or should I say Michael? While I was upstairs alone, I began thinking about what I should be doing with the rest of the time I have on Earth. Whether it be a short or, with God's blessing, a long life, I have come to the conclusion that the 'Big

House' is really such a waste of space for a boring old cretin like me to rattle around in and is actually designed to be a family home. It needs children's laughter to bring it alive. So, after giving much thought to what to do next, I have decided to move out and give the 'Big House' to you and Rose as a wedding gift. Oh, I almost forgot to mention it will come with a permanent fixture that you will find very useful. Mrs Beddoes," joked Ernest, knowing that it really was best his loyal housekeeper stayed and worked for Quinn and Rose.

"Ernest, for now at least, please continue calling me Quinn. I can barely get used to my mother calling me Michael. More importantly, let's get back to your generous offer and think in depth at all the consequences that could come with it, some of which I personally think is an arrangement that wouldn't work. Do you really think the people in the village would accept Me as the new proprietor of the 'Big House'? The gossip would come out in force and probably start spreading rumours that I had murdered you or something," said Quinn, making up any old excuse as he began feeling upset at the prospect of living in the impressive mansion without his best friend.

Feeling Quinn's sadness, Ernest went on to explain and lay out his plans and how it really was the perfect solution for all concerned.

"Quinn, I am not leaving the country nor actually intend to move very far away. There will be a few legalities to get over, but basically, I am going to try and acquire Wells mill house. I'm sure old Huxley will be finished with it soon and will be able to release it from his investigation. I'm so excited about the prospect, you think about it, it's the perfect property for me. Secluded enough not to be bothered by the village busy-bodies, it has a private waterway for easy access to London and comes with a magnificent fully equipped workshop. Everything a restless inventor could ever need. Now enough on this matter, it's settled: get married, live here with Rose and have at least three children. That's an order," said Ernest, joking, speaking in his most authoritative tone.

Quinn gave his kind and generous friend a huge hug. Unable to control his display of gratitude, sent a telepathic wave of appreciation directly into Ernest's brain that almost knocked his dazed friend to the ground. Once Ernest pulled himself together, he suggested to Quinn that now was the perfect time to tell Jack about the important developments and also confront him about the long-running problem of his inappropriate feelings towards Rose.

Walking over to a large gathering, they found their mechanical 'son' as usual being the centre of attention, so without looking rude, Ernest and Quinn made a few excuses and politely 'pulled' Jack away and eventually managed to get him to themselves.

"I'm not in any trouble, am I? I've tried to keep my theatrical quotes to a minimum of late. I know I can come over as a bit boorish, but have no fear; I've made it my New Year's resolution to tone myself down a tad. Either that or I'll let you and Quinn have a mess about in my old noddle," said Jack, switching his speech seamlessly between an educated, articulate speaker and a cockney costermonger.

Ernest went on to tell Jack of his plans for the future and got down to the sensitive matter of Jack's out of control emotions that had to be addressed.

"No, Jack, you are not in big trouble, but there is an issue with your personality that needs to be dealt with. To 'mess about in your noddle' is not an option any more as you are your own man and that's the way it will stay. There is one thing, though, that Quinn and I have discussed and that we both come to realise is something you are really struggling with," said Ernest, leaving Jack scratching his head, wondering what on earth he was talking about.

"Let's all have a walk over to that grass mound in front of the conservatory and make ourselves comfortable," said Ernest as the three of them settled down in the secluded spot.

"Jack, in the past, when you used to live here, I have watched you from afar on many occasions sitting on this grass mound and wondered for a long time why you love it here so much. Just recently, I worked out that the conservatory windows were the perfect place for you to see your reflection exactly as others see you. As you sat there sometimes for hours at a time, I couldn't help noticing on those occasions, you always looked so forlorn," said Ernest as he noticed Jack drop his massive head, visibly upset at being 'found out'.

Ernest turned his head to face his 'son' and, reaching up as high as he could, just managed to give Jack a couple of comforting pats on his giant iron shoulder. "What are we to do with you? None of this is your fault. OK, it is Quinn and I that built you, but in some ways, we have created a monster," continued Ernest as worryingly he saw Jack fidget and turn his eyes a deep crimson red at the word 'monster' being used.

"Jack, I'm sorry, that was stupid of me; I shouldn't have said monster; that was so insensitive of me," said Ernest as Quinn intervened and managed to calm Jack down. Choosing his words more wisely, Ernest approached the subject again.

"Jack, it is a fact that Quinn and I put you on this earth and it is solely our responsibility to look after you as best as any parent could. Your complex brain was built, factoring in as much human emotion as possible, so it was not a big surprise to both of us when your human traits began mirroring Quinn's. We should have realised it was inevitable that in due course, your feelings towards Rose would grow in an unacceptable way, but Jack, we cannot let this situation fester and frustrate you any more, so earlier on, when I sat in my library and I had time to think about the worrying predicament we had got ourselves into I believe I have found the perfect solution.

The first job Quinn and I will tackle in the new year will be to invite you, along with Samuel and Freddy, to join me in my new house and draw up plans for what I propose should be our next iron guardian. Jack, of course, you will have full control over how the final design should look, but I've already thought of what we should call her. How do you like the sound of 'Iron Jane'?" concluded Ernest enthusiastically as Michael Quinn, the man with virtually no features, somehow managed to look stunned. Iron Jack seemingly lost for words ran off, his arms swinging wildly as his huge metal top hat blew out intermittent short bursts of steam, causing it to whistle loudly, releasing just enough pressure to stop his massive iron body from blowing up with excitement.

The End.